To Jenia,

Thank you

and best wishes,

ANGEL

OF

AMBITION

A NOVEL

Glenn Kaplan (signature)

GLENN KAPLAN

woodhall press

Woodhall Press | Norwalk, CT

woodhall press

Woodhall Press, 81 Old Saugatuck Road, Norwalk, CT 06855
WoodhallPress.com

Cover design: Jessica Dionne Wright
Layout artist: LJ Mucci

Library of Congress Cataloging-in-Publication Data available

ISBN 978-1-954907-34-8 (paper: alk paper)
ISBN 978-1-954907-35-5 (electronic)

First Edition

Distributed by Independent Publishers Group
(800) 888-4741

Printed in the United States of America

ANGEL

OF

AMBITION

JUST TRY TO STOP HER

A NOVEL

NEW YORK TIMES BESTSELLING AUTHOR

GLENN KAPLAN

TWO PROLOGUES

Jack Price

This was worse than one of those bad dreams.

You know how they unfold. Your worst fears assemble like an evil army. The misdeeds you keep buried under cover of daylight pop up in darkness with terrifying hallucinations of persecution and imprisonment. You are banished from the rest of humanity as punishment for all the sins you committed and even the ones you just thought about. You wake up in a sweat, gripped by the horror, haunted and quaking. As soggy bedsheets materialize around you, you shudder with gratitude that it was only a dream.

Yes, this was much worse. It was real.

Just the night before, I'd been a guest on a gigantic yacht moored off the tropical paradise of Antigua. Now I was in Her Majesty's

Prison in the capital of St. John's. With no running water. Toilet facilities a personal slop bucket for each prisoner.

As I sweated in the heat, I wondered how the sins of my forty-eight years could have rightly led me here—sleeping on the floor with accused thieves, rapists, drug dealers, and worse. Holding my nose against the ungodly stink. Paying prison guards for bottled water after they warned me that the well water would kill me before they or the inmate gang members did.

Wasn't everyone guilty of a few dark deeds? Sure, I had racked up a few. But no more and no worse than anyone else. I'd been a decent guy who tried to do the right thing. Well, most of the time.

How could this be happening to me? Until a few weeks ago, I was a New York advertising executive at the top of my game, living the Manhattan high life.

Then my whole life went to Hell. Literally.

There was blood on my shirt. My lip was split. My throbbing right hand was swollen. I certainly looked guilty. The police and the magistrate thought so. Even if I had been too drunk to remember whether I did or did not murder the old billionaire, I knew I hadn't meant to.

All I could remember was the toxic mixture of too much alcohol, way too much money, and the machinations of that woman. Angela.

I shudder at the irony of her name.

Some goddamn angel. More scheming, more ruthless than any man I've ever known. Heart as cold as absolute zero and cunning beyond imagining. In place of oxytocin, her veins must run with battery acid.

I found a place in a corner to be by myself. Lay down on the gritty floor. Closed my eyes. And waited. For what, I dared not imagine. Maybe I fell asleep. Or just zoned out.

VIII

After a while I heard the scuffling of feet and felt the presence of people looming over me. I half-opened one eye for an instant. Saw shadows of legs all around. Hugged my arms to my chest. Braced myself for the kicking and beating I was sure was coming.

A shoe nudged me gently. I looked up and saw a face smiling down at me. The last face on earth I wanted to see. With the cruelest smile I could imagine.

Angela's.

Angela Hanson

To the daughter I hope to have someday—

When you are grown and learn about how I made my way in the world, you may end up hating me. Daughters of exceptionally strong women often do.

Was I cruel? Immoral? Evil?

Maybe. But no more than I had to be to get by in a world that is cruel, immoral, and evil. I learned to look at life without any of the sugarcoating people use to delude themselves. That's how I was able to do things other people don't dare to do.

I would never try to tell you that I did it all for you. No way. I won't saddle you with any of the self-serving guilt mothers use to pummel their children into gratitude.

Everything I did was for me, for my own life.

XI

But because of me, you will never see what I saw when I was growing up. A world without hope, your loved ones squashed like bugs, nothing but defeat in the eyes of everyone around you.

No, my precious girl, you will never feel the world you tell you what it tried to tell me. That all you deserve is a shitty little life, whether you play by the rules or try to break them.

Unlike me, you will never know what it's like to be desperate for money.

Never have to grovel for it the way I did. Right after I finished high school, I got a job at a fancy hair salon on the Upper East Side. I was a foolish girl chasing what I thought would be a life of glamour.

I swept hair off the floor, ran the coat closet, and cleaned the bathrooms for a tribe of rich, bitchy, entitled—mostly white—Manhattan women.

The worst bitch of all was a triple-process blonde who'd had too many facelifts. Mallory Drummond.

She let everyone know she hated me. Maybe because I was young and pretty. Maybe because my hair is naturally blonde. Or maybe because my job was to wait on her. And she knew she could get away with it.

When it came time for me to make the coffee run, Mallory always made a big show of ordering the most complicated half-caff-half-soy-medium-foam thing. When I'd return to hand out the lattés, she would dangle a five-dollar bill in the air. I can't tell you how much that lousy $5 meant to me.

Mallory would sit there frowning, her face framed by the black vinyl cape, her hair glopped up in foil layers. She would take her stupid coffee concoction, inspect it suspiciously, and take a test sip. If she approved, she would nod and extend her hand with

XII

the five, letting go just as I reached for it. If I didn't time my grab perfectly, I'd have to pick it up off the floor. She'd smirk whenever that happened.

This one day, she took her test sip and spat it out. "It's cold, damn it," she barked. "Cold!"

I had checked the cup below the cardboard holder; I knew it was hot. But I kept my mouth shut. I kept my fake grin of gratitude in place, hoping to look worthy of her goddamn tip.

She balled up the five in her fist and spun around in the chair. "I don't like that girl," she stage-whispered to her colorist. "She's not respectful."

After closing that day, right after I had cleaned the last toilet, they fired me.

I managed to hold back my tears until I got out onto the street.

Then they flooded out of me. Tears of anger, panic, and fear. Tears of every desperate hurt, resentment, and confusion an eighteen-year-old girl can feel. By the time I got to the subway station, I was all cried out. Through my sniffles, I made a vow. Nobody would ever have the power to make me feel like that again.

Then it hit me. That miserable job had been like school. The beginning of my education. I knew I'd never see the inside of one of those fancy colleges with ivy-covered halls. But I realized that the rich bitches at the salon had been my professors. Professors of how the world of money and power *really* worked.

All those conversations I had listened to while pretending to be human wallpaper–they were my lectures. All their dishing and griping and bragging contained knowledge a girl like me could use. I wished I'd had a secret recorder to capture it all. But I remembered and began to catalog all the things they'd said – about their husbands and their big jobs, their own careers, their husbands'

XIII

affairs, their revenge affairs, their vicious competitive social climbing, their ugly divorces. OMG, their divorces! Their divorces were the bloody wars that revealed the truth about what everyone was up to. Their divorce lawyers were hired killers in the knife fights over money, houses in the Hamptons, and the children. Those poor little rich kids were the most valuable of all the poker chips in their heartless game.

My sweet girl, I promise you with my whole being, I will never *ever* let you be used the way those kids were used. Still, those awful women knew exactly how the world worked. And they knew how to win.

I made up my mind in that stinky subway station on that steamy August day. I was going to learn everything they knew. Absolutely everything. And figure out how to get everything they had—and more. I was going to be tougher and smarter and richer than all of them. I would let nothing stand in my way.

And I got what I wanted, didn't I? Oh yes, and then some.

But, my dear girl-to-be, I accomplished something more, something very few people ever do. I became the person I was always meant to be.

Did my journey make me cold? Hard-hearted? Maybe even something of a monster?

You will make up your own mind when the time is right.

But know this — my dearest wish for you is that you will walk through this world feeling safe. Feeling entitled. Not just to the glittery things. Yes, the glittery things are wonderful. But you will learn, the way everyone does, that they can't fill you up inside.

More than anything else, I want you to feel entitled to the one priceless luxury *I* could never afford – the luxury of giving in to the power of love.

Hoping I'll be your mom. Someday.

XIV

CHAPTER 1

The train wreck that shattered Jack Price's life started in a stately Georgian mansion just off South Audley Street in Mayfair, London's most exclusive neighborhood.

A chauffeured Range Rover pulled up in front of the headquarters of Globalcom, the giant marketing services holding company. Before the driver could come around to open the back door, a beautiful American woman in her early thirties stepped out. She strode on stiletto heels toward the yellow eighteenth-century front door. She wore an expensive jade-green silk wrap dress and carried a small handbag.

Tagging behind her, shouldering her briefcase, was a twenty-four-year-old wisp of an Englishman in skinny jeans, a floral print shirt that looked like it had time-traveled from 1960s Carnaby Street, and purple suede Chelsea boots. His brown hair was done in a dramatic mullet—long at the nape, shaved close along his

1

temples, with a stripe bleached pure white over his crown, styled upward like a rooster's comb.

"Angela, Angela," he called breathlessly to her back, "do you want me in the meeting? I can take notes. Handle papers. I can be quieter than a houseplant if that's what you want, you know that." Angela's assistant, Eric Ainsley, enunciated with great care in his best posh accent, trying never to let the Derbyshire twang of his hardscrabble upbringing show.

Angela stopped short a few feet before the front door. Eric nearly crashed into her. "No, Eric, not for this meeting," she said, staring straight ahead. "This is the chairman and the chief financial officer." She added, mumbling to herself, "The captain and first mate of the *Titanic*."

She turned around. Looked Eric up and down. Then shook her head no, emphatically no.

"They're dinosaurs, luv. Besides, we're here to plan . . ." Then she mouthed the words "mass executions" and made a gun-firing gesture with thumb and forefinger.

Eric gasped.

She put a fingertip to her lips. "You'll wait for me outside the conference room. I want you to memorize everything you hear on all the phone conversations around you. Absolutely everything."

Eric bobbed his head up and down obediently.

Angela took two steps forward and raised the heavy brass ring of the door knocker. She held it for a moment, staring up at the elegant brick facade. She felt a knot in her stomach and sweat in her armpits. No raising your arms in there, she warned herself. Once again, she had to tell that poor, insecure girl inside her to shut the fuck up. She *did* deserve to be here, running with the big

2

dogs, running the show. Act like you belong here, she told herself. Keep up the front and maybe someday you really will belong.

She let go of the knocker. She flinched when it clanged louder than she had anticipated. Mercifully, the jarring noise silenced her anxious thoughts.

A uniformed butler opened the door.

She took a deep breath and put on the face of confidence and poise she had mastered after untold hours of practice in the mirror.

"Angela Hanson to see Sir Alban," she said. She gave the butler the slightly condescending smile she had learned from the privileged women she had waited on years before at the hair salon.

On her journey to this doorway to power, Angela had worked in all sorts of jobs, serving the rich, from maid to manicurist to waitress to boutique salesgirl to secretary. All the while, she was studying the accents and mannerisms of her masters. A talented mimic, she learned to impersonate their ways, hoping it would help her to win the privileges they enjoyed. Many nights she would collapse into bed, exhausted from playacting all day, wondering who she really was, what she was becoming, and whether her masquerade would really work.

The butler gave an elegant bow of the head. "Of course, Miss Hanson. Sir Alban is expecting you." He led her past the foyer toward the double pocket doors of what had once been the dining room.

Angela gestured at Eric who had already planted himself in a straight-back Queen Anne chair against the wall near the desks of the two secretaries. "My assistant," she said.

"Certainly," the butler said as he slid the doors open and ushered Angela inside.

Two pale-faced English gentlemen rose from their chairs at the far end of a long Regency dining table. Both had thinning white hair and wore bespoke chalk-stripe suits.

Angela walked across the room to greet her bosses.

"Sir Alban," she declared in her best fake warmth as she took the chairman's hand.

Sir Alban Reade offered a limp grip with his right hand and, with his left, gave her a fatherly pat on the shoulder.

Angela beamed at him. Turning quickly to the finance chief, Simon Woodleigh, she pretended to be equally delighted. "And Simon, *so* good to see you!"

After a few more pleasantries, they sat down, Reade at the head of the table, Woodleigh to his right, Angela to his left.

Reade said, "Next stop for Angela is New York." He nodded imperiously at Woodleigh. Woodleigh bowed his head in return and handed out a deck of spreadsheets. "Are you prepared for this?" Reade patted Angela's arm, again very fatherly. "It's going to require immense strength on your part."

"Yes, absolutely." Angela gave her bosses another well-practiced facial expression—steely determination. She felt sure she had this one down pat. It was the foundation of what the business books called "executive presence."

Angela's looks were a striking combination of seemingly impossible opposites. She had pale golden hair as fine as corn silk and slightly hooded crystal-blue eyes set in a decidedly swarthy complexion. Her paradoxical beauty was testament to a motley collection of ancestors from both the warm and cold parts of Europe. Her blonde and blue-eyed bits came from the pure Nordic DNA of an American father who bolted soon after she was born. Her dark olive skin was from a mother descended from a mash-up of immigrants from the southernmost parts of Italy and Spain who got to the United States after generations of couplings in Venezuela, Puerto Rico, Cuba, and Trinidad. Angela's 23andMe DNA analysis showed a lineage of Scandinavian, Sicilian, and Andalusian with trace amounts of Taino, African, Arab, Jewish, Bengali, and Chinese blood.

She felt sure that Reade and Woodleigh must be thinking of her as a "wog." After all, that's how upper-class Brits of their generation were brought up to organize the human race—with themselves at the pinnacle. But now, in this era of diversity and political correctness, in exchange for big pots of money, they would never dare to utter that word. At least not in front of the wog.

In her meetings with these smug aristocrats, Angela would fortify her confidence by imagining two strains of her long-dead ancestors—the ancient Romans who conquered the British and the Vikings who regularly kicked the shit out of them. Even though they were nameless, faceless ghosts to her, she decided they could give her inner strength to draw upon.

Woodleigh said, "Angela, you should know that we have a sizable reserve fund for severance costs. But if you can bring in the cuts for less, your bonus will reflect a rather nice percentage of whatever you save."

In other words, Angela thought, I get a cut of every dollar I can screw out of the employees. Their loss, my gain. She was amazed that the higher she rose in the corporate world the more she could be rewarded for cruelty. Of course, she had learned that in business they called this particular heartlessness "the ability to make tough decisions."

Woodleigh pointed at his spreadsheets. "The New York salary liabilities are rank-ordered, starting with the most expensive," he said.

Angela glanced at her copy. She flipped through the pages, pretending to study them. She spoke with practiced calm, calculating what she thought her bosses wanted to hear. "All I see when I look at these names are numbers I have to change."

Woodleigh sighed with admiration. "Ah, Angela, you have a temperament that is exceptionally well-suited for business." He glanced admiringly at his boss. "Hiring you as chief culture officer was yet another stroke of genius on Sir Alban's part."

"Bah. I deserve no credit whatsoever," Reade said with false modesty. "It was so obvious. I just looked at the credentials you earned at our competitors'. Good God, that ability of yours to bend all those unruly employees to the will of their leaders. To say nothing of the speed with which you rose through their organizations. You are the youngest C-suite executive Globalcom has ever had. But I can tell, oh yes, I can tell." He wagged his index finger in playful accusation. "Angela Hanson, you have an old soul."

Old soul? she thought. Old soul and how. Growing up poor on the streets of New York, she had learned to survive in a world of unrelenting fear, insecurity, deprivation, and desperation, a world that drove people to drugs, violent crime, prison, and early death. All because no one had *any fucking money*! She shuddered inside and thought, I've seen more bad shit than these pampered marshmallows could begin to imagine.

She shook her head and ordered herself to focus. She looked more carefully at the first page. The name Jack Price was at the top of the list. His salary, bonus, benefits, and severance guarantees made him the costliest employee on the roll call of the doomed. She blinked for an instant, incredulous. Jack Price! She had to catch her breath. She hoped it didn't show. Her thoughts were exploding in all directions. Jack Price! Jack-*Fucking*-Price!

Jack had hired her for her first job in advertising five years before. She had charmed him into becoming her mentor, extracting from him everything he knew about the glittering world of success. To make sure he was holding nothing back, she seduced him into an affair. Then she made the mistake of falling in love with him. How stupid she had been back then! He had promised to leave his wife for her but had backed down at the last minute. Her girlish, starstruck passion had turned to bitter, angry gall that she still tasted to this day. That burning heartbreak had helped fuel her meteoric rise to the pinnacle of the industry. In a weird way, she was grateful for the pain.

Now Jack Price was to be the next victim of her globe-trotting firing squad. Sweet! Already she could feel his presence in her memory start to shrink.

But revenge was just the beginning. What put her over the moon was the stunning realization that Jack Price was also the answer to her very own, totally personal, incredibly urgent billion-dollar question.

It was Jack who had taught her: Always be on the lookout for your next job. Never stop maneuvering for your next step up the ladder. She had followed his advice. At this very moment, she was looking for a talented adman for her very rich friend. The very rich friend she would use as her rocket into the stratosphere of success. Miles above her life as a mere corporate salary slave. She could hardly believe her luck. Talk about the circle of life. Jack Price was perfect. Jack-Fucking-Price!

She dared not look up from the spreadsheet for fear that her euphoria might show. She took one deep breath, then another, to make sure she had restored her facade of executive calm. There, now.

Angela turned the papers over and gave them a little pat, as if putting them to bed. "I promise. I will take care of things."

Reade smiled, cleared his throat. He announced, as if addressing a large audience, "Now, we all recognize that we would *never* make personnel judgments based on age."

"No, never on age," Woodleigh echoed.

"Indeed," Reade said, agreeing with himself, "not in this company. Never."

Angela joined the game. "No, of course not. This is not at all about age. It's about digital transformation. Nothing else."

"Precisely," Reade said, "digital transformation. Not age. Never." He sounded relieved, as if the crowd that wasn't there had finally been convinced and quieted.

Angela knew what this meant. Her job would be to fire all the older employees. But artfully. The way a clever chief culture officer should. She could feel the pain and panic of the forty- and fifty-something employees she would terminate at the very moment when they needed their jobs most to pay for their kids' colleges and build retirement savings. She knew they would be finished forever in the industry. She also knew that if she did not deliver Woodleigh's savings, *she* would be out on her ass.

She put on her mask of bulletproof executive confidence and took control of the meeting. Just the way Jack Price had taught her.

"Gentlemen, our vision for digital transformation is more than being comfortable in the digital age. The kind of employees who can take us into the future do not get into marketing communications because they love money. Money is incidental to them. They don't understand it. And they don't need much. Their reward is belonging, being accepted into the right tribe. They will sacrifice everything to be . . ."—she paused for emphasis—". . . *cool.*"

"So, they still use that word?" Reade asked innocently.

"Oh, yes," she said, delighted that the big boss could be so clueless. More proof that her youth gave her power. "What's more, the cool factor can be bought on the cheap." She gave Woodleigh's hand a comforting pat, letting her fingertips linger just a nanosecond longer than necessary. "I know what my generation wants, and how to give it to them."

"Of course you do, Angela," Woodleigh said, perking up at the beautiful young woman's touch.

She flashed them the smile she used on older men. Sweet and faintly seductive.

"Consider this work done," she said. "Done," as she patted each man's hand in turn, again letting her touch linger just a tiny bit too long. "And done." She could almost feel their aging hearts beating faster than their doctors would recommend.

"Th-thank you, Angela," Woodleigh stammered.

"Why, yes, Angela, thank you very much indeed," Reade added.

She was sure she saw their pasty white faces flushing slightly pink. Older men are so easy, she thought. And so grateful.

After Woodleigh asked about more potential savings, Angela cheerfully agreed to fire even more people.

The meeting ended.

As Angela walked to the double doors, the two men were huddled over the speakerphone for the call that was their next agenda item.

She paused for an instant, thinking about the secretaries she was about to face in the reception area. She had been a secretary herself not that long ago. She knew how people treated secretaries. How they would look right through them. Or, when they needed something from the big shot they babysat, shamelessly suck up to them. But hardly ever did anyone treat them like actual human beings.

Would she stop and get friendly with them? Talk about their shared experience and create a warm human bond? She thought that would feel good. It might even make her feel less alone in her scary new role. And the genuine connection she could make with them would certainly be helpful in the future.

But no, she decided, not this time. Fear was better than love, Jack Price had taught her. First, be feared. Then people will be grateful when you show them a little shard of anything that feels like warmth. You will look like more of a leader to the people below you *and* above you in the hierarchy.

She slid the doors open.

Eric leapt to his feet.

She did not acknowledge him. She could see the two secretaries look up to see if there would be a chance to make eye contact. Resisting temptation, she stared past them toward the foyer. She marched forward, one arm extended, with Woodleigh's list dangling between thumb and index finger exactly the way Mallory Drummond had held out her $5 tip. Just as she was about to let it drop to the floor, Eric plucked it from her fingertips and inserted it into the briefcase he carried for her.

She could feel him tagging eagerly behind. Exactly the display of power she wanted the secretaries to see. Let them feed the company rumor mill and build her brand. Spread the word that Angela Hanson, the girl who was secretly racked with self-doubt and insecurity, is a force to be reckoned with. With bitter irony she thought, Jack Price would be proud of my performance.

Next visit, she would make friends with them.

Outside at the curb, the liveried driver stood by the big Range Rover, holding the rear door open. Angela stopped. Eric moved to step in to take his usual seat behind the driver, where there was less leg room. She stuck out her hand to block him.

"I think you'd better get your own ride to Biggin Hill," she said, referring to the general aviation airport where the Globalcom jet was waiting to take them to New York. "I have to make a *personal* call."

Eric protested with a flutter of theatrics. "A taxi? A *mere* common taxi? Is my next humiliation to be flying commercial?"

Angela shrugged. "You'll survive, my dear. Call a black cab, a limo, a stretch, whatever. Who cares what it costs? Just don't be late. Wheels-up at exactly three p.m."

He gave a big huff and turned his back to her. With Angela's briefcase hanging off his shoulder, he took his phone out of his pocket and began typing, pretending that the taxi app required his total concentration.

She patted him lightly, thinking how dear he was to her. "Now don't be hurt," she said affectionately. "I have a matter that's beyond confidential. If you found out about it, I'd have to shoot you. Really. And we wouldn't want that, would we?"

He turned around, his face beaming. All was forgiven.

She leaned in close to him and whispered in his ear, "Did I ever tell you about my secret history with Range Rovers?" She tapped the roof of the vehicle.

"No," he gushed. "I love secrets."

"Well," she continued, *sotto voce*, "when I was a kid in New York City, I used to stand on the corner in front of the projects where I grew up."

"Projects?" Eric looked puzzled.

"Council estates," she said, translating for him. "Low-income housing projects. You know, shitty little government flats for poor people."

Eric nodded.

11

"Well, on the other side of Tenth Avenue, there was this crazy-expensive private school filled with rich kids. And a lot of them used to get driven to school in Range Rovers just like this one. I could see that they were just kids, little people no different from me. But when I'd wave to them, they never waved back. They looked right through me. Like I didn't even exist. I knew they'd get cushy rides to wherever they went for the rest of their lives. I was like, 'Hey, what did *they* do to deserve all that? Why not me? Why . . . not . . . *me?*'"

Eric snickered, "Ha! In Britain, we call that proud tradition of injustice our class system."

Angela climbed into the backseat. "Except," she said with a smirk, "here I am, being driven around in my very own Range Rover. Just like one of them." She wondered what those snotty rich kids would say if they could see her now.

"Well done, you," Eric said. He stepped back to let the driver close the door.

Angela lowered her window and leaned toward Eric. "Don't fret about traffic. I won't let them take off without you. Promise." She blew him a little two-finger kiss, then raised her window.

My dear Eric, she thought. Dear vulnerable Eric. Dear irreplaceable Eric. How we have grown to need each other. He needs my protection. I need his devotion.

She also knew what made them brother and sister under the skin—the worry that some unintentional slip might expose their low-rent roots. And the fear that one of their slimy entitled colleagues might push them off the merry-go-round of success and send them back where they came from.

Yes, she thought, my dear Eric. He could be the closest thing to a friend I may ever have.

CHAPTER 2

Jack Price was charming two pretty young women at the crowded reception. At least he hoped he was. They had just seen his presentation at the marketing industry conference and were gushing admiration.

"Come on, tell us, Jack," the taller one teased, poking a finger into the center of his chest. She had a cascade of pink hair with neon-blue ends. "What's the secret of your success?"

He shrugged. Grinned with false modesty. Maybe flirting back. "Well, how does anyone get ahead in our business?" he said. He leaned in to tell them his secret.

They moved in closer to hear him.

He whispered, "The thing is . . . I'm really good at . . ." He paused again. ". . . Lying." Then he raised his right hand as if being sworn in. "Honest."

For an instant, they were silent. Then they started laughing. Blue Ends touched his elbow and gave it a little squeeze. Jack wondered, was she really flirting? Or just indulging this older guy who might help her land her next job? She gave him her business card and another little pinch on the arm. The women giggled and melted into the crowd.

He didn't know what to make of them. Once he had been a confident ladies' man. But that was twenty years ago. These days, he was never sure about reading the signals.

He looked at his watch. No matter. It was time to meet Sandra and Luke outside the conference center. His ex-wife and their thirteen-year-old son. Luke was staying at his apartment tonight. At moments like this, he regretted the joint custody stuff and wished they were still a family. Sandra's love had been the best he'd ever known. Probably ever would know. And he had fucked that up with his affair with Angela.

He made his way through the crowd, getting kudos from people he did and didn't know. Nice, he thought. I've still got my business mojo. Even if I'm not sure how to navigate the young hotties the way I used to.

Once outside the towering glass doors of the conference center, he scanned the swarms of people making business contacts and scouting car services and taxis. Then he spotted that special backpack in the distance. It was festooned with Luke's changing array of stickers and doodads. But there was one toy Luke never seemed to outgrow. It was Marlin, the cross-eyed cartoon clownfish from the early-2000s movie *Finding Nemo*. The father who swam to the ends of the earth to rescue his lost son.

"Luke! Luke!" he yelled. "Hey, dude! Over here!" He snaked his way toward him.

Jack could see his boy's face light up, even under the gray hoodie. "Hey, Dad! Dad!"

Jack pointed to an empty patch of sidewalk a few yards away. Luke gave him a thumbs-up. Jack felt an overwhelming rush of emotion every time he saw Luke. A jumble of pride and worry, hope and fear, and a thousand feelings of attachment—some desperate, some euphoric—that could only be expressed in a great big hug. He felt it the moment he'd seen his newborn son and he knew he would never get over it. Before Luke, he'd had no idea that love could so completely overtake him.

As if by magic, Sandra was suddenly standing with them. Jack could never figure out how she managed to appear like that out of nowhere.

"Hi, Sandra," he said, smiling politely.

"Hi, Jack," she said, smiling back the same way.

He took in his ex-wife, noticing that she was starting to show strands of gray in her dark brown hair. The little crow's feet and smile lines she was getting were kind of sexy, he thought. Her pretty face was ageless to him. Her big dark eyes shone with natural warmth, along with that X-ray vision she possessed. That uncanny, often annoying, ability to see the truth behind people's bullshit. Especially his. Yes, he thought, I really fucked up the best thing I ever had. And the dick pic that Angela had sent in her fury to Sandra's phone, well, that finished their marriage.

Sandra reached up to pull back Luke's hoodie and fix his hair. "I haven't seen you guys together in a few weeks. Pretty soon, Luke's going to be almost as tall as you."

"That's the plan," Jack crowed, "taller, smarter, bigger. Any way you measure it, better than his old man." Luke was lanky and gawky, moving like a baby colt trying to get his long limbs to work together. Jack marveled at seeing bits of himself and Sandra emerging in the boy's looks and mannerisms.

15

Sandra stroked Luke's arm affectionately. "Now remember, Luke's got his game in Riverdale tomorrow morning at eight-thirty sharp. You can have your boys' night out. But not too late."

Jack nodded. "Got it," he said, and turned to his son. "What'll it be tonight, dude? Steak? Lobster? Pizza?"

"I really like that steakhouse down the block from your condo." Luke turned breathlessly to his mom, "That's where we saw J.Lo and A-Rod!"

Sandra gave Luke a fist bump. "Okay, you A-listers, have fun." She turned to Jack. "I know you said you've got to be in the office to work on the pitch this weekend. Are you sure you can get away to pick him up and drive him home after the game?"

"Yeah, no prob. I can slip out of the office for an hour. Hey, I'm the boss. What are they gonna do, fire me?"

Sandra shrugged. She blew a kiss to Luke and headed for the subway.

CHAPTER 3

Alone in the backseat of the Range Rover, Angela tapped Favorites on her iPhone to FaceTime with Charlotte Townsend. It jingled for a moment, then the ticket to her brand-new life appeared on the screen.

"Yoo-hoo, Charlie," Angela cooed, "it's me. I've got great news."

"And I've got sad news," Charlie answered with a pout.

Angela switched immediately to a show of concern. "Oh, poor baby, tell Mommy where it hurts." Charlie's troubles, whether imagined or real, always came first. Angela never stopped feeling on tenterhooks with her, never sure if her petulant friend would turn on her, or worse, just lose interest.

"I'm at Hermès in Paris," Charlie said. She waved her phone around to show Angela the main floor of the stupendously expensive boutique. "I dragged myself all the way over here to be at the source, where the magic happens, to show them my undying loyalty." Charlie put her angry face back in frame again. "Then they tell me there won't be a waiting list for the next new Birkin. Which means I can't bribe anyone under the table to reserve mine. How depressing is that?"

"Oh, *very* depressing," Angela said. She stared solemnly at the screen, letting her BFF see how sincerely she felt her pain. Then she tried brightening her tone. "Maybe I can cheer you up with the news I've got?" She paused, watching her rich friend very closely for the tiniest reaction. It was impossible to predict what Charlie's next whim might be. Angela hoped that the gurgle from her nervous stomach did not register over speakerphone.

Charlotte Townsend was the first billionaire Angela had gotten to know. Actually, her father Clifford Townsend was the billionaire; Charlotte was his only child. But still. A decade and change older than Angela, she was a woman of the world somewhere in her forties. Angela never dared to probe Charlie about her actual age. Divorced three times, at least one facelift or maybe two, homes on three continents—Charlie had gone through all the landmarks that Angela was just embarking upon, and she was triumphantly on the other side.

Angela had glommed onto Charlotte Townsend and was not going to let go until she got herself her own piece of that rich world. She worked tirelessly to find every emotional crack in her rich friend's life so she could fill them with the balm of her sisterly love. She was faking it, of course, just the way she was in business. But the heiress, like her agency bosses, seemed to be buying her act. As a result, Angela was beginning to let herself hope that someday—maybe even someday soon—she might really have enough money and power to feel safe and secure.

Charlie waved away Angela's news with a somewhat lesser pout. "I'm also annoyed about something else."

"Tell me, sweetie, tell me."

"Well, I was planning for Cliff and me to take the jet from London very early tomorrow morning to get me to New York by late afternoon. In time for the gallery opening of this very important new artist tomorrow evening. Then Cliff got a last-minute invitation to go golfing in Scotland. Now, I have to go back to London tonight, wait for Cliff to finish his eighteen holes, and *then* fly to Dundee, of all places, to pick him up. It will be the dead of night by the time we get to New York. And I will miss the artist's opening. He's a very hot item—in all ways, I might add. Can you believe it?"

"Well, it *is* Cliff's jet."

"It's the *family* jet, lovey," Charlie said. She paused, then took a deep breath. Angela thought she saw the dark clouds over Charlie passing. Sad whim might be fading, happy whim might be appearing. As usual, for no apparent reason. A smile began to form.

"So," Charlie asked, suddenly cheery, "is our favorite chief culture officer also on her way to New York?"

"As we speak," Angela said brightly. She held her phone up to the car window to show Charlie the traffic on Park Lane.

"Great!" Charlie said with a big smile. "We're going to have sooo much fun at the gala Saturday night. It's at the Pierre, you know. All the most glamorous parties happen there. And the crowd that shows up for this disease, well, it's all the right people."

"Really? What disease is it?"

Charlie looked puzzled. "Uh, I don't remember exactly. It's something awful. They have a video to show how heartbreaking it is. But they always end it with hope. I guess that's to prime the crowd for

19

the live auction right afterward. I've seated you between Cliff and me. We've bought one of the top-tier tables."

"How much does that cost?" Angela asked.

Charlie gave a tsk-tsk and wagged a finger, "Nah-nah-nah, you're not supposed to ask, you know."

Angela paused. She held her breath, not sure if she had broken another one of those unwritten rules no one ever told you about. Sometimes it was okay to mention prices. Why not now? Every time she talked to Charlie, she feared that one of her innocent, ignorant missteps might get her banished forever. She wished there was a pill she could take to fill her with everything she needed to know about the subtleties that the rich understood tacitly.

"Uh, I'm sorry, Charlie," she stammered. She put on her best apologetic smile and hoped her *faux pas*—the French phrase she had learned from committing mistakes regularly—was not a fatal one. It was nerve-racking, trying to navigate the hidden twists and turns of people with money.

Charlie made a big theatrical frown that morphed into a big grin. "Aw, hell! It's right there in back of the gala program. Two hundred and fifty thousand, if you must know. It's an investment, really. I've been trying to get on this benefit committee for years. And this year, I think they'll vote me in. That is, if I get the nod from Susanna, the chair of the committee. I really hope it'll happen . . ."

Charlie's voice trailed off. She wrinkled her brows with what looked like worry.

"I'm sure you'll get it," Angela said, relieved and grateful that she still had her job as Charlie's cheerleader.

Charlie crossed her fingers, then took another deep breath to clear the deck for her next new whim. "Say, don't you just love that Alexander McQueen number we picked out for you?"

Angela nodded obediently. "It's a dream."

"I'm telling you, it was a steal at that price."

Angela swallowed hard. She was still not accustomed to spending $15,000 on a dress. She hoped desperately for the day when she might get used to it.

"My personal shopper," Charlie said, "she's the best. The absolute best." She seemed to beam with pride at this extravagance.

"Yes, she is," Angela agreed enthusiastically, trying hard to banish her worry over the price tag. She thought it might be safe to change the subject. To something *else* that was all about Charlie. Angela understood her role in the relationship. It was not fun. It was work, the hard work of a servant. Not much different from her agency job. "Listen, I've got great news. I've found the perfect man for our project. He's a top adman with all the right credentials. I can hardly believe our luck."

Angela envisioned Jack Price sitting in his corner office, gloating over the awards and trophies that proved what a creative genius he was. And not having a clue of what was about to happen to his brilliant career.

Charlie wrinkled her brow and peered into her phone with great concern. "Please, *please* promise me that you will vet him very carefully. This is the most important thing I've ever wanted in my entire life. My whole future happiness depends on it. Failure is not an option. Check him out *thoroughly*."

"No worries. I know him well." Angela grinned. "Very, very well."

Charlie was intrigued. "*How* very well?"

Angela grinned wider. "Dick pic well."

Charlie giggled. "Really?"

"Yes, and then some. We had a thing for a while. About five years ago. I even fell for him. Well, sort of. Thought I could get

21

him to leave his wife for me. But he said no. Then he lost both of us, poor dear."

"Ooh, I love it when that happens," Charlie said, her laugh tinged with the bitterness of one who gets genuine pleasure from the romantic misfortunes of others. "Was it the dick pic?"

"How'd you guess?"

Charlie wagged a finger. "Bad girl."

"Actually, I'm very good. Best of all—and he doesn't know this, of course—he's about to become unemployed. So, he's going to be looking for work. The prospect of doing a creative project for a billionaire on a superyacht in Antigua will be, well, impossible to resist."

"Say, girl, you *are* good."

Suddenly, Charlie's face turned worried again. "Are you absolutely sure this adman of yours can make a business presentation that will get Cliff to change his mind? I mean, absolutely, positively sure."

"Oh, he's the best. Really." Angela paused for an instant, recalling Jack's words of caution about what to call his professional skill. Never call it lying, he said. Always call it persuasion. "He's a world-class persuader. He can sell anybody anything. He's perfect for what we need."

She thought about Jack's gargantuan ego. His need to be admired, especially by pretty women. His need to prove he was a champion at nearly everything, including the orgasms he gave her (that she often faked). They were her best ever, right? She thought about his blind spots and bad habits. Especially his drinking.

"He has all the right strengths," she said, "and even better, all the right weaknesses."

CHAPTER 4

Jack Price knew he'd had too much to drink. But, hey, it was champagne. And if anything could make the world a happier place, it was champagne. There wasn't anything that good champagne couldn't fix. Even a dull party like this one.

Across the room, he glimpsed an old woman seated against the wall. She had a champagne flute in one hand and a small plate of hors d'oeuvres on her lap. She saw Jack and smiled.

It was his mother.

He made his way through the crowd to her.

"Mom, what are you doing here?"

"Aww, Jack," she sighed. She offered her cheek for him to kiss. "I'm sorry, honey. I was supposed to be part of the surprise. You're getting an award later on."

He sat down beside her.

"An award? For what?"

"For being an outstanding professional liar."

"Really?" he asked, confused.

She motioned at the hububb round them. "Jack, we are all so grateful for the world you created. The world of lies. Movies, television, books, they're all lies. The business world? Lies, lies, lies. Same with politics, same with religion. Even what they call true love. People can't live without lies. The world can't function without them. That's why the work you do is so important. I'm so proud of you, Jack. We all are."

"Is this for real?" he asked urgently.

She took his hand and squeezed it. Her loving touch reached back to his earliest memories. "Of course it is. I wouldn't lie to you. I'm your mother."

He stared deep into her eyes. And he knew she was lying.

His mother had died ten years ago.

She grinned. Her grin started to grow wider and wider. Like the painted smile of a creepy carnival clown. Then her skin peeled away to reveal the bleached bare bones of a skull.

Jack heard himself scream, felt himself bolt up from under the covers, gasping for breath in the dark.

His bedroom door flew open.

Luke ran to his bedside. "Dad, what's wrong? What's wrong? I heard you scream all the way out on the balcony."

Jack fumbled for the remote. The blackout curtains cranked open to reveal the morning sun over the East River, from the twentieth floor.

"Bad dream. Thought I saw my mother."

Luke stood by the bed. "You never talk about Grandma. She died when I was still a baby. Why won't you tell me what she was like?"

Jack rubbed his eyes against the sunlight. "She was a nice lady," he mumbled.

"Oh, come on, Dad, no one's mother is just a nice lady. It's compli-cated. Moms and dads and kids. For everyone. You know, I used to have scary dreams about you and Mom after you guys split up. That's when I started waking up so early. Mom says everyone in your life can be a pain in the ass, especially the people who love you. Come on, what was your mom like?"

Jack was in no condition to wade into the perilous swamp of his memories of Vivian Price. He ignored Luke's question.

"What on earth were you doing on the balcony?" he asked, squinting.

"Selfies," Luke said urgently, "amazing selfies. With that view of the river and the skyline behind me, I'm going to get a shitload of likes."

"Hey, watch your language, dude." Jack swung his feet out of bed onto the floor.

Luke leaned over the night table and picked up the empty glass. He raised it to his nose. "Ewww! How can grown-ups drink that stuff? Smells like sh—"

Jack raised a warning finger before the boy could finish the word.

"Smells awful," he said, backtracking. "Mom says the people in your business all drink too much. She says they use work pressure as their excuse. But it's just an excuse. Do the guys at your agency go drinking, like, every single night?"

"No, Luke." Jack shook his head. "No, we don't."

Luke raised the offending glass with a questioning look.

"That was just one little nightcap," Jack muttered.

"Really? One? Come on, Dad, I heard you going back and forth to the liquor cabinet last night. Like three times before I fell asleep."

"Well, maybe a few more than one."

"Like, how many more, Dad?"

Jack looked down guiltily. "A couple, I don't know. It helps me get to sleep."

25

Luke grimaced and put the glass behind his back, as if to prevent his dad from using it again. "I figured out a way to help you stop drinking," he said. "Just wait. You'll see."

Jack shrugged. "Uh-huh, okay, yeah, great," he mumbled as he climbed out of bed. "Thanks, dude."

Luke stepped in front of his father, blocking his way to the bathroom.

"I mean it, Dad. Drinking's not good for anybody. Everybody knows that. I want to help you stop it. I talked about it with Mom. She said I could try. She says she tried before. She said you might listen to me. She said it worked sometimes. She said it would be for your good and my good—for all of us. So, I'm asking you, okay?" He put his free hand on his father's shoulder. Father and son looked into each other's eyes. "Will you promise to try? Will you?"

The gravity of his son's plea woke Jack from his hungover fog. He reached for Luke, amazed that the boy really was almost as tall as he. They held each other at arm's length, looking into each other's eyes for a long moment.

"Yes, Luke, I promise—I'll stop. I'll try."

"Starting when?"

"Starting now."

Jack pulled his son to him and hugged him tightly, both to show his affection and to end the discussion. They disengaged and Jack headed for the bathroom.

Luke followed behind him. "You promised, right? Mom says it's really hard, but if you know you've got support from your family, it's, like, a lot easier."

Jack stopped and turned around. "Yes, all right. I promised. I've done it before. I can do it again."

"It's for *you*, you know. It's not for me. It's like when you ask me to do something that I don't want to do but I oughta do it and I know it but I still don't want to do it, but I try anyway because you ask me, like, really seriously. You know, like that—like, for my own good. It's the same thing."

"Yes, Luke." He gave the boy another hug. "I know." He let go and finished his walk to the bathroom. Yes, he told himself, he would give it a really serious try. Yet again.

"So, what about Grandma?" Luke asked, following him to the open door. "You never talk about her."

"Please, some other time," Jack groaned. "Okay, dude?"

Luke stood in the doorway, talking while Jack peed and washed up.

"Come on," the boy insisted, "you can talk about grown-up stuff with me. I'm not a little kid anymore. You know, I used to be able to hear Mom yelling at you. I could hear through the wall. I thought it was all one word—Gofuckangela. Gofuckangela. Ha! It was three words! Go . . . fuck . . . Angela. Boy, was I a kid back then."

Jack flinched at the mention of Angela. He remained silent, hoping the topic would evaporate.

Luke walked beside him toward the kitchen. "I made you breakfast, a really nice one," he sputtered. "Just like I do for Mom. It's important for you guys to know that I don't show favoritism. I love you both the same, no matter what. Now, come on, you have to take me to soccer camp. If we don't get started now, we're gonna be late."

Jack stopped in front of the table in his breakfast nook, speechless for an instant.

"Luke, you've outdone yourself!"

The table was resplendent with formal placemats and linen napkins he did not remember he owned. The plates and coffee cups came from the fancy set that was a wedding gift Sandra never

27

liked. The smell of espresso and cinnamon toast filled the air. He pulled Luke in for a hug.

"Thanks, dude. I don't deserve this kind of treatment."

"Yes, you do," Luke said.

Jack sat down at the place of honor his son had prepared for him, amazed at what a remarkable person Luke was growing into.

Over breakfast, Jack asked him about school, friends, the songs he was listening to, the computer games he was playing.

Luke insisted on doing the cleanup.

In the garage beneath the apartment tower, Luke admired his dad's brand-new BMW 650i coupe in blue.

"Why'd you get rid of the red one? That red was really cool."

"The lease was up. Besides, the cars aren't mine. They're company cars. One of my perks."

"Perks," Luke mused as he ran his hand over the sleek dashboard. Like every teenage boy, he was fantasizing about driving.

They rode in silence up FDR Drive toward Riverdale. Luke fidgeted in the seat, one leg bouncing up and down. Finally, he blurted, "Why do you have to go to the office *again* on a Saturday?"

"Because, it's a huge crisis. New business pitch. It's do-or-die."

"Geez Louise, Dad, you always say that."

"Hey, watch your language, kiddo."

"That's not swearing."

"Technically not. But only technically."

"You didn't answer my question. Why are you in there today when you should be watching *me* in the game?"

"Because this pitch really is a big crisis. And because they tell us, 'If you can't be bothered to come to work on Saturday, don't bother to come in on Sunday.' "

"Is that supposed to be funny?"

28

"Only a little. It's mostly serious."

Jack Price had been doing this for nearly twenty-five years. In spite of all his awards and the bravado he put on for public consumption, he still felt he had to prove himself. Everyone did. Everyone was desperate for their next win, no matter how many wins they had scored before. Nobody ever gained any ground. Every day everyone started again at zero.

What Jack did not mention was the new chief culture officer at his company, the wunderkind who had rocketed her way up through bigger and bigger jobs at one agency after another. The woman he had not seen in five years.

Angela Hanson.

CHAPTER 5

Angela handed her copy of The List to Eric, who sat beside her in the conference room of Globalcom's largest New York agency. Eric put it into the briefcase he carried for her.

Angela had learned never to carry papers out of any meeting. Assistants and middle managers carried papers around. Not C-suite executives. Angela carried only her iPad and, for the last two months, the smallish $10,000 Hermès 2002-20 handbag that Charlie had teased her into buying.

"Just what you need to show them who's boss at the office," her rich friend had said, wrinkling her nose at Angela's worn, no-name everyday purse.

Once she'd recovered from her sticker shock, Angela came to love the bag. The Hermès icon had become like a knight's armor to her. It made her feel strong, protected, maybe even almost invincible in the warfare of corporate life. Maybe it really did help to protect her from rivals and from her own nagging doubts about herself.

She turned to Daniel, the CEO of the New York office. "So, are we in sync?"

"Yes, Angela, hundred percent," he said obediently.

She turned to Ira, the chief legal counsel, and Jennifer, the head of human resources. Angela raised one eyebrow, a power gesture she had learned from a son-of-a-bitch restaurant manager who had tried to grope her. Then fired her.

"Yes," the two answered, nodding in unison like twin bobbleheads.

"Any more questions?" Angela asked.

"Well, yes, one," Daniel said, a bit hesitantly.

She answered with another raised eyebrow.

"If we don't win this VeRity new business pitch, it will be easy to explain all the layoffs. Especially the senior people. But if we win the account, everyone will ask questions. I mean, this office would be getting a big boost in revenue."

Angela shook her head. She had the official company lie all teed up and ready.

"No worries. It's all part of our digital transformation. Doing more with less. That's the beauty of technology, isn't it? We'll make sure that the employees we keep are grateful to be members of our new tribe. We'll use their pride in belonging and their fear of being expelled to keep them in line. That's how we'll build a new corporate culture. At a lower cost."

She turned to Jennifer and Ira.

"It's up to you guys to identify other personnel cuts that will make the layoffs feel impartial. So, add enough cuts at junior levels. Now that I think of it, cut even more than we actually need. It will be good for maintaining anxiety and uncertainty."

Not long ago it would have weighed heavily on her conscience, ordering such cruelty and injustice. But once firings had become part of her job description, she knew she had to choose between employee heads on the chopping block or her own. Then it became kind of fun. This was power. Yes, power.

Hey, she told herself, working hard to brush aside her qualms, I'm just doing my job as a senior executive. I'm helping my company by taking on the "tough decisions." Welcome to the C-suite, girl.

She looked into the eyes of her colleagues to see if her words were doing what she hoped they would. Yes, she thought, these three people were now terrified for their own jobs. Satisfied with her unspoken threat, she went on.

"Working late nights and weekends is part of our tribal code of belonging. The ones who don't complain, or don't dare, are the ones we want to keep. They won't think they're missing out on anything. After all, their family is here in the office. And the people who don't feel that way? They can leave on their own." She looked directly at Ira and smiled. "Without expensive lawsuits."

Ira flinched for a second. Then looked up and said, "That's right, Angela."

She put her Hermès bag on the table, signaling that she was ready to end the meeting.

"Can you give Eric and me a little privacy? We need to go over some global business."

The three executives hurriedly collected their papers and left, closing the door behind them.

As soon as the door closed, Angela raised a finger to her lips. Eric mimicked her. They waited in silence for a long moment. Then she mouthed, "Go check," pointing at the conference room door.

Eric rose, tiptoed to the door, opened it a crack, looked out in both directions, closed the door, and returned to the seat next to Angela.

They were safely alone.

Gleefully, he whispered, "Did you see the looks on their faces?"

Angela smirked and whispered in return, "What did you think?"

"I think you scared them half to death."

"I hope so," she said, no longer bothering to whisper. She gave Eric a wink. "They know I could just as easily have them fired."

"Would you?"

"No, not now. Not useful. But they don't know that. Fear is what makes the corporate world go 'round."

"And our job," Eric said, rubbing his palms together hungrily, "is to create even more of it!"

"No, luv. Our job is to *manage* the fear. We gin up fake camaraderie and community. That's how we create 'the culture.' First, we help the poor frightened employees think they belong to a great company. Then we delude them into believing that their great company also cares about them. If we do our job well, the employees buy into it. And they obey. What's more, they really do come to love the company. Can you imagine? *Love* it?" She smirked. "But here's the best part: The company never has to love them back. At any moment"—she raised her hand in a gun gesture and pulled the imaginary trigger.

"Bang!" Eric said, with a big grin.

CHAPTER 6

Charlotte Townsend was slightly disappointed that the mirrors in the bathroom of the Gulfstream IV weren't kinder to her. After all, at these prices, you'd think they'd find a way to make the coddled passengers look better than if they were peering into another ordinary mirror. But no. All the mirrors in this little room—and there were mirrors everywhere—told the whole truth and nothing but.

She was sure she did not look forty-five. The last facelift had seen to that. Still, she began to catalog a few spots where she would have her dermatologist freshen up her Juvéderm when she returned to New York after Antigua. She was the master of all the artifice that went into her look, holding all her aestheticians to the highest standards as they cared for her filled-in wrinkles, triple-process blonde hair, sculpted eyebrows, extended lashes, bronzing, facials, peels, makeup, waxing, and mani-pedis. And all that was before she even got started with her wardrobe. Yes, maintaining Charlotte

Townsend was a full-time job. But Charlie, hypervigilant and absolutely uncompromising when it came to her appearance, was up
to the challenge. In fact, she reveled in it. Although she knew she
could not stop time, she was proud of her accomplishments in
slowing down its ravages.

She checked herself in the full-length mirror one last time. Yes,
still a beauty. And yes, absolutely, still *hot*.

She emerged from the bathroom and was hit with a shock.
Suddenly she saw proof that her father was shrinking with age.
He had never been able to stand up to his full six-foot-two height
inside the Gulfstream. He'd had to scooch down a bit to keep his
head from bumping against the ceiling of the cabin. But there he
was, standing fully upright in the center of the aisle, with a fraction
of an inch clearance. His head did *not* touch!

Finally, the distant, often scary, tall man whose favor she had
negotiated with such care all these years was getting smaller.
Maybe, she hoped, the power he wielded would start to dimin-
ish as well.

As she took her usual seat in the center of the plane, she looked
at him with fresh eyes. Seventy-five-year-old Clifford Townsend still
had the blunt, plain features of an American descendant of hearty
Yorkshire peasants. His straight white hair was parted a little too
far down on the left side in order to achieve some comb-over at the
back of his bald head. Those big, round, wire-rimmed eyeglasses
still defined his look—the look of a *very* predatory owl—even if
the eyes were starting to sink inward, appearing smaller. But he
still vibrated with the antsy impatience of a teenager. He boasted
that, during his three marriages and divorces since her mother's
untimely death, he had also retained the sexual energy of a teenager.
Or damn close to it.

36

He flopped down into the big, lavishly padded leather seat across from Charlie. He stretched out his long legs and sighed. "Ah, best golf in the world, here in Scotland. Even if the weather is lousy. Got to get up here more often."

Still annoyed that Cliff's golf had blown her plans, Charlie did not respond.

With just the two of them in a cabin that could seat fourteen in extravagant comfort, there was plenty of room all around. Annie, their regular stewardess, pottered around them as the pilots prepared for wheels-up. As always for takeoff, she brought out two big crystal goblets of bubbly Badoit mineral water, no ice, and a slice of lime. Champagne, wine, and cognac would flow later on with the meal, and long afterward.

Cliff mused, half to himself, "You know, I really like your friend Angela."

"I'm so glad," Charlie said. "Sometimes she feels like the little sister I never had." Charlotte was Cliff's only child, despite his four wives. "Angela is so eager to learn. And I have so much fun teaching her. She's a very quick study."

"She sure is. That girl is whip-smart," Cliff said admiringly, "and a good listener."

"I'm sure," Charlie said with a smirk, "you never noticed how beautiful she is, you dirty old man, you."

"I am *not!*"

"Yeah, right."

"Charlie, come on," he protested. "I like her because she's a fighter. Nobody ever gave her anything. She knows the value of a dollar. Got a good head for business. Believe me, I can spot management talent. She knows what it's like to go without, to have doors slammed in her face. She knows the feeling of being the underdog with no one to help. No one. That's how you learn to rely on yourself and your wits. Like I did. I hate to say it, but she's the opposite of you. You've had everything handed to you on a silver platter."

Charlie made a show of taking umbrage. "Well, excuse me!"

Cliff waved it away. "Not your fault, not your fault. I did it for your mother. She made me promise. You have no idea how your mother had me spoil you. I did it willingly, of course, don't get me wrong."

Charlie did not want to go down that tired old path. Too many land mines. A long moment later, she said, "I'm working on the foundation idea. Will you promise to listen? Angela's helping me, you know. She's going to recruit a top communications expert. We want to make a very serious presentation to you."

Cliff shrugged. "Sure, I'll listen. But you're not a businessperson. You've never worked at anything." He reached his hand across the aisle to calm her before she could balk. "Like I said, you're not to blame for that. It's all on your mother and me."

Charlie waited until Annie had gone into the galley and closed the door.

"Cliff," she said, then paused. She started again in an urgent whisper, "Dad, it's time we sanitized the family fortune."

"Charlie," he answered in a needlessly loud voice, "there's nothing to sanitize. It's all honest money. How many times do we have to go over this?"

"But it's sleazy money. Pawn shops, bail bonds, payday loans, factoring, bottom-of-the-barrel businesses—I don't even know what they're called. The articles still talk about how you started out in porn video rentals. Remember when they put you on the Forbes

400? They dubbed you the King of Sleaze. You know what the girls at Miss Porter's started calling me? Princess Charlotta von Sleaze."

Cliff was annoyed. "I sent you to that pretentious girls' school because that's where your mother wanted you to go."

Charlie sat silent for a while. "Now that you're selling off your companies, isn't it time that we—"

Cliff interrupted her. "That's *my* business. I'm doing strategic liquidations, estate planning," he muttered.

"Exactly! So, it's the perfect time to create a foundation. Take all those hundreds of millions and do some good in the world."

Cliff shook his head and looked down at his shoes.

Charlie reached across the aisle again to pat Cliff's arm.

"You know, every time I go down to Antigua, I ask that banker of yours, Mr. Beresford, where he puts all that money you send him. And he just stonewalls me."

Cliff smirked. "That's his job."

She leaned across the aisle and whispered in his ear, "Tell me, are you *laundering* your money down there?"

Cliff sat back, removed her hand, and again answered her whisper in a voice louder than necessary. "You don't *need* to launder money when it's already *clean*."

Charlie swiveled her chair around to face him.

"Daddy, I want to create our own family foundation. I want to *run* it. I want to do good in the world. Sure, I've wasted time and money. But now I know what I want to do, what I was *meant* to do."

"My dear, you can't run a business. And a foundation is a big complicated business with all sorts of regulations and reporting requirements. Lawyers, accountants, complex tax regulations, mountains of paperwork. You have no idea how to manage that."

39

"I'll hire people to do all that boring stuff. I just know I can be the head of our foundation."

"Charlie, I believe what you want is to go to fancy parties and hobnob with snobby people."

That remark set her off. "And *you* like to embarrass me at those parties."

"I don't feel comfortable around phonies," Cliff said defiantly. "If they can't take me as I am, they can go stick it."

They descended into one of their ritual arguments.

As the pilots fired up the Gulfstream's engines to take off from Dundee Airport, Charlie and Cliff's bickering reached its usual stalemate.

Charlie got up and moved to the farthest seat at the back of the cabin.

"We'll finish this later," Cliff called to her, his usual closing remark.

Charlie gave him her usual response—a melodramatic huff—and fell into her seat with her back to him.

She was thinking about revealing the secret her mother had kept, years after her death. The secret that gave her power over the scary man who called himself her father. And her fear of what he might do if she tried to use it against him.

CHAPTER 7

Stewart Foley looked out over the expanse of open-plan workstations, all of them occupied. He asked himself how many Saturdays he had pissed away like this, slaving over lies and catchy jingles. Desperately trying to sell crappy products in order to make other people rich. Saturdays, and Sundays, too. He was fifty-six. Could this really have been how he had spent most of his adult life? Was this job with the mediocre salary and constant worry the best he could do for his family?

He felt so fucking old. Every day, as he got older, the people around him seemed to get younger. They wore their youth with arrogance, flaunting it, flinging it in his face along with their dating apps, tattoos, and sexting.

All he had was his ability. He was so good at the work. The kids would come to him for help. They were nice to him when they wanted something. God knows what they called him behind his back. But they came to *him*, all right. He would write for them

41

and show them how to craft that tweet or post into a zinger that would reverberate for a nanosecond inside the cold, hollow chambers of social media.

Stewart couldn't remember ever feeling this afraid. This time the rumors of mass firings sounded truly ominous. While worker genocide was a regular ritual of the agency business, Stewart had always been able to count on protectors like Jack Price to save him from the firing squads. Jack had shielded him in various agencies over the years. But suddenly, Stewart could see that even Jack—yes, even golden boy Jack Price—was starting to look old. And he could overhear the kids in the group bitching about having to submit to Jack's rule.

If Jack Price was getting too old, then Stewart knew he was doomed. Lately, when his mind would go blank with panic, he would dream of going postal. He would slay these snotty, entitled kids. With a torrent of words. Like bullets from a machine gun. Words that could kill them. And save him and his family. But they were only written words. Because S-S-Stewart c-c-could b-b-b-barely speak.

CHAPTER 8

By the time Jack had dropped Luke off and gotten to the agency, the sea of workstations was fully populated, as was typical for most weekends.

Jack waved to his team of writers, designers, coders, and staff assistants. His group filled the southeast quadrant of the thirty-third floor around his big corner office. Jack's position entitled him to one of the few enclosed spaces, even if his walls were glass.

Jack's people were a motley collection of men and women in roughly equal numbers, almost all in their twenties and thirties. They dressed to express their fierce individuality by conforming rigidly to one of the fashion templates current on the creative side of media world. There were hipsters, rockers, punks, preppies, and a few others in indefinable costumes that might signal the beginning—or the end—of one arcane trend or other. There were assorted hair buns, faux hawks, piercings, and lots of tattoos.

By mid-morning, the last of the faux hawks and man-buns had presented their ideas to Jack. In a half-hour or so, he was supposed to slip out of the office to pick up Luke and drive him back to Sandra's apartment.

Stewart Foley, a small, plain, middle-aged man with thinning gray hair, clearly out of place in this department, stood waiting with yellow legal pad in hand.

Jack waved him inside and motioned for him to close the sliding-glass door.

"You got taglines for me?" he asked.

Jack was sitting behind his enormous black Parsons table desk, empty except for a laptop computer and one of the virtual reality headsets they were pitching.

Stewart took his usual seat on the other side of Jack's desk. He held up his legal pad triumphantly. "C-C-C-Cannes L-L-Lion," he said, pointing it at the crowd of trophies on Jack's windowsill. Lions, Clios, Muses, Effies, Mobius loops, Hermès wings, and more.

"You always say that," Jack smiled, "you bullshit artist."

"Y-y-yes. B-b-but I am a *g-g-great* bullshit artist."

"You certainly are." Jack reached across the desk for a high five.

How many times had he saved Stewart's job? He was happy to do it. Time and again, he'd had to justify keeping this odd older guy who made three times what a newbie did. He had to explain over and over how Stewart was still a bargain. He produced five times more than the kids in less than half the time. His ideas were consistently creative and on-target. Unlike the kids, whose ideas, while crazy and fun, were, more often than not, unusable. What's more, as a—ahem—mature employee, Stewart was grateful for his job. He was compliant and passive. Easy to manage. Very *unlike* his entitled, whiny younger colleagues. Jack's final argument was that Stewart's speech handicap had to be good for diversity numbers.

"Show me what you got," Jack said eagerly. "Let me see what's on that magic legal pad of yours." Stewart did all his writing in longhand, using his office computer only for e-mails and Internet searches to feed his imagination.

Instead of handing over the yellow pad, Stewart laid it facedown on the desk. He put his hands on his knees, leaned forward, and gave Jack a grim stare.

"What's the matter, buddy?"

Stewart said nothing.

"Come on, what's up?"

Stewart took another deep breath. "L-l-l-layoffs. Th-th-that's the word." He pretended to fire a machine gun at an invisible crowd. "M-m-mass e-e-executions."

Jack held up the VR headset. "Hey, we're going to win this account. We'll all get rich."

"M-m-maybe you guys will. N-n-not me."

Stewart looked down at the floor. His shoulders rose and fell with labored breaths. When he looked up, his eyes were watery, his expression, pure panic.

"J-J-Jack, th-this is a-all I'm g-g-good at. N-n-nobody's g-g-gonna h-h-hire an old w-weirdo like me."

"Stewie," Jack said warmly, "I'll take care of you. I always do."

Stewart shrugged.

Jack knew what was worrying him. The agency's global holding company had announced, in oblique business jargon, a "strategic restructuring to implement a total *digital transformation.*" A fancy way of using this catchall term—which could mean anything—as an excuse for cost cutting. The holding company's newly appointed global chief culture officer—Angela Hanson—was leading the charge. Jack's Angela. The wonder woman who'd risen in record time to the dizzying heights of the C-suite. She was making surprise visits all across the network. "Friendly little audits of our digital culture," people said she called them. No one knew when or where she might pop up next.

"I-I'm n-not a d-digital native," Stewart said, invoking the catch-phrase that put you on one side or the other of the great divide.

"Stewie, take it easy." Jack reached across the desk and gave Stewart's arm a comforting squeeze. "You're the go-to guy for all the digital natives on this floor. They come to *you* to sharpen their tweets. Jesus, *you're* the guy who writes the zingers that get them the most likes, shares, and retweets. I'd say that makes you pretty goddamn digital."

Stewart waved away the compliment. He inhaled deeply and held his breath for a long moment. Then he spat out his words with not a trace of stuttering. "Fuck digital, Jack. I'm worried about my life insurance."

Jack did a double take. "Life insurance?"

Stewart's shoulders sank again. His stutter returned.

"I-I-I signed up for the d-d-double death b-b-benefit w-w-when you hired me. Th-th-they d-don't do it anymore. N-n-no one w-will i-i-insure me now." He tapped his chest over his heart. "B-b-bum ticker." He sniffed back a sob. "If I g-g-get fired, I lose it. M-m-my wife . . . m-my kids . . . it's all I g-g-got for them. J-Jack, I h-h-have to k-k-keep this shitty job."

"Stewie, relax. I'm not going to let them fire you." Jack lowered his voice. "Hey, I'll tell you a secret. I know this Angela woman."

Stewart lit up. "Y-you do?"

"Yeah, she worked for me five years ago. She was new in the business."

46

"Th-then m-maybe you c-can help me?"

Jack racked his brain to formulate a comforting lie to reassure Stewart. All he could muster was a fake smile and a thumbs-up.

CHAPTER 9

Angela and Eric left the conference room and took the curved architectural stairway one flight down to the creative department. They stood by themselves on the landing, looking out over the expanse of workstations.

"See that big glassed-in office in the far corner?" she whispered. "Go check out the man behind the desk for me."

"Who is he?" Eric whispered back eagerly.

She waved away the question. "Just go see what he's doing. Act like you belong and come right back."

"If I need to look like I belong, I should *not* be carrying this." Eric took the briefcase in both hands and presented it to Angela.

"Oh, all right," she snapped, taking it from him. "Now go! *Go!*"

Eric ambled his way through the workstations. He did a credible flyby of the corner office, wandered around the perimeter, and returned.

Angela immediately shoved the briefcase back into his arms.

"Well," he said quietly as he took it, "whoever he is, he is definitely a hot one."

"I didn't ask you to rate him," she whispered peevishly. "I asked you to tell me what he's doing."

"Ooh, aren't we touchy! Say, who *is* he?"

"He's Jack Price," she muttered angrily, "the head creative." Then she looked away.

Eric reached out and touched her chin gently. He turned her face to him. "Who is he to *you?* Come on, sister, you can tell me."

Angela was fighting off a flood of memories. Jack Price kissing her madly. Jack Price devouring her passionately. Jack Price inside her. Jack Price swearing he loved her more than life itself. Jack Price promising her everything forever. Spending countless hours imagining the rest of her life with Jack.

She looked down and whispered, "I almost married the bastard. Five years ago."

Eric lifted her chin again to make eye contact. With great tenderness, he asked, "What happened?"

"He was going to tell his wife he was leaving her. We had it all planned. We made love one last time to seal the deal." Angela narrowed her eyes. Old rage returning. Her voice turned cold. "No, he *fucked* me one last time. Then he said there was no way he was going to leave her. Not with their little boy, not with the life they had built. He said it was time to break it off. He said I knew it would end this way all along. He said I *had* to know. I mean, how could I *not* know?"

She remembered him standing there, a dark shadow looming over the bed. Just like every other man who had taken what he wanted. And then was done with her.

50

She pursed her lips.

Eric touched her shoulder. "It's okay, luv. I understand."

She stared hard at Eric. "That's confidential," she said through gritted teeth. "Con-fi-den-tial."

"Into the vault," Eric said, and zipped his lips.

They stood in silence for a long moment.

"So, are you going to, uh . . . ?" Eric made the pistol-shot gesture.

"Not today. We need him to finish the new business pitch on Monday. Then."

"Then when?"

"Wednesday. That's the big day."

"Do these people have any idea?"

"No," she said. "At least, I'm pretty sure they don't. There's nothing they can do about it, anyway. Tell me, what did you notice about the man in the office with him?"

"He's some gray-haired older chap in vintage Dockers, of all things, worn with absolutely no irony, I might add. Can't imagine what he's doing here."

"Oh, I know who he is. He's a copywriter. I have him in the database. Very convenient timing. I'll pay them a visit. Kill two birds with one stone."

"But I thought you said Wednesday?"

"Just a figure of speech." She pointed to an unoccupied workstation not far from them. "Go sit down and pretend to work. I have to handle this myself."

Eric gave a mock salute and headed for the workstation.

Angela pulled back her shoulders, straightened her spine, and took a deep breath through her nose. Whenever she faced a situation that might threaten her path to success, she summoned up the memory of the vestibule of the public housing tower where she grew up. The acrid stink of stale piss. It attacked everyone first thing every morning on their way out into the world. It welcomed everyone back home at night. A foul, stinging reminder that there was neither hope nor safety if you lived in the projects.

She shook her head to clear out the memory. It had done its job. She was determined to win, no matter what.

She thought of how foolish she had been with Jack. How weak, how emotional. Now she treasured the scar tissue the hurt had left. She was stronger for it. And she would never let her feelings get the better of her again. Imagine if she had become Jack's little wifey? Sharing with him the humdrum middle-management life that was about to be blown to bits.

She reviewed her objectives: One, Scare the shit out of the old copywriter, in hopes that he would quit on his own. Two, Keep Jack in the dark until the moment she would take control of his destiny.

She didn't feel bad for Jack.

Well, not too bad, anyway.

He was a dead man here, no matter what. She would actually be doing him a favor. Taking away his current job as a professional liar and giving him a new one.

Yes, a favor. For old times' sake.

CHAPTER 10

Jack saw her out of the corner of his eye. Her approach had that sudden slow-motion sensation people say they feel as they hurtle into a car crash.

Angela knocked on the glass door.

Jack waved her in.

Angela slid the glass door open.

"Mind if I join you?" She was not asking.

She walked across Jack's office as if she owned it.

Jack studied her. It had been five years. She had the same beautiful round face and high cheekbones, the same naturally blonde hair, the same hooded blues eyes set incongruously against her light brown skin. But girlish Angela was gone. She looked taller than the five feet, four inches he had once adored, from head to toe. Maybe it was the stiletto heels. Or her aura of absolute confidence.

No longer wearing cheap designer knockoffs, this Angela sported an expensive, sophisticated look that the rank-and-file women in the agency could never afford. Black watered-silk capri pants from Prada, royal blue Hermès tunic, genuine Verdura jewelry—necklace, wrist cuff, and ear-clips of gold strips woven like straw—and Christian Louboutin black patent-leather peep-toe pumps with signature red soles, her toenails and fingernails painted to match. She carried an iPad and a small, quietly elegant handbag that looked like it cost a small fortune.

She pulled up the chair beside Stewart and sat down. She put her expensive handbag on Jack's desk. As if it were *her* desk.

"Welcome, Angela," Jack said, trying to sound neutral and professional. He had no idea what to expect. "Been a long time."

She settled back in the chair. "A lifetime, Jack." She looked him squarely in the eye. "Several lifetimes."

When Jack had known her, she'd had a tentative, inquisitive air. Now she was pure laser-focus and ice-cold purpose. Of course, *he* had tutored her in the fine art of putting up a bulletproof facade. How to out-bullshit the other bullshit artists she would contend with in business. Clearly she had mastered this skill, and then some.

She rested her iPad on her lap and swiped a finger across the screen. "It's great to be back in New York," she said, half to herself, as she scrolled through screens. "I just don't think I'll have any time to enjoy it."

Jack knew she lived in London now. A whole new life he could only imagine.

She crossed one leg, keeping it parallel with the floor for an instant. Just long enough to show off the red sole of her pricey designer shoe. Or, Jack wondered, was she showing off the little tattoo cradling her ankle bone? He could not make out what it depicted.

She turned to Stewart. He was visibly quaking.

"And you must be . . ." She studied her screen for an instant. "Stewart, yes? Stewart Foley?" She used the fake-friendly tone of an authoritarian middle-school teacher.

Tongue-tied Stewart nodded.

Jack jumped in to help. "Stewart is one of our top writers. He's our go-to guy for great ideas and copy. The whole company depends on Stewart."

"Uh, thanks, Jack," she said, switching to a more grown-up variety of condescension. "Why not let Stewart answer for himself."

There was a moment of uncomfortable silence.

"J-J-Jack is m-my s-s-spokesperson. I've g-got him under c-contract." Even in his frightened state, Stewart tried to be light. In their world, good banter was the surest display of confidence.

"Clever, Stewart. Well done," she said approvingly. She gave a single tap on her tablet. "You live up to your reputation." She studied the screen a bit more. "But I see you are not at all active on social. No Twitter, no Instagram, no Snapchat—not even a Facebook page, like everyone's grandpa. Is my information correct?"

Jack interceded again. "Stewart writes the best posts and tweets in the agency. All the kids go to Stewart for social copy for clients *and* their personal pages. It's an open secret. He writes the zingers that get the most likes, shares, and retweets."

Angela gave Jack the faintest of smiles. "I wonder, does he also write the big ideas *you* take credit for?" She tapped on her tablet and clicked her tongue.

Suddenly Jack squirmed. His phone chirped once in his pocket. It was the text tone assigned to Luke.

"You want to get that?" Angela asked.

"No," he said uneasily. He was thinking, *Jesus, no!* Not now. Not a collision between Luke, the victim of my biggest mistake, and

Angela, the cause of it. "Uh, it's okay," he said. He reached into his pocket to silence the ringer.

"You sure?" she asked. "Really. It's all right." Her strained politeness said that the interruption was *not* all right.

Jack took the phone out of his pocket, powered it off, and put it facedown on the desk.

"No problem—go ahead."

He had no choice but to put Luke off for the moment. He felt a pang of guilt so sharp it was almost physical.

"I'm eager to meet the whole agency," Angela said. "As you probably know, I've been doing culture audits all around the network. Of course, I already know Jack."

Jack hoped the poker face he put on would reveal nothing. He wondered how the hell she was going to handle this.

She turned to Stewart. "Jack was my first mentor, you know. He taught me so much at the very beginning of my career." She smiled at Jack. "I'll always be grateful to you for teaching me about the business."

Jack nodded graciously, relieved at what would now become the official lie about their relationship.

"I was a wide-eyed newbie," she went on, "a nobody. He was this big deal with a corner office." She smiled at Stewart. "He still is. I'll never forget what I said."

Angela switched to a coarse street-accent impression of her younger self. " 'Yo, Jack, teach me how to get my slice a this.' At first, he gave me some bullshit answer like, 'Well, young lady . . .' " She slipped into a very good impersonation of Jack as her wise elder, giving her a lecture. " 'It takes a lot of hard work, initiative, and determination. You'll need resilience, lots more hard work, and then a little luck.' And I said, 'Get outta here. That's just a bullshit way of saying nothin's easy.' "

She turned to Jack. "Right?"

Jack nodded. She remembered everything.

"And I said, 'Jack, tell me what the real deal is. How things really work inside those big shiny towers. How those people *really* get ahead. The *real* deal.' And he said, 'I don't think you can take it.' And I said, 'Yes, I can.' Like nine or ten times. Finally, he said, 'Okay, I'll tell you.' Remember, Jack?"

Jack nodded again. She left out the fact that they were naked, and he was inside her during this particular conversation. He shot a look at Stewart that he hoped would give his colleague some optimism.

Angela set her iPad on Jack's desk beside her handbag, completing her conquest of his territory, then got up and walked to the window. She picked up one of the Clio trophies from the windowsill. She held the base with one hand while idly running her other hand up and down the length of the standing figurine.

No, Jack thought, she can't possibly be reminding me of that. He looked away.

"How's the VeRity pitch going?" she asked as she dropped the Clio onto the windowsill with a loud *thunk*.

Stewart looked pleadingly at Jack. Jack shook his head to signify no worries.

"Good," Jack said, hesitant for an instant. "No, it's going great!" He picked up the VR headset. "Got it nailed."

"Just the way you always do. Right, Jack?"

"You bet," Jack said, putting on a cheery face for Stewart's benefit.

"To *whom* does Stewart report?" she asked, suddenly sounding like a pretentious English teacher conducting an exercise.

Jack knew she was referring to the grammar lessons he had taught her in bed, usually after bouts of Olympic-level sex. He answered in the same pedagogical tone, just as he had done back then. "I am the one to *whom* Stewart reports."

Angela gave him a little smirk.

Jack returned the look.

Even though Angela had barely gotten through community college, she had, through her fierce native intelligence, her gift for mimicry, and Jack's lessons in bed, mastered the impeccable diction and grammatical precision of an Ivy League English major, along with the full set of social skills he had taught her—table manners, polite small talk, the works. His tutoring had transformed the crude street girl from the projects into a reasonably creditable forgery of an uptown debutante.

She bent down and spoke into Stewart's face. "Stewart, ever seen a bucket of crabs?" She made a frantic snapping motion with both hands. "Snap, snap, snap!" Stewart tried to recoil but had nowhere to go. "The crabs climb all over each other, trying to get to the top of the bucket. Snap, snap, snap! Snap, snap, snap! They fight and chop each other up. Some get maimed, some get killed. They don't care. Snap, snap, snap!"

She let her hands fall to her sides and stood up straight.

Stewart whimpered.

"That's our company. That's everybody's company. We're all nasty, murderous little crabs."

She placed a hand on Stewart's shoulder. "Stewart, may I see one of your business cards?" Stewart looked up in terror. He reached into his back pocket for his wallet, a sorry bulging flap of cracked, battered leather. He rifled inside it, searching through his personal crap. Finally, he found a lone business card. With shaky hand, he gave the pitiful dog-eared thing to Angela. He lowered his head as if he were naked under a paper gown, about to undergo a humiliating medical exam.

Angela held the card up in the air. "Here we all are, carrying our company identity around in our wallets. Then suddenly, the company takes it away."

She grabbed the card with her other hand and crushed it into her fist.

Stewart hugged himself and leaned forward, as if he had stomach cramps.

"Maybe for good reason. Maybe for no reason. Maybe it's a new boss who wants his—or *her*—own team. Maybe it's a phony made-up reason. Maybe it's just bad luck. Or maybe, just maybe, one of your fellow crabs fucked you over in some way you'll never know about."

She opened her fist and looked at the balled-up card. She made a mock frowny face and gave a sad little snivel. She took a deep breath. Gave her shoulders a little shake.

"Wouldn't it be great to get away from all of this, once and for all? It's something *I* dream about all the time. Just quitting and walking away from it all. Don't you, Stewart?"

She pressed the mangled card against her leg with great care, ironing it back into a wrinkled semblance of a rectangle.

"Ohhhh," she said with exaggerated sadness. She handed it back to him. "Forgive me. I got carried away."

Stewart stared at the sorry thing in his hand. He looked at Jack in horror. Then he jumped to his feet and ran out of the office, leaving the door open.

"Jesus, Angela!" It was all Jack could do to hold back his anger. He knew all too well how cruel she could be. But he also knew why. She detested weakness in others and attacked it. Because she was so terrified of the slightest weakness in herself.

Angela walked to the door and slid it shut, then turned to face him.

"Jack, we have to find a way to conduct our business relationship like adults. We need a fresh start."

"I agree." He got up and walked over to her.

She took a deep breath. Then another. In that fleeting moment, her icy demeanor seemed to melt away. She peered up into his eyes with something that looked like the warmth he had once known.

"Jack . . . I'm sorry. Sorry about everything in the past." She gave him the hesitant little smile she used to give him when she was looking for his approval. "We both acted kind of crazy back then. Didn't we?"

Then she looked down and shook her head. When she looked up, her stone face was back.

"Now we have to live in the present and be effective." She extended her right hand. "Peace?"

Jack took it. He felt none of the electricity that had once passed between them.

"Okay, Angela. Peace."

She shook and let go. Then turned to leave.

Jack spoke to her back. "Uh, Angela, did you really have to be so tough on Stewart? He's a good employee. Productive. He's just not a power player—more of a gentle forest creature."

She did not turn around. "A gentle forest creature?" she asked, repeating the phrase quizzically, as if confused. She took a step toward the doorway.

Jack knew damn well she was pretending not to remember. He had taught her that phrase to describe withdrawn creative types who nonetheless produced a lot of good work.

She spun around abruptly and faced him. Aggressively.

"See this expensive necklace? See it? Do you?" She lifted one of the gold links with a fingertip. "If I don't deliver a total transformation to digital culture, and fast"—she gave the necklace a little yank—"this will turn into a noose."

She cocked her head to one side for an instant, as if being hanged.

"Believe me, Jack. You may have a soft spot for gentle forest creatures, but management does not. In the new world I have to create, gentle forest creatures end up as only one thing."

"What's that?"

"Roadkill."

She slid the door open, turned on her bright red soles, and walked out, closing the door behind her.

Jack shuddered. She's the perfect corporate monster, he thought. And I created her.

CHAPTER 11

Jack sat down at his desk. His mind was racing.

Angela is here to clean house. She's making a list. Checking it twice. Nothing personal, Jack. Just business. Yeah, right. Except she wants a little more revenge for the way I dumped her five years ago.

He realized when he had told Luke that this VR pitch was do-or-die . . .

Shit. Luke!

He powered on his phone. Luke's texts flooded the screen. There were emojis everywhere:

> Hey I won!!
> I scored the winning goal!
> Dad, when are you going to pick me up?
> LIKE NOW??????
> Hey where are you?????

????????
WTF Dad?????

Jack called. Luke picked up immediately. Before Luke could finish his first syllable, Jack jumped in. "I'm so sorry, kiddo, believe me. Crazy shit at the office. Really crazy shit. Luke, I can't leave. I can't. I know you've heard that before. But this time, this pitch, it really *is* life-or-death. This is your tuition, that new bike we talked about, the next vacation, all that and more. Can you please call Mom? I promise I'll make it up to you. Promise, cross my heart and hope to die, honest! Please, Luke. Please call Mom."

Jack heard a distant, disheartened "Okay." His son clicked off.

Guilt, Jack thought. More guilt for Jack Price. Go ahead, pile it on. We're talking about a Mount Everest of guilt on my head. What's yet another failure, one more disappointment for my only child?

Stop it, he ordered himself. That doesn't help anyone. Just fucking stop it and get to work.

He stood up and shook his whole body up and down. He reached into his briefcase for his AirPods. He slipped them into his ears, scrolled through his music library, and tapped his favorite Philip Glass playlist.

He sat down to focus. Opened his laptop. Concentrate, Jack, concentrate.

He began by rereading the top-secret, password-protected product briefing, all the confidential stuff for which everyone in the agency had had to sign NDAs. Leak any of this shit to anyone, per the nondisclosure agreement mumbo-jumbo, and lawyers will descend on you like a plague of locusts and destroy your life.

Blah, blah, blah. This new virtual reality headset has innovative software developed by an elite team of computer animators, gaming mavens, and hardware and software engineers. Nothing special about that. Blah, blah, blah. It's a unique combination of AR, augmented reality, and VR, virtual reality. It puts the wearer of the headset in his own personal action movie. The camera works with the animation software to combine the real environment with a fantasy landscape of the wearer's chosen action movie. In a perfect illusion, the wearer will have the feeling of flying, crashing, doing whatever super feat they want their invincible action hero avatar self to do—in their own real-but-altered environment.

Different? Meh. Not all that different.

We did test drives of all the VR products on the market. They're all pretty cool. And pretty much the same. So what?

The big difference was that this developer team also included neuroscientists. The extra thing is what the neuroscientists built into the user experience. Proved it with brain scans. This VR gaming headset will trigger all the brain chemicals that promote—not just fun and excitement—but addiction. This was the thing everyone had to keep secret. This was the real reason for the NDA.

Addiction! Every marketer's dream. A product that customers *have* to have.

Is it mind control? Who knows? Jack wondered, Is it even true? Clients always inflate their claims. They bullshit their agencies and their agencies bullshit the public. There are laws and regulations that keep it more or less honest. We are all relieved of guilt, right?

Yeah, right.

It's not like we're selling cancer the way they did with cigarettes back in the day. Or opioids, more recently.

Jack asked himself, Who's bullshitting who? Then he shuddered.

His mind flashed on an image of Angela correcting him at the very moment she put the gun to his head. "Wrong, Jack," Dream Angela says as she cocks the trigger. "It's who's bullshitting whom. *Whom!*"

He could almost hear the shot splatter his brains across the wall. Then the image vanished.

Who? Whom? Who gives a shit? As long as we can make the customers buy and buy and buy.

He picked up Stewart's legal pad and started reviewing the list of ideas written in his buddy's tight, nervous scrawl. He studied all three pages. Slowly. Deliberately. Once. Twice. He sat back to absorb and reflect. He studied his view from the thirty-third floor. He studied the dust particles floating in the beam of sunlight. He emptied his mind. He filled it again with his own thoughts on selling the product. Then the three or four ideas from Stewart that had stuck in his memory. On his third pass through Stewart's pages, he spotted it. Philip Glass provided a little crescendo at just the right moment.

Twenty-five years in the business, and he knew it when he saw it.

The big, beautiful, simple, memorable, totally believable lie.

Jack drew a red circle around Stewart's killer theme line. Around the solution. The answer. His and Stewart's salvation. The Big Idea. The Big Lie that will save their jobs.

Jack could see the campaign in his mind's eye—the YouTube videos on their dedicated channel, the ads plastered everywhere, the Instagram movie snippets, the insidious Facebook posts, the flood of hashtags, the frantic handheld Snapchat videos, the whole package. The big, beautiful lie that gets repeated over and over until it touches the nerve that creates . . . desire. Desire for something nobody asked for. Desire for something nobody really needs. But now they want it. They have to have it.

Can our lie get past the lawyers? Of course, it can. It's a great lie. Not just a good lie. A great lie. We can frontload it with a disclaimer that will make the lawyers happy and keep us morally pure. We'll just keep the disclaimer very small.

Jack knew at once how he would spin the presentation at the big meeting with the clients on Monday. How he would woo them. Spellbind them with his legendary powers of persuasion.

Ha! No one in this place can sell the way I do. If I can get credit for this big win, I can send Angela back to Corporate and out of my life.

He started typing his notes for the presentation and assigning the pieces of it to his creative staff for them to craft over the rest of the weekend. He paid no attention to the distant noises outside his office. Philip Glass's insistent repetitive rhythms helped take care of that.

Until one loud knock got past the music.

He looked up to see his door open. It was Paul Angelos, one of his top creatives, red-faced and out of breath.

"Jesus, Jack! Didn't you hear anything? Jesus! Fuck!"

Jack was annoyed at the interruption. He removed his AirPods. "What?"

"It's Stewart! He threw up in one of the men's room stalls. He just lay there on the floor. He wasn't breathing. We called the ambulance. They tried to revive him. They say he's dead. Said it looks like heart attack. They're getting ready to bring him out."

Before Paul could finish, Jack had flown out the door and was sprinting toward the men's room.

He pushed his way through the crowd.

The scene unfolded in disconnected snippets. Jump cuts. Like bad film editing. One jarring shot interrupting the next.

67

The men's room floor. Harsh lighting. Two uniformed emergency medical technicians. One EMT snapping up the big suitcase of medical gear. The other strapping a pale, waxy mannequin that sort of resembled Stewart to the gurney. The mannequin's face gray and expressionless. Shirt sliced open? Pale chest? Where was Stewie? The mannequin looked so much smaller than Stewie. How did Stewart get so small? EMTs moving everyone aside. The crowd buzzing.

Jack walking.

Stunned.

He found himself back in his office.

He sat down in the chair Stewart had just run from. It was cold. No trace of his talented little buddy's life force.

Jack looked at his watch. Just a few sweeps of the hands ago, just a few of those seconds that tick-tick-tick themselves into nothingness, just minutes ago, sweet stuttering Stewart was right here. How could he be gone? Dead meat. With no good-byes. Just gone. Like that.

Jack sat frozen in his friend's chair.

CHAPTER 12

Angela and Eric were waiting in the conference room. Daniel, Ira, and Jennifer were due any minute for the emergency meeting.

"Ewwww," Eric said. "Did you see them carrying out the body?"

Angela shrugged a no.

"I couldn't help but stare." He rambled on as he did when he knew that Angela was not listening. "I know it's terribly rude to stare, but it didn't matter to *him*, now, did it? That older chap. The body, I mean. Just think—I was spying on him a few minutes before. I saw that he'd wet those vintage Dockers. Must have happened when he died. The body lets loose at death, I hear. You were actually just talking to him. My God, you were, along with that former Romeo of yours." He paused. "Tell me, have *you* ever seen a dead body?"

She shrugged again. "Yeah." She turned and faced him.

"Really?" Eric seemed pleased to have her attention again. "How perfectly awful for you. Where? When? Tell me, tell me."

"In the projects. Somebody down the hall who didn't come out for a week and then the smell got the neighbors' attention. Gang killings. A friend in high school, I saw her get shot by a stray bullet one summer night."

Eric winced.

"I've had people dying on me since I was little," she said, talking more to herself than to Eric. "Like my shithead father." She pointed at her eyes and blonde hair. "The guy who gave me my Swedish genes and last name. I met him once. Once! I was seven. That same night, he drunk-drove his car into an embankment. For years, I thought it was my fault."

"I'm so sorry," Eric said.

"Don't be." She turned away and looked impatiently at her watch. "Where the hell *are* they?"

Eric hesitated, then said, "Well, at least you had your mum to make it all right."

Angela gave him a blank stare.

"You had your mum, right?"

She sat silent for a moment. "Yeah. Until I was nineteen. Then she joined my parade of dead people."

Eric winced again. He took her hand urgently and squeezed it.

She let him hold it as she thought of poor abandoned Sonia Hanson and her only child, Angela.

"I watched her die in the hospital," Angela said softly.

"Of what?"

"You know what sepsis is?"

Eric gasped. "Infection?"

"Improperly sanitized instruments," she muttered as she stared out the window. "It's horrible. Happens all the time in hospitals. Especially to poor people."

She remembered her mother's guilt at her sin against her beloved church. She'd had the abortion to kill the baby inside her that came from the rat-bastard owner of the factory where she worked. All the pretty women on the production line had to give that fat white pig whatever he wanted. And he got away with it. Probably still did.

"How old was she?" Eric asked meekly.

"Thirty-nine." Her tone was flat and robotic; she was remembering. Her mother's death had been her introduction to the business world. The boss who could fuck his workers any way he wanted.

She was still haunted by her mother's cries from her hospital bed—a bloodcurdling mixture of pain, guilt, shame, and helplessness. Angela felt the soft and loving parts of herself die along with her mother, and the birth of the hard-hearted fury that propelled her.

"Do you want to talk about it?" he asked tentatively.

"No," she said, withdrawing her hand. Not because she wanted to let go of Eric. She did not. She liked this moment of intimate sharing. It felt easy and right. She loved her brotherly bond with Eric. But the time and place were wrong.

They were in the middle of a shit storm.

They needed to focus.

She needed to focus.

She had a plan almost entirely worked out in her mind. She thought it was inspired, maybe even brilliant. She imagined herself like the safe-cracking jewelry thief in a heist movie. She had her stethoscope against the metal door and was turning the dial ever so slowly, listening for the cogs of the tumblers, expertly coaxing them into clicking together in just the right way to give up the secret code and let her open the millionaire's vault. To steal the priceless gems inside.

The conference room door flew open.

Daniel burst in, Ira and Jennifer right behind.

"Oh Jesus, oh Jesus," Daniel said, holding his head as if it might explode. "I've never had an employee literally die on me *in the office*."

Ira tried to calm his boss as they sat down at the table. "They said it looked like a heart attack. Hey, this stuff happens. My father-in-law died that way. Nobody had any idea he had a problem. Then one day he just keeled over." Ira snapped his fingers. "Just like that. He was sixty-eight. Never knew what hit him. There's a kind of mercy in that, you know." He snapped his fingers again. "That's how I'd want to go."

"Me, too," Jennifer said. She put a folder down on the conference room table. "Here's one piece of good news. Stewart had the double death benefit life insurance. We stopped offering that years ago. Good thing for his family."

"Yeah, good," Daniel said halfheartedly. He went back to holding his temples to keep his head intact. "We've got the new business pitch, the layoffs," he fretted. "Jesus, what do we do?"

Angela maintained her studied calm. "Let's strategize," she said.

Jack Price had taught her that the big shots in business always kept calm. Even if they didn't have the answer, they always *looked* like they did. In this case, she was pretty sure she did have the answer. That is, the answer to the question, "How can Angela Hanson make goddamn sure she gets an even bigger bonus?"

Daniel shook his head. "I'm worried about the pitch—morale, blowback from the firings, what the trade press will say, what our other clients will think. Jesus Fucking Christ."

"Worrying never helps," Angela said. "Just give me a sec here." She drummed her fingers on the table. Then peered off into space. "It's a terrible shame that Stewart died. Just terrible. We all feel awful."

She looked down, pretending to honor Stewart's memory and their shared sadness. She knew that nobody gave a shit about Stewart or his family. She just needed to lead them through a hypocritical ceremony that fulfilled the group's obligations to decent humanity. She kept her head down in a silent mourning pose for a good two minutes. Angela intended it to feel like forever. And it did. Once the human decency box had been properly checked, they could all get back to business.

Finally, she looked up. "But—we *can* make this work for us. Really, I'm sure of it. Stewart can help us solve several potential problems. Except for being in his fifties, he was the perfect role model for our new tribe. He was talented, passive, compliant, and undemanding. Fear kept him working nights and weekends with never a complaint. Let's make him our hero. Without actually saying so, we will be demonstrating that we value older employees. Let's make Stewart Foley the answer to all the questions of our catechism. That way, how could anyone dare accuse us of age bias after the layoffs?"

Daniel and his colleagues stared at her, dumbstruck.

Eric looked on with admiration.

Angela was on a roll and she knew it.

Did she feel that maybe, just maybe, she had caused Stewart's heart attack by going after him so viciously?

No, she told herself, giving her conscience a big fat shove. No way. No more than she had caused her girlfriend's death from the street gang's stray bullet that night in the projects. It had taken twenty years of screaming nightmares for Angela to get over her guilty horror. But she had finally made peace with it. Well, on most nights. Yes, she had teased Eva. Eva, her true bestie forever and ever. Shamed her like a mean girl to get her to join her in the courtyard to escape the un-air-conditioned heat of the apartments they occupied with their sad single mothers. But now, she had accepted that the collision between the bullet and poor Eva's skull was an inevitable act of destiny. Not her fault anymore. At least, not *all* her fault.

The mass firings she had come to New York to execute were also not her doing. She was merely an instrument of Fate, the Grim Reaper with a handbag from Hermès and stock options. If Stewart Foley had a heart condition and had stayed too long in a job that ate people alive before they could reach middle age, that was *his* problem. He had been doomed one way or the other.

What mattered to everyone in this conference room was how to get out of this mess with their careers intact. And by serving herself, Angela had a way to save them all. End of morality play, she told herself, ordering the guilty murmur in the back of her mind to pipe down.

"Let's plan a big party for the whole agency," she said, her voice brightening. "Daniel, do you have a place where you guys celebrate new business wins?"

"Uh, yeah, sure," he said hesitantly. "Vlad's Vodka House."

"Tell me all about it," she said urgently.

"Well, uh, the kids love it. They get a free open bar into the wee hours and we pay for car services home for everyone."

"Great! Let's arrange a big bash for Monday right after work. No matter what happens in the new business meeting, we are going to celebrate our hero Stewart Foley. Can we get a Stewart Foley tribute video cut in time for Monday evening?"

Daniel nodded a puzzled look.

She glanced at Eric for support. She felt his secret smile when their eyes met. She could always depend on Eric to feed her confidence. He was her touchstone. With him at her side, she could get through anything. She turned back to Daniel.

"Then get it done, my friend! Get it done!" She gave him a pat on the shoulder to buck him up. He forced an obedient smile, hesitantly getting on board her fast-moving train.

"Daniel, my man, first we have to help the troops get over their shock. Then, get them back to work on the pitch. Let's call an all-hands meeting in, say, half an hour. I know just what to tell them."

She raised her hand for a high-five gesture.

Daniel raised a hand hesitantly.

She gave it a good hard slap like a regular bro. "We can *do* this!"

CHAPTER 13

A sudden noise brought Jack back to reality. It was coming from his desk. The ringtone assigned to Sandra. Shit! He could feel the phone vibrating with her anger. He lunged for it, imagining the pissed-off voice mail she would leave if he did not answer.

"Let me guess," Sandra said before he could say hello. "You couldn't make it to your son's victory celebration when you were supposed to be spending the entire day with him, acting like his father." Sandra didn't sound hugely angry. Just a little peeved, which meant she was actually flat-out furious at him. "Why? Because you have no choice but to be at the office. It's not your fault, right?"

Jack had learned long ago never to answer an angry woman's rhetorical questions. That only made things worse.

"Tell me, Jack, do you have any idea how much that boy loves you? Do you know how much he idolizes you? He's at a critical point in his development. He needs his father to be his role model.

His father. Remember? Uh, that's you. God help him. Do you have any idea the kind of excuses I have to make to preserve your image as world's greatest dad?"

"Hey, come on," Jack said, trying not to sound lame and defensive and knowing he was. "I have taken him to soccer camp a hundred times. I take him to movies, the circus, ball games, the natural history museum, you name it. He stays at my apartment all the time. We hang out in the park together. We pal around all the time. I love him just as much as you do. True?"

"Yes, Jack, it's true. You can be a good dad when you make the time."

"Okay then," Jack sputtered, hoping to raise himself out of the dark pit of guilt where Sandra had rightfully tossed him. Still, he knew he had fucked up. Again.

"But Jack, this one really mattered to him," she said. "He won the damn game, for Pete's sake. I bite my tongue ten times a day to keep him convinced that his dad loves him as much as he loves his dad. I do it for him, Jack. Not for you. I covered for you again. I picked him up and brought him home. You are officially off the hook. Okay?"

"I'm sorry, Sandra. Really." He cringed at his words.

"I know, Jack. You're at the office and you're going to have to crunch into the night because, if you can't be bothered to come in on Saturday, don't bother to come in on Sunday. And later tonight, after all your hard work, maybe you guys will go out for drinks. You think? And maybe you'll find some cute young thing who desperately needs mentoring. And you, out of generosity, will take her under your wing and teach her everything you know in an all-night"—she paused, preparing to give her next bit ironic emphasis—"an all-night *tutoring* session. Have I got that right?"

Not that this is a contest, Jack told himself, but Sandra has sunk me again. And she was right, of course.

"I know my apologies are lame, Sandra."

He could almost see her nodding. Looking way down at him from the unassailable heights of her moral high ground.

"I'm not trying to make excuses," he said. "It's just that . . . well, I'm a little fucked up at this moment. My best friend at work—remember Stewart?"

"Yes," she said coldly, knowing the excuse was coming. "The older guy with the stutter."

"That's right, him." Jack took a deep breath. "He just dropped dead. Heart attack."

Sandra gasped. "No!"

"Stewie, my Stewie," Jack said, suddenly hit by a wave of grief. "I guess the pressure . . . uh, he'd told me he had a heart condition." Tears filled his eyes.

"Oh, poor man!" Sandra was genuinely distressed. "Did he have a family?"

"A wife, two kids."

Sandra groaned.

"He was sitting in my office just a short time ago. Suddenly, he went pale as a ghost. Hugged himself and doubled over. Ran to the men's room. They said he was probably gone before he hit the floor."

"Oh, Jack," she whispered, chastened.

"So, I'm sorry, but I . . ."

He wiped his eyes with his sleeve and sniffed back the tears that wanted to flow. Real tears.

Sandra gave a sigh. "It's okay. Don't worry," she said softly, "I'll take care of Luke."

Jack had a sick feeling of guilt. It was awful to be breaking the news of Stewart's death like this. That wasn't why he had failed to pick up Luke.

Suddenly, Paul Angelos appeared in the doorway. Seeing Jack with the phone to his ear, he mouthed his words with silent exaggeration. "All-hands meeting. Now!" He pointed frantically in the direction of the communal break room. "Now!"

"Sandra, they're calling an all-hands meeting. I gotta go. Thanks for covering for me. I promise I'll make it up to both of you. Promise."

CHAPTER 14

As Jack walked down the hall toward the break room, he heard Daniel introducing Angela to the group.

The room was full when Jack arrived. He was thinking about Stewart. In his way, Stewart had managed to do the impossible. He had quit before they could fire him. And he still held onto the double death benefit for his family. Extreme, yes. But he did get everything he wanted. Weird.

He assumed that the purpose of Angela's rant had been to encourage Stewart to leave on his own. Save the agency the trouble of a messy firing with a possible ageism lawsuit. If so, she had certainly accomplished her goal. Had she actually killed Stewart? Nah, not really. Did she know he had a bad heart? How could she? Jack was pretty sure that personal medical records were strictly confidential. Still, you could say that Angela did scare Stewart to death. Like Stewart, Angela got everything *she* wanted, too. Even weirder.

Then he saw Angela do something that showed her mastery of power. She gave her handbag and iPad to a skinny young man with a stripe of white hair and purple suede Chelsea boots—no doubt the British boy toy and executive gofer Jack had heard about in the rumors. She raised one foot toward the seat of a chair, indicating she wanted to hoist herself up to stand on the table to deliver her remarks. Without so much as looking at Daniel, she extended one arm in front of him. Daniel, a very in-charge guy, acted just like a footman tending the carriage at an English great house. He grasped her forearm and elbow. In one quick motion, she went from floor to chair and was standing on the big white table. She gave Daniel neither thanks nor the slightest nod for his help.

She commanded the room from on high in her expensive red-soled stilettos. Projecting her voice effortlessly, she filled the room as expertly as a stage actress.

"If we were normal people," she said, "we would all hug each other and say that life is short, and love is all that matters. Then we would call off this crazy weekend work and let everyone go home to mourn the loss of our friend, Stewart Foley. Daniel, your CEO, would call the VeRity client and ask to delay the Monday meeting. And if the client said no, he'd say, 'Then I'm sorry, we can't play. We are human beings first and marketing creatives second.' "

She paused, took a deep breath, and looked around at the crowd. Silence.

"But, hey, from what I can see, we're not normal. *I'm* not normal. Anybody here normal?"

"Not meee!" Boy Toy exclaimed, with a big laugh. The crowd followed his lead.

"That's what I thought," Angela said. "Nobody here is normal. And neither was our friend Stewart."

82

A little buzz of relief.

Angela caught her breath, as if holding back tears.

"I had no idea how lucky I was earlier today. I was with Stewart, just minutes before the tragedy. We were in Jack's office. Just talking, bullshitting a little, having a few laughs to ease the pressure."

She pointed to Jack at the far wall of the room and gave him a little wave.

Jack waved back, playing along.

"Of course, I knew all about Stewart. His talent, his years of service, and how so many people in this room loved him and depended on him. Am I right?"

The crowd did not react.

"Come on! It was an open secret. Stewart was the go-to guy to sharpen your social media copy." She raised her hand, indicating she wanted a show of hands. " 'Fess up. Who got help from Stewart? Come on, let's see."

A few hands went up hesitantly. Boy Toy raised his arm and waved it enthusiastically. More hands went up. Then more still.

"Yes! Stewart was our guy. I'm glad I got to know him a little bit. I feel grateful for that. He joked about how he had Jack under contract as his spokesperson. Stewart gave Jack pretty good grades for presenting his ideas as if they were his own." She made a big "Oops" face and clapped her hand over her mouth. "I'm sorry, I meant to say, Jack presented Stewart's ideas with his brilliant skill and won business for all of us."

Boy Toy tittered. A few people tittered with him.

"Hey, we are all feeling this terrible shock. Sadness. Loss. We will miss his wry sense of humor. We will miss his generosity. He asked for little in return. Just to use his talent to help us all win together. Stewart was, and I'm not afraid to use the cliché, Stewart was a team player."

83

Her eyes were starting to water. She sniffled.

"Let's win this pitch for Stewart and for the team. It's what he would have wanted."

Boy Toy started cheering, "Stew-art, Stew-art!" The crowd joined him.

She waved to Jack. "Jack, will you have work from Stewart to show? Do you have Stewart's last ideas?"

"Yes, of course I do," Jack announced like a cheerful team player.

He was thinking, If I win this account, she is laying the ground-work for denying me credit. If we lose, they could blame me, but they'll have to share some of that blame. But if we do win, there will be a battle for credit. And that will be even uglier. Gotta love this business.

By now Angela's eyes were filled with tears.

"We're going to work, day and night, until the clients walk in here Monday afternoon. We'll blow them away. We've got to give this our best. We'll win this"—she choked up—"for the wonderful creative man I was lucky enough to meet today." Tears began to stream down her elegant cheekbones, some streaked with mascara. "For Stewart!" she shouted.

"Stew-art! Stew-art!" the crowd answered, with Boy Toy leading the cheers.

Angela took a step toward the edge of the table and did a convincing impersonation of someone who was terrified of falling. In a flash, Daniel was there. He reached up to give her balance and support, guiding her down with great care. While she utterly ignored him.

Wow, Jack thought, she's really good. Meaning, of course, she's really bad.

CHAPTER 15

Angela was thrilled with the way she looked in the Alexander McQueen dress Charlie had railroaded her into buying. It was a smashing combination of blatant sex appeal and impeccable elegance. Beneath her bare shoulders was the black leather bustier that laced up like an antique corset; it held her in and pushed up her breasts. From the waist down was a cascade of white lace and more black leather in overlapping layers. The look would command old Cliff Townsend's undivided attention, she hoped.

She paused at the revolving door of The Pierre to take a deep breath and gather her confidence before venturing into the fabled hotel.

She remembered what her mother once told her when they had walked past this very doorway. As they stole a glimpse at the elegant partygoers inside, her mother gave scrawny preteen Angela a little shake.

"Look! Look at those people! Someday, you find a way to be one of *those* people. Don't you dare be like us or the people we live with. You learn how to be like *them*. Get what *they've* got. Get yourself out of our world and never look back. *Never!*"

And now, here she was, about to go inside The Pierre as a member of the elite she had once gawked at. She had finally become one of them. Well, almost. Once again, she wished for the magic pill that would infuse her with perfect knowledge of all the unspoken do's and don'ts of Charlie's rarefied social milieu. Short of having that kind of guaranteed internal confidence, she decided she would smile a lot and try to say as little as possible. Do *not* take any chances.

At the reception desk outside the ballroom, she gave her name to the young woman minding the G-through-L place cards. "There you go, Miss Hanson, you're at table number two."

"Table two?" an older woman beside Angela said, barging in. "That's the very top tier. My, my, how lucky of you to have such nice friends."

Angela turned to face her. And froze.

It was Mallory Drummond. Mallory Drummond! The nasty, entitled hedge fund wife who had stiffed her out of her $5 tip and gotten her fired from the Madison Avenue hair salon.

Angela held her breath, wondering if the bitch recognized the girl she had abused years before. Her mind went blank. Speechless. Then it hit her. The bitch was impressed with her pricey table. This gala was a high-society smackdown for competitive social climbers. Angela, the salon's toilet scrubber, was at table two! She had already won.

In that instant, she knew just what to say and how to say it. She formed the same snotty, snarling half-smile Mallory had once used on her and said, "I beg your pardon."

86

Mallory flinched ever so slightly. Angela could detect no recognition in the woman's cold eyes. The stinging humiliation that had stuck with Angela all these years had been nothing to Mallory Drummond. Nothing. Angela was nothing to her. Literally nothing.

Suddenly, Mallory sounded hesitant and defensive. "I, I, I, uh . . . well, uh." She smiled at Angela, conciliatory, maybe even sucking up a bit. "Well, we all know this is such an important event in the social calendar, I, uh, was just wondering who bought the table you're sitting at."

She knew enough about Charlie's world to be completely assured in the way she'd work this little moment.

"Close friends of mine," she said in her best la-di-da accent. "Clifford Townsend and his daughter Charlotte. We're inseparable pals from London, actually. It's my first time back in New York in ages."

She studied Mallory for some kind of recognition of what she had done to that teenage servant girl. Still nothing? Okay then. She gave Mallory Mallory's own this-conversation-is-over smirk, then turned and walked away, her spirits buoyed by this sudden, unexpected settling of a painful old score. Maybe there really was justice in the world, she thought, just maybe.

She stopped in the doorway of the ballroom and scanned the noisy cocktail reception, looking for Charlie in the crowd.

When she found her, they exchanged gushing admiration for each other's outfits.

"Follow me, sweetie," Charlie whispered in Angela's ear, "I'm going to introduce you to absolutely everybody."

Angela repeated her mantra to herself. Smile a lot. Say as little as possible. Do *not* take any chances.

Charlie seemed to know people everywhere. Angela watched as she and the elegantly dressed people she called her "dear, dear friends" exchanged air kisses, almost touching in a way that hinted at, but was not quite, a hug.

Angela studied the eyes of these people as they shared breathless pleasantries. They didn't really look at each other. Their eyes were darting around, looking furtively over the shoulder of the person they were talking to. Everyone seemed to be on the lookout for someone else. Someone who was more important, more connected, someone with more of something than the dear, dear friend in front of them.

These people are awful, Angela thought, feeling very alone in this crowd. How could I ever have let myself feel inferior to them? Why are they all so hot to hang out together? It's pretty clear they don't even like each other.

"Isn't this just perfect?" Charlie said as they took a pause from socializing. She gave Angela's arm a little squeeze. "Are you having fun?"

Angela faked a grateful smile. "Yes, this is the best! Thank you." She watched Charlie's eyes searching the crowd. "Charlie, are you looking for someone in particular?"

"Yes, as a matter of fact," Charlie said. She seemed edgy and anxious. "I'm looking for Susanna Stratsman. She's the Stratsman heiress. You know, *the* Stratsmans. They've been rich and important for generations. Talk about exclusive. She's been the benefit chairperson for years. Incredibly prestigious, you have no idea. I've been working on her since forever. I finally got her to put my name in to be considered for the committee for next year. I told you we bought their most expensive table and threw in a staggering contribution on top of that. I know she's here somewhere. It's *her* event, after all."

Suddenly, Cliff appeared, cocktail in hand. He stood between Angela and Charlie.

"Hi, ladies. This is some big do," he said flatly. "Looks like they spent a fortune on this tropical theme, banana leaves and whatnot dripping from the ceiling."

Angela gave Cliff a smile and a gentle touch on the arm. A simple plain touch, rather than the not-quite-seductive touch she used on older men. That would be for later.

"Isn't it fun?" Charlie gushed at her father. "It's so creative."

Cliff shook his head. "You'd think, if they were serious about finding a cure, they'd put all that money into research instead."

"They do, Cliff, they do," Charlie insisted. "I'm sure they're raising millions tonight. Millions. It's a wonderful cause."

"I'm just saying," Cliff shrugged. "Seems a waste to have to spend all this dough on foolishness to pry money out of rich people who could afford to just give it."

Suddenly, a sixtyish woman in a glittery red cocktail dress barged in between Cliff and Charlie. "Well, if it isn't my family. Excuse me, my ex-family." She was tipsy.

Not sure what the woman meant or who she was, Angela gave her a bland smile, kept her mouth shut, and observed carefully.

"Oh, hi, Judy," Cliff said. "I think of you every time my accountant shows me those canceled checks."

"Our little *billets-doux*," she said, with a theatrical French accent.

"Bee-yay what?" Cliff said.

"That's French, Cliff. French for alimony."

"Why, Judy," Charlie announced, as if that were a complete thought.

"Why, Charlie," Judy said in return. Then she gestured at Angela. "Aren't you going to introduce me to your beautiful young friend?"

"Angela," Charlie said, giving her a possessive little hug around the waist, "this is Judy Townsend, one of my many ex-stepmothers.

Judy, this is my dear friend Angela Hanson. She's like the perfect little sister I never had."

Again, Angela used her silent, plain vanilla smile, hoping she would not have to do any talking with this nasty, unhappy family.

Judy eyed Angela up and down.

"You know, Angela," she said, slurring, "between the three of us Townsends here, we have burned our way through nine marriages. Three for Cliff and three for Charlie. And two more of mine, if you count my matrimonial disasters before and after the Townsend clan. But who's keeping score?"

"The lawyers," Cliff said with a smirk, "that's who."

Wishing she could be invisible, Angela just kept smiling.

Judy grinned at Cliff. Then turned to Charlie. "Charlie, I see you took my recommendation and went to see Dr. Baker. Isn't he just the best?" Judy ran a fingertip down the side of Charlotte's glowing, wrinkle-free face, highlighting the artistry of the prestigious plastic surgeon. "Why, my dear, you look as fresh and young as the day Cliff and I sent you on that Junior Citizens World Art Tour. What was it, thirty years ago?"

Charlie pulled Judy's hand away. "I get flashbacks of my panic attacks like it was yesterday," she snapped. "A dozen angry teenagers chained together by kidnappers and dragged, kicking and screaming, though dusty museums across ten countries."

Angela took a half-step back to get herself out of the line of fire. Her dumb smile was starting to hurt.

Judy sighed, "What I remember is an entire summer of peace and serenity." She looked down at her empty glass, hiccupped, and shrugged sadly. "Ta, loves," she muttered, and wandered away toward the bar.

"Oh, Charlie!" another woman inserted herself into the group. She looked to be in her mid-fifties. Elegant. High cheekbones, wrinkles untampered with. Long, silver-gray hair pulled back in a chignon. A beautiful woman unafraid of her age, Angela thought.

"Susanna!" Charlie beamed. "You totally outdid yourself with this year's decor!"

"Why, thank you," Susanna replied.

Charlie turned to her father.

"Cliff, Susanna is the creative genius behind this wonderful event. Susanna, let me present my father, Clifford Townsend. Cliff," she said breathlessly, "*this* is Susanna Stratsman."

"Hi, Susanna," Cliff said calmly, "nice to meet you."

"The pleasure is all mine, Mr. Townsend."

They shook hands.

"Oh, come on," Cliff said, "it's Cliff."

"Why of course," she said brightly, "Cliff it is."

Angela, the keen student of accents, recognized the woman's precise diction as old-school uptown aristocratic. So, *this* was the society queen whose approval Charlie was so desperate to win. She seemed pretty chill, not at all the snob Angela had been expecting.

Angela felt Cliff's hand on the small of her back, gently nudging her into the center of their circle. "Susanna, have you met the newest member of our little family?"

"Why, no," she said, smiling and looking directly into Angela's eyes. Her gaze seemed to radiate genuine warmth.

"Allow me to present Angela Hanson," Cliff said proudly. "She's a big-shot executive at Globalcom and our best pal in London."

Susanna extended her hand to Angela.

"Welcome, Angela, I'm delighted to meet you."

91

Susanna's hand was warm and dry, her momentary grip just friendly enough. Her hand also radiated athletic strength. Judging from the faint calluses, Angela decided she probably played a racquet sport like tennis or squash. In that instant, she managed to make Angela feel that she really was welcoming her. Angela's intuition told her that Susanna was different from the crowd of phonies with their darting, evasive eyes.

Susanna turned back to Cliff.

"Cliff, I want to thank you *so* much for your generosity. It means so much to the foundation. As I'm sure you can imagine, it's very important for an old charity like ours to recruit people with new fortunes to the cause."

"Well, you know," Cliff said, cracking a little grin, "I made my first fortune way back in the seventies. I'd say that qualifies me as old money. Don't you think?"

"Well," Susanna smiled again and gave Cliff a little wink, "now that you frame it that way, I guess it does."

Cliff mused, half to himself, "Made my first killing in VHS video rentals. Triple-X-rated. God, I miss the seventies. It was the golden age of the full bush."

Stunned silence.

Susanna turned to Charlie with a pained smile and fled back into the crowd.

Charlie flushed red with anger and stomped away.

Angela was delighted. Suddenly she had Cliff all to herself. She gave him a playful little nudge.

"You naughty man, you. You really are too funny, Cliff."

"I'm afraid Charlie doesn't think so."

Angela stood up on the balls of her feet and whispered in his ear, blowing just a little more breath than necessary. "Well, Cliff, just between us, I don't think she fully appreciates what an amazing man you are."

"I think you're right."

Cliff gave her arm a little squeeze as he peered down into her pushed-up breasts.

Delighted, she inhaled a bit to make her chest expand inside the bustier. Thank you, Mr. McQueen, she thought, wherever you are now.

Quickly looking up again, Cliff said, "Say, uh, you know, Charlie's taking the jet to Antigua tomorrow." He hesitated again. "Why don't you come over for a quiet dinner at the apartment next week? Charlie's finally done with the damn decorating. We can break in the new dining room chairs. What do you say?" He held his breath expectantly.

He's nervous, she thought. He's afraid I might say no. The all-powerful billionaire is nervous. Nervous and hot for me. Perfect.

"Why, Cliff," she said coquettishly, "there's nothing in the world I'd like better." She switched on that special smile she reserved for older men. Blasting him with all the extra wattage she had.

He patted her on the small of her back again, this time just a bit lower. Almost but not quite patting her ass.

A tall tuxedoed man in his late thirties, movie-star handsome and athletic, slowly passed in front of Angela and Cliff. He was carrying two champagne flutes. He stopped for an instant and scanned the crowd as if looking for the person whose drink he held. Angela sensed it was a ploy; he was trying to make eye contact with her. When she let their eyes meet, she knew she had been right. He gave her his gorgeous warm smile. With a quick snap of her head that signaled rejection, she looked away. No, she told herself, *no!* You're here on business. When she looked back, he was gone.

She sucked in her breath for an instant and held it, asking herself if she was really ready to have this boorish old man ravish her with his icky old body. Was she prepared to share a bed and a bathroom with him as old age made him steadily lose control over his bodily functions?

Yes! a part of her replied. *That, girl, is the cost of your ticket to freedom.*

The other part of her countered with another resounding, *Ick, ick, ick!*

Then, as she felt the old guy give her another creepy little pat, this time right on her butt, her business mind took decisive action. It replayed a montage of the horrors, fears, sights, sounds, smells, and humiliations she had endured as a result of growing up in poverty.

Yes, she told herself again, ordering her reluctant *Ick* half to get lost.

Yes!

At least for now.

CHAPTER 16

Monday afternoon, Jack was in top form in front of the clients. Like an athlete who had been training for this moment his whole life, his mind and body were perfectly synchronized. He felt propelled by an almost magical force as he aced one move after another in this game that he loved. His words of persuasion were like a magic spell he cast over the clients. Yes, he thought, when it came to pitching a group of human beings burdened with a multimillion-dollar marketing budget, Jack Price was still the gold-medal champion at convincing them how to spend it.

At the end of his presentation, he held up the VeRity headset like a priest raising a sacred chalice. He whispered, "This is not mere technology." Keeping the clunky, sawed-off helmet at arm's length, he pretended to stare into its goggle lenses. "This is the portal through which users will be transported to a whole new world. An intoxicating combination of the world they know and

95

the world they thought they could only dream of inhabiting." The three clients on the other side of the conference room watched with rapt attention.

Stewart's death had given him an explosion of desperate energy. It powered him through two all-nighters and a long Monday morning of rehearsals. He was still in shock at seeing Stewart's stuttering life force suddenly vanish, leaving behind an inert sack of flesh. The omen was clear: Even Jack Price could be snuffed out at any moment. Not in some gradual fade to black in a distant senior-citizen future, but in a sudden cut. Abrupt. No warning. Everything unfinished. Unresolved. Just blackness. Forever.

Jack clicked the next-to-last slide of the presentation deck. The client's logo—the name "VeRity," with the capital V and R writ large, in a futuristic design—and Stewart's tagline beneath: "The thrills are totally real."

"As we've shown you," Jack said, moving in front of the screen, "we can customize this brand promise for every possible customer demographic, every psychographic, every mind-set, across every platform and every medium, from Snapchat to the Super Bowl. We can frame this versatile, compelling, sales-driving brand promise in the language consumers themselves would use. The thrills are . . ."—he began quickly counting on his fingers—". . . totally real, absolutely real, one hundred percent real, epically real, twisted real, crazycool real, sickyfresh real . . . The list goes on. The possibilities for pool-outs are endless under the umbrella of the simple, unifying, unforgettable brand promise for VeRity. *The thrills are totally real.*"

Jack moved away from the screen and clicked the final slide, saying "Thank you." He went back to his seat on the agency side of the table, in between Daniel and Angela and their three supporting players.

The head client, a handsome blond guy in his late thirties who looked like he had gotten a permanent California tan as part of his Stanford MBA, nodded to his two junior colleagues. They nodded back obediently. "If you could leave us for a few minutes. We'd like to confer."

"Of course," Daniel said, rising and leading Jack and Angela and the others out. He closed the conference room door and silently motioned for them to walk out of earshot.

They huddled on the far side of the hallway.

"Great job, Jack," Daniel said in a whisper. "You were brilliant. As usual."

"You had them spellbound," Angela added. "They hung on your every word."

"Think we got it?" Jack asked.

Daniel shrugged. "Clients? You never know. You just never know."

"So, tell us, Jack, now that it's over," Angela said. "That brilliant tagline. Was it Stewart's?"

Jack paused, considering his options. It could be days before they found out which of the three agencies had won the account. One-out-of-three odds. That was at best. Maybe one of the other agencies had an inside track. Maybe the whole thing was rigged and already decided. Maybe one of the other agencies had come up with a magic bullet idea they had somehow missed. Credit and blame. Blame and credit. If they won and Jack took full credit, it would give him tremendous leverage. But if they lost and Jack had taken full credit, he would get full blame. And then some. There was risk either way.

Stewart never got credit for his ideas because it wasn't his role to get credit. He was a lowly worker bee who stayed in the background. Besides, Jack evaluated all the creative work, selected the best, and did the presentations. The presentations were what sold the ideas. And that was Jack. All Jack.

"Yes," he whispered, "I found it on his legal pad after . . . after he was gone. It was on page three of his scribbles." For once, Jack thought, the truth was not only believable, it was emotionally satisfying. And politically very savvy. He could generously share credit with a dead man in case they won. And insulate himself from some of the blame in case they didn't.

The conference room door opened. The junior client, an ebullient preppy woman in her mid-twenties, gave a big smile and waved for them to come back inside.

Stanford Tan stood up to greet them. "Congratulations," he said. "You have won the VeRity account. And I have to tell you guys—for us, the thrill is *totally* real."

CHAPTER 17

"No, Eric," Angela said firmly, "you can walk to Vlad's Vodka House." She pointed down the avenue. "It's only three blocks in that direction. When you get to the corner of 49th Street, turn right. Daniel says there's a red canopy with a big hammer and sickle. You can't miss it."

"But Angela," he whined, pointing at the Town Car idling beside them at the curb.

"No! *I'm* going back to the hotel to change clothes. It's in the other direction."

"But you just said," he made a frowny face, "it's only three blocks."

"No! I have a secret mission."

"Tell me, tell me!"

"Silly boy," she said, "then it wouldn't be a secret. And then . . ." She fired the imaginary pistol at his head. She lifted the briefcase off his shoulder. "Here, I'll take this. It's got The List and other confidential papers inside. We can't risk anyone seeing it while it's hanging in the cloakroom at Vlad's. Now, you've got to go make sure that all the preparations for the party are in perfect order. Perfect, I said. You understand?".

Eric nodded obediently.

"And you know what you've got to do once the party starts."

Eric snapped his heels together and gave her a British army salute.

Angela made a little shooing motion and opened the rear door of the Town Car.

Eric turned and walked toward Vlad's. She watched him for a moment, feeling a wave of affection for him. She could trust Eric as much as she had ever trusted anyone. No, she felt she could trust him more. He was the devoted little brother she'd always wished she had.

As her Town Car pulled away from the curb, she was seized with a sudden, heart-stopping panic. A faceless ghoul in black was coming to punish her for all the bad things she had ever done. This guilty specter invaded her consciousness without warning from time to time. She closed her eyes and forced herself to take four deep breaths. One, two, three, four. When she opened her eyes, she saw the blue and red sign down at the end of the block. That brought her back to reality.

"Please stop!" she told the driver. "Over there. At the Duane Reade. I'll just be a minute," she said as she bolted out of the car.

The dull mundanity of the drugstore calmed her jangled nerves. She knew just where to go. Down the beauty aisle to perfumes. There it was, right where she remembered it. Forbidden Kiss in the skinny little vial. Only $4.99 marked down from $8.00. The cheap perfume she wore to every one of her trysts with Jack Price. She laughed inside as she held the little bottle in her hand. Laughed at her younger self who thought this fragrance with its "seductive notes of vanilla, bergamot, cherries, and musk" was the height of sophistication. It was all she could afford at the time.

A girl who could have been that younger Angela appeared beside her. About twenty, olive-skinned, dressed for her low-level office job in poignantly cheap, out-of-date designer knockoffs. She eyed Angela up and down, taking in the expensive clothes and accessories. She reached for her own vial of Forbidden Kiss and held it out in front of Angela.

"Do *you* like this fragrance?" she asked with an earnest curiosity that Angela recognized.

She wondered for a moment about the girl. She could hear in her question echoes of her own hunger to learn. She could feel her own hopes and dreams in the girl. Angela wished she could tell her something useful, something helpful. But there was so much—too much—even to begin to try.

Angela said, "Yes, it's a lovely scent."

The girl brightened. "Really? What do you like about it?"

Angela gave her a warm smile. "It's very sophisticated. And sexy. In just the right way."

The girl held up her Forbidden Kiss as if it were a winning lottery ticket. "Gee, thanks!" she said, and hurried away down the aisle.

Angela declined the plastic bag the cashier offered and slipped the little bottle into her Hermès bag. She was not about to walk through the lobby of the Four Seasons displaying the Duane Reade logo.

She was certain Jack would remember this fragrance. And once she had him disoriented with enough alcohol, it would trigger powerful, if not overpowering, memories of their former passion.

As she got back into her Town Car, she felt strong again. The momentary panic had passed. The black ghoul of justice was not coming to get her. At least, not yet. Tonight, with Eric as her wingman, and with a little luck, she hoped her plan would come off perfectly. Then later on, with a little more luck, her even bigger plan might also come off. And she could kiss her life of corporate bullshit good-bye.

CHAPTER 18

Luke was sitting at the kitchen table on West End Avenue, nibbling on an orange and staring at his backpack, giving Marlin the clownfish little flicks with his index finger. He was thinking about starting his homework. Maybe.

The phone on the wall rang. When the readout lit up with the words "Jack Cell," he jumped up and grabbed the handset.

"Dad!" he said excitedly.

"Dude!" Jack crowed, "I won the VR account. I won it! I'm going to make it up to you for Saturday, you hear? Just name what you want. Box seats at Yankee Stadium, a Broadway show, hiking trip to the Catskills—you name it."

"That's great, Dad!"

Suddenly Luke felt Mom appear from out of nowhere. She had a way of doing that whenever he said "Dad" aloud. He turned to face her. She pointed to the phone in his hand and mouthed the word "speakerphone" emphatically.

Luke pushed the button and put the handset on the table. Jack's voice filled the smallish kitchen of the 1920s-era apartment.

"I crushed it, kiddo. I crushed it! This is the biggest of all the VR accounts. Their devices are going to be everywhere. We're going to set a new standard of rad for the whole industry. I'll bring you a freebie to play with. Your friends will be so jealous. You'd like that, wouldn't you?"

"I'm sure he would," Sandra interjected, smiling at Luke to soften the spoilsport role she was about to play. "But we wouldn't want him to use it as yet another distraction from his schoolwork, would we?"

"Oh hi, Sandra. Hey, thanks again for Saturday. I was just telling Luke that I crushed this new business pitch."

"I heard," she said. "That's great, Jack."

"I'll come by to drop it off later tonight, okay?"

"Sure," she said, "about when do you think that'll be?"

"Well, we're having a victory celebration for the whole agency. We're taking over Vlad's Vodka House, so I guess, uh, it may be a little late."

"I don't suppose anyone will be doing any drinking," Sandra said sarcastically, "this being a victory celebration and all, with a hundred thirsty agency people at that legendary industry watering hole. What d'you suppose?"

Luke interjected, his voice cracking with determination, "No! Dad promised me he's going to stop drinking. He promised me, we had like a man-to-man about it. Right, Dad? Tell her, tell Mom— go ahead, tell her, tell her!"

"That's right," Jack said. "I promised Luke. I promised myself. I promised for all of us."

"See?" Luke said, "See? He promised. See, Mom? See?"

It was Sandra's turn to speak. But she was silent. The silence ripened quickly and started to rot.

Finally, Jack spoke, "And I won't stay too late, either. I promise that, too."

"Okay," Sandra said with a weary sigh. "Just remember it's a school night for some of us."

She gave Luke a mom-look. He made a prune face in return.

"Got it," Jack said.

"And Jack?"

"Yes?"

"Congratulations on your big win. We're proud of you."

"Thanks, Sandra."

"Yay, Dad!" Luke jumped back in. "I can't wait! See you tonight!"

CHAPTER 19

The workstations outside Jack's office were mostly empty. By now most of the agency had departed for the party at Vlad's. The tradition for new business wins was for everyone to walk the few blocks in packs of office buddies—twos, fives, tens, sometimes more. Or sometimes, almost the entire agency would swarm in one giant migration. Over one hundred people would fill the sidewalks like a crowd of demonstrators with no placards and nothing to protest. Just buzzing with the shared ambition to get their asses over to Vlad's and get rip-roaring drunk on the company's nickel.

Jack's office phone rang. It was Jessica, Daniel's executive assistant. Jack scooped up the handset. "Jessie, what's up?"

"Hey, you," she said. "Congratulations on the VeRity win."

"Thanks."

"Uh, it's, uh, so great that it was Stewart, uh . . . I mean, it's so good you made sure he got . . . well, you know . . . credit."

"I know, I know. Stewart's our hero," he said brightly, trying to relieve her unease. "He'd be thrilled." So, he thought, it's official. This is poor dead Stewart's win. And I'm a generous statesman. Jack considered agency politics for a moment. Hmmm. I can play the sympathy card as part of my strategy. Have to, actually. But that's all right. Heartfelt emotion covering my naked grab for power. Nice. Or, to be more accurate, covering my desperate grab for one more day of survival.

Jessie switched back to her formal executive assistant voice. "Jack, I'm calling for Angela." Of course, he thought. When Angela visits an office, she has the run of the place, including the use of the big boss's secretary. "She asked me to ask you if you would like to ride in the car with her to the victory celebration." Jack knew there was nothing optional about "would like to." It was a command.

"Sure," he said, also knowing that "the car" meant her dedicated full-time Town Car and driver. Just for her. Only the big shots from the global holding company had them. Even divisional CEOs like Daniel had to get by with car services or sometimes yellow cabs, or even, in a pinch, the subway.

Jack had a habit of friendly kidding with Jessie. "Aw, come on, can't she walk over with the rest of us? It's only five blocks."

"Nuh-uh, I don't think so," she said. "Have you seen those heels she wears?" He could almost see the smirk on Jessie's face. "Those shoes are strictly for limos."

"Right as usual, Jessie." The unspoken rule was that you could joke around with Jessie—she expected it from the senior managers—as long as you gave her some measure of appropriate deference in every conversation. That, too, was expected.

"She says she'll meet you in the lobby in five minutes. Is that okay?"

Another question that was not a question.

"Of course," he said with a salute in his voice.

"Thanks, Jack. And congratulations again." She sighed. "I wish Stewart was here to celebrate with us. I miss him."

"We all do, Jessie. We all do."

Jack went down to the lobby and waited, exchanging high fives with the last few stragglers departing for Vlad's. Then he waited. And waited. And waited a bit more, thinking that the party would be well under way by the time he got there with Angela. Not that it mattered. He was going to stick to bottled water.

He was thinking about men and women. How women always end up making men wait. And how uncomfortable it can be to be with a woman with whom you used to have passionate sex.

Angela appeared. But not from the elevator bank. From her Town Car at the curb. She must have gone back to her hotel to change her clothes. He watched, as if she were a stranger, as she walked across the lobby. Camera-ready for a chic party, she wore a white silk blouse buttoned at the neck, small black Gucci handbag with thin cross-body strap, black Chanel pencil skirt with golden double C's at the waist, and Manolos made of little more than thin straps and towering heels. He observed, as if for the first time, the way high heels pitch a woman forward. With every click, click, click, she is battling forces that are trying to make her fall flat on her face. Forces strong enough to make planets spin and galaxies implode. She's not just walking, he thought. With every stride, a woman in high heels is fighting a war against gravity.

She greeted him with a smile and a thumbs-up.

"There's nothing like winning," she said.

"Yeah, there's nothing like it," Jack agreed.

She pointed at her waiting Town Car and led the way.

"No, no," she said over her shoulder, "I don't mean there's nothing *like* winning. There's nothing *but* winning. Nothing less is acceptable. Winning is all there is. Winning is what we're paid to do."

The driver held the rear door open. Angela motioned for Jack to get in first. To give her the extra space behind the front passenger seat, set all the way forward.

They settled in for the short ride to Vlad's.

Angela stretched out her bare legs and wiggled her toes, relieving tension. "There now," she sighed and gave Jack's arm a friendly little pat.

She crossed her ankles.

The ankle with the tattoo was facing him. He pointed at it. "The tat is new, right? Is it a snake?"

"Oh that? Old by now. Ugh, it's supposed to be an asp. You know, Cleopatra? She's a hero of mine. But guess what I found out after I got it? The asp came from one of Shakespeare's inaccurate sources, a popular myth. Note to self—before you put a permanent mark on your body, do your freakin' homework. Believe me, when Cleopatra meant to do something, she'd have used the surest, most efficient way to get it done. Snake bite? Nah, no way—hit or miss. She was an amazing woman. Really. A beloved ruler, a skillful administrator, a wily politician, a fierce warrior, a wife, a mother, and absolutely the equal of the great men who ruled the ancient world. She understood the power of women, the power of money, and the power of, well, the power of power."

Jack gave an impressed nod.

"I read a lot. I'm on the jet all the time." Meaning, the holding company's corporate jet. "Backfilling the holes in my education. You got me started, you know." She patted Jack on the arm again. Then gave it a little squeeze. That little squeeze could have been just friendly. Or, Jack thought, it could have been a reminder of the way she used to touch him all over. His body knew that squeeze. His body would never forget it.

Another brief silence.

Her phone vibrated. She fished it out of her little handbag.

Jack could read the text screen. Daniel wrote: "Got Jack??" She quickly typed: "CU in 2." Then tapped Send and put the phone away.

"Listen, Jack," she said urgently, "this party is important. This is *your* win. Everybody knows that. But the agency needs you to share the spotlight with Stewart. You're okay with that, right?"

Another order posing as a question. He shrugged. "Sure, of course."

"Whew, thanks," she said, apparently relieved. "We want to make Stewart our hero, the role model for the new culture we want to build."

Jack was puzzled. "But it looked like he wasn't going to make it in the new world of digital natives."

Angela waved away that notion. "Doesn't matter. Now he's a symbol of everything we want from our employees."

The Town Car arrived in front of Vlad's. Angela put her hand over the door handle. She wasn't quite ready to exit the car. She looked intently at Jack.

"You ready to lead these kids in some serious partying? I assume you're still the champion when it comes to shots."

"Uh, Angela, I, uh, promised myself I would lay off the sauce for a bit. I really can't do shots tonight."

Angela peered at him, *into* him, her brow wrinkled in concern. "These kids *love* to drink. It's their big reward. Their release. The way they bond. They have a million words for what they do—drunk-calling, drunk-texting, drunk-munchies. They've earned this party. And so have you. Just look at what you've been through in

111

the last three days. We need you to inaugurate the toasts. Just get them started, that's all."

Jack wrestled with how much to tell her about his pledge to Luke. "I, I really can't."

Suddenly, she looked exasperated. "Tell me, how long have you been on the wagon?"

"I'm starting today."

"Well, Jesus, Jack, start tomorrow! What difference does it make? These kids look to *you*. Have a shot to get the party going." She pointed at the door of Vlad's. "The whole agency is in there waiting for you. Come on, just one drink. It's your responsibility. You're their leader."

CHAPTER 20

Vlad's Vodka House played the Russian thing to the hilt. The wait staff dressed in *kosovorotkas*, the classic high-necked tunics popular with Russian peasants since the twelfth century and with fashionistas in the twenty-first. In between giant flat-screens and dance-club speakers were life-size portraits of famous Vladimirs—like Lenin, Putin, Horowitz, Nabokov, Zworykin, Vlad the Impaler—all painted heroically in mock Soviet Social Realist style. Vodkas of all kinds flowed like the waters of the Volga from numerous bars all around the dark, cavernous space.

Daniel greeted Angela and Jack as soon as they passed through the heavy red curtains that separated the entry foyer from the club.

"Hi guys, check this out!" He waved at the big table overflowing with boxes of VeRity headsets in VeRity-labeled gift bags. "One for everyone," he said proudly. "The client had them messengered over." He gave Jack a fond nudge with his elbow. "See what you and Stewart have done?"

A leggy young woman in a red *kosovorotka* not quite covering her black micro-mini skirt handed Daniel a microphone.

"Ladies and gentlemen, ladies and gentlemen," his voice boomed and ricocheted, "friends, Romans, countrymen! Boys and girls. Hey, guys—guys . . . hey!"

The crowd finally quieted down. The music lowered to a distant background beat.

"Before we start this celebration of our latest new business win, I want to thank everyone for all their hard work and dedication on this account, and on all our accounts. This is a huge victory for all of us. We have earned the right to . . . *party!*" He paused to allow cheers and hooting. "I have one important policy directive. Car services are on the company tonight. Everybody rides. Nobody but nobody gets behind the wheel after we're done here." The crowd gave a happy roar. "Now I want to introduce a special guest from our corporate headquarters in London. If you were in the office working on the pitch this weekend, you've already met her. If you haven't, I'm pleased to introduce our global chief culture officer, Angela Hanson!"

Cheers and clapping.

Eric appeared with a wireless mic and handed it to Angela.

She took the mic and stepped forward. The low background music stopped, the video screens went dark.

"Thanks, Daniel. I'm glad I got to meet so many of you this weekend. I'm looking forward to meeting everyone by the end of my stay here." She lowered her voice. More personal. "I hope that all of you will come to understand what my role as chief culture officer really is. Think of me as your chief caring officer." She patted her heart. "That's right. My job is caring. Caring about each and every one of you. Caring about how we work together and support each other. Caring about your professional and personal growth. And yes, caring about your happiness. You guys are all very special people. Every single one of you."

Deep breath, holding back a sob.

"Tragically, one of our most special people"—she raised her right hand high, one finger pointed heavenward—"isn't here to celebrate with us."

Suddenly the video screens popped on to reveal a candid photo of Stewart, taken at an agency holiday party a few years before. In the shot, Stewart is smiling awkwardly, his hand raised, probably to shoo away the photographer. "I'm talking about our friend and colleague, Stewart Foley. As we all know, he died on Saturday, doing the job he loved. Working with the people he cared about. Creating and contributing to the very end. By now, you all know that it was Stewart who wrote the tagline, *The thrills are totally real*—the big idea that won this new business pitch. We will all miss him more than we can say."

A hush fell over the room. A sweet melancholy tune sounded softly over the speakers, a touching soundtrack to accent the emotion of Angela's speech.

"Stewart had a lot to teach us about caring. All the different kinds of caring. Right now, I'm asking myself, 'How can I be more like Stewart?' I hope all you guys ask yourself the same question. How can *all* of us be more like Stewart? Hardworking. Dedicated. Generous to others. So generous. Tonight, as we celebrate, watch the screens for this picture of Stewart." She turned and pointed a nearby screen. "When Stewart appears, the music will stop." Perfectly on cue, the music stopped. "That's when we should all raise a toast to Stewart."

Suddenly a dozen costumed wait staff carrying trays of icy shots appeared and started walking among the crowd.

"I want you to grab your shot and walk over to our legendary Jack Price, whose amazing presentation skills helped win this client."

Angela extended her free hand into the air. Eric rushed to her side with a shot glass. Without acknowledging Eric, she took the glass and stared directly at Jack. "Raise a toast to Stewart with Jack." She raised her glass in the air in Jack's direction, her eyes burrowing into him. "Jack was Stewart's boss, his mentor, his biggest supporter, his friend."

Daniel came up behind Jack and grabbed him fondly by the shoulders. He took Jack's right hand and raised it like the referee declaring him the world heavyweight champion. "That's right," Daniel shouted, compensating for not having the mic, "raise a toast to Stewart with Jack!"

Eric grabbed two shot glasses from a tray and gave them to Daniel. Daniel handed one to Jack and turned to the crowd. "To Stewart!" he cried, raising his glass. He turned to face Jack.

Jack held his shot glass. Daniel clinked their glasses and downed his shot. "Now, let's celebrate!" Stewart's photo dissolved away. The pounding soundtrack of dance music returned. Hot music videos filled the screens.

Jack held his glass in front of him. Daniel gave him a questioning look. "What's the matter?"

Angela came over and put a hand on Jack's shoulder. "Jack," she said, concerned, "Daniel just toasted *your* friend in *your* honor."

All around them, people were downing their shots.

Jack stared at his glass. Angela patted his back, like a coach encouraging a star athlete.

Daniel gave him a hurt look and a shrug.

Jack stood still, frozen. Eric walked up to them, shot glass in hand. "To Stewart!" he said raising it in Jack's face.

Jack looked at Angela, then at Daniel.

"Jack," Angela said. "We're all toasting Stewart. The whole agency loved Stewart."

Jack stared at the three people waiting for him. He took a deep breath. Then downed his shot. Then looked down at his shoes. He heard a cheer. Felt a hand take his empty glass and replace it with a fresh icy one.

A chorus of three more young employees came up to him, chirping, "To Stewart! To Stewart!" Without looking up, Jack drank another shot. That warm feeling began to rise inside him. Suddenly there were people all around him toasting Stewart. And more shots being handed to him.

Jack felt two waves crashing over him.

First, a wave of guilt. Luke. His promise. His word.

Then, a much bigger wave, washing over the first one. It was one shot after another. A wave of relief. And release.

He found himself swimming in waves of small talk. Congratulations. Handshakes, pats on the back. Dude, how'd you do it? Let's have lunch sometime. Stewart was some guy. Yeah, he sure was. And when the music suddenly stopped, another toast to Stewart. The random pauses were the only markers of time passing in the noisy celebration. To Stewart! Again, and again.

Before he knew it, he had lost count of his shots. And he didn't care. He was exhausted from lack of sleep. Guilty about disappointing Luke. Shocked by Stewart's death. Saddened. Haunted by the sight of his buddy's lifeless body. Chilled at the thought of the Grim Reaper coming after him at any moment. He was also elated at winning the new account. High on himself with the biggest rush of being in the business.

He was on overload. Just wanting a break from it all. A little moment of feeling good after feeling so goddamn bad.

The alcohol was giving him exactly what he needed. Every time he turned around, it seemed, Eric appeared with big smile and a fresh, icy shot.

"Here now," Angela's boy-toy would say as he took the empty glass from Jack's hand and replaced it with a full one. "You deserve it, sir. You've bloody well earned it!"

He could feel that lovely dissociation from his conscious, controlling brain.

Watch out, he told himself, you're at work. But hey, his other self answered, this actually *is* my job at the moment. After all, I'm their leader. When I raise a shot for Stewart, I am doing my employer's bidding. Fulfilling my responsibility as a member of management. Doing my work as a skilled professional liar. Lying about Stewart and how he felt about working here. Lying about how Jack Price feels about working here. To protect my big income for Sandra and Luke. To hold on to my glamorous lifestyle and all my perks. To maintain my status as a big, bold-face name in the business.

Soon, he was standing outside himself. Just watching. Even kind of admiring the bullshit he heard Jack Price putting out.

The alcohol heightened the moments worth remembering while erasing the boring downtime in between them. One minute he was chatting up Naomi, the head of video production, making her laugh. Next thing he knew, he was razzing Chad Littleford about his new tattoos.

Where had he been in between? What had he been doing? He had no idea. What did it matter? He was experiencing only the peak moments. And acing them one after another. Jack Price and his alcohol buzz, working and playing together like champions.

He found a dark corner. Turned his back to the party to take a little breather.

118

CHAPTER 21

Angela waited for the two drunk girls to finish reapplying their lipstick. They were sloppy and slow, taking forever. Finally, they giggled their way out of the ladies' room, tottering on their high heels. Silly white chicks, she thought. They had no idea how lucky they were, floating through life on their cloud of privilege.

Reaching inside her little handbag, she extracted Forbidden Kiss. Began to spritz it on the way she used to. On the inside of both wrists, behind each ear, and, after unbuttoning the top three buttons of her blouse, in the hollow between her breasts. She checked in the mirror, adjusting the blouse to provide a nice glimpse of her lacy black bra. She fixed her hair, touched up her mascara. Checked her armpits—a bit damp from nerves—but odorless. Fortunately, the dress shields were doing their job, keeping her white Fendi blouse bone-dry. Touched up her lipstick and made sure there were no smudges on her teeth. She chewed three mints, moving the little pieces all around her mouth, waiting for them to dissolve. Blew into the palm of her hand, making sure that her breath was sweet. Checked herself out one last time in the mirror, grateful that she still had the bathroom to herself.

She reviewed her plan. One hundred eyewitnesses out there. All of them frightened for their jobs. All of them taking it as a matter of faith that whenever there's an accusation of sexual harassment, the man is always guilty. Always. The balance of power had finally shifted.

Would she be able to get away with it?

"Yes, goddamnit!" she told herself, "Yes!"

She had to.

Did she have any fears? Any doubts? Any feelings of guilt? Any hesitations?

"Yes," another voice told her, "you can stop now. Don't do it. Don't!" It was the one voice she did not want to hear.

She forced herself to think about her projected ROI. Everything came down to Return on Investment. In the religion called Business, ROI was the Holy Grail.

If Jack Price got fired for cause, instead of just laid off, the company would not have to pay one penny of the $1 million in severance guarantees in his contract. And a piece of that savings, as pasty old Simon Woodleigh had promised her, would go into her bonus. Maybe an extra $100,000, maybe more.

Her investment was a five-dollar bottle of perfume.

She stared into the mirror. Slowly, she raised her right arm, pointing an imaginary pistol at the woman in the white Fendi blouse.

"Sorry, Jack," she whispered, "but business is business. Just like you taught me."

She pulled the trigger. Her hand jumped wildly as if there'd been a violent kick.

It was, after all, a double murder.

With one pretend bullet, she killed Jack Price's career. And the conscience of the woman in the white Fendi blouse.

She turned and went out to the party.

CHAPTER 22

Jack felt a tap on his shoulder. He turned around. It was Angela. Looking up at him with those big, exotic crystal blue eyes.

"Tell me, Professor Higgins, what do you think?" Her voice was playful. Like the Angela he once knew. "What do you think of your handiwork?" With outstretched hands, she presented her chic, expensive self with a little ta-da. He thought the neckline of her blouse was more open than he remembered it being in the car. Or maybe, when he was sober, he was more careful not to look at the exposed slice of the breasts he once knew.

He shrugged.

"Jack, don't you get it? 'Enry 'Iggins?" She gave him a little poke in the chest, her finger lingering a fraction of a second longer than necessary. "You were Professor Henry Higgins. And I . . ."—she touched herself between her breasts—". . . was your Eliza Doolittle." Jack's eyes had no choice but to follow her hand there. Her fingers—and Jack's eyes—lingered there. "I finally saw *My Fair Lady*. Had front-row seats. That was *our* story, right?"

"Yeah, right." He was pretty sure he wasn't staring. Well, maybe staring a little. But definitely not leering. No, no way. But he did let his mind wander from those breasts to memories of the rest of her. The specter of dead Stewart gave his imaginings a sharp-edged urgency. Every pleasure could be your last. At least he'd had intense pleasures with Angela that he could remember before he died.

She leaned in closer to make herself heard above the music.

He could feel her breath in his ear. A minty scent tingled his nostrils.

Her breath had once been an overpowering weapon of arousal. With her lips barely touching him, she used her breath to inflame every sensitive nerve ending he had. Driving him crazy with desire.

As she leaned in to talk more about how he had civilized her, the way Henry Higgins had done with Eliza, he thought he recognized her perfume. Wasn't that the same scent she used to wear during their affair? A part of him said, Nah, no way. But something in his limbic brain said yes. He hadn't noticed any perfume when they were in the car. Had she put it on since then? Had she put it on for him? He tried not to think about that.

As she talked in his ear, he watched himself nodding politely. While having more flashbacks of Angela naked and open to him, inviting him to indulge his every urge. The Angela he once loved. Yes, loved. It wasn't that he had stopped loving Sandra. He had loved her then; loved her still. And would forever. They had Luke and always would. It was just the way motherhood and the baby had changed both of them. Dynamited their sexy, carefree life together.

Jack heard Angela say something else in his ear. The pounding music made it hard to know exactly what it was. Was it, "You're the best," talking about the new business presentation? Or was it, "You *were* the best," talking about their affair?

Then she said, "We're great together." Talking about office team-work. Or, maybe it was, "We *were* great together." Talking about their sexual chemistry.

He remembered doing more polite nodding as she talked. Yes, definitely more nodding. While thinking about how he used to reach for her when they finally closed the door of their hotel room. The way he would scoop up her breasts and, in one continuous motion, reach down to take in her whole sexual being with hungry fingertips. He was just thinking about that. Just thinking, that's all. That's what he thought. Really.

Then he heard Angela scream. Felt her fists pounding on him.

"Jesus, Jack! Get off me!" Felt her hand slapping his face. Pushing him away. Her blouse was ripped open, her bra was torn, one breast exposed.

Did he do that? Or did he see her do it to herself?

Everything had happened so fast. And his brain was so slow.

He had never torn a woman's clothes before. And was sure he never would. He took too much pleasure in removing them slowly.

Angela was screaming through tears. "Jack! Get off me!"

Suddenly, a crowd stood around them, gawking. Angela pulled at her torn blouse to cover her chest.

The music stopped. The screens lit up with the shot of Awkward Stewart. The bar went silent. But no one raised a toast.

A man's arms grabbed Jack from behind and pulled him away. It was Daniel.

"What the hell are you doing? Jesus, Jack—what the hell?"

Then snippets. Jump cuts. Like the death of Stewart. But now it was the death of Jack Price and his brilliant career. Three people surrounded him. A woman and two men. Jennifer, the head of HR. Ira, chief legal counsel. And Daniel. Angela stood behind them, sobbing, holding her blouse closed.

Ira barked in Jack's face, his breath acrid. "We'll prepare papers in the morning. But you have to go now. You can try to fight this, but all you'll do is make some lawyer rich. We've got a hundred witnesses here."

Jack's mind went blank. He heard the word "cause" repeated over and over. *Cause* meant no severance, no vesting. Nothing.

"Here, take this," Daniel said as he dragged him toward the door. He put the VeRity gift bag in Jack's hand and pushed him out. Out through the heavy curtains into the foyer. Then out the door onto the sidewalk.

Jack took a deep breath of cool night air. Alone. Dazed. Confused. With a gift bag in hand. And his life in ruins.

CHAPTER 23

With tears streaming, Angela held her blouse closed and ran into the ladies' room.

The girls by the sinks turned to her, wide-eyed with concern, mouths open in shock.

"Please," she sobbed, "can I have a minute?"

One of the girls reached for Angela to give her a comforting hug.

"No, please," Angela said, stepping away and fighting back more tears. "I just need a little privacy."

The girls headed for the door.

"Thanks, guys," she sniffled as they exited, "I'll be fine in a couple of minutes."

The instant the door shut, Angela stopped sobbing and reached for the box of tissues on the shelf beneath the mirror. She wiped her eyes and blew her nose. Grimaced in the mirror at her smeared eye makeup. Her heart was pounding the way it did when she was a teenager and had gotten away with shoplifting on a dare.

Yes, she'd gotten away with it. Yes, she really had!

She stared at that face in the mirror. She had just done a horrible, hurtful, life-destroying thing to another human being. She had to look away. As she stared at the floor, she reminded herself that other people had done horrible, hurtful, life-destroying things to *her*.

She turned back to her reflection. Hadn't Jack Price taught her that people in business did horrible things to other people all the time? He sure had. What's more, he had said that everyone more or less accepted it because, well, *It was business*.

She went into the center stall and took a deep breath as she locked the door. She found pleasant release in peeing. Felt her whole body letting go. She lowered her head and closed her eyes. For a nice long moment, she breathed in and out.

When she opened her eyes, she surveyed the damage to her thousand-dollar blouse. It was ruined. Cost of doing business. Worth it. Her plan had gone off perfectly. She let her mind go blank.

Suddenly, she heard the ladies' room door fly open. Eric's voice echoed off the bathroom's hard surfaces. "I'm here, luv! I'm here! It's me!"

She looked down and saw Eric's purple suede Chelsea boots on the other side of the stall.

Eric started rapping on the door, rattling it, shaking the metal partitions that surrounded her.

"Are you all right? Did he hurt you? Did he?"

"Get out, will you! Leave me alone! And stop that damn banging!"

Eric spoke tenderly, "Tell me, luv, are you all right? I did everything you told me to do. I got him drinking. Kept him drinking. You saw, you saw! I'm here for you, you know that. Oh, that

128

horrible, horrible man! Ugh, what a pig! You said he was a bastard, you said so. But I had no idea. What a perfectly horrible man. A shit, a total shit. To think, after all these years, he just *assumed* he could grope you like that. In front of everyone. What an absolute, irredeemable, horrifying swine . . ."

"Shut up!" she snapped. "Shut the fuck up!" Then she heard words gushing out of her that shocked her even as she spoke them. "Don't you dare talk about him like that! Don't you fucking dare! Ever! Do you understand?"

She heard Eric gasp. Saw his feet step backward away from the stall.

"I was just giving you moral support," he said meekly.

"Don't! He's none of your fucking business. Now leave me alone. Now! *Now!*"

She hadn't meant to hurt Eric. But she had been overpowered by feelings she didn't want to have, didn't mean to have, and didn't understand.

She heard Eric's feet shuffle across the tile floor, heard the door bang shut.

Another deep breath. Trying to let the twisted knot of her emotions about Jack Price unwind. Big exhale. There, now. The quiet and solitude of the stall was comforting.

Focus on actions, she told herself. Actions, not feelings.

She reached into her little handbag and extracted her phone. The next step in her plan was to text Charlie, who had flown to Antigua the morning after the gala. She typed:

DALE WALDMAN is headhunter Cliff's office must contact.
Office on Madison Avenue.
Waldman will definitely call Jack Price.
Jack Price now free to work for us.

She put the phone back in her purse. Before she could close the snap, the phone rang. She extracted it and saw that it was Charlie.

"Hi, it's me," Charlie said.

"I know," Angela said, grateful that Charlie had used the phone and not FaceTime. She looked underneath the stall partition to make sure she was still all alone in the ladies' room. "I just texted you the name of the headhunter."

"I saw," Charlie said. "But give me his name again. I don't trust these digital things. I want to write it down."

Angela spelled it out for Charlie. "Dale Waldman. Office on Madison Avenue. He and Jack go way back together. If Cliff's recruiter calls Dale with the job, Dale will definitely call Jack Price."

"Dale Waldman," Charlie repeated.

"Yes, he's the guy to get us Jack Price," Angela said.

Listening to Charlie gave her a sudden sick feeling in the pit of her stomach. What was that expression about a chain being only as strong as its weakest link? If anybody could screw things up, it was Charlie. Spoiled, flighty dingbat Charlie.

"Got it," Charlie said, "I'll leave a voice mail for Cliff's executive assistant tonight. She'll get the right people working on it first thing in the morning." Charlie gave an exhausted sigh, as if she had just completed a very arduous task. Then her voice turned mischievous. "Say, girl, I've been checking out this Jack Price guy online. He's really cute! You had yourself a hottie."

Angela pulled her torn blouse closed. "Yeah, I guess so. I don't see him that way anymore." She wanted to scream at this silly rich woman, tell her to focus for once and get serious. Demand that she not be like, well, like Charlie. Angela shook her head in resignation and hoped for the best.

130

"Well," Charlie prattled on, "I'm looking forward to having him all to myself down here. I plan to work him very hard on the pitch for the foundation. But as they say, all work and no play makes Jack a dull boy. I think we can have a nice time together in paradise. Achieve some of that work/life balance all the articles talk about."

Angela was exhausted. But she fought against her fatigue. She had to stay alert to keep juggling all these balls in the air.

Charlie said, "You know, Cliff really likes you. I heard he invited you over for a private dinner."

Angela hesitated, unsure how to answer. This was the biggest of the balls she was juggling. Or hoping to juggle. She held her breath.

Charlie paused.

Angela remained silent. Unsure what to expect. Worried.

After what felt like an eternity, Charlie burst out, "You know, sweetie, I think that's great. Just great!"

Angela let herself exhale. Finally. "Really?" she asked tentatively.

"Really," Charlie said warmly, "really and truly."

"Thanks," Angela said softly. Then added impulsively, "Love you."

"Love you more," Charlie cooed.

Angela sighed. No competition for Cliff's attentions. At least not yet.

"A little warning, sweetie," Charlie said, "just so you know. He's very impulsive with women."

Angela decided to play up to her big sister's worldly wisdom. Putting on the closest thing to virginal innocence she could muster, she asked naively, "Oh dear, should I be scared?"

"No, no, silly girl. Just don't be surprised if he brings up marriage."

Thinking quickly, Angela decided it was time to use the plead-the-opposite-of-what-you-want ploy, the strategy Jack said usually worked like a charm. "Marriage? Now, Charlie, *you're* the silly girl!"

"No, I'm not. Just wait and see. He proposed to all his wives after my mother practically after shaking hands for the first time. After all the stepmothers I've had to endure, I'd welcome you. Really. We could be a team. You and me, managing Cliff. This could be a good thing."

"I'll do whatever you say." Angela was so relieved. "Whatever you say, Charlie. You know him best."

"We'll take turns wrangling him," Charlie said with conspiratorial delight. "Two against one."

"Yes! Like tag-team wrestlers on TV."

"Uh, sure, I guess so. Is that what wrestlers do?"

Angela shook her head, thinking, She's so clueless. What planet does she live on?

"Yup," she said brightly, "that's exactly what they do."

There was a knocking sound on Charlie's end.

"Come in, darling!" Charlie said in a loud voice.

"Am I interrupting anything?" Angela asked.

"No, no. It's just Josef." Her voice went distant, talking to her guest. "Do open the champagne. And please, darling, take your clothes off." Her voice came back. "You'll meet Josef on the yacht. He's very handsome and, uh, talented. Gotta run, sweetie."

The line went dead.

Angela put her phone into her handbag and closed her eyes. She let her head and shoulders go limp, letting the rest of her tension drain away.

CHAPTER 24

Jack wasn't exactly sure how he got to his former home on West End Avenue. He definitely remembered the yellow cab waiting just outside Vlad's. Like it had his name on it, he had announced with fake mirth to the driver. Yeah, he remembered that. Lucky me. Said he should buy a lottery ticket. Said he'd split it with the driver. He and the driver laughed. Yeah, funny, ha-ha. That memory was pretty clear. He vaguely recalled the taxi crossing through the underpasses of the Central Park transverse at 66th Street. Or was it 79th?

Anyway, there he was at the locked front door of the building where he used to live, waving to the overnight porter to come over and let him in. He did not recognize the worn-out man in his ill-fitting uniform. "Denny," the oval label on his shirt proclaimed. Only a few of the guys he had known still worked there.

Jack shook himself a little in an effort to pull mind and body together. He felt certain he could hide how drunk he was. He had this down. Nobody would suspect.

Denny opened the door a crack. "Yes, sir?"

Jack tried to step in. Denny held the door, blocking him.

"Hi, Denny," Jack said, trying to pretend they were buds, "I'm Luke Price's dad. You know, Luke from 3-C." He held up the bag with the big VeRity logo. "I promised I'd bring him up this virtual reality headset. It's gonna be the latest, greatest thing. He's waiting for me."

Denny stood his ground. "I'm sorry, sir."

"What do you mean? I told Luke's mom I'd come by to give it to him." Jack hoped he was not coming off as belligerent. When he was in this state, he made a point of acting extra calm and gentle. Jack Price was definitely not a mean drunk. He never lost control. At least as far as he remembered.

"Sir, it's past one a.m. Mrs. Price called down an hour ago. She said if you came by to tell you that she was going to bed and to please not disturb her."

Jack took a deep breath. He looked at his watch. Shit, it was later than he thought.

"Mr. Price, if you leave the bag with me, I'll make sure the morning crew delivers it to Luke." He reached his hand through the door to receive the bag.

Jack pulled the bag to himself. Be nice, he thought. Not nasty. Even if you'd like to punch this guy in the nose. He's just doing his job.

"Well . . . let me . . . let me call Luke's mother," he said, speaking ever so slowly and carefully. To be sure he wasn't slurring his words.

Denny closed the door a few more inches and stepped back a bit. If Jack tried to push his way in, he could slam the door in his face.

Jack slipped the shopping bag handle over one arm and reached into his pocket for his phone. When he clicked it awake, he saw Sandra's text filling the screen:

> Luke waited up for you until 11. I finally made him go to bed. I told you it's a school night. I waited up till past midnight. You can leave the VR thing with the doorman. Luke will get it in the morning. I don't mean to make you feel guilty, but you should know. Luke was really looking forward to seeing you. It wasn't the toy he was excited about. It was you.

Jack looked up at the porter, who stood in readiness for whatever might come next. Jack handed him the bag through the crack in the door.

"Thanks, Denny. Thanks for getting this to Luke," he said.

He turned and walked away, watching his feet carefully to make sure his steps went in a straight line. A voice in Jack's head asked him, Is there anything else you can possibly fuck up tonight?

Once out of sight of the building, he stumbled to Broadway and found another yellow cab. Collapsed onto the backseat and lay flat. Watched the lights above blur past. Said nothing to the driver.

Back in his apartment, he let his public defenses fall away. Let the alcohol take over. The room started spinning. The floor was pitching up and down like a boat in a storm. He needed sleep. He needed oblivion. A chance to forget before he had to wake up tomorrow and figure out what he could possibly do next.

Yes, he needed sleep. But to get there, he needed a little something more. Just a drop or two to ease his way to Nowhere Land. He spied the liquor cabinet. It was pulsating at the far end of the gyrating living room. Next thing he knew, he was on the floor in front of it. He opened the cabinet door. There in the front row of bottles, taped over the label of his Johnnie Walker Black, was a note. In Luke's handwriting: "Dad—Don't. Please."

Jack wanted to stop the room from pitching. He planted both hands solidly on the floor. Okay, sort of. He stared at the note. And started to cry.

CHAPTER 25

As soon as Angela closed the door of her hotel suite, she kicked off her shoes and yanked off her torn Fendi blouse. As she walked toward the bathroom, she began to tear it apart at the seams. Yanking and pulling violently, she tore it to shreds, leaving a path of white rags on the floor.

She stood in front of the glass door to the shower enclosure, breathing hard. With her chest heaving, she pulled off the rest of her clothes and threw them, piece by piece, out into the living room, not giving a shit where they landed.

She stood naked before the wall of mirrors and looked at herself as if inspecting another person. Her shoulders were slumped with fatigue. That won't do, she thought. She breathed in from her diaphragm, straightened her spine, and held her head high.

She did a second inspection of her naked self.

This is what I have, she told herself. It's not bad. No, it's pretty good, all things considered. And as for my flaws, my many, many, many flaws? Her eyes went up and down her body, doing an inventory. She stopped, closed her eyes, and took a deep breath.

Don't do that female thing, she chided herself. Just *don't!* Don't over-focus on your flaws.

She opened her eyes again. There now. They're no worse than any other woman's flaws.

She raised her right arm and pointed her index finger at her image. "Make the most of what you've got *now,*" she commanded aloud. "You're only going to get older."

She turned on all three showerheads and switched on the steam. She stood with eyes closed, surrendering to the cascading water and billows of vapor. She lost track of time, trying to stop her mind from replaying the events of the evening.

She tried to focus on this wonderful shower. So much of what she loved about the showers in the bathrooms of four-star hotels like this was the absence of everything she had grown up with. Like sputtering water that went scalding hot, then turned ice cold. Then disappeared altogether—for weeks at a time. Faucet handles that broke and fell off in your hand; just try getting them fixed. And that cramped little tub. Chipped, stained with god-knows-what grossness, enclosed by a torn, mildewed curtain.

This shower was an enclosure big enough to host a small party. With gleaming walls of marble and thick glass. Not just pretty faucets that worked, but a custom temperature setting, three showerheads, and blasts of steam at the touch of a button. This shower soothed and pampered not just her body, but her soul.

Still, she could not stop replaying the evening that had just ended.

Was she some kind of monster—or merely effective? She was getting what she wanted, after all. It did seem like things were lining up on her side. So why did she feel so—she searched for the words— so dark, so uneasy, when she should have been happy? She was full of hope and anticipation. And at the same time, full of sadness and guilt.

Wasn't Jack Price the one who had taught her that she had to do whatever she had to do? He'd said it time and time again: "Angela, you're starting out with so many strikes against you. You can't afford to play by the rules. Nobody who wins ever does. Do whatever it takes. Whatever it fucking takes."

That's what he'd said.

And that's what she's done.

It wasn't wrong. She did what people who understood the game did. Because they were smarter. And they did what they *had* to do.

Even though she knew she was clean from the hot water and the steam, she reached for the loofah and the little bottle of hotel body wash. She covered her body in thick soapsuds, scrubbed her skin all over, and rinsed clean.

She replayed her conversations, her deceptions, her victories.

She covered herself in more suds again. She scrubbed and scrubbed with the lather and rinsed clean again.

She thought about her upcoming plans with Charlie and Jack. And Cliff. All the things she *had* to do.

She made more suds, scrubbed herself all over with the loofah, and rinsed again.

She kept thinking. And kept scrubbing and rinsing.

She wanted all the soapsuds in the world. She thought her skin must be glowing from all the scrubbing with the loofah. By now, her body must be covered by only fresh new skin. As if she were a whole new person, cleaner than ever before.

139

When she saw that she had gone through all four of the little bottles of body wash, she was afraid she might be done. Then she spotted the little bar of soap through the dense steam. And covered herself again in suds and scrubbed some more.

It felt so good to feel clean. Cleaner than clean.

She knew she'd finally had enough when her skin started to tingle at the touch of the loofah. Her fingertips were wrinkled like prunes.

Next, she craved the delicious feeling of the thick, yummy terrycloth of the hotel bathrobe. This, she thought, is how the rich treat their bodies. She wrapped her hair in a towel, put on the robe, and tied the belt around her waist. Yes, this is how the rich treat their bodies every single day. As many times as they like.

She stepped back into the shower to reclaim the empty body wash bottles. She lined them up very carefully on the marble countertop for the maid to collect in the morning.

Her mother's sister Veronica had been a chambermaid at the super-posh Hôtel Plaza Athénée on East 64th Street. She used to tell stories of how guests would leave their rooms like pigpens. Go out of their way to do it, she said. And the super-rich clients in the biggest, most expensive suites? They were some of the worst pigs of all. The shitty messes they left behind. Literally, shitty messes. Animals, she said, they were like animals. And often the cheapest tippers, to boot.

Angela always left her hotel rooms on the neat side to make them easy to clean up.

And she always left extra big tips.

Even before she could really afford it, she left big tips for everyone who waited on her. Big tips were her small way of righting an unfair world. And assuaging her survivor's guilt at having escaped the fate of the people she had left behind.

She savored the feeling of the padded carpet under her bare feet as she walked to her panoramic view from the forty-fifth floor. The only light in her living room came from the nighttime cityscape. She could see through a gap in the Midtown towers a slice of the rooftops of the projects downtown. *Her* projects.

She pulled the robe tighter against her body, reassuring herself that she was here.

Here in the tower of the Four Seasons on 57th Street. Here to stay. Never going back there. Ever.

She told herself that she was doing what all successful people do. They—no, she corrected herself—*we* do whatever it fucking takes.

CHAPTER 26

The early-morning Caribbean sun peeked through the curtains of Charlie's stateroom on the second upper deck of *King of Pawns*, the custom-built 300-foot Christensen mega yacht. But the sun wasn't waking her. Her phone was.

To answer it, she had to cut through the hangover from last night's champagne. It felt like a hatchet in her skull. She'd had lots of yummy champagne. And lots of yummy Josef. Dear, yummy Josef, the yacht's hunky lead deckhand. And her devoted, on-demand fuck buddy.

Fumbling with eyes closed, she reached for the bedside table where the phone was ringing. She felt dampness under her. She had fallen asleep in a wet spot. Just conked out dead.

As she opened her eyes ever so slowly, she saw several dark Rorschach blots of drying love goo across the expanse of her

California king-size bed. Josef must have been *very* glad to see her. Very glad indeed. Her darling Slavic Superman.

She rolled to the edge of the bed and planted her feet firmly on the polished tropical hardwood floor. She wanted to feel completely grounded for this call, even if she was naked. She gave her head a shake, cleared her throat, and raised the phone to her ear.

"This is Charlotte Townsend," she announced with imperial hauteur.

"Uh," a young man said hesitantly, "I'm John Parsons. From, uh, human resources. At Mr. Townsend's holding company?" His voice rose in a question that was not a question. It was terror. "I'm the, uh, recruiter you asked for? My, uh, boss's boss, Ms. Evans, the head of HR, gave me your number. You're Mr. Townsend's daughter?" Again, not a question.

Charlie put a smile of kindness in her voice. "Yes, that's right. Thank you so much for calling. It's John, is it?"

"Y-y-yes, it's John, thank you. Is this a good time to talk? If it's not, I can call back later."

"No, no, this is the perfect time. I have the name of the head-hunter we want you to contact." Now fully awake, she reached for the pad where she had written the name. "It's Dale Waldman," she said slowly. "Dale Waldman. I'm told his office is actually on Madison Avenue. He's one of the top headhunters in advertising. He's terribly important, at least in that business."

While the recruiter clicked away on his keyboard, Charlie glanced into her bathroom. She saw the pile of towels Josef had left on the floor. His long showers usually woke her, but not this time. Yes, it must have been a great night.

"Ms. Townsend, I have his business information right here. Dale Waldman Associates. We haven't worked with him, but he is well-established in his field. Can you e-mail me the job specs?"

144

"Specs?" All Charlie had was the headhunter's name.

"Uh, job specifications . . . so we can draw up a rec?" Again, not a question. "You know, a formal job requisition? Do you know which one of Mr. Townsend's companies will be filing the rec so we can get all the paperwork in order?"

"Oh dear." Suddenly, Charlie was confused. Annoyed that she was confused. Irked that she was annoyed and confused. And bored with all these complications that were getting in her way. "Oh dear. Say, John—it *is* John?"

"Yes, Ms. Townsend, it's John."

"John, I'm afraid I'm not very good at paperwork. That *is* what your department does, yes?"

"Yes, Ms. Townsend."

"Can you get those details done for me? Mr. Townsend and I are looking to hire a particular adman to prepare a very important presentation for Mr. Townsend. It will be here in Antigua on our yacht. The adman will be our guest. I mean, our employee, with all his expenses paid. Are you with me, John?"

"Yes, Ms. Townsend, yes."

"Well, I have no idea what that costs or what a job spec is. Can you research that for me? Let's pay him whatever the market pays for a big important freelance job. Let's plan for success. Say six months, with an option to extend. Then sweeten the offer a bit. Can you work that out for us? Figure out the details? I'm no good at administration and I'm terribly busy right now."

She looked around her. Empty champagne bottles, sweating ice buckets dripping puddles onto the floor, crystal champagne flutes lying here and there.

"We have to make this happen. Very soon. Can you do this for me? That is, for Mr. Townsend and me."

145

Silence. The only sound the clicking of the functionary's keyboard.

"Yes, Ms. Townsend, we can process this. Do you have particulars we should put in the online application?"

"An online application? Yes, great idea! I mean, no, I don't have the particulars. But an online application would be wonderful. We want this Dale Waldman to recruit this one particular adman who he's known for years. Can you set up all the correct employment things? I'm sure you know how to make it very professional and all that. Look, we know he is going to call this one adman. And we are very keen to have him do the job."

"Uh, would you call this a consulting engagement?"

"Yes, yes, that's it! A consulting engagement. Exactly. Communications consulting. Marketing, creative work, branding, all that kind of thing. Can you just make it happen? The process, the paperwork, his fee, and so on? I'll be sure to tell my father how incredibly helpful you've been. Just set up all the things necessary for this Dale Waldman to get this one man to apply. Then we can put him in front of Mr. Townsend for an interview and then hire him to work for me here on the yacht. Can you make all it very professional, to make it look like a real executive search?"

"Yes, uh, we sure can."

"You'll fill in all the correct details, right? My father and I *really* need this to happen. I can't begin to tell you how important this work will be. It will have a positive impact on millions of lives. You'll be helping countless people, honest. It's about creating one of the world's most important philanthropic foundations."

Charlie had a flash of her favorite new daydream—she and Melinda Gates onstage at a very important conference, discussing how they are saving the world together. Charlotte Townsend and Melinda Gates!

She bubbled with enthusiasm. "We really need this adman to get this initiative off the ground. Are you with me, John?"

"Yes, Ms. Townsend. Is this the best number to reach you?"

"Yes, John. Just please make this your top priority."

"Yes, Ms. Townsend, it is my top priority."

"Oh, thank you, John! Thank you so much!" Charlie couldn't wait to put the phone down. "We'll talk more about it later. Just please get this started."

She spotted an empty champagne flute lying on the floor near her right foot. She started rolling it around with her toes.

"John, I'm so overbooked this morning. I'm already running late for my next two meetings. I'm going to hang up now. Is that okay?"

"Yes, Ms. Townsend. It's okay."

CHAPTER 27

Jack was passed out on the floor of his living room when the cruel light of dawn woke him. He had the worst hangover of his life. After a shower and a fistful of aspirin, he e-mailed the headhunter who had gotten him all of his big jobs. The man he considered his best friend in the business, his trusted advisor, his promoter, his biggest fan, and a workaholic early bird. Dale Waldman.

Dale replied instantly. "I'm at my desk. Get your ass in here IMMEDIATELY."

By 7:00 a.m., Jack was sitting in front of Dale, woozy but awake.

"What do you mean," Dale asked for the third or fourth time, "you're not exactly sure what happened?"

Jack held his splitting head in his hands and mumbled at his shoes. "Like I said, I'm not sure."

"Listen," Dale barked, his patience wearing thin, "either drunken Jack Price did something completely unacceptable, or Angela

Hanson did something even worse. If you actually did grope her, you're an idiot. If she actually did what you think she may have done, she's some kinda psycho."

Jack shook his head no. "Not psycho. Just a person who'll do anything to win in business."

"Sounds psycho to me," Dale said. "Remember, when I placed you there, I got you a great package. If they wanted to get rid of you, your contract gets you total vesting, a solid-gold parachute, extended benefits, the works. But if they fire you for cause, you get exactly nada. If they were looking to get rid of you, they just saved a shitload of money."

Jack looked up. "Do you think they set me up?"

"If they did, you couldn't have been more cooperative. You were an even bigger patsy than they dared hope for." Dale leaned forward. "Are you absolutely sure you're not sure? Because you could fight this. Your chances would be a million to one, no, ten million to one, and you'd just end up making your lawyer rich, but you might—"

"That's what Ira said."

"Who's Ira?"

"The general counsel. He said if I tried to fight it, all I'd do is make my lawyer rich."

"So, you remember *that* clearly?"

"Yeah, very."

"Too bad your memory is so selective."

"Ira also said they had a hundred witnesses."

Dale snickered. "Every one of them scared for their jobs."

"Exactly."

"Jack, you are so fucked. So completely fucked. Done. Finito. End of story. Sorry. Would you like to wallow in silence for a while before I—like a true friend who will tell it to you straight—explain reality in all of its ugly detail?"

Jack gave a heavy sigh. "Thanks, I'm done wallowing."

"Okay. You have just joined the ranks of the untouchables. The #MeToo criminals. The assholes, the male sex pigs. It doesn't matter if your misdeeds are true and corroborated or not. It's like the Spanish Inquisition out there. The very fact of being accused makes you guilty. But in your case, it's your boozed-up memory against the word of the entire senior management team and one hundred eyewitnesses. When the release about your firing for violating the code of conduct goes out in the trades this morning, you will be toast. Like, right about now."

Dale raised his watch arm. It was 7:15.

"Everyone can read between the lines and know it's for some kind of sex offense. And the way gossip spreads, by ten o'clock everyone will know the specifics. The way stories snowball and get distorted, your reputation will be worse than Jack the Ripper's. You won't just be toast; you will be off-the-charts radioactive. You will never work in this business again. That's reality. Do you understand?"

Jack nodded.

Dale shuddered. "Oh Jesus, Jack, how could you?"

Jack was silent.

Dale took a deep breath. Then he brightened a bit. "But there is a silver lining. Of sorts."

"Really?"

"I said of sorts."

"What could the silver lining possibly be?"

Dale hesitated for a beat, collecting his thoughts. "This unfortunate event only hastened the inevitable."

"What do you mean?"

"What I mean, brother, is that you are fucking old."

Jack sat up straight. "I am not. I'm in my prime—my skills, my talent, my competence. I'm at the top of my game. Do you have any idea how good my pattern recognition is? Besides, I've got a network of connections. Do you know how many people I mentored who are now in positions of power? These people owe me."

Dale interrupted him. "Jack, I promise you, not one of them will return your call. No one will have lunch with you. No one will talk to you. Yesterday, you were a big shot. Today you are literally nobody. You don't exist anymore."

Jack had a flashback of Angela taunting Stewart about what happens when the company takes away your business card. *No one will have lunch with you . . . afraid you could be contagious . . . Without your business card, you are literally nobody . . .*

"Jack, I'm not supposed to ask, so you never heard me say this, but . . . exactly how old *are* you?"

Jack paused. "I, uh, I just turned forty-five."

"Bullshit! You're forty-seven. No, forty-eight. Don't forget, you and I grew up in this business together. Jack, you've been an old guy in this game for a long time now."

"But you never said anything to me?"

"I was making money off you, placing kids in your creative group. Why would I say anything? My friend, you've been living on borrowed time. Nobody gets to be your age in your kind of job. It's amazing that you've lasted as long as you have. Those years were a gift. The silver lining is that you've been a dead man walking for years and you didn't even know it."

Jack had had recurring dreams of a phantom hitman pursuing him. Finally, he could see his executioner face-to-face. It was Jack

Price. Me. Me all along. Bang! Smash cut to black nothingness. The End.

"Jack." Dale reached across his desk and touched Jack's arm. "Say thanks to the gods. You've had a great run. Now start learning to adjust to your new status. And the, well, different range of opportunities that society reserves for old people."

"Such as?"

"You like shuffleboard? Bingo?"

"Fuck you! You make it sound like I'm ready for a retirement community in Florida."

"No, maybe not yet. But you have officially joined the ranks of The Old. You are too old to be in this game. No one is going to let you play anymore. And if you're too young for shuffleboard—"

Jack's phone sounded. Luke's ringtone.

"Oh, Jesus, Dale. I have to take this. It's Luke."

"Want some privacy?" Dale started to stand.

"No, you might as well hear this." Jack waved at him to sit. "I'm going to need your advice."

Dale sat down.

CHAPTER 28

Jack tapped the speakerphone button and set his phone on the edge of Dale's desk. He took a deep breath.

"Dude?" He tried to sound surprised but cheery.

"Dad?" Luke sounded on the verge of tears.

"Hey, buddy, aren't you supposed to be on your way to school?" Jack's attempt at matter-of-fact was not convincing.

"Dad? I-I-I just saw all headlines in the trade magazines. What happened?"

"Luke, how do you—?"

"Oh, I have a ton of alerts out there with your name as keyword. Anybody writes anything about you anywhere, I see it the second it's published. They all say"—Luke swallowed hard—"they all say you were terminated for violating the company code of conduct." Another silence. "That's really bad, isn't it? What happened?"

Jack looked at Dale. Dale shrugged.

Jack felt his natural instinct to lie pop up like an evil jack-in-the-box. Very deliberately, he pushed the little demon back down into its dark hole and carefully secured the lid.

He took a deep breath.

"It was a party, a victory celebration for the new VR account." He stopped, hoping to collect his thoughts. But he had none to collect. "There was a lot of drinking. Everybody was drinking. Doing shots. Everybody had too much to drink." Jack paused. Okay, he told himself, enough with excuses. "I did, too."

Silence.

Finally, Luke spoke. His voice halting. "But, Dad? You promised."

Deep breath.

"Luke, I broke my promise. I'm sorry. It's complicated, what happened. How it happened. They asked me to start off the shots. It was . . ."

Jack stopped himself before he could finish his excuse.

Another silence.

"They said I groped one of the women. That's the violation they, uh, they, uh—"

"W-what?" Luke asked.

Then Sandra's voice. Of course, Jack thought, she's standing over Luke. He pictured them in the small kitchen, finishing the breakfast Luke had made so carefully. Getting ready to walk to school together.

"*Did* you grope one of the women?" Sandra asked. Jack could hear the strain in her voice. "Did you, Jack?"

"I don't think so, Sandra." He said it in the same way he had said it on countless nights of her questioning him. Nights when he would come home late from business "entertainment" in one degree or other of alcohol impairment.

"You don't *think* so?" she repeated slowly.

"Uh-huh."

"Which means you can't be sure?" Sandra asked the question the same way she had asked it all those times back then.

"I'm pretty sure I didn't. It's not the kind of thing I would do. I mean, I've never—"

Jack stopped himself again. He knew Luke was fully clued in about sex. That was something he and Sandra had done in a series of delicate, coordinated conversations. Under Sandra's direction, of course. Sometimes the two of them together with him. Sometimes each parent alone, supplementing what they knew he was getting at school and correcting what they feared he might be getting from his peers. And God knows what from the Internet. They had tried to make sure there was no mystery and no shame. But tearing off a woman's clothes in a drunken lunge and grabbing her breast? No, he wasn't going to talk about that in front of Luke.

"It doesn't matter what I think I did or didn't do," Jack said quietly. "They say that I did it. And they say they have a hundred witnesses from the party who will also swear that I did. They are firing me for cause. That's the bad thing. A really bad thing. I could try to fight it, but there's no way I could win. I'm finished in the business. Done."

He went silent again.

"Geez, Dad! You can recover!" Luke's cheerleading sounded desperate. "You told me—you told me that winners always bounce back. No matter how they get slammed. Everybody gets knocked down. The winners are the ones who get back up and keep fighting. That's what you told me."

"I know, Luke. That's true." Jack had never felt more disappointed in himself. "But sometimes, things get broken so badly, they can't be fixed."

Jack told himself to stop making it sound like an external force, like the weather had happened *to* him.

"Luke, I really screwed up, I did. And I can't fix it this time."

"Not ever, Dad?"

Jack looked at Dale. Dale's eyes told him to tell it straight. Jack felt like a vise was crushing his chest. "Not ever. No one's going to hire me. I'm going to have to figure out some other kind of work. Somewhere else. I don't know what that will be yet."

Silence.

Finally, Sandra spoke. "We have to get moving now. Luke's going to be late for school."

Another silence.

Then Sandra spoke softly. "Tell me, are you still dating that lawyer?"

"No."

"Do you have anyone to be with tonight?"

"No."

"Why don't you come over for dinner. You shouldn't be alone now."

Jack looked at Dale.

Dale mouthed the words, "Lucky guy."

CHAPTER 29

The morning sun flooded Daniel's corner office, lighting up the spines of the management books on the shelf behind his desk. Words like Leadership, Teamwork, Values, and Excellence glowed brightly in colorful publisher typefaces.

"I have Jack Price's termination papers all drawn up," Ira said. "He gets nothing. Nada. I'm pretty sure he won't feel like coming into the office to sign them. I'll have a process server deliver them."

Jennifer from human resources added, "We'll clean out his office this morning and have the boxes sent to his apartment."

Ira turned to Angela. "Do you want to take any legal action against him? You are more than within your rights. God knows he deserves it."

Behind her solemn expression, she was wondering what they might think if they knew she had a job for Jack all lined up. They probably wouldn't hear about it until weeks or months later. Or maybe never. Either way, it wouldn't matter.

Right now, she had to close out this transaction. She had to focus on executing her next very necessary charade. She shuddered with her whole body, pretending to relive the horror. It was the kind of thing a woman who was traumatized would do. She hugged herself and took a deep breath. Pursed her lips tightly as if holding back tears, making a show of pain and courage. She looked down and shook her head emphatically, no. Took a long moment to compose herself. Looked up and spoke haltingly, "I . . . I just want to put the whole thing behind me."

Daniel patted her shoulder. She gave him a grateful smile. "Thank you," she said softly, "you guys are the best." Deep breath. Big sigh. "Let's just get back to work. Work is all that matters."

Daniel nodded. "You're so right." He turned to Jennifer. "When will you finish the paperwork for the layoffs?"

"End of day today," she said.

"By four?" Angela asked, her businesslike composure returned.

Jennifer looked at her watch. "By, uh, 3:30. Okay?"

Angela asked, "Did you add the extra terminations we discussed?"

Jennifer nodded.

"Random?" Angela asked.

Jennifer nodded again.

"Undeserved?"

Jennifer nodded. But with a wince of discomfort.

Angela looked away. She thought of the drunken girls giggling in the ladies' room and the hipster boys they hooked up with. Their idea of a big problem was how to get their new pair of raw denim, selvedge jeans broken in just right. Those kids had no idea how lucky they were. A sudden shock of failure might begin to teach the little brats a lesson about how the world works.

160

She turned to Daniel. "I think *you* should do the senior terminations, Daniel. Give those people a feeling of dignity." She put
on an expression of gravity, while snickering inside. "You know,
show them that the CEO cares enough to talk to them personally.
Uh, when you fire them."

"Good idea," Daniel said solemnly. "Ira and Jennifer and I will
start at four and we'll be finished by five. Angela, do you want to
be part of the team?"

"No, I think I should be out of the building today. Be sure not
to give any reassurances that there won't be more firings to come.
Keep them guessing. I'll be here first thing tomorrow morning. If
they walk in full of anxiety after a sleepless night, they'll be more
receptive to my message of building the new culture. I'll love them
up and welcome them to the new tribe. They'll be grateful."

Angela looked for fear hidden in the eyes of her senior management colleagues. She was pretty sure she saw it. She could just as
easily have *them* fired, too. And they knew it. Like most employees,
they spent their lives fearing for their jobs.

It never ceased to amaze her, this world of big corporations. Here
she was, organizing cruelty and injustice. And it was building her
credentials as a top executive. She glanced up at the titles of the books
on the wall behind Daniel—*Leadership, Teamwork, Values, Excellence.*
Yeah, right, she thought. The corporate world was yet another insti-
tution built on lies. She was merely playing this distasteful game the
way everyone else played it. Everyone, that is, who won big.

By this time next year, she hoped, she would be out of this
stupid corporate swamp and enjoying her next new life. As Cliff
Townsend's fourth wife. Or fourth ex-wife. Or, with any luck, after
not too many years, his widow.

CHAPTER 30

Jack spent the rest of the morning in shock, walking around Manhattan. He wandered from Dale's office in the Flatiron up through Midtown toward his apartment building. He made a circuitous journey through memories, seeking out buildings where he'd once worked or had important meetings or job interviews. He would stop and stare upward like a tourist.

The buildings still resonated with the dramas he had lived inside them. Wins, losses, disasters, Hail Mary passes, camaraderie, competition, office politics—all twenty-five years of it rushing by, ending suddenly in this awful moment. Now that he knew how the brilliant career of Jack Price came to its abrupt conclusion, he relived his time in "the business" with a mixture of nostalgia and regret. Memories of triumphs would pump him up with a rush of arrogant pride, only to be crushed an instant later by overwhelming pangs of shame. He was grateful he did not bump into anyone he knew.

How could he have been so good at this game? Such a winner. A player. And now be such a loser. A nobody.

Jack Price *was* his work. His work was *him*. Just yesterday, he'd had all these things that reinforced how important he was. The big office, his title, the meetings where people hung on his every word, his status as an industry star. He realized that all the things that reinforced his importance were mirrors. The Jack Price he knew was the man he saw reflected in them. He had depended on them to tell him who he was and what he was worth. Repeat, *was*.

Who was he now? And what was he worth?

As he approached his own block, he realized he would have to start looking for a much cheaper place to live. He took out his phone. He'd been afraid of this moment all morning. He wanted to prove Dale wrong about no one taking his calls. He searched his Contacts for the direct line of Tim Walsh, the guy he had mentored long ago and for whom he'd given solid-gold references over the years as Tim moved up the ladder. As Jack *helped* him move up.

Tim was now CEO of the second-largest agency in New York. He and Tim were still tight. Once a year, they would meet up after work to drink and bullshit. As they would get into their cups, Tim would promise Jack he was going to hire him away and, together, they would take the business by storm. High fives, bro hugs, blood brothers forever.

Jack tapped Tim's direct line, the personal line that only Tim's closest friends and colleagues had.

"Mr. Walsh's line," the woman said.

"Hey, Colleen, it's Jack Price!" he chirped, the way he always did.

Long silence. Was her hand over the receiver, or had she put him on hold?

"Uh, I'm sorry, Mr. Price . . ." She always called him Jack. "Mr. Walsh is not available." She always called him Tim to his friends. "I'm supposed to ask you not to call again."

"But, Colleen, please tell Tim that it's not what—"

"I'm sorry. I've been instructed to do this."

The line went dead.

He stared at his phone, lost. His thoughts were shattered by the angry roar of a truck engine. He looked up toward his apartment building. Emerging from the underground garage was a big flatbed tow truck with a car on it.

His car. *His* blue BMW.

But it wasn't his. It never was.

What on earth would he tell Sandra and Luke tonight?

CHAPTER 31

Luke Price completely forgot that he was in his room in the apartment on West End Avenue. He was fighting off the combined armies of continuously mutating alien metallic lizard monsters and ancient Egyptian warriors. He was unleashing deadly atomic laser pulses from his fingertips, vaporizing his opponents one by one as they attacked him from all sides.

He could still make out the contours of his room. But his bed, his desk, his dresser, and even his wall-mounted Nerf basketball hoop had been transformed into the mountains, mesas, and plateaus of the ash-covered postapocalyptic landscape in which he battled. A perfect marriage of VR and AR.

He was having more fun than he had ever had with any gaming technology. Ever.

He lost track of time. Forgot who he was, where he lived, what he worried about at school that day, and what homework he was supposed to be doing. He had changed into a whole new Luke. With light-speed reflexes and superpowers that flowed from his every move. He was the master of a whole new universe of violent death, instant rebirth, and thrills he had never imagined before.

Suddenly, there was an explosion at the far end of his world.

A blast of blinding light.

A new monster approaching. A monster with a huge head. Snakes for hair. Armor plate all over its body. The monster was getting bigger, bigger, bigger in his field of vision.

He fired at the beast. Blasted it with his laser cannon. One blast after the other. Gigantic bolts of atomic laser lightning accompanied by deafening thunderclaps. He had slain other monsters with it, cut them to shreds.

Pow! Pow! Pow!

But this beast was unharmed. Unaffected. It just kept getting closer. And bigger. Oblivious to the massive firepower he was directing at it.

Suddenly, the beast filled his field of vision. Covered up his entire world. Shrouded it in total darkness. Something grabbed his head, shook it, shook his world, pulled at him. Yanked his headset off.

There was blinding light everywhere. He covered his eyes and tried to catch his breath.

He heard a voice shouting. A woman's voice. "Jesus, Luke!"

He uncovered his eyes.

It was Mom.

She was holding the VeRity headset at arm's length the way he had seen her hold a snapping lobster at The Clam Shack when they were on vacation in Montauk the previous summer.

"What on earth are you doing with this thing?" she asked.

168

"Uh, killing aliens?" Luke knew he was in some hot water. Not boiling hot, but still hot.

"Enough for one night," she said. "I don't know how you and I and that thing are going to coexist in this apartment."

"Aw, Mom," he pleaded. "It is soo rad."

"Do you have any idea how much noise you were making?"

"Well," he said, trying to score points with a little charm, "you know they haven't perfected silencers for the atomic laser cannons, but they're working on it."

"Wise-ass," she said, "just like your father. You told me you were going to put it away and do some homework. What happened?"

"I, uh, just wanted a little more. It's so much fun, I couldn't resist."

She shook her head and muttered, "Uh-huh. Also just like your father."

CHAPTER 32

"So, you're going out to a posh Manhattan dinner," Eric said, almost bursting with frustration, "but you won't tell me where. Or who you're going out with."

"Whom," Angela said offhandedly, "it's *whom*." She stepped into the slinky black Stella McCartney dress and turned her back to Eric. "Here, zip me up." Her little brother.

"Why won't you tell me?" he whined as he pulled the zipper ever so carefully.

"Not won't," she said. "Can't. It's too soon. Besides, well, pain of death and all that. You know the drill."

"Yes, all too well," he said, disappointed.

She slipped on her Manolos and did a little pirouette for him. "How do I look?"

Eric put on the voice of a tough-guy American movie detective. "Ya look like a million bucks, babe. Like a million bucks."

She scanned the view out of her forty-fifth-floor window. "I was thinking more like a billion. Or two or three."

"Now *this* is getting more interesting," Eric said, switching back to the posh accent he had mastered to cover the accent he had acquired growing up.

She wondered if she could take Eric with her on the next leg of her journey, if her plans worked out. She really hoped so. She wondered if he would want to join her, and what she might have to offer him to make it worth his while.

Angela began transferring critical items from her Hermès handbag to a tiny Judith Lieber purse in ruby-colored alligator. "Sorry, that's all you get for now."

"You're just going to walk out of here without telling me more?" Eric sounded exasperated. "You absolutely cannot. I refuse to allow it."

"Sorry, that's exactly what I'm going to do."

"Well, then, you owe me another secret. Tell me something deeply personal that you've never told me about."

She closed the snap on the little purse and started walking toward the door. "Don't forget to close the door behind you and make sure it's locked," she said over her shoulder.

"Oh, come on, Angela," he whined. "*You're* going out on the town and *I'm* here with nothing to do. Give me something juicy to chew on. Tell me. Tell me. Tell me. Tell me. I've got it! Tell me about your first time. Your first official shag. Come on, let's hear it. The deflowering of young Lady Angela."

She stopped. Took a deep breath and turned around slowly.

"If you must know, it wasn't much of anything. I was fifteen. After listening to my girlfriends, I thought it was time to get it over with. He was sixteen. He was awkward and scared. We both were. I'm sure he lied about not being a virgin himself. It hurt a little. I wondered, Am I supposed to enjoy this?"

Eric peered at her eagerly. "Did it make you wonder about gir—?"

Before he could finish saying "girls," she shook her head no and wrinkled her nose.

"Nah, too soft and mushy. And all those tears? Nah. Besides, it didn't take long to figure out once I found the right boy."

"You liked it?"

"Of course, silly." She had a fond, fleeting recollection of Shawn and their clumsy athletic bouts of teenage lovemaking.

"So, tell me, did it ever feel like fireworks? Like I-feel-the-earth-move? That kind of utterly, impossibly over-the-moon crazy-good?"

She nodded. "You're asking who was my best one?"

"Yes! Yes! Who?" Eric asked urgently. "Who was it? Who *was* it?"

She zipped a finger across her lips. "I have to go." She turned and walked toward the door.

"Hah!" Eric almost screamed. "It was him! I just know it! It was *him*, wasn't it? He was your best ever, wasn't he?"

She stopped at the door and turned around.

"So what? Sex is just"—she paused—"well, just sex. Sometimes it's good, sometimes it's not. Sometimes there's caring. Sometimes there's not."

Eric pointed an accusing finger. "Sometimes, there's *loove!* The kind we never quite get over."

She smiled at him and opened the door. Gave a little wave over her shoulder and let the door close behind her.

When the elevator came, she was grateful it was empty. As it plummeted down those forty-five flights, she felt like she might explode. She had been dying—*dying!*—to share her plans with Eric! Dish with him about Cliff Townsend and their dinner date. Talk it over and get his advice. It had taken absolutely all her willpower to keep from spilling her secret to him.

But she knew she had to wait. She dared not tell another soul. Nor yet. Not even Eric, her confidant with whom she wasn't shy about sharing almost *anything*. This was just too monumental. Until she had proof that her plan was more than a pipe dream, she had to keep her mouth shut.

All afternoon, she had been worrying. About her outfit, her hair, her makeup, her nails, her breath. Everything had to be perfect. *She* had to be perfect. And she knew she was sooo far from perfect.

Would she in some way disappoint Cliff Townsend—only realizing it *after* it was too late? Like maybe he'd notice her earlobes were a bit odd and get turned off. Or she'd have a hair out of place, or stumble in her stiletto heels. She might do something that would hit him the wrong way and ruin her chances with him.

She agonized about all the things she could try to control, and then worried that she was trying too goddamn hard. Then she obsessed even more about the things she knew she hadn't thought of and could not control. She had bottomless anxiety about tonight and what Cliff might think.

Then there were *her* very mixed-up feelings about Cliff to worry about. Trying to snare a rich old man for his money. Her very first time at this game. Was he the billionaire of her dreams? Hardly. But he was the billionaire fate had thrown her way. Could she hold out for a better one? Maybe. But for how long?

Now was her moment to strike. Every day, the clock was tick-tick-ticking away her youth and beauty. She had also been considering Cliff's physical attributes. His seventy-five-year-old body. His veiny hands dotted with liver spots, his stained, eroded teeth, his sags and bags. How bad could it be, really? If sex was just, well, sex, especially in the dark (she would insist on keeping the lights out—or hoped she could), how much did it matter? Besides, Cliff was gentle with her. Protective. Shy, in his way. She knew she had power over him. She was succulent fruit. He was almost drooling with desire for her.

She had been thinking about the kind of women who married much older rich men. How, for those women, their attachment could not possibly have been hot physical attraction. She had seen these wives, ex-wives, and widows at fancy events. They were important people. No one would dare call them the whores of geriatric tycoons. At least, not to their faces. And even if they had, did she think the women would have cared? No way. They had their money and power.

She knew the score among the rich. If you had it, nobody cared how you got it—within certain bounds of decency and the law, of course, or at least behind well-constructed façades of decency and the law. And if you were high enough in the status hierarchy, you could even get away with violating the rules as long you kept it secret. Yes, discretion, always.

By the time the elevator doors opened, she had pulled herself together and felt ready for her mission. As she walked across the lobby of the Four Seasons toward her waiting Town Car, Angela told herself she was an actress.

Not just any actress. A great actress.

A great actress about to audition for the role of a lifetime.

CHAPTER 33

Luke jumped through the apartment doorway to give his dad a hug, almost knocking him over.

"We love you, Dad," Luke said, wrapping his arms around him and holding on tightly, "no matter what."

Jack wondered if his son's use of "we" reflected something he and his mom had discussed. Aching for affirmation, he would take it any way he got it and enjoy acting as if he were still inside a family he had not destroyed. He did not have the heart to bring up his broken promise to Luke. At least, not yet. He did not want his weakness to shatter this moment of domestic closeness.

Over the simple roast chicken dinner that Luke proudly said he had prepared with "only a minor assist from Mom," the grown-ups ate mostly in silence. Luke filled the vacuum with his enthusiasm for his new VeRity headset.

"You're right, Dad! It is so incredibly rad! It's like I was flying around my room like a superhero! I could stay on it all day!"

Sandra groaned and shook her head. "Gee, thanks, Jack. We really needed this. Especially at the end of the school year when Luke's got exams."

"It's okay, Mom," the boy insisted through a hurried mouthful, "I won't screw up."

Jack decided it was his turn to play the role of parental killjoy.

"Dude," he said patting Luke's arm, "for one thing, please slow down. This is not an eating contest. For another, please watch your language. And most important, your schoolwork. School comes first—okay?"

"Sure, yeah, okay." Luke looked back and forth between his parents, who stared back at him, a united front.

Jack said, "Promise?"

"Yeah, promise."

"Good." Jack squeezed the boy's arm, sealing the deal.

He savored this momentary feeling of family unity, watching Luke take another bite. The boy did an exaggerated slo-mo display of eating and chewing. Jack decided to ignore his son's wise-ass fake obedience.

"So, dude, have you decided what we're going to do together after you ace those exams? Is it the Yankee game, the Broadway show, or our hike in the mountains upstate? Or maybe what's behind door number four?"

"No contest," Luke smiled. "The ridge climb at Mohawk Mountain."

"If that's what you want." Jack looked at Sandra for approval. She nodded. "Done deal. Mohawk Mountain."

Luke finished the last remnants of his chicken and put his hands down. He looked at Sandra. "Can I go to my room now?"

With a glance and a head bob, Sandra indicated Luke's plate, the sink, and the dishwasher. Luke took his plate to the trash can, cleaned off the chicken bones, rinsed his plate and cutlery in the sink, and carefully put them in the dishwasher.

"If you need me, you know where I can be reached." He grinned and bolted for his bedroom down the short hallway.

After a comfortable uncomfortable silence, the kind they had gotten used to over the years, Jack began the remarks he had been preparing all day.

"Sandra, I have enough saved so that I can cover you guys the way I always have for at least another year and a half. Maybe two years. No problem, really. And I'm going to cut back on my own expenses—I mean, really cut back. So, it may be even longer."

Very tentatively, Sandra began. "You could apply to the court to—"

"No. No way," Jack insisted. "No way I'm going back into that viper's nest of lawyers and judges. I'm telling you—I can keep things the way they are now for quite a while. My problems don't have to become your problems."

Sandra was positive in her neutral kind of way. "Sure, okay. Sounds good."

Another silence.

"You know," Sandra began slowly, "with Luke headed for eighth grade, I've been planning to go back to work full-time. Remember Michelle, my office mate from the old production company? Well, she's got her own production company now. You must have heard of it. Double-X Omni-Channel Media?"

"Really?" Jack said, "It's *that* Michelle? I didn't connect the dots. They're really hot right now."

"They sure are. She says the hardest part of running her own company is finding people she can really trust. She knows how good

I am and how hard I work, and she's happy to give me flexibility around Luke's schedule. She and Roberto have two kids, so she gets it. I'm really looking forward to working again."

"That's great, Sandra," he said, knowing he sounded halfhearted. He really *was* happy for her, and relieved he would not be the only source of support. But it was odd that she was going back to work now that he had none. Was part of his hesitation jealousy? He wasn't sure. Everything was too damn painful and confusing to sort out at this moment.

Sandra reached across the table and touched his hand. Just for an instant.

"Jack, what are you going to do?"

"Well, first thing, I'm going to stop drinking."

Silence. Deep breath. "You've said that before."

"This time I mean it. I put a padlock on my liquor cabinet. Really. And when I move out of this place to someplace cheaper, there won't *be* a liquor cabinet."

Sandra shrugged.

Banging noises filtered down the hall from Luke's bedroom.

"Superhero flying, no doubt," she said. "He has barely taken that thing off since he got it this morning. I'm going to have to put that VR toy in a cabinet and padlock it."

More banging noises.

Jack said timidly, "Sounds like he's having fun. The product briefing said it was designed by neuroscientists to be addictive."

Sandra raised an eyebrow in alarm. "That's terrible!"

Jack waved away her concern. "All clients make up bullshit about their products. I don't believe any of it."

There was another silence, and then Sandra sat up straight and cleared her throat.

Jack knew what was coming.

"Jack, how could you do it—to that woman? Knowing what it would do to you—to us?"

He looked down at his plate. He thought about whether he should tell her that it was the infamous Angela of the dick pic. Or that Angela may have tricked him. Framed him. Ruined him. Or not.

Then, after agonizing over it all day, he decided no. It was not necessary to tell her. This was not a lie. It was an edit, that's all. It didn't matter who the woman was. It only mattered how stupid *he* was.

"I don't have any excuses," he mumbled. "Like I said, I'm not a hundred percent sure, but I don't think I would do something like that. Even if—"

"Even if you were drunk as a skunk?"

"Even then."

"Shouldn't you get professional help?"

"I can manage this myself."

They'd had this discussion countless times. There was no point in going back over it.

Sandra gave a deep sigh. They had very separate lives now. Even though Luke would always be theirs together, their lives were about to get even more separate.

"Do you know what you're going to do next?"

"No, not really. It's only been one day. I need a little time to recover."

"Of course you do," Sandra said with genuine sympathy.

She picked up her plate and Jack's, cleared them at the garbage can, and took them to the sink. The sound of her rinsing the plates filled the little kitchen.

Jack took his phone out of his pocket just to fill the empty moment. Suddenly a text chimed and filled the screen.

"Whoa, Sandra! It's from Dale Waldman, my favorite headhunter. He's got a job opportunity." Jack read the text aloud. "Wanted: World's best liar for world's worst job. Call me ASAP."

Jack put his phone down, shell-shocked.

Sandra turned around from the sink. "What are you waiting for?"

Jack tapped Dale's cell number and the speakerphone button. He was getting used to sharing all of his important phone calls.

Dale's voice boomed from the kitchen table.

"Jack, my man. I told you, you are one lucky guy. This just came in over the transom. An opportunity for someone who is so good at lying he can make *anyone* look good. Even the King of Sleaze."

"Who?" Jack asked.

"Clifford Townsend. You must've heard of him. Made his first fortune in video porn rental stores. Got out of porn right before VHS died and got into pawn shops. Grew a chain of them like crazy. Expanded into bail bonds, payday loans, factoring, low-income housing—a whole empire built on fucking over poor people. Think of every shitty, disreputable, exploitive, but legal business you can imagine, and he's there, big-time. Guy's a billionaire several times over. The assignment is to turn him into a pillar of respectability, a philanthropist, a paragon of conscious capitalism. What do you say?"

"I've told bigger lies for worse scumbags."

"Good. The project driver is Townsend's daughter Charlotte. I Googled her. His only child. Mid-forties. Divorced three times. Wants to sanitize the fortune. Looks to me like she wants to buy herself a place in fancy society. She works hard at getting herself in those party pics at benefit balls. The pay is about half what you were making. They are okay with your recent, uh, problem. I assured them you're not a creep. In fact, they like the idea of negotiating with someone who doesn't have a lot of other options. And get

182

this—the winning candidate will live and work on Townsend's humongous super-yacht with him and the daughter.

"Townsend's first wife died when the daughter was a girl. The old man burned through three more marriages and his daughter did the same. Now they spend a lot of time together, the two of them. Weird, huh? You still up for this, Jack?"

"Yeah, sure. Why not? I mean, yes. Absolutely. Yes."

"That's the spirit.

"Great! I e-mailed you the link to their application process. There's a lot to fill out—your experience, NDAs, plus a fuck-ton of essay questions about your qualifications in communications for philanthropy." Dale paused for a moment. "Jack, do you know anything about philanthropy?"

"No, but I can do some homework. I'll make myself an instant expert."

"Then go for it, buddy." Dale rang off.

Jack jumped up from the table. "It's a job, Sandra. A job! I can start fresh. And I promise to start changing things."

"Like what?" she asked.

"Like everything," he said breathlessly. "*Everything!* I'll start tonight."

He wanted to kiss her cheek and even give her a good-night hug, but he just mouthed a thank-you and walked down the hall. He said a hurried good-bye to Luke, who barely noticed him from behind his new VeRity headset.

Out on the street, his mind was racing with new possibilities.

Work.

A purpose.

A place.

Philanthropy?

Of course, philanthropists need liars, too. Probably even more than marketers.

He would make these resolutions and *keep* them. Like quitting the alcohol! He could do it. He was sure he could.

Jack Price was going to reinvent himself into someone new.

Never in his whole life had he felt more determined to succeed. Or more frightened that he might fail.

CHAPTER 34

"I think it's possible I may never marry," Angela said tentatively as she turned the stem of the gilt-edged crystal wine goblet between her thumb and forefinger.

She glanced out over Central Park at night from the sixtieth-floor $50 million condo of the Townsends. She turned back to Cliff, who sat across the dining room table from her. A stunning collection of crystal, silver, and fine porcelain filled the space between them.

"But I'm absolutely sure I'll never stop working. Never. I need to make my own money, have my own real-world responsibilities. I have no interest in staying home and being some man's little wifey. Besides, I like being the boss. And I'm really good at it."

She looked carefully at Cliff to gauge his reaction.

The old man gave her a warm smile. "In a lot of ways, you sound like me," he said.

"What's wrong with that?" she asked.

"Nothing. Absolutely nothing." He raised his goblet in a toast. She clinked hers against his. "Here's to people who understand work," he said, "people like *us*."

Angela kept her eyes riveted directly into Cliff's eyes as she took a micro-sip of the insanely expensive 1980 Château Lafite Rothschild he'd had the butler bring out for their intimate dinner.

Yes, she thought, it's working. It's working. First, showing him that I'm the complete opposite of Charlie. It's essential that I replace her as the woman in his life. Then, showing him how well I understand him and the world he comes from. Prove to him that the last thing I want is to be dependent on him and his money. Convince him I want the opposite of everything he is accustomed to women wanting from him.

Reverse psychology, just like Jack Price taught her. When you really, really want something, make the other guy think you don't want it at all. Nine times out of ten, it works, Jack had said. And the one time it doesn't work, well, you weren't going to get it anyway.

She had a moment's regret about Jack and what she'd put him through. Then she decided she had finally gotten her full revenge. And besides, she was saving his ass with the new job he would get from Charlie. Maybe that finally evened the score between them. Or came close enough.

Cliff took a long, noisy gulp of his wine, draining his glass yet again. He was already half into his second bottle. Angela was beginning to understand why Charlie complained about his uncouth ways. If the next thing he did was burp, or even fart, she would pretend to be charmed. This was work—hard work. She was determined to succeed at this dirty job and get justly rewarded for her hard labor when the time came.

"So, Angela," he said, without releasing any gases, "what do you think of our new place?"

"It's nice," she said with deliberate understatement. She did not want to seem too impressed or too eager. In fact, the girl from the projects was utterly blown away. Here she was in one of *the* premiere new condos on Billionaires' Row on West 57th Street. The panorama of Central Park from sixty stories went on forever. The picture windows were two, maybe three stories high. The soaring space felt more like a cathedral than an apartment. Minimalist sculptural furniture, all custom-made. Enormous abstract paintings highlighting the towering expanses of glass. Tens upon tens of millions of dollars had been poured into this movie set of Manhattan glamour. Everything was perfect. No, beyond perfect. OMFG! *Oh, My Fucking God!*

But Angela wasn't about to let him know that.

"Yes, Cliff, it's very nice," she said, playing the role of the very polite young lady, employing all the formal social graces Jack Price had taught her. Then, while maintaining her prim expression, she leaned forward to let Cliff see a bit more of her breasts. Squirmed a little in her chair to draw attention to her hips and the mysterious treasures she was sitting on. And even gave Cliff's veiny old hand an ambiguous touch, all the while keeping her face a mask of pleasant indifference. She was counting on the unsettling power of mixed signals.

Through the rest of the main course and for quite a while after they had finished dessert, Angela probed Cliff with detailed business questions about how he had built his empire—something she knew Charlie would never, could never have done. She listened with wide-eyed admiration to his every word. She'd heard many of his stories before, but she was careful to pretend they were all new and absolutely fascinating. She could see that Cliff was visibly thrilled to have such an attentive, well-informed, admiring listener.

She made him feel attractive. Powerful. And, of course, sexy. She didn't have to do much, really. Just fake it enough to encourage him a bit. His monumental opinion of himself did the rest. She felt sure that he believed her bullshit. Because she knew he believed his own bullshit about himself.

When he had finally run out of stories, Angela slid her chair back from the table.

Cliff looked disappointed. "Wouldn't you like to stay for a little after-dinner cognac? I like to have a snifter or two. Settles the stomach after a big meal."

"I'm sorry, Cliff, I really can't. Tonight has been just wonderful. Magical." She stood up. "But I'm afraid it's a work night. Tomorrow's going to be a very tough day. My company has hit a slump and we have no choice but to do some serious layoffs. I've got to go in there bright and early and start rebuilding morale. Those employees, I care so much for them. Maybe too much. I feel like, like, they're my *children*. They'll need a lot of love and support from me. I need a good night's sleep."

Cliff stood up from the table, a little unsteady from two bottles of the heavy red wine. "Well, of course you do. It's so important how you handle things after layoffs. You should have said something sooner."

Angela, who'd had barely a sip from her wineglass, stood and beamed her best older-man smile. "No way. I was having so much fun I lost track of the time. That feeling is so rare." She took three steps and was right beside him, close enough to be touching. But not quite. She looked up at him. "You are a very vibrant man. I love your life force."

Cliff reached out with open arms, surrounded her, and pulled her close. With an abrupt, jerky motion, he bent down and put his mouth on hers. Angela kissed him back but kept her lips shut.

What a clumsy pass, she thought. No finesse. But then, he's probably never needed finesse. He just reaches for the women he wants. And they let him do whatever because he's so fucking rich. With the old man kissing her clumsily, she closed her eyes and thought of the expression men use about getting laid. All cats are gray in the dark. She thought of the parade of her own cats. From her clumsy schoolboys to Jack and the other lovers after him. Just close your eyes, she told herself. In the dark, all cats are gray.

"Oh," she said demurely when he tried to reach a hand between her legs. Clumsy again, she thought, removing his hand gently but firmly. "I really have to go."

She wondered how many of the haughty society ladies had gone through this same experience. Maybe it was a rite of passage they had endured but never spoke about. Maybe, after they had graduated into widows and divorcées, they sat around over drinks to dish about the first feel their old geezers had tried to cop from them. Angela felt confident she was well on the way to joining their exclusive little club and finding out. After that, she could learn from them how they used their handsome pool boys to have sex they actually enjoyed.

Cliff stepped back from her, arms dropped to his side.

She leaned forward, stood on one tiptoe, took his face in her hands, and gave him a lingering kiss with a little dart of her tongue at the very end. Then let go of him and stepped back.

"I hope you understand," she said with all the virginal modesty she could muster.

"Uh, of c-course," he stammered. "Of course I do."

189

She watched the old man struggling to catch his breath and regain his composure.

Yes, she thought, perfect. *Perfect!*

Now, Charlie, my dear, dear BFF Charlie, just try to compete with that. Just fucking try.

CHAPTER 35

Exactly one week after filling out the online application, Jack got the e-mail, informing him that "Mr. & Ms. Townsend" would interview him in person.

He thought it odd that father and daughter would refer to themselves in the same way a married couple would. He was to appear "at precisely 2:00 p.m." at the address on West 57th Street. It was one of those spiky new towers for billionaires that offered sweeping views of Central Park to anyone rich enough to buy on the floors above the roofs of the neighbors on Central Park South. The e-mail included a QR code to present at the concierge desk along with his valid ID.

"Please arrive no more than five minutes early," it instructed. "If, for whatever reason, you are more than one minute late, the QR code will expire. You will be denied entry and the interview will be canceled. Mr. & Ms. Townsend will be waiting for you in Apartment A on the sixtieth floor."

Jack had watched that tower going up. It was way too tall and skinny for the flow of buildings around it. As he approached it, he thought of the slogan the developers had plastered everywhere—"Soaring to new heights of opulence." Jack added "and vulgarity" to the slogan when he saw the lobby, overdone with glitter and crystal.

At precisely three minutes before 2:00, he presented himself to the elegantly uniformed concierge at the front desk. He scanned Jack's QR code and driver's license.

The elevator whooshed him nonstop to 60. The small hallway presented two doors facing each other, A and B. "A" must be the park-view side, he thought. No self-respecting billionaire would live on the B-side of anything.

Before he could ring the bell, the door opened.

A small Filipino man in a butler's uniform held the door wide open. Caressing his consonants in his Tagalog accent, he said, "Wel-l-l-come Mr. Price. Please come in."

In spite of himself, Jack was impressed. The view of the park was stunning. The ceiling had to be three stories high. Custom furniture, ten-foot-high abstract paintings. More like the lobby of a very grand hotel than a living room.

"Hello, Mr. Price, I'm Charlotte Townsend." She had appeared, it seemed, from nowhere. She extended her hand. "You can call me Charlie. May we call you Jack?" Her perfectly manicured hand looked like it belonged to a woman heading toward fifty. But her face, framed in cascading ringlets of three shades of blonde, had a strange, unnatural smoothness. Fillers and plastic surgery made it look like she was trying to imitate the face of a twenty-four-year-old. She was a very trim five-foot-six in strappy stiletto sandals and a clingy silk dress that screamed pricey. Her thin bare legs were taut and toned but starting to show the stringiness of middle age. She was tanned from head to toe in bronzed perfection. As if she had just arrived from the tropics.

"Yes, please, uh . . ." Jack said, pausing.

"Charlie," she offered. "If we end up working together, you'll get used to it. I must say, you come highly recommended, Jack."

"Over here!" an older man's voice crowed from far across the room.

Clifford Townsend stood up from one of the white chairs in a semicircle grouping right next to the window and the panorama. Townsend was a tall man who had once been taller. The stoop at the neck and slumping curve at the shoulders brought his six-foot-something height down a bit. Big round eyeglasses, plain features, white hair in a comb-over atop his bald head.

Charlie touched Jack's elbow as they walked the considerable distance to her father.

There were three chairs facing each other in the semicircle.

Cliff took Jack's hand; Jack shook firmly.

"A pleasure, Mr. Townsend," Jack said, trying to sound respectful and confidently cheerful. The old man grunted his acknowledgment and sat down.

As she took her seat, Charlie made a show of crossing her legs. And another show as she pulled her hem down, pretending to make sure she covered the top half of her trim thighs. She thrust one leg out. Her elegantly arched and perfectly pedicured foot bobbed up and down. Jack got it. She was daring him *not* to stare at her legs.

Cliff crossed his arms across his chest and huffed at his daughter, "You go first. This is your project."

Charlie cleared her throat. "Well, Jack." She said his name emphatically then paused as if that alone were an important communication.

193

Her eyes wandered up and down him. Jack could have sworn she was checking him out.

She cleared her throat again and began in a very formal tone, "Mr. Townsend is creating a number of very significant liquidity events—"

"Liquidity events?" Cliff squirmed in the chair. "You sound like one of those private equity assholes. She means I'm cashing out of my companies, consolidating my assets, and getting ready for the next phase in my life. You know, when I get feeble and senile and need full-time nurses to keep me from drooling all over myself. Or, I keel over and die. Whichever comes first."

Charlie patted his arm with apparent fondness. "Not for many, many years, Cliff. Really."

Cliff snorted and peered out the window.

Charlie continued. "This time of asset consolidation is the perfect time to consider how to deploy this very substantial amount of cash. Creating the Townsend Foundation could be the perfect vehicle for us going forward."

Cliff snorted again.

Jack nodded. "Makes sense," he said.

"But," she took a deep breath and got a troubled look on her face, "we've been told by experts in the field that when a family decides to devote a certain portion of its wealth to philanthropy, they have to make a choice. Do we want to look good, feel good, or do good? They've told us we can only have one. But I disagree. Why do we have to choose? Why can't we do good, feel good, *and* look good? I mean, really, why can't we?"

"Because," Cliff muttered, "the whole charity thing is hypocrisy and bullshit. Carving your name all over buildings, to impress who?" He hugged his arms closer to himself.

Charlie ignored him. She leaned forward, pointing her bobbing leg directly at Jack.

"Jack, we would like to engage a communications and persuasion expert to help us create the brand for the Townsend Foundation. We want to do good, be properly recognized for it, and allow at least some of us to feel good as a result. Do you think a person with your skills and experience could accomplish that?"

Jack leaned forward, trying to look, and not look, down at her legs.

"Yes, Charlie, absolutely."

Cliff unfolded his arms. He gazed upward, musing.

"I'll tell you something I'd fund. How about this for a joint venture? *Sesame Street* and Harvard Business School. Teach little kids what business is really like. Teach 'em how to chisel and screw each other while they're learning their ABCs. Show 'em how some kids get rich by poisoning their classmates. Oops, a little dioxin got in the groundwater from the class mining project. Sorry about that lemonade we're selling with the cookies! Guess a few of your classmates will keel over dead. But hey, we're showin' 'em how the free market works. Kids, high time you learned that shit happens. Show 'em how a few kids end up owning everything while the rest own nothing. Teach 'em how to swindle on a really grand scale and win awards for being model citizens. I'd write a check for ten, maybe twenty, million to fund *that*."

He turned to Charlie. "I bet you'd have a ball, waving a check that size in front of those prestigious names. You'd meet a lot of nice people, make a lot of fancy new friends. And I'd show the next generation the kind of skills they're *really* going to need in this world."

He turned to Jack. "See? Your job could be easy."

195

Charlie rolled her eyes. "Oh please, Cliff."

Jack noted that she did not call him some variant of "Father."

"I'm just saying," Cliff muttered.

"Please excuse him." Charlie leaned over and touched Jack's arm. "He's had some bad experiences with institutions that didn't fully appreciate his, uh, unique personal style."

Yep, Jack thought, just what Dale said. A family fight.

"Tell you what I learned about life by running pawn shops," Cliff said. "Everybody with something they need to hock walks in thinking about the deal they want. The deal they deserve. Guess what? Everybody walks out with the deal I give 'em. That's the deal they get. Period. Everybody. Including me."

Cliff pinched the skin from the back of one hand in two fingers. His skin was loose, almost translucent, streaked with blue veins, flecked with age spots. "Think this is the deal I want?" He let his hand drop. "I got bathrooms made a' marble and onyx in this place." He indicated the grand apartment around them. "Faucets a' gold and crystal. But every time I sit down on the crapper, I get pain and humiliation. Pain and humiliation. Think them gold faucets can change my deal? Think again."

Charlie shook her head and quickly changed the subject, talking about the nobility of giving back. Cliff talked more about big egos looking only to glorify themselves.

Jack, taking cues from Charlie, talked about the power of image building to pave the way for doing good. How changing minds could create the conditions necessary to effect positive change. Taking cues from Cliff, Jack talked about how tough, unglamorous businesses were the true proving ground of grit and character. Cliff and Charlie bickered back and forth through Jack for another fifteen minutes.

196

Finally, father and daughter turned to him as one.

Charlie said, "Jack, you're the communications expert. Can you help us? Tell us the truth."

Cliff said, "That's right, Jack, you're the communications expert. Tell us some lies. Make 'em good ones."

Jack took a deep breath. Okay, this was the big moment.

He had spoken to Dale that morning. "Kiddo," Dale had said, "this may be the worst job on earth. But believe me, it's your very last chance. Do whatever you have to do. Just get this fucking job!"

"Well," Jack began, gesturing at Cliff, "I know for a fact that you deserve more recognition than you have gotten. I'm confident we can beat the snobs and assholes at their own game." He turned to Charlie. "I am also confident that you and I can sift through the world of causes to find ones where Townsend Foundation can make a meaningful difference. Together, we can prove to the founder," he turned respectfully to Cliff, "that we can deliver results in his name with no hypocrisy or bullshit."

There, Jack thought, a nice combination of lies and truth, pandering to this couple's weaknesses, insecurities, hopes, fears, and gargantuan egos. He put his hands in his lap and stared at his potential employers, waiting for a reaction.

Father and daughter were poker-faced.

Cliff stood up abruptly. "We'll let you know in a week or two." And walked away.

CHAPTER 36

Charlie did not budge. She sat smiling at Jack. He's definitely the one, she thought. He can turn Cliff around, I'm sure of it. Cliff engaged with him for fifteen whole minutes. I've never seen that before. She checked her watch. OMG, it was almost twenty. That's a lifetime for Cliff. He has no patience for anyone he doesn't think is useful.

"Should I do anything in the interim?" Jack asked. "Anything more I can provide to help with your decision-making process?"

"Oh, no," she said. "We have all your contact info, right?"

"Yes, I'm sure you do. From the, uh, online application I filled out. But is there anything more I can show you? I can send you more samples of my work. Or maybe you'd like me to develop an idea or two. I have no problem working on spec. Really. Just say the word. Whatever you need."

How sweet, Charlie thought. He's nervous about getting the job. So eager to please. He's just perfect! And he is even cuter than his pictures. He'll be all mine to play with on the yacht. I can hardly wait.

"No need, Jack," she said comfortingly. "We won't need you to do that. Your credentials are just great, really."

Very slowly, she uncrossed her legs, watching his eyes carefully to make sure he was watching her do it. He was. Satisfied that she could command his attention as a man, she stood up.

Jack jumped to his feet.

She took him by the elbow and held on. "Here, Jack, let me show you out." Before they completed the long walk to the foyer, the butler appeared. "Thanks, John Rey," she said, "I'll take care of Mr. Price." The butler melted back into the cavernous apartment.

Charlie opened the door, still holding on to Jack. She wanted so much to feel around for his biceps—and so much more—but restrained herself.

Jack stepped backwards into the hallway to maintain eye contact.

"Seriously, if there's anything more you'd like from me, just let me know. E-mail, text, phone call, whatever."

Charlie loved his vulnerability. She could have almost kissed him right there in front of the elevators. But no, that would have to wait. "My father and I will definitely be in touch." She knew she could not promise him the job until Cliff gave his okay. "Thanks *so* much, Jack."

"Thank you, uh . . ." He paused.

"Charlie. Remember, it's Charlie to you." She reached out and touched his forearm. We'll talk very soon," she said in a breathy whisper.

"Thanks, Charlie." He turned and pressed the Down elevator button.

She closed the door and hurried across the living room. Opened the French doors and walked into the dining room.

Cliff was standing by the window with one arm around Angela's waist.

"Cliff," she gushed, "you liked him, didn't you? You liked him?"

"He's okay," he muttered as he hugged Angela closer to him. "My girl here tells me he's the best in the business. That's good enough for me."

Charlie clapped her hands. "Wonderful! I'll let him know right away he has the job."

"No, no, no, Charlie," Cliff grumbled. "No! I told the guy a week or two. That means a week or two. In this case, it means two. Let him stew a little. It'll give us more leverage in negotiating his fees. Besides, Angie tells me he's not getting any other offers anytime soon, so just relax."

"That's right," Angela said, snuggling against Cliff, "we don't have to worry about him getting snapped up by anyone else."

"This is *so* exciting!" Charlie said. "I can hardly wait to get the foundation plans going."

Cliff let go of Angela. "Don't get ahead of yourself, girl. I said you could hire the guy. I didn't agree to any foundation plans."

"Not yet," Charlie said, winking at Angela.

Angela winked back.

Cliff checked his watch. "I've got to take a conference call with some investment bankers." He turned toward the French doors. "They're selling Payday Heyday for me. What a business, payday loans. Those thousand crappy little storefronts have been a gold mine. Probably paid for this condo and half the yacht. Looks like we've gonna have a battle of the buyers. Drive that price up nicely."

Cliff walked to the French doors. Then turned around.

"Charlie, I've asked Angie to come with me when we meet on the yacht. She said yes. She's rearranged her vacation to do it. From what she tells me about the terrible pressures of her job, she's earned some fun in the tropics. And she wants to bring her executive assistant."

"He's a dear man," Angela said. "You guys will love him. He's charming and fun. And he knows exactly when to disappear into the woodwork."

Cliff looked at his watch again. "Angie tells me they have to take their vacations at the same time. It's company policy."

"Well, not exactly," she said. "But we have so much confidential personnel information in my department. And Eric is wonderful, but he's very junior. So, it's best if I'm on vacay for him to be out-of-office, too. And besides, he could use a little Caribbean sun, too. I work him *so-o-o* hard."

Cliff gave a shrug and wandered off toward his study.

Charlie waited until they heard the distant sound of the door to his study closing. Then she walked to the French doors and closed them carefully.

She turned to Angela and spoke in a whisper, just in case. "He calls you Angie? *Angie?* Really?"

Angela gave a little giggle and whispered back, "Yeah, he does."

"You told me you hate being called Angie."

Angela giggled again. "Uh-huh. Like fingernails on a chalkboard. But I'll get used to it."

"Has he asked you to marry him yet? I told you how he jumped into marriage with the others. He can't stand living alone. He's very impulsive with beautiful women who seem to be able to put up with him."

Angela nodded. "I told him I need more time. I wasn't saying no, I wasn't saying yes. She took Charlie's hands in hers and stared deep into her eyes. "I want you to understand, I never in a million years expected your father to, well, you need to know that I never tried to—"

Charlie cut her off. "Of course, you didn't. I know that. This is great for *all* of us. Cliff was really starting to fade. He was really

202

getting old. I mean, he's shorter than he used to be. I just noticed it the other day. But since you've appeared, he's bouncing around and happy like I haven't seen him in years. You're going to be the favorite of all my many stepmothers—just imagine that. Plus, my dear little sister, and, most important, my secret weapon. What a combination."

Charlie gave her a hug, then held her by the shoulders. "But I am concerned," she said, hesitating, "about, well, about *your* needs. I mean, it's great for him to have a beautiful young woman. Jesus, a woman young enough to be his granddaughter. But you, sweetie, what about you? He's my father and he's awfully, uh . . . well, he's old."

"Actually, I like older men. I really do. Maybe it's from not ever knowing my own father or my grandfathers, for that matter. It's just, uh, really, I'm good. Really. Love comes in lots of varieties. It can be such a funny thing."

Charlie gave her another hug. Then released her. "I just needed to ask, that's all. Has he had the lawyers show you his standard prenup? It's like a nice severance package with a pension. He practically includes that with the diamond ring."

"No. And no ring yet. I was very clear. I told him if I said yes, I would sign whatever he wanted. No lawyers on my side, no negotiating. Whatever deal he wants. I told him, 'I'm not after your money.' And I mean it. I told him I plan to keep my job and keep working. No matter what."

"How did he react?"

"Shocked. I think. Not what he expects from women."

"Good," Charlie said, "keep him off guard."

"He wants to show me your old house up in Westchester next weekend. He says that's where you grew up."

Charlie shuddered. "It was my mother's house. I haven't set foot there since I was a teenager. I don't know why he keeps it. It's a shrine to my mother. Creepy. Nobody lives there. It's haunted."

"Haunted?"

"Someday, I may tell you. My mother's ghost. Secrets between them."

CHAPTER 37

Eighteen-year-old Charlotte Townsend had just had another birth-day. All by herself again. She had received another faked birthday card and another stupid necklace, supposedly from her father. She knew damn well that his secretary sent them. As usual, the hand-writing on the card was clearly feminine. Lots of love to my big girl, from Dad. Yeah, right.

Cliff Townsend's newest wife saw to it that he somehow could not arrange his schedule to visit her at her prep school in Farming-ton, Connecticut. Like it was somewhere in the wilds of Mongolia.

But on this birthday, she had a visitor in the parlor of her dorm. A gray middle-aged man in a gray suit. A lawyer from New York City, with a letter for her. It was inside a sealed envelope inside another sealed envelope.

When Charlie got to the letter itself, the lawyer asked her if she would like to be left alone. Charlie shrugged. She had no idea why he should go away while she read the letter. The gray man nodded politely and looked out the window.

Charlie opened the folded paper and saw the handwriting. Her mother who had died of ovarian cancer eight years before.

> My darling baby girl,
>
> I hope you are reading this letter on your eighteenth birthday. And I hope you are growing into the wonderful young lady I know you can become. It breaks my heart that I am not there to see you and hug you and be the mom you need as you grow up.
>
> I am making plans to make sure you get what you deserve even though I can't be there for you. There are important things you need to know now that you are a grown-up. Terrible but necessary things.

Charlie looked up from the letter.

"Sir," she said to the lawyer, "I think I need to be alone, like you said."

The gray man gave her a polite smile. He got up and walked out of the parlor.

Charlie clutched the letter in both hands and continued reading.

> Clifford Townsend is your father, but not your biological father.
>
> We kept trying to get pregnant after we got married. That's how we learned that Cliff is sterile. He can't father a child. We wanted a baby so much!
>
> I know you must be a woman by now. And I hope what you've learned about men and women and sex and love

is good and positive. You must know how complicated it all can be.

Your biological father was a man I loved before I met Cliff. His name was Michael de Furia. I invited him to our house one night when Cliff was traveling on business. But Cliff came home unexpectedly and found us together. He was angry, very angry.

When Michael drove away, Cliff followed him. Cliff was gone for hours. When he came home, he said that Michael was speeding and lost control of his car and died when he crashed into a tree. He told me the police said it was an accident.

When we learned that I was pregnant with you, we decided to count our blessings and tell no one what we both knew.

I hope you remember your childhood with happiness. You have no idea how much joy you gave us! You should know that Cliff loves you. He did his best to be a good father, but he worked all the time. He is a hard man. He makes a lot of his money in businesses that take advantage of people when they're desperate. He can be cold and heartless. He cheats and lies in business all the time. But I will *not* let him do that to you. Ever.

After I got my cancer diagnosis, they said I had very little time. I knew I had to protect you and make sure you will have the life you deserve.

After my chemo in the hospital last week, I hid a small tape recorder under the covers. I asked Cliff about the night of

207

the car crash. I told him I needed to know the truth before I died. He admitted that he drove Michael's car off the road. Murdered him. He admitted that he paid off the police to say it was an accident. He admitted it all.

That tape is in safe keeping with the law firm that is bringing you this letter on your eighteenth birthday. If Cliff ever denies you your rights to his fortune, if he ever tries to cheat you out of your birthright, you must go to the lawyers and have them release the tape recording of Cliff's confession. There is no statute of limitations on murder.

I made Cliff promise to take care of you always. But people do not always keep their word.

At the time you are reading this letter, Cliff will also get a letter from me telling him just enough to make sure he will keep his promises to you.

It breaks my heart that I have to tell you all of this so long after I'm gone. But now that you're a grown-up, you need to have this information so you will be able to protect yourself and get what you deserve.

Be strong, my baby. I love you forever.

Mom

CHAPTER 38

"Aw, come on, Dad!" Luke protested. "Just one shot? Me in front of this incredible view will get me a sh—" He stopped before saying shitload. "I mean, a ton of likes."

Jack smiled. "Now that's better language. But hey, we promised each other. No screens on this hike. No phones, no texts, no tablets, no Internet. Just us hiking together. We made a deal."

Sandra had told Jack she was concerned that Luke was spending way too much with the VeRity headset. Jack assumed that the boy would have no need for virtual reality on the glorious outdoor expedition he had chosen over the other guilt presents he'd been offered.

Luke kicked the dirt and sent some stones hurtling down over the edge of the Mohawk Mountain outlook, the rocky cliff vantage point over the breathtaking panorama of lushly wooded Catskill Mountains and glacial lakes.

"Just one shot! *Pleeeeeze?*" Luke could practically taste the jealousy he would incite in all the friends and followers who would see his post. Here's another perfect moment in my perfect life, you assholes. Just try and measure up to this total coolness. Just try!

"We can take the shot on our way down," Jack said. "An hour from now the sun will be facing us. We'll get better lighting on the lake and mountains behind you. If we take it now, your face will be in shadow."

"Promise?" Luke kicked a little more dirt to express his disappointment.

"Promise." Jack had to smile. What a great kid. What a great time he was having with him. Why hadn't he done this more often? Soon Luke would be all grown up. He saw Luke in a flutter of stop-motion shots, transforming from little baby to now, this beautiful boy on the verge of manhood. It goes by so fast, he thought. So goddamn fast.

Luke scampered back from the cliff edge to the trail. "I'll lead," he announced, striding ahead.

"And I, sir, will follow," Jack said with a smile. He watched the boy's backpack bouncing up and down. Especially Marlin, the little cartoon clownfish toy, symbol of the super-dad.

They hiked upward along the trail in contented silence for a while.

Then Jack's phone started vibrating in his pocket. Not wanting to break his own rule, he tried to ignore it. He let it go to voice mail once. Then it started vibrating again immediately. He reached into his pocket and looked at the screen. It was Dale Waldman. Dale! The Townsends must have made a decision! What do I do? Dale's words clanged in his brain: *Your last chance . . . Do whatever it takes . . . Get this job!*

He answered the call. He whispered into the phone, hoping Luke would not hear him.

"Just a sec, Dale. Hold on, okay?"

210

He called to Luke, "Dude, hold on, will you? I have to take this call!" He stopped, phone at his ear.

Luke stopped and turned around. "What the f—?" he asked, visibly miffed, cutting short his full WTF question. He stood with hands on hips, defiant and accusatory. "What about our deal? How come *you* get to use your phone but I can't use mine?"

Jack waved his phone at Luke, then pressed it against his chest before answering.

"This is my job call," he pleaded. "I have to take it. I'm sorry, Luke. Really, I am. It's for you and mom. For all of us. Just two minutes, okay?"

Before he turned to go behind the big pine tree and talk to Dale, he saw Luke kick the dirt angrily. Very angrily. Heard him say, defiantly and intentionally loud enough to be heard up and down the trail, "Fuck!" It was yet another time that work had overruled his time with Luke. But what else could he do?

"Dale?" Jack huddled behind the tree, whispering into the phone, hoping his voice did not carry. "What's the verdict?" He held his breath.

"You got it, Jack. You got the job."

Jack didn't quite dare to breathe. Not yet.

"You are the official mouthpiece, marketing genius, and family therapist of the crazy rich Townsends, father and daughter. It's a six-month contract. I got you a slightly better base salary. But more important, there's bonus opportunity if you make them really happy."

Jack took a deep breath. He had work again. Real work. Well, real enough. At least he wouldn't have to get a job washing dishes or selling aluminum siding. He wondered, giddy with relief, if they even sold aluminum siding anymore. He would make amends with Luke in a couple of minutes.

Dale explained, "A week from now, you will fly on their private jet to St. John's, the capital of Antigua. From there, they will put you on their motor launch to the yacht's mooring at some little archipelago nearby. Wheels-up at noon next Tuesday, buddy. You're going first-class all the way. Soon as you docu-sign the papers, they'll e-mail you your flight info. Naturally, they'll send a car to take you from Manhattan to Teterboro.

"Jack, if you can make a go of this, you could well come back from the #MeToo leper colony and be employable again. You just might be able to continue your career as a top-gun professional liar. Congratulations, buddy!"

"Thanks, Dale," he whispered.

"Say, where are you? Why are you whispering?"

"On a hike in the woods upstate with my son. We're supposed to be in a no-screen zone. Just us together in person. But for your call, I broke our pledge."

"Go back to your father-son vacation this instant. That's real life. This is just work. Later, man." Dale rang off.

Jack stared at the phone, his mind racing in a million directions.

"Hey, Luke!" he called. "Luke!"

He felt the urge to ask for forgiveness. Forgiveness for this unavoidable disappointment. And everything else he had ever done to let his son down. Which was really a lot.

He came out from behind the tree, looked up at the trail above. "Luke! Hey, Luke!" Looked at the trail below.

No Luke.

He knew what he would do as soon as he saw Luke. A great big bear hug for the best son any man ever had. The son he did not deserve. The son who loved him in spite of everything. Very likely the only person on earth who loved him.

"Luke! Luke? Dude, where are you? Luke? Luke?"

CHAPTER 39

Angela, who grew up in the gritty chaos of Manhattan, always found the suburbs weird. Too quiet, too neat, too isolating and lonely.

The neighborhood where Cliff brought her was the most bizarre of all the ones she had seen. Edgecliff Estates was a pretentious gated 1980s housing development where all the streets somehow managed to be cul-de-sacs. The big houses, jammed too close together, were festooned with arches, columns, gables, turrets, and other architectural geegaws randomly mashed up in weird combinations of brick, stone, and wood.

With great pride, Cliff gave her a tour of this house where no one lived. It was filled with chintz, golden oak furniture, glass-topped tables, and expanses of wall-to-wall carpeting, mostly in teal or mauve. At first, Angela was confused by the decor. Then it hit her. It was as if she had walked onto the set of one of the old movies she remembered from television. Like *Pretty in Pink* or *My Stepmother Is an Alien.*

She tried to make a little joke. "Gee, Cliff," she said, giving him a little tickle in the ribs, "Was that Molly Ringwald I just saw? Or Kim Basinger?"

Cliff didn't get it. "I love this house," he said. "It was the first house Julia and I ever bought. Nothing has changed in it since the day she died. Nothing."

Angela didn't try to push her ironic humor about the retro-ness of it all. She wasn't surprised that Charlie refused to visit. The place really was a shrine, a museum. No, more like a mausoleum. Creepy, she thought, very creepy. But loving and devoted. Cliff's Julia had a hold on his emotions that had not diminished with the years. She must have been quite a woman. Or Cliff must be even stranger than Angela thought. Or both.

"I hardly ever stay here anymore," Cliff explained. "You know, with my travel schedule and our places in London and New York, the ranch in Montana, and the yacht down in Antigua." He lowered his head. "Poor Julia," he whispered sadly, "she never got to enjoy any of that. Poor, poor Julia."

"Yes, poor Julia," Angela repeated with solemn obedience. She was here on an intelligence-gathering mission. She would listen and learn as much as she could.

Clearly, she thought, this man is capable of deep and abiding love. *And* deep and abiding weirdness. Cliff was proof that when you have money to burn, you can indulge both tendencies to wild extremes. This is what people mean when they talk about rich people who are very "eccentric." If a poor person tried to do all this, the neighbors would report him to the mental health authorities.

Cliff walked Angela to the master bedroom suite. It was all 1980s Laura Ashley—wallpaper, paint, curtains, bedspread, rugs. Explosions of flowers from the Cotswolds in mauves and creams. He brightened as they entered.

"See how the housekeeper keeps the place looking like it's brand-new? Anita, she's one hard worker. She's Rina's daughter, you know. Rina took care of us from the day we moved in. She helped raise Charlie from a baby. And she helped with poor Julia right down to the end. When Rina passed away, Anita took over for her."

Cliff leaned down and whispered, "I've put her in my will, you know. Gonna take good care of that girl. Of course, she doesn't know that. Never asks for a thing, Anita. She does a great job, don't you think?"

Angela forced a warm smile. "Yes, Cliff, the place is immaculate." She stared at the wedding pictures of Julia and Cliff on both bedside tables. She felt her heart stop with alarm.

"We're not going to sleep in *here*, are we?"

"Oh no," he said, "this is Julia's bedroom. I use the guest room on the third floor."

Angela was relieved. And even more creeped out. Definitely no sex tonight, she thought. But then, she had made that decision long before she'd seen the wedding pictures. She had other plans for this evening.

When it came to sex with Cliff, Angela had tried to make it bearable by closing her eyes and repeating her mantra. "All cats are gray in the dark, all cats are gray in the dark, all cats are gray in the dark." And it quickly did become bearable—in a way. She accepted it as just another one of those icky things a woman's body had to endure. Like discharge, menstrual cramps and bleeding, yeast infections, and the occasional UTI.

Cliff's clumsy enthusiasm was tempered by his extreme eagerness to please. His gratitude was poignant, evoking in her a feeling of gentle pity. Sometimes. Her skin didn't crawl at his touch the way it had at first. Well, not quite as much. As she had gotten used to physical intimacy with Cliff (and, mercifully, despite his bottomless stash of Viagra, he did not require the frequency a young man would have demanded), she found herself developing a certain fondness for him that made the mismatch of their bodies somewhat easier to tolerate.

Or maybe it was just her determination to get her hands on his billions that made her able to endure it gracefully. She decided, after her initial revulsion to him pawing her all over and grunting and thrusting inside her, this must be the cruel discipline all women who marry for money learn to master.

Anita had made a dinner of pot roast and vegetables before leaving and left it warming in the oven. Cliff downed almost two bottles of Merlot over the hearty meal. And proposed again.

"I want to say yes," Angela said tenderly, "but I still need some time to think about."

Say no to get to yes, she thought. Say no to make him want yes even more.

"I get that," he said. "*You've* got all the time in the world. But some of us at this table don't."

She took his hand and gave it an affectionate squeeze.

"I'm working out my issues. My need to be independent. My career. You know, I can't just up and quit and throw away everything I've worked for."

"I'm not asking you to." He pulled his hand away.

Inside, it was killing her to put off snaring her very own captive billionaire. A billionaire begging her to get married. But she knew this was the right psychological approach to get the power she wanted.

"I'm just asking for a little more time. Just a little. Honest."

She reached out and took back his hand, this time holding on tighter. Say no with words, she thought, say yes with touch.

"Oh, all right," he said, resigned. "Let's have an after-dinner cognac."

"Yes, let's. That would be lovely," she said brightly. She had no intention of drinking anything.

In the library, filled with leather-bound books that had never been opened, Cliff poured two snifters of expensive cognac from the glass cocktail wagon, then flopped down in his big leather club chair. Angela sat on the couch by his side.

She kept him rambling on as he drank. About the house, about Julia, about Charlie, about anything and everything he wanted to ramble on about. All the while, she kept getting up and walking to the cart to refill his snifter. She thought about men with a weakness for booze. How it was such a stupid weakness. Angela had no interest in the fuzzy oblivion people got from alcohol. It didn't feel that good and she hated the thought of losing control (to say nothing of the puking and hangovers). She didn't crave it, ever. And while she was totally turned off by the sloppy spectacle of men in their cups, she was grateful when she could use their weakness for her own purposes. Like she'd done with Jack Price. And now, with Clifford Townsend.

For the fourth refill, she stood with her back to him, blocking his view of the cart. In her hand she had a little folded paper with four Benadryl tablets ground to very fine powder. She dropped the powder into the bottom of the snifter, refilled it with cognac, and swirled it until the powder had dissolved.

She brought him the classic date-rape cocktail.

219

"Here, my big guy," she said putting the snifter into his hand, "one for the road." Sure to knock him out.

Cliff took it, his hand wobbly.

She watched him down it in a few big gulps. Then she waited. Just a few minutes. And he was out cold. His head back. Snoring loudly.

She tiptoed upstairs. To Julia's bedroom.

What were those secrets Charlie had alluded to? What could she learn from the perfectly preserved time-capsule bedroom tomb of Julia Townsend? Where would Cliff's first wife, knowing she was dying, have left clues to a mystery before the end?

Angela, a determined combination of marital archaeologist and cat burglar, began to snoop around. She was hunting for something—anything—out of the ordinary. What would Julia have hidden? Where? Why?

She went through the dressers quickly, making sure not to disturb the carefully folded underwear of the long-dead woman. Julia's underthings were immaculate but inexpensive. This was a woman used to saving money. At least on the things that didn't show.

Angela was careful not to disturb any of Anita's perfectly folded piles and rows. She found nothing unusual. Nothing but clothes, accessories, and cheap jewelry.

There were two closets. One was completely empty, not even coat hangers on the rods. That must have been Cliff's. As he said, he had moved to the guest room on the third floor.

She turned to Julia's closet. Another perfectly maintained time capsule. Her dresses, slacks, blouses, and sweaters hung neatly, waiting patiently for almost forty years for her to return.

Angela's inspection of the rows of clothes on hangers revealed nothing unusual.

She turned to the shelves. There were stacks of flat boxes from stores more expensive than wherever Julia had bought her no-name underthings. Many of the stores were ghosts like Julia. Henri Bendel, Lord & Taylor, Bonwit Teller. The boxes she peeked into contained blouses and sweaters, all perfectly folded. Nothing else. Nothing unusual.

Then she saw it. In the corner behind a stack of black boxes from Saks Fifth Avenue. A stack of slim boxes from Hermès. Hermès! Of course, Charlie's favorite fashion brand. A passion passed on from mother to daughter.

She opened the first box with great care. Inside was a colorful silk scarf, still wrapped in the elaborate layers of tissue paper that the store lavished on all its merchandise. There was also an envelope from the store with a receipt in French, and care instructions printed in several languages. A trip to Paris, maybe a very special trip. Maybe with little-girl Charlie in tow. Interesting but not amazing.

Angela persisted.

It was in the fourth of the six boxes that she found something else that had been carefully hidden in the Hermès envelope. Folded in with the receipt and care instructions was a two-page, handwritten note heavily edited with cross-outs and insertions. What must have been the draft of a letter. It was addressed to "My ~~dear~~ darling ~~daughter baby~~ baby girl." Plus, the one-page Quick Guide to something called a "Dictamite" from a company called Dictaphone. "The smallest dictating machine ever made," it proclaimed, "it fits in the palm of your hand."

Angela read the letter carefully. Then took pictures of it with her phone. She wanted to capture all the specifics. The story was breathtaking. Terrifying. Confusing. Charlie's biological father murdered by the man the world knew as her father. The dying wife's recording of her husband's murder confession. The mother's gift of the power of blackmail, delivered by a law firm on Charlie's eighteenth birthday. From beyond the grave.

Angela could hear Cliff snoring downstairs in the library.

She was planning to marry a murderer. A murderer who had gotten away with it.

Suddenly, whatever traces of guilt she'd felt about deceiving the old man evaporated. What was her little misdeed compared with his monstrous crime?

She knew she would not get much sleep this night. There was so much to think about. So many angles to consider. And how she might play them.

CHAPTER 40

Jack ran uphill, shouting. When he heard nothing from that direction, he stopped short. With heart pounding, he told himself to think.

Where would Luke have gone?

Of course!

He ran downhill in a panic, trying not to slide on the gravel or twist his ankle. He rushed toward the outlook where Luke had wanted to have his picture taken.

He got there. Out of breath.

"Luke! Luke!"

Nothing.

He called out to the view of the mountains and lake. "Luke! Luke!"

Still nothing.

Then he spun around and saw it. Luke's backpack leaning up against the pine tree at the edge of the trail. It looked like Luke had placed it there carefully. Like he was coming back for it soon. He ran to it.

Luke's phone was in the left-side outer pocket, where it belonged. His aluminum water bottle was in the designated pocket on the other side. All the zippers were closed. He ignored the emojis and other crap. All he saw was Marlin the clownfish staring up at him with his big, dopey, slightly crossed eyes. The dad who went to the ends of the earth to rescue his son.

"Luke! Luke!"

Silence.

Jack grabbed the backpack, tore the main zipper open, and looked inside. There was Luke's hoodie, crumpled up. A baseball cap. A couple of paperback joke books with goofy covers. A curled-up issue of *Mad* magazine. His iPad. Two pairs of clean sweat socks. A plastic dispenser of hand sanitizer. A crushed box of Skittles. And three charger cables. One for his phone. One for his iPad. And the one with a plug much larger than the other two. It had the VeRity logo embossed in the plastic. VeRity? Oh shit! The headset? Where was the headset?

Jack rummaged through the backpack. No VeRity headset. Just the charger cable and plug.

Jack set the backpack down on the ground.

"Luke! *Luke!*"

He walked toward the rocky outcrop where Luke had stood a few minutes before, pleading to have his picture taken. He walked to the very edge, afraid of what he might see.

He looked down.

Time stopped.

Luke lay facedown on a ledge about thirty feet below. The VeRity headset was shattered into pieces on the rock where Luke's head rested.

He was not moving. He just lay there. There was blood on the rock. But not a lot.

Jack gasped. The voice in his head started screaming, The headset! The headset! The goddamned headset! Whether Luke was angry or bored with waiting, or trying to fly, or—

None of it mattered. Whatever Luke had done, or why, it was his fault.

My fault! *All my fault!*

Jack felt his chest constrict. He had no breath to catch. In a frenzy, he studied the cliffside to see how he could climb down to Luke. There was a descending ridge almost like a ramp. He slid down on his butt, feetfirst, trying not to kick any loose stones that might fall on Luke.

"Luke, I'm here. Don't worry. I'm here. Dad's here," he called softly on his way down.

When he reached Luke, he bent down to inspect his face. His eyes were closed. A small cut over the left eyebrow. Not in the eye. A fragment of plastic had cut a red patch open just above his hairline. The headset in pieces, all around.

All my fault! All my fault!

Luke was breathing. Breathing! Very slowly, but regularly. In, out, in, out. Like he was sleeping. Yeah, like he was sleeping. He touched Luke's hand. It was warm, not cold. He didn't dare move his arm. He was afraid to do anything that might disturb Luke's neck or spine.

All my fault, all my fault.

"Luke," he spoke softly. "Don't worry. I'm here." He heard himself muttering, chanting, "My boy, my baby, my Luke, please be okay, please." His hand was shaking furiously as he took out his phone.

All my fault. All . . . my . . . fault.

It was all he could do to make his quivering index finger hit the numbers 9-1-1.

Jack felt only partially awake inside the nightmare. There were gaps in memory, moments of apparent magic, sensations of reality and unreality clashing violently with each other. He was a dreamer imprisoned in a netherworld of heartache and horror where all time was suspended.

Yes, the 911 operator knew Mohawk Mountain outlook. Yes, the regional hospital had rescued hikers before. But it would take a little time for the EMTs to get to him and Luke. No, don't move him. No, don't do anything. Just wait and watch the boy closely.

The EMTs moved like mountain goats inhabiting the bodies of exceptionally strong, caring humans. Three men and a woman with superpowers scampered down the cliffside and levitated Luke's stretcher up to the trail.

Then back down to the ambulance.

Then to the regional hospital.

Doctors and nurses swooping up the sleeping boy to take pictures of his insides. Jack standing numb under fluorescent lights, clutching his son's backpack. Holding it close to his heart. Nearly crushing it when they talked about the medevac helicopter and the spinal operation Luke would need at the big hospital in Manhattan. Something about a long, complicated surgery. Many months to recover if all went well. If.

The voice in his head repeating, All my fault. All my fault.

Finally calling Sandra. Her screams echoing in his ears. His own voice, distant as a stranger's, trying to tell her about the innocent boy and the unwitting evil stupidity of his father.

The ungodly racket of the helicopter. Luke sleeping. No, unconscious. The skyline of the city suddenly popping up on the horizon. First a distant outline. Then a dense, menacing forest beneath them.

The second hospital. Huge. Shiny terrazzo floors. Luke swooped up by a new team of people in scrubs.

Sandra in the waiting room. Crying. Waiting. Not speaking. Crying. Nightfall. Fluorescent lights.

Finally, Sandra speaking quietly. The low rumble of a volcano about to explode.

"You gave it to him. You gave him the fucking VR toy. They *told* you! It's *addictive!*"

Jack barely responding, talking at the floor. "I never believe them. They all lie."

Sandra quietly, half to herself, "That makes your lies even worse."

Jack, too heartsick to say, If I didn't do it, someone else would.

Sandra accusingly, "Jack, do you know why you're so good at telling lies to the world?"

No answer.

"Because you're so good at lying to yourself. Not because you're afraid of the truth—because you're afraid of life. You're afraid that life might not be fun. Or glamorous. Or make you look impressive to strangers. You're afraid of anything that might be difficult and smelly and tedious and boring. You're afraid that life might be grindingly hard work that no one will ever notice or praise. Don't you see? Having a child was a test. A test of how much you can endure for love without angling to get anything in return." She went silent for a moment. "You failed." A cascade of Sandra's quiet tears. The worst kind.

The spinal surgeon appearing, telling them the good news. The VR helmet had saved Luke's life. It absorbed the worst of the impact

227

and protected his brain from damage that would have been fatal. Then the bad news. The operation could take six or seven hours. Maybe more. Months and months to recover if . . . if.

Go home and get some rest. That's the best thing you can do for him. We have your numbers. We'll have someone call you as soon as we know anything.

CHAPTER 41

Angela saw Charlie's name light up her iPhone with a FaceTime call.

"Yoo-hoo," Charlie said, wide-eyed. "Did you survive the Addams family mortuary?"

Angela fell back onto the couch of her suite in the Four Seasons. She was relieved to have escaped the haunted house.

"Barely," she said. "You gave me a hint, but I had no idea it would be so totally creepy."

"Is everything still just the way it was? Her clothes perfectly folded in the drawers?"

Angela thought quickly. She could imagine little Charlie, grieving and confused, invading her dead mother's bedroom, hungering for some trace of her, for the smell of Mommy. For weeks after her own mother's death, Angela had breathed in pieces of her clothing to feel her presence and the memory of her love.

"Gee, I don't know." Angela hesitated while deciding on the lie she would tell. "I don't know about the drawers. But Cliff showed me her closet with everything all lined up, untouched from thirty years ago. That was enough for me."

She wondered; would her mention of the closet trigger any sign of recognition from Charlie? Did she know about the special box from Hermès? If so, what then? She was hoping to give Charlie the chance to open the vault of dark secrets.

"So, does Rina's daughter still keep everything exactly the same?" Charlie asked. "He told you about Rina, I assume?"

Angela nodded yes at the screen.

"Well," Charlie said, "I told you it would be creepy." She waved away the subject. "Now, let's talk about the future. The deliciously immediate future."

"Okay," Angela said.

Charlie had not taken the bait about her mother's closet. She would have to wait to open the vault.

"I'm getting things ready for the yacht and Antigua. We're going to be one big happy family as we all convince Cliff to give me my foundation."

"Well, yes, that's the plan." Angela wondered if Charlie was actively blackmailing Cliff now. And if so, when she may have started. Both father and daughter seemed to be very talented at masking their true selves. More lives built on lies. There's so much I can learn from these awful people, she thought. All their money has given them so many more opportunities to fuck with each other. Maybe that's the reason the rich are different from the rest of us.

"But tell me, "Charlie said, "should I let Jack Price know that *you* have been pulling the strings behind the scenes? Arranging his life without his knowing it?"

"No, no, don't say a word about me. Or Cliff and me. It will confuse him and distract him from the work we need him to do. Really, really, *don't.*" She hoped her panic didn't show. "Besides," she said, trying to put on a mischievous smile, "I want to surprise him."

"Okay, I got it. Now for the fun part." Charlie gave a wicked little laugh. "Now, since you and I are going to be Eskimo sisters, you need to tell me"—big pause—"what are Jack Price's favorite things to do in bed? I want all the details, a complete instruction manual for turning him on. Tell me *everything.*"

Angela was relieved that this was all Charlie wanted from her. At the same time, she felt a twinge of jealousy. Not that she wanted Jack for her own again. But a part of her did *not* feel like sharing him with another woman. Still, she knew the rules here. Whatever Charlie wants, Charlie gets—at least until it becomes Angela's turn.

Dutifully, she said, "Okay. Do you want to get a pencil and paper to take notes?"

CHAPTER 42

Back at his apartment, Jack fidgeted as he wandered from room to room. Movers' boxes were everywhere, some still folded flat, others partially filled, still others all packed, taped shut, and ready for the storage warehouse where all of it would go during his time on the Townsend yacht. He had no idea where he would live when he returned. If he returned.

Not that it mattered now.

Not that anything mattered now.

He kept coming back to the living room, where he had put Luke's backpack on the couch. Carefully. Like it was a little person. Back side out. With clownfish Marlin, the hero father, watching him.

All my fault, all my fault.

He stopped at the backpack, unzipped the main compartment, and reached inside. His hand found Luke's hoodie. He seized it and brought it up to his nostrils, inhaling the scent of Luke. With great care, he refolded the garment and put it back inside. His hand touched the VeRity charger plug in the backpack. He grabbed it.

All my fault, all my fault.

Holding up the black plastic brick, he looked at the padlock sealing the doors of his liquor cabinet. He started smashing the plug against the padlock. But the damned rubber-coated thing just kept bouncing back at him.

It hurt his hand.

He liked that. He pounded harder. Hurt his hand again. There, even better. He did it again, this time drawing a little blood.

The padlock laughed at him. Unbroken. Unimpressed.

He threw the charger plug across the room, punching a hole in the drywall.

Beside the couch was an open movers' box filled with his professional trophies. He grabbed a Clio statue in one hand and a Mobius "8" loop in the other and attacked the padlock. He cut deep scars into the cabinet. Smashed the handles. Knocked them loose from the wooden doors. That made the damn padlock fall to the floor. He threw the Clio, then the Mobius, at another wall and knocked out two more chunks of plaster.

He opened the cabinet doors. There were the bottles he had not touched since that night after Vlad's. He had thrown away Luke's Post-it note when he got the padlock. Now he wished he had saved it. He would add that to his long list of other wishes that would never be granted.

He turned to look at Luke's backpack. Was Marlin staring at him accusingly? You couldn't tell where the clownfish was looking with those stupid crossed eyes. Very carefully, he turned the backpack around. To make sure Luke's little characters would be unable to see what he had to do next.

He bent down and reached for the bottle of Johnnie Walker Black.

He unscrewed the cap and brought the opening of the bottle up to his nose. He inhaled deeply. Maybe he could really smell the notes of charred oak, peat smoke, toffee candy, vanilla, butterscotch, and glazed pecans that the maker of the Scotch promised. Or maybe he just smelled the all-forgiving, unconditional mother-love aroma of alcohol.

Holding the bottle by the neck, he walked into his now-empty kitchen. He put his hand on the freezer door and thought about the ice cubes inside. Thought about the way ice melted into the golden liquid, chilling it and softening its burn.

He turned from the fridge and took three steps to the kitchen sink.

He took a deep breath. Held the bottle over the sink. Then turned it upside down. Poured the liquid into the drain. The glug, glug, glug sound rang like a panic alarm in his ears. He thought about smashing the bottle into a million pieces. Then thought of all those shards of glass.

He put the empty bottle on the kitchen counter and walked to his bathroom.

He had not yet packed up the contents of his medicine cabinet. He found the yellow prescription jar behind a fancy shaving balm he never used. There were two little white pills in the bottom of the jar. They were the remnants of one of his previously failed attempts to stop drinking. He remembered what the psychiatrist had said: "The Ambien is the same thing as the alcohol. A drug. But it can become a temporary substitute. And then, with hard work . . ."

Jack swallowed one pill. Took a deep breath. Then stared inside the jar at the lonely little pill remaining. Fuck it, he thought. No, fuck me. No, fuck everything. Then he swallowed that one, too.

He walked to his bedroom, kicked off his shoes, and fell fully dressed onto his bed. Hoping sleep would come and give him oblivion.

It did.

Next thing he knew, he heard his phone calling him from a world far away. A world where Luke was fine and nothing bad had happened.

He opened his eyes. *Whaaa?* The phone was where it always was, on the night table.

He was afraid to answer, afraid of what the caller might tell him.

The screen showed that he had missed four previous calls over the past hour. Slept right through them. Three from Sandra and another from a number he did not recognize. He answered this time.

A woman's voice told him to come to the hospital. *Now.* She did not say why. She gave him a room number. Now, Mr. Price. *Now.* Call ended.

Was Luke dead? What was the news the woman would not tell him over the phone?

He stumbled to his bathroom sink and put his head under the tap. The mirror told him to comb his hair and brush his teeth. Then to his closet. Fumbled out of his wrinkled clothes and into fresh ones.

Jack and his feeling of dread made it to the hospital in record time.

Stepping carefully out of the elevator, he could see Sandra down the hall handing a clipboard to a woman who had a folder full of papers. Talking but making no sounds. At least that he could hear. As he neared, he saw Sandra's eyes. Red and swollen, her cheeks flushed.

"Where the hell have you been?" she barked. "You were supposed to get here an hour ago. The surgeon has come and gone."

"Sorry," he mumbled, "sorry." Lame, he knew. He looked over Sandra's shoulder into the hospital room. Saw Luke sleeping quietly, arms at his side. Lot of tubes in him. Lots of monitors with lines and beeps.

"They say he's going to live. For now. But he's in a coma," Sandra said. "Could be days or months before he wakes up. Or never. They don't know."

Sandra's lips quivered. Her mouth started moving but no sound came out. Until she heaved a deep breath and screamed, "You ruin everything! Everything!" Then came a terrible howl. He had heard her yell for hours when she was in labor with Luke. This noise was deeper, like an animal gravely wounded. "I can't look at you!" Her whole body heaved.

She stormed past him and stood by the window in the corridor, sobbing.

Jack stood looking at Luke for how long, he did not know. He stood frozen, feeling the pain of love and the weight of guilt, literally pressing on his chest. He could hardly breathe. He wept in silence, not even trying to wipe his tears, his only sound a sniffling once in a while.

He finally turned around when he felt someone touch his arm. It was a nurse.

"There's nothing more you can do for him right now," she said gently. She handed him some Kleenex and escorted him out into the corridor.

He dried his cheeks and approached the window where Sandra was still crying. She did not turn around.

He spoke to her back. "Sandra, I—I'm going to cancel my freelance gig. I can't go off to Antigua now. No way. I won't. I'm going to stay here with Luke. With you. I'm going to sit with you by his bedside. Until he gets better. Until *we* make him get better."

He reached out and touched her shoulder.

She flinched and moved out of his reach.

"I can't leave now," he said softly. "I won't."

He watched Sandra carefully. She took a deep breath and straightened her shoulders. She gave her head that shake she did whenever she wanted to clear her thoughts. After a few more deep breaths, she turned around to face him.

"You can't help Luke recover," she said, with that calm determination she had whenever shit hit the fan. Jack never knew if she was actually controlling her panic or just faking calm to cover it up. "Neither can I," she said, her voice cracking and more tears flowing. "I think . . . I think," she clenched her jaw to stop a sob, "I think the best thing for you to do—the best thing you *can* do for Luke—is to go to that job. You can't help him. Just sitting around here waiting won't accomplish anything."

"But I need to be here," Jack insisted. "At his side. By your side. He's our baby."

She gave a weary nod, then a big sigh.

"The best thing you can do for Luke right now is to put your life back together. Work is the best thing you can do. This crazy freelance gig fell out of the sky. It's a piece of luck. Don't squander it. Having a job again is the best thing you can do to get back on your feet. That's why it's the best thing you can do for Luke. You'll be no good to him if you're a wreck."

Jack raised his hand to speak. Sandra held up her hand to stop him.

"Jack, I promise to keep you posted every day, every minute. If anything happens, I promise I will let you know. It's up to the doctors now. We can't do anything for him."

Jack sputtered, "But my guilt—my guilt . . ."

Sandra took him by the shoulders and gave him a shake.

"No guilt," she said, staring into his eyes. "No guilt, understand? Guilt won't help Luke. Or me or you. Shit happens. It's awful, but

238

it's nobody's fault. Go to work. Don't blow this opportunity. It's the only positive thing you can do now. It's the right thing. For all of us."

When she let go of him, his shoulders dropped.

He asked in a whisper, "Really?"

"Really. Now go."

She turned and faced the window again.

Jack walked to the doorway of Luke's room. He stood in silence, staring at his son for a time he could not measure.

Finally, he turned to look at Sandra. She hadn't moved; her back was to him. He knew she would not turn around until he had done what she had told him to do.

As Jack walked to the elevator bank, he whispered to himself, "Dude, I'm going away for a while. Could be a few months. Cool assignment on a rich guy's yacht. I'll keep you posted with texts and pics. In the meantime, I'll hold on to your stuff for you. Okay?"

Jack was pretty certain he heard something in his head. It sounded like Luke's voice. "Yeah, sure, Dad. You hold on to my stuff. Good idea."

CHAPTER 43

Charlie Townsend watched the small motorboat approaching the yacht. She felt a tingle of anticipation, thinking of everything she was about to accomplish—and all the fun she planned to have in the process. Under the glorious Caribbean sun with the mountains of Antigua on the far horizon, she could see her two hunky men through the spray the boat was kicking up. Jack Price was holding onto the railing next to Josef, who gunned the engine and made the boat zigzag with the same bravado he displayed in bed.

Whenever she had an important guest coming for a stay on *King of Pawns*, she also had a twinge of regret. Why, oh, why hadn't she put her foot down and forced Cliff to order their yacht with a helipad on it? The cost of that lovely extra would have been maybe a few hundred thousand dollars. And at these prices, what would it have mattered?

Not that there was anything shabby about this 300-foot superyacht. But just think what an impression the helipad would have made. What an unforgettable entrance for an A-list guest. Someone like Susanna Stratsman, for instance, who would recount it breathlessly to her elite circle of friends back in Manhattan, telling them what a privilege it was to have joined the board of the Townsend Foundation.

At the time, Charlie had thought about using the "nuclear option" to force Cliff to add the helipad to the design specs. She had thought about calling her mother's law firm, getting the tape recording of Cliff's murder confession, and playing it for him. And then playing hardball.

But then she thought better of it. If she was going to use it to get something she wanted, it would have to be for something totally monumental and life-changing. She had to be prepared for her blackmail to end their relationship once and for all. The helipad, tempting as it was, was not worth that risk.

But the foundation, *her* foundation, her launchpad into her rightful place in society, her mission for the rest of her life—*that* would be worth incinerating her relationship with Cliff over. But only if she had to. She was counting on the genius salesmanship of Jack Price to sway the old man and let her keep her powder dry. Besides, she had no desire to get Cliff thrown into prison. That would shatter her social ambitions once and for all.

As the boat neared *King of Pawns* at its mooring just off the cluster of little islands, two miles off Antigua, she hurried down three decks to greet her men. As she flew down the stairways, she had a passing fantasy. Maybe, after her foundation was promised and everyone was happy, she might have *both* of her stud muffins in bed with her at the same time. How delicious.

When she got down to the waterline, Josef was giving Jack a hand to steady him as the little boat bobbed up and down in the waves.

"Careful," Josef said, "on boat is many ways to die."

"Oh, Josef!" Charlie said playfully, "don't scare our guest. This yacht is the safest place on earth. Nothing bad can possibly happen to us here." She offered Jack her hand. "Jack!" she said, squeezing his hand more than necessary as she guided him onto the deck, "Welcome!" She leaned in and wrapped him in a brief hug, carefully pressing her breasts firmly against him.

"Don't take Josef seriously," she whispered in his ear. "He's just an alpha male defending his territory. But you, *you* are our guest of honor for this cruise."

Jack went to reach for his suitcases back on the boat. Charlie waved him away.

"Don't be silly, Jack." She nodded to Josef. "Josef has a team of deckhands to carry your luggage to your stateroom. I want to give you the grand tour."

Jack turned to Josef. "Uh, Josef, can you toss me my backpack there? On top of the suitcases." Josef obliged. Jack caught it in midair and hung it over his shoulder. "Thanks, man."

Charlie looked at the backpack. It had a collection of juvenile-looking pins and doodads. Hanging off the main zipper was an orange-striped toy fish with crossed eyes. She put her hand under the fish and gave Jack a puzzled look.

"Is this yours?" Maybe, she thought for a second, hiring Jack Price wasn't such a great decision.

"Oh that?" Jack was embarrassed. "No, no, it's not mine. It's my son's. He's a teenager. I'm, uh, holding onto it for him. I promised . . . uh, it's, it's complicated. No matter, really. It will stay in my room. No one will see it again. Don't give it a thought."

"Okay, Jack." She noticed a tightness in his face when he mentioned his son. Like a sharp pain. She hoped his son's problem, whatever it was, wouldn't get in the way of her plans.

Jack made a visible effort to switch to bright and cheery. "Now, Charlie, how about that tour you promised?" He looked around, wide-eyed. "This yacht is fantastic, fabulous. Really, it's amazing."

Charlie liked it when he touched her forearm. She wagged a finger in a come-hither gesture. "Follow me."

She walked him up and around through all three levels, pointing out each amenity like a broker showing a prospective buyer. All six sundecks. The garage-like hold for storing all sorts of fun little toys—jet skis, sunfish, kayaks. The lap pool. The Jacuzzi. The other Jacuzzi. The alfresco dining area. The indoor dining room. The coffee bar. The giant-screen home theater. The spiraling interior staircases. The fully equipped gym with sauna and steam room. The gaming parlor. The elevator. The library. The parade of guest staterooms.

"It's like a five-star resort," she said, "that can take you anywhere you want to go."

Jack gave the appropriate oohs and aahs, she thought.

She paused for a moment. "I think money is a form of magic, don't you?"

"Magic?"

"Yes. Just this morning, you were in your apartment in Manhattan. Then, abracadabra! You are whooshed to Antigua on a private jet, then a boat to an enormous floating playground in paradise. It's magic, no?"

Jack nodded.

"I do love money," she said. "Really, I just love it. But it carries a lot of responsibilities. I think it's really important to spend it well. Spend it the right way. I mean, any slob can just buy things. But buying beautiful things, the finest things, and really appreciating them, that's an art. I work hard at it, believe me."

Jack nodded and smiled.

When they got to the business conference room, she ushered Jack in first. Then stood behind him, just touching his back with her fingertips and breasts. "And here is where Jack Price will work *his* magic."

The mahogany paneling and vast conference table had the desired effect.

"Wow, it's like the boardroom of a Fortune 100 corporation," he said admiringly.

She gave him a little tickle in the ribs, "Only with a lot more fun waiting just outside the boardroom door."

He seemed not to react. He broke away and paced around the room.

"So, this is where I'll present to your father. Can I make this my workspace as I prep?"

She nodded yes.

"Great. I see we have all the screens I need. Do you have a—"

She cut him off. "Tech specialist? Yes, of course. You'll meet him tomorrow. He's one of our crew members."

He paced some more. "You should know that I've done a deep dive into the world of foundations. I've completed an extensive competitive analysis, and I have some strong ideas and video sketches to present. If you can validate my assumptions about Mr. Townsend and his objectives and tastes, I can—"

She cut him off again. Raised her hand like a traffic cop. "Let's start work tomorrow, okay?"

"Uh, sure," he said. "I just want you to know that I'm ready to hit the ground running. Sprinting, actually. One more question:

I'm going to need a production budget. I'll need money to work with a producer and a video house or two back in New York. It's not cheap."

"Money, Jack, is no object. *No object*. You can see that, no?" She gestured at the lavish room around them.

Jack nodded, yes.

"Spend whatever you need to make it happen. Okay?"

She reached into the pocket of her paisley-print Lilly Pulitzer beach cover-up and flashed a shiny credit card. "There's $100,000 prepaid on it. As the saying goes, don't spend it all in one place. But if you need more, just holler, okay?"

She smiled and dropped the card on the table in front of him. He's so sweet, she thought, wanting to show how professional he is. Perfect. She gave his belt a little tug.

"Tomorrow morning, I'll be all business. But now, for the best part of the tour, let me show you the VIP stateroom. Your home away from home."

She walked him up to the third deck and flung open the door of a grand bedroom suite done in sleek contemporary style.

"Note the bar," she said with a sweep of her arm. Against one mirrored wall was a shrine to super-premium liquors of all kinds. Above the rows of pricey bottles, etched in the mirrored glass were the words "Infinite Pleasure," reflected backwards and forwards from the mirror on the wall facing it, the bottles and the two words receding, smaller and smaller in both directions, into infinity.

"And above that giant, comfy bed," she said with another sweeping gesture, "note the lovely oval moonroof, for inspiration under the stars. Even my stateroom doesn't have a moonroof. I sometimes sneak away to sleep here." She let her fingertips brush lightly down his right arm.

"Well," Jack said with a deep breath, "I'm raring to get to work tomorrow." He removed his backpack, walked to the closet, and opened the door.

"Geez," he said, seeing his clothes neatly hanging, "I'm already unpacked!"

"Of course, you are," she said. "That's why I gave you the long version of the tour."

Jack put the backpack on the shelf.

"You know," she said, watching him make himself at home, "Cliff won't be arriving until next week. That means we'll have lots of time for work. And lots of time to play and enjoy this island paradise. I would hate to see us lose sight of the work/life balance. It's so critical to a healthy life. Don't you agree?"

She kept hoping he would turn around from his inspection of the room. He did not.

She cleared her throat to get his attention. "I'm thinking dinner under the stars tonight. Around eight?"

Jack turned to face her. He hesitated. "Uh, if it's okay with you, I'd like to turn in early. It's been a crazy week for me, with some big sleep deficits."

She gave a big sigh and made a little pouty face. "Okay, Mr. Price. Well, you've come to the right place. I always sleep like a baby in this bed. I'm sure you will, too."

"I hope you don't mind," he said tentatively.

"No, it's all right."

"Really?"

She was happy to see him trying to please. "Yes, of course. Get the rest you need. I want my marketing genius fresh in the morning."

"Oh, I will be. You can count on that."

"See that little button above your night table?"

He turned and stared at it.

"Anything you want, just ring and ask for it. Ab-so-lute-ly anyyyything. Welcome to paradise, Jack."

Jack smiled. "So, what do you say we start work tomorrow morning in the boardroom? How about 8:30?"

Charlie wrinkled her nose. "You can start whenever you like. I'll see you around 10:30 or so." Clearly disappointed, she turned and walked out, closing the door behind her.

Jack pulled his phone out of his pocket and immediately texted Sandra. He had texted her repeatedly from the limo to Teterboro, throughout the flight to Antigua, and for part of the drive from the St. Johns airport to the motor launch. Then the signal had given out.

He knew he was starting to annoy her, but the constant check-ins made him feel as if he were doing *something*, and the contact with her helped to calm him.

In just the one day since he'd left her at the hospital, they had gotten into a very efficient shorthand system.

He would text: ????

At first, Sandra would reply: **No news is no news.**

But as Jack's inquiries multiplied, she condensed her response to: **NNINN.**

After getting Sandra's no-news message this time, he began snapping shots of the grand stateroom, especially the crazy oval moonroof that floated over the bed like a UFO. He made a point of not snapping any pics of the booze or the etched invitation to drink. He scrolled through his new shots, found three he liked, and texted them. He looked up from his phone expectantly. When he heard the *ping* sound coming from the phone in Luke's backpack, he smiled to himself.

"What do you think, dude?" he said to the backpack. "This is some movie, isn't it? The private jet, this crazy yacht. And what did you think of that muscleman who drove the motorboat?"

He paused.

Luke's voice told him, "That guy–wow, he's like a freakin' Frankenstein."

"You said it, dude, a freakin' Frankenstein. We're going to steer clear of him."

Jack wandered around the stateroom, acclimating himself to his surroundings.

"And that woman, Charlie. My new boss. What do you think?"

"W-T-F," he heard Luke say.

"You're right, dude."

Jack saw no reason, under the circumstances, to enforce polite language anymore.

"Absolutely! What . . . the . . . *fuck?* You know, even with all this luxury, Dale wasn't kidding when he said this could be the worst job in the whole world. But I have to make a go of it, no matter what. This is your dad's very last chance. I'm not going to blow it, Luke. I promise you."

CHAPTER 44

Daniel was very solicitous of Angela as he walked her to the elevator bank. Eric followed behind, making himself invisible.

"Thank you, Angela," Daniel said. He started to reach out to touch her, then decided not to. "Thank you for everything. After the layoffs, you got the place humming with that feeling of belonging to the new tribe. People are really excited."

Angela stopped just outside the double doors of the wall of frosted glass. "Of course they are." She reached up and patted Daniel on the shoulder. "And you are the leader of that tribe."

She was thinking about Simon Woodleigh's promise of her cut of the million-dollar savings from the severance package Jack Price never got. Plus the extra firings she had strong-armed Daniel into doing. Her year-end bonus could go up by another $200,000, maybe more. Unless, of course, she was Mrs. Billionaire by then. Then she'd be in line for a bonus far bigger than that. As much as she hated the bullshit of corporate life, she had come to love the clean, unemotional way that business let a person measure just about anything in life.

"Will you, uh, be talking to Sir Alban soon?" Daniel asked, barely masking his anxiety.

"I already have," Angela lied. "And even more important, Simon knows that you've exceeded Globalcom's expectations." That part was true. She had spoken to Woodleigh. But, of course, Angela had framed it in such a way as to make her, not Daniel, the hero of the savings. Which was truer than true.

Daniel's smile looked to her like a smile of relief.

"Now," she said brightly, "it's up to you to keep that tribal drum-beat going." She gave his shoulder a friendly little squeeze, then let go. "Keep them believing in the shared values, the higher purpose that keeps all of us working so hard. It's all about the values."

"You said it, Angela," Daniel said obediently.

Eric had walked to the elevator and pushed the button. The doors opened with a *pong* sound. Eric stepped inside and held out his hand to keep the doors from closing.

Angela stepped in beside Eric. "Next time, I'll call before I visit," she said, giving Daniel a little wave.

Daniel stood frozen in front of the elevator. "Whatever works for you, Angela. Whatever works for you."

Eric removed his hand and the doors closed. They were alone for the descent.

"That was quite a lovefest," Eric said. "You were spectacular."

"Why, thank you, sir," Angela said in a playful schoolgirl voice. Then in her normal voice, "There's nothing like raw fear to keep people in line. Plus, the abject gratitude of the survivors who still have jobs. They'll buy anything we sell them."

"Even, for example"—Eric cleared his throat and, in a mock American accent, did an impersonation of Angela from the meeting just ended: "*A tribe that is united in a culture of shared values is driven by a higher purpose that leads all of us selflessly to greater and greater accomplishments.*"

"Yeah," Angela smirked, "even that."

The doors opened to the lobby of the office tower. They walked toward the Town Car waiting at the curb.

"We're flying commercial," Eric sniffed. "I can't believe it."

Angela said, "Tsk-tsk, dearie. Sir Alban has to be in Singapore to speak at a conference. He's got the jet. We're in business class. We'll survive."

Angela reached into her Hermès handbag. "I had our tickets printed out. Here's yours."

Eric stopped short. "Hullo?" he cried. "This ticket says coach. *Coach?*"

Angela shrugged. "Sorry, luv, I thought you were sitting next to me. Must be the corporate hierarchy. Every day in every way, we do everything we can to reinforce the pecking order. I promise you, when we go to Antigua next week, we're both flying on the Townsend private jet."

"You won't make me sit outside on the wing?"

"Promise. Inside the pressurized cabin, complete with oxygen."

"And champagne?"

"I assume so. But in moderation, please."

They walked through the revolving glass doors and down the steps toward their black car.

Angela stopped before they got within earshot of the driver, who was waiting behind the wheel.

"You should know that on the yacht there's going to be someone from the agency, someone you've already met."

"Really? Who?"

She took a deep breath. "Jack Price."

Eric was gobsmacked. "No. Really?"

Angela raised her hand. Stop. "I got him a freelance gig working for my friend Charlie. A creative assignment for the Townsends."

Eric shook his head with astonishment. "After everything that happened? After you had me make sure he got drunk. After he groped you and got himself fired? What *is* it between the two of you? I am utterly mystified. Have you seen him since that night?"

Angela shook her head no.

"Does he know you're coming?"

"No, he has no idea. He also has no idea that I got him his new job."

Eric grasped her by the shoulders. "Are you sure, I mean absolutely sure, there isn't something going on between the two of you? Some kind of weird unresolved love/hate connection."

She shrugged out of his grip. "No, not love. Not hate either. Just utility."

"Utility?"

"You know, usefulness. Getting things done—things that need to get done. The universe has brought us together again. I didn't ask for it, but there's no point in fighting it. It was fate. And for me, good luck."

"What on earth are you going to say to him?"

Angela began walking the short distance to the car. She replied over her shoulder, "I'll start by telling him I forgive him."

Eric reached for her with both hands. "*You* forgive *him?* But you and I were the ones who got him drunk and set him up to lose control and ruin his life."

She pulled out of his grip, opened the rear door, and gestured for him to get in first.

"But he doesn't know that. At least, he doesn't know that for sure. What I'll tell him is, later that night, I thought it over. And I forgave him. And when I heard about this opportunity, I wanted to help him in his hour of need."

Eric asked, "Did you plan it this way all along? Tell me, tell me. Did you?"

She smiled at Eric with genuine affection, wondering what it would take to keep him by her side as she built the great big new life she hoped to build.

"Girl," Eric said as he slid into his place behind the driver, "you are very, very bad."

"Oh no, I'm very, very good. Just watch me."

CHAPTER 45

Jack sent his first text of the morning to Sandra before getting out of his enormous bed under the moonroof. He'd had a restless night, not finding the switch that brought the shade across the big glass oculus until well past 2:00 a.m. Sandra's reply at 5:07 a.m. was:

NNINN
Jesus jack its 5 am WTF

He promised he would not text her again until the afternoon. She replied with a thumbs-up emoji. He could almost see her flopping back into her pillow.

Jack rang the galley for an in-room breakfast. A cheery young Australian woman brought him a tray with the eggs, toast, and coffee he'd requested, plus a lavish assortment of tropical fruits and copies of the *Financial Times*, *Wall Street Journal*, and *Antigua*

Observer. He took his time eating and reading, then showered and got dressed.

Steeling himself for Day One, sure to be filled with surprises from his new boss, he stepped out of his stateroom into a perfect tropical morning. He thought he might look a bit ridiculous, in Bermuda shorts, tropical shirt, straw hat, and sunglasses, while carrying the leather briefcase he had carried to his office jobs for the past decade. But no matter. He was here to work, not to vacation.

He thought he knew all about handling high-pressure jobs. Somehow he had always found a way to manage, maneuver, or finagle his way to success. Until now.

He had no idea what to do with Charlotte Townsend. Of course he'd had difficult, demanding, unreasonable bosses before. But none like Charlie. His fate was in the hands of this kooky woman who seemed to think that the reason the universe existed was to indulge her every whim. As he walked down the deck of this fortress of over-the-top luxury, he realized that life had taught her to think this way.

He strolled around a bit in the sunshine. Crew members, busy with chores, would greet him with a cheery, "Good morning, Mr. Price." Beneath their smiles of professional hospitality, Jack thought he sensed fear. Or maybe it was just a projection of his own fear.

At precisely 8:30, he entered the boardroom. The lights went on automatically. Maybe Charlie really didn't care what time he started. Or maybe she was having his every move closely monitored. He took a seat at the head of the mammoth slab of shiny mahogany that was the conference table. There was a PBX phone with multiple lines and an Iridium satellite phone. The PBX unit must connect to local phone lines, he thought. The Iridium phone was for use out at sea. He reached for the PBX handset and dialed Dale Waldman's private line.

Dale picked up after one ring. "Jack, is that you?"

He was glad to hear Dale's voice. "Yeah, how did you know?"

"The readout said Antigua-Barbuda, so I figured, who else could it be? How's it going?"

"I just got here yesterday."

"Is everything fabulous?"

"Yeah, totally fabulous. And totally weird."

"Hey, I told you."

"Listen, Dale, I need a producer who can help me put together videos for my presentation to Mr. Townsend. It's next week. I'm assuming no one in the business wants to talk to me."

Dale was silent for a long moment. "Uh, you got that right."

"Well, can you find me a freelance producer who can work with a production house and *not* tell them it's for the industry's latest sex criminal?"

"Lemme think," Dale said. Jack heard him clicking away at his digital address book. "Hey, remember Stan Noble?"

Jack thought for a moment. "Wasn't he head of production at Addison and Morris? I think he was just leaving when I got there."

"Yeah," Dale said, "he managed to hang on to staff jobs until the Age Police finally got him, at fifty-five. He freelances now. He's one of the best. And he's got great relationships with production houses all over town. He'd be happy to have the work. And he'd have no trouble acting as your beard. No one will know it's you."

"Great, Dale. Have him call me."

"At this 268 number?"

"No, Jesus, no. My cell."

"One question, buddy. You got a budget for this? A big one?"

Jack laughed. "You should see my working conditions. Don't worry." He quoted Charlie, using her intonation, "Money is no object. *No object.*"

"You got it," Dale said, and rang off.

After making a tour of the boardroom for the surveillance cameras, if there were any, he sat down and extracted his idea notebook from his briefcase. He picked up where he had been scribbling on the jet the day before, dreaming up concepts, losing track of time.

He was startled by the feeling of two hands gently grasping the trapezius muscles between his neck and shoulders.

"You're working so hard," Charlie whispered behind him. She began to massage him in earnest.

"Oh, Charlie," he said, feeling at once alarmed and relieved of a bit of tension. He spun around in the chair to face her. That stopped the neck massage. "I've got some great concepts going," he said.

She took off her sunglasses and sat down beside him. She made a display of peering over his notes. "I'll bet you do."

"Listen, I've got a video producer in New York all lined up. It's going to be a lot of work to get a good show ready in time for next week. Overtime costs for him and the production house."

"I told you," she said with a little wave. Then with a French accent, "*Coûte que coûte.*"

"Huh?"

"Spend," she said. "Spend whatever. Just make it great."

"I will, Charlie, no worries. But I need some insight into your father. Can you tell me what he's like in business? You know, his management style, the way he leads. What kind of boss is he? That kind of insight is critical when presenting to a client."

She frowned and folded her arms across her chest. "Well, I've made it a point to stay away from the world of his businesses. As you know, they're sleazy. They prey on poor people. Pawn shops, bail bonds, payday loans, other low-rent things. I don't even want to know about them. That reputation for sleaze is one of the problems we're hoping the foundation will solve."

"Yes, Charlie, I know all that. But I'm sure *he* doesn't think of them that way. Does he?"

"Oh, no. He's, uh"—she waved a hand in disgust—"proud of them. Certainly not ashamed or embarrassed."

"That's what I thought. But he's the client, right?"

She nodded yes.

"So, we're coming to him with a deal proposal, just the way executives would do inside one of his companies. What can you tell me about how they manage him?"

She fidgeted in her chair.

"Any insights you can provide could really help the cause." He leaned over and touched her arm. "*Our* cause."

She smiled and put her hand on top of his, holding it there for a long moment. He withdrew his hand to get his pen poised over his notebook.

"Well," she said, then paused. He thought he could feel her distaste.

"Yes?" he said eagerly, touching the tip of his pen to an empty page of his notebook.

"Well, uh, I did once have a brief, uh, friendship with one of his top executives." She bit her lower lip. "An affair, actually."

"And?"

"And he swore me to secrecy."

"Charlie," he touched her again, "this is critical intelligence gathering. Come on."

She looked down at his hand on her arm, looked up, and smiled. "Well, I suppose. He moved on to another company a few years ago."

"So, tell me what he said about Cliff in business."

She zipped her mouth shut with her index finger.

"I promise," Jack said, "nothing leaves this room. Nothing." He put his pen on the table and closed his notebook. Again, he wondered what kind of surveillance might be going on as they spoke.

"Justin told me that Cliff is just impossible. He's a bully. He's abusive. Totally controlling."

Jack shook his head. "Not helpful. All those billionaire founders are impossible. What else did he say? Why did Justin quit?"

She stared at him. "He had balls."

"Balls?"

"Yes, *balls*. The balls to stand up to my father. And if you must know, an absolutely beautiful dick that also stood up tall and proud."

Jack pretended not to hear about Justin's dick. "Where did he go?"

"To run a gaming company out west. I haven't heard from him since. Someone told me he married a cocktail waitress. Some bimbo who's now head of the Junior League of Reno. Or maybe she was a lap dancer, I don't know." Charlie gave a big sigh that seemed full of memories. And regrets.

Jack pressed on with his diagnostic question. "How would Justin describe Cliff in one word?"

Charlie looked down and talked half to herself. "Well, he takes advantage of people when they're desperate. Bleeds them dry with no pity." She looked up. "Cold? Hard-hearted?"

Again, Jack shook his head no. "Nah, too obvious."

Charlie thought for a long moment. "Well . . . Justin used to say that Cliff was completely . . . cynical."

Jack was encouraged. "How so?"

"He said Cliff assumed that everyone else's motives were as evil and selfish as his own. That everybody else was up to no good. Just like him."

Jack nodded. Cynical was promising. He could deal with cynical. Work with it. The clients who were a pain in the ass were the ones who believed their own sanctimonious bullshit.

"That's very helpful, Charlie. Really."

"Jack, have you dealt with clients like him before?"

He smiled. "Oh yeah, I sure have." He could feel a flood of new ideas coming. He knew exactly how to build a pitch for a cynical bastard. Boy, did he ever. What's more, it would be fun.

Suddenly, his cell phone rang inside his briefcase. He reached for it urgently.

"This is Jack," he said. "Stan! Glad to have you on board. Can I call you back in five? Yeah. Uh-huh. Thanks, man."

He rang off. Turned to Charlie. "That's our producer for the videos. We've got to hustle like hell to make everything we need for the Cliff meeting next week. You're welcome to sit in on my call." He hoped she would not, of course.

She stood. "No, Jack, that's okay. You go work your magic." She put on her sunglasses and headed for the door. "But I insist you join me for lunch on the alfresco deck. And after that, a little swim and a snorkel and a jet ski ride. And later this week, we'll sample some of the posh British culture of Antigua. The cricket matches, yacht clubs, private estates of some friends of mine. This island is one of the last bastions of aristocratic elegance." She wagged a finger at him. "Remember, all work and no play makes Jack a dull boy."

He forced a grin in response, then tapped the producer's callback number and brought his cell to his ear. With his free hand, he gave Charlie a military salute as she turned and left the boardroom.

CHAPTER 46

Charlie had Jack right where she wanted him. Well, almost. This dinner under the stars was a lovely prelude to the treat she was planning for later on.

"Don't you like this champagne?" she asked. "It's Cristal. How can you take such tiny little sips when it tastes so incredibly yummy?"

"Just pacing myself," Jack said. "I'm on duty, you know."

"No, you're not," she teased him. "Your workday was all morning. We had sports time all afternoon. Now, we're on evening fun time."

Before flying to Antigua, Charlie had gone to La Prairie Spa to get her intimate grooming done according to what Angela said turned Jack on. That meant waxing in some places and not in others, with special bits of trimming here and there. She could hardly wait to have him feasting on the delights she had so carefully prepared for him.

She finished yet another round of bubbly in her gilt-edged flute.

Jack reached for the bottle in the ice bucket and refilled her champagne yet again. It was their second bottle. After dessert, Charlie had shooed away the help to ensure their complete privacy.

"Why, thank you, sir," she said with practiced coyness.

"You are most welcome, ma'am." He smiled. "So, tell me more about this fascinating, complex woman named Charlotte Townsend."

"My favorite subject," she said.

"Mine, too," he said.

Now this is more like it, she thought.

"You can be charming," she cooed, "when you want to be."

"I want to be," he said, taking another one of his tiny sips.

She patted his knee under the table.

"Well, now that you're responsible for creating the Townsend family's future greatness," she said, leaning toward him, "I can share some of our secrets with you."

He leaned in closer to her. She put her hand back on his knee.

"Start from the beginning," he whispered. "Tell me *everything*."

Yes, that's definitely more like it, she thought. He moved his leg; she took back her hand.

"Well, I hate to sound like the poor little rich girl, but that's kind of my story. Mommy died of cervical cancer when I was just about to become a woman. Daddy was a distant presence at best. But he was getting us rich. Very rich. Before she died, Mom made him promise all sorts of things for me. The first promise was Miss Porter's School. You know, where Jacqueline Kennedy Onassis went?"

He nodded yes.

"I didn't make a lot of friends there. Very snooty place. They found the source of Daddy's wealth, well, sleazy. Not at all what they were taught to aspire to. But when I listened to them, I mean, really listened, what I heard was something very revealing. A lot of those girls had been brought up to want nothing but a rich husband. The richer, the better. They didn't have the term 'sex worker' back then, but I wondered: What's the difference between these snobby girls and lowly prostitutes? They both trade their bodies for money. The only difference is how much they get paid. Instead of a hundred bucks for a quickie, my classmates were planning on a lifetime of payments in big houses, country club memberships, charity balls, and the clique-y friendship of other girls like themselves.

"And, from what they said about their own fathers, it was clear that the most successful husbands had other women on the side. For every indiscretion, their moms got another expensive bauble from Cartier or Van Cleef and Arpels. 'That's why God created jewelry,' was the favorite quote of the prep school moms when they talked about their cheating husbands. As far as I was concerned, it was all an arrangement of respectable prostitution. Well, I wanted no part of it. Not that they would have accepted me anyway."

She put her hands over her heart and said with mock melodrama, "I, on the other hand, believed in romance. Pure romance! I eloped with the most dashing, handsome polo player in Argentina. Ha! I know it sounds like a Harlequin romance cliché. It was. But I was nineteen. It was real to me. And I was escaping, well, everything. Absolutely everything. It turns out Raul loved three things, in this order. His stable of polo ponies. His stable of other women. And beating the shit out of his wife—me. Black eyes, contusions, broken bones, the works."

Jack patted her arm sympathetically. "I'm so sorry." He seemed to mean it.

She gave him a courageous smile. "Next was the society boy from Palm Beach. He had a collection of the most delicious sherbet-colored cashmere sweaters. He wore them tied elegantly around his shoulders. He was gentle and sensitive in bed. Hesitant, almost embarrassed. It turned out the reason was that he preferred boys." She banged her forehead. "Well, duh! Of course! Sorry, but my life has been plagued with cliché relationships."

"No one's life is a cliché," Jack said earnestly.

"Dear Jack," she said wryly, "nearly everyone's life is cliché," as she waved away the thought.

"My last bad choice was a hardworking trusts and estates lawyer from an eminent, old-line law firm." She sighed. "He was straight and nonviolent. Not bad at sex, actually. Dutiful and nicely athletic. But all he was interested in was getting his hands on my trusts and Cliff's estate. Finally, I got one of Cliff's corporate IT guys to hack into his phone and laptop. When I showed Cliff printouts of some of his texts and e-mails, we threw him out together. It was our first actual adult bonding experience. At the time Cliff was in the throes of divorcing his third wife since Mommy. After that we became sort of an odd couple. Globetrotting together for lack of better companions. The odd couple that you met at the condo back in New York."

"I see," he said.

"So, here I am at this point in my life. I know what I want, and I know how to get it. No romance, no illusions. I let nothing stand in my way. Nothing."

"Good for you, Charlie." He refilled her champagne flute again.

"Let's just be quiet for a while," she said. "Listen to the waves."

He smiled at her. She put her hand back on his knee. He let it rest there.

She liked his smile, even if it was a little forced. It felt good to confess to him about her love life, such as it was. It would help him to understand what would happen later that night. Her story would free his mind about her. Help him to perform better, she hoped.

The Cristal warmed her in such a nice way. She downed another. He refilled her flute again. And again. And again.

She had that delicious feeling of floating, which made her more aware of the faint rocking of the yacht in the nighttime tide.

"Now, Jack, for what I'm about to tell you, I need to swear you to secrecy. Do you swear to tell no one?"

"I swear," he said and crossed his heart.

"Pain of death, understand?"

"Yes, I understand completely."

"Good." She held out her empty flute. He refilled it.

"Cliff, my father Cliff—and that's a complication I can tell you more about sometime—that man you met, is keeping his will and estate plans secret. He says his heirs will find out when the time comes. Heirs? *I'm* his only heir. What the hell is he talking about? And when the time comes? I say, 'The time is now. *Now!*' That's why we have to create the foundation. *Now!*"

She took Jack's arm urgently. Leaned in and whispered in his ear. "I'm convinced that Cliff is secretly laundering millions. Tens of millions for sure, hundreds, for all I know. I've got forensic accountants trying to keep track. He funnels money to a little offshore bank here in Antigua. He's got this banker, a tight-lipped local man named Mr. Beresford. He won't tell me a thing. He's the one who sends the money down an accounting rabbit hole to nowhere. I'm convinced it's some kind of money laundering. Cliff denies it. But of course he would."

Jack refilled her champagne flute again.

"Jack, I want to do good in the world. I really do. I need your creative magic to persuade Cliff to become a philanthropist. So

269

I can take my rightful place with the kind of people who really matter." She gritted her teeth. "This . . . is . . . the most important . . . moment . . . of my . . . entire life. Do you understand?"

She squeezed Jack's hand in hers. He squeezed back. "Yes," he said.

She whispered again, "There's something else. I know something very, very dangerous. It's something Cliff is afraid of. Very dark. Very dangerous. Maybe later I'll tell you about it. If we become really close."

She pressed her index finger to Jack's lips. "Can I really and truly trust you?"

He nodded yes emphatically. Took both her hands in his. "Absolutely."

She thought it would be a good moment for a kiss. Then decided no, that's for later.

He let go of her hands and stood. "I'm sorry, but I have to make a call to New York. It's about my son."

She didn't like that. He got that pained look whenever he mentioned his son. She definitely did not want him distracted from *her* needs. She was paying to have *her* needs attended to, 100 percent. She felt like ordering him to sit back down, but she didn't want to emasculate him. At least not tonight.

"Thank you for a beautiful dinner, Charlie," he said. Then he whispered, "And thanks for sharing with me. I will do everything I possibly can to help you." He reached down and took her hand one last time. "Everything."

CHAPTER 47

Jack did not want to appear to be fleeing his dinner with Charlie, even though he was. He was filled with dread, hoping against hope that Charlie would not show up in his stateroom later, intent on doing more than just flirting. He had never in his life imagined having a boss who made sex one of the preconditions of employment. In his panic, all he could think of was how much he needed this goddamn job.

He made a point of walking slowly—ambling, actually. On the outside, he was a man enjoying a leisurely stroll on a floating pleasure palace. Inside, he was running at full sprint. The trip up to the third deck to his luxurious moonroof prison cell felt like it took for-fucking-ever.

He closed his door and ran to the charger where his phone sat. He texted his question marks to Sandra and got the usual response, just as he had gotten from her a couple of hours earlier, before dinner: **NNINN.**

271

He wanted to know more, wanted to hear Sandra's voice. She'd been with Luke, watching him breathe, talking to his doctors. He couldn't stand being so isolated. The absence of Luke, the inability to touch him and feel that he was still alive, was an actual ache. His fingertips throbbed with it.

He picked up his cell phone. Why the hell not?

He dialed Sandra. It rang. Twice. Then he heard a man's voice. "Is this Jack?"

"Of course it's Jack," he snapped. "Who the hell are you? And what are you doing with Sandra's phone?"

"Oh, I'm sorry," he said. "Sandra's in the hall, conferring with the doctors. She'll be back in a minute."

"You didn't answer me, goddammit! Who the hell are you?"

"Hello, Jack," the man said warmly. "I'm Ned. Ned Robbins."

"Like I said before," Jack said, not caring how nasty he sounded, "who the hell are you, and what are you doing with Sandra's phone?"

"Oh, I'm sorry. I thought Sandra had told you. We've been, uh, seeing each other for several months, Sandra and I."

"No, she never said a word about you."

"I see. Well, I, uh . . . Oh, here she comes now. I'll just hand the phone back to her. Jack, I want you to know how sorry we all are about Luke. We're all praying for him to recover. Me and my son Ken. He idolizes Luke, you know. Luke's been like the big brother he never had. He's been such a stabilizing influence on him. Uh, here's Sandra now."

A pause, then he heard Sandra. "Jack, I told you in my text, there's been no change. He's stable. The doctors tell us that it's actually good for his brain to have this healing time. They say all we can do now is be patient and hope."

Jack took a deep breath. He projected himself into the hospital room, standing beside Luke's bed, whispering encouragement through the boy's coma, into his soul. He was there, not here on this ridiculous yacht. Suddenly, against his will, he was sobbing.

"I love Luke," he stammered. "I love him. And I want him to get better."

Sandra spoke softly, comfortingly. "I know you do. Luke knows you do. He loves you, too."

Jack sniffled, took a deep breath, and regained partial composure.

"I didn't know about Ned. You never told me. That's his name, for real—Ned?"

"Yes, Ned. I was planning to. And then the accident happened."

Jack felt a sudden wave of possessiveness. It confused and upset him.

"Is he good to you?"

"Yes, Jack. Ned is a wonderful man. He's wonderful to me, and to Luke. Ned's wife died two years ago. His boy Kenny was only five at the time. He's had a lot of troubles since then. Luke has been so good with him. They've become like brothers, helping each other."

Jack didn't know what to say. He thought Sandra might not know either. There was a long moment of silence between them.

Sandra spoke first. "You can call and ask about Luke anytime you like. You know that. But I promise to text you every day. And if anything happens, anything at all, you know I will call you immediately. You know that. Don't you?"

"Yes, I do."

"Luke loves his dad. You know that, too?"

"Yes." He paused, unsure about whether to ask his next question. Then he plowed ahead. "Are you happy with Ned? Really happy?"

"Yes, Jack. I really am."

"Then are you—?"

"I live day to day now. That's all I can say for sure."

"I understand. I do, too."

"Jack, I'll let you know the second anything changes. Okay?"

"Okay, Sandra."

He wanted to hear something more, but she had hung up.

He looked across the room at Luke's backpack on the closet shelf. The orange clownfish looked at him with those goofy crossed eyes.

He felt exhausted, totally wrung out.

He opened his windows to let in the cool breezes of the tropical night. Hit the switch that pulled the shade back, to see the starry night sky. Slipped out of his clothes. Collapsed onto the enormous bed. And fell into a deep sleep.

CHAPTER 48

A gentle stirring sound, like tall grasses in the wind, half-awakened Jack. He turned his head toward the sound. In the moonlight shining down through the giant glass hole in the ceiling, he saw Charlie standing naked, holding open a long silk robe.

His worst fear had come true.

He looked her up and down. She was toned and fashionista-thin, not a trace of fat anywhere, the tips of her hip bones protruding slightly and a few ribs visible, her small breasts seemingly untouched by the gravity of her forty-plus years. She seemed to be watching him looking at her body. She dropped the robe off her shoulders. It made a puddle of silk around her feet. She opened her legs a bit and let her hands hang down, drawing his eyes to where her thighs met. "Something tells me," she said softly, "you're the kind of man who likes a good, old-fashioned American bikini wax."

He looked at the perfect triangle of her pubic hair and the bare skin precisely defining her panty line. He had no idea what to say. How did she guess he had a thing for that style? He felt panicky about what he knew he would soon be expected to do. His could not tell if his flaccid dick would perform.

Without another word, she slid onto the bed. Sitting up on her knees, she straddled his legs. Then started running her fingertips up and down the length of him. Then began kissing and licking his limp penis.

His first reaction was resentment. How dare she? Then resignation. She's my goddamn boss. Then worry. If he had no choice but to submit to her, what would happen if he could not get it up for her? He looked down and saw he was as limp as if he had been sitting in an ice-cold bath.

"Just lay back and enjoy," she said between motions of her mouth and hands. "Close your eyes and concentrate on your sensations. I'm very skillful, you know, and I'm pretty sure you're really going to like this. Just concentrate on your pleasure and go where it takes you. Remember, Jack, we're in paradise. Now close your eyes and relax into it."

He did as she told him. He did his best to forget that she was his boss. That she held his future in her hands. And now in her mouth. He tried to forget that he was desperate to succeed in this, his very last chance to rescue his career. And that an erection would now be key to his performance appraisal. He lay back. At first, feeling defeated. Then, telling himself he had no choice, he slowly began letting himself enjoy the sensations.

What the hell? What the fuck?

Her technique, her wet ministrations and strokes, were almost exactly what he liked most in a blow job. With each little lick and tickle and tease, he found himself rising. Throbbing with arousal. How did she know so exactly what to do to make him hard?

Could he now forget that she was his employer, if only for a few minutes? Oh boy, could he ever! Any thoughts he'd had about not being able to perform had evaporated. His throbbing boner had a mind of its own. And he knew it would stand proud until it got its chance to come inside Charlie's pussy.

She slid up farther, pressing the tip of his dick ever so lightly against her labia for a fleeting moment. Her thighs were straddling his chest. Her curly hairs just brushing against his sternum.

"Now you seem like a real gentleman to me," she cooed. "Am I right?"

He gawked up at her as she loomed over him. Speechless.

"Ladies first, right?"

"Right," he gasped.

She slid up further and straddled his face, blocking out the moonlight. "Gentlemen," she whispered playfully, "start your engines."

He took her butt cheeks in both hands to steady himself and began licking. He lost himself in his quest to tease her clit and bring her to orgasm. She was no longer his employer. She was every woman he had ever wanted. He was the universal man, fueled by lust, devouring every succulent pussy in the world. His whole world consisted of her tender lips, her wetness, her wiry hair, her intoxicating smell. She moved with him, sighing and gasping, smothering him with her tender flesh, drowning him with her juices.

She gave him directions from time to time. A little more here, a little less there, yes, yes, like that. Never giving orders, just asking sweetly but urgently for more pleasure. After the waves of her orgasm had finally subsided, she leaned over him and gave him deep kisses. Ardently, he returned them, stroking her body all over.

Then she slid back down and sucked him some more to recharge his erection to the point of near bursting. She mounted him in the cowgirl position and slid him inside her. She ground her way atop him to another orgasm of her own.

"Let go," she said breathlessly, "let go. Come inside me. Come on."

He grabbed her hips and began thrusting. They bounced together, rocking the giant bed.

"Let go," she gasped, "let yourself go!"

He obeyed, abandoning himself to the sensations of skin and hair and smell and slippery friction. Once again, his universe collapsed into a few inches of flesh. Nothing existed but his dick and her pussy.

Finally, he was coming. And coming. And coming.

After he slipped out, she rubbed against him and worked her fingers inside herself. Then she was coming. Again.

She fell on top of him. They kissed lightly and stroked each other gently. Felt the electricity of skin against skin, the contrasts of man against woman. Sex. Satisfaction. Release.

After a while, she slid off the bed, picked up her silk robe, slipped it over her shoulders, and walked to the door. She put a hand on the doorknob and turned back for a quick glance in Jack's direction. She said nothing. Just walked out, closing the door behind her.

Jack did not know how long he lay there in the moonlight. At first, he had no thoughts. Just the pleasure of afterglow mixed with gratitude for the moments that had let him forget the pain and loss of the last few weeks.

Then, gradually, he began replaying what had just happened.

Then, wondering what was going to happen next.

His feelings of defeat, of resentment at being used, gave way to something else. He began laughing inside.

I can't report this incident to Human Resources, he told himself. Because there *is* no human resources to report it to. My boss wants to fuck me. Insists on it. And I must let her get away with it. Why? Because I need this job. I've joined the ranks of those who've been fucked by their bosses. Me. Me, too. Hah. That's right, Jack Price, the #MeToo offender. Me, too. He had to laugh.

He jumped out of bed and started pacing the room. He desperately wanted to text Sandra. But it was the middle of the night, and if anything had happened, she would have let him know. He knew what he wanted was contact with the world outside. His world. The real world, not Charlie Townsend's fucked-up world.

He turned to the backpack. There was Marlin, the cross-eyed clownfish who had witnessed the whole thing. Luke's little mascot.

"Dude," he said aloud, "we always used to joke about being whores in our business. But Luke, buddy, it was just a way of saying we had to give our clients anything they wanted. Now, for the first time, I actually have to *be* a whore."

CHAPTER 49

Jack sat alone at breakfast on the alfresco dining deck where he had poured Charlie all that Cristal the night before. He fidgeted over his fruit salad, wondering when she was going to show up and what she was going to say after their midnight sex. He had no idea what to expect.

Would she be warm to him? Kittenish? Cold? Had he given her what she wanted? Satisfied her? Or disappointed her? Were they supposed to acknowledge the sex they'd had—or pretend that it never happened? Was it supposed to remain a secret? Or was it totally cool, normal, and out in the open? No more dramatic than two people eating ice cream together. How would it affect their relationship as employer and employee? What were the rules on this crazy boat? What were the fucking rules? The rules for fucking?

He checked his watch. He had calls starting in a few minutes. Production plans, a check-in of his storyboards, reviews of video

281

signatures from established foundations. Old Man Townsend was scheduled to arrive for the big meeting in only five days. He had to crunch the way he used to for new business presentations.

Suddenly there was a shadow over his plate. He looked up. The vast bulk of Josef was blocking out the Caribbean sun.

"Oh, hi, Josef," Jack said uneasily.

The wall of muscle grunted. "Is gone, Miss Charlie. Gone to St. Barth's. She says she visit friends there. She says you have to work. Work hard. You need anything, you ask me. Just ask. Anything." As best he could, he forced a smile. "Okay?" Josef offered his fist for a bump.

Jack obliged with his fist.

Josef banged it harder than necessary. Then smiled again, this time with no awkwardness. He gave Jack a look that seemed to say *I beat the shit out of you anytime I want*, then turned and walked away.

Why had Charlie fled to St. Barth's? She had promised him a tour of Antigua and her aristo pals. Had he done something wrong? Was she embarrassed? Or worse, was she disappointed in his sexual performance? Was he going to be fired by one of her lackeys? How could she have sex like that with him and then just vanish? Just split without a word.

Again, he thought of the irony of it. Men did this to women all the time.

Jack retreated to the boardroom to make his calls and video conferences. He kept refining his presentation materials, sending his producer to meetings in New York as his cover, arguing with video editors on Slack, reading everything the Internet could show him about the world of philanthropy and family foundations. Revising and re-revising his charts and text slides.

He spent all day shut away in the boardroom, ignoring the tropical paradise just outside the door. Hour after hour, he fretted,

GLENN KAPLAN

worried, and obsessively reworked his sales pitch in hopes that his redemption could be won if only he could build a presentation that was absolutely perfect.

Skipping lunch, he stayed inside working until well after sunset. He ordered a modest in-room dinner. For the third time that day—or was it the fourth or fifth or eighth?—he texted Sandra and got the same no-news message.

He climbed into bed and talked to Luke's backpack until he drifted off to sleep. Not for a moment was he tempted by the overstocked bar on the other side of his stateroom. He had stopped seeing it. For Jack, it did not even exist.

He repeated the same routine for four long days. Charlie did not return, and there was no word about her, at least that he got. He was the only guest on *King of Pawns*. Of course, he was an employee just like the eighteen crew members. But he had the super-duper stateroom and enjoyed the status of a Townsend intimate. Crew members would ask him why he didn't take advantage of the many toys and pastimes on board. He would shrug and say he had too much work.

On the morning of the fifth day, Jack's breakfast was interrupted by a hubbub among the kitchen crew. His deckhand waitress Sally came bolting up the spiral staircase.

"Mr. Townsend is on his way from the airport in St. John's," she said in her Aussie accent, "with a party of his friends. They should be here in a half-hour or so."

Jack gave a noncommittal nod. He was, in equal measure, nervous, scared, bored, and totally sick of this fucked-up so-called job.

He dropped his spoon into his empty bowl and stood up.

"Thanks, Sally. I'll be at work in the boardroom if anybody needs me. Okay?"

Sally answered with her wide grin and a thumbs-up.

283

CHAPTER 50

Angela stood in front of the door to the boardroom. As soon as she and Cliff and Eric had stepped off Josef's motorboat onto the yacht, she had asked where she could find Jack Price. From behind her, Josef grunted, "In boardroom. Is where he works. There all the time."

Jack had the blinds down and the room darkened. For video viewing, no doubt. She didn't need to summon up unpleasant childhood memories before this encounter with Jack Price. This time, she summoned up lessons Jack had taught her about how people succeed in the glittering world of skyscrapers. The one she remembered now was very specific. She could still hear his voice that day as they lay naked on the bed in the hotel room, with him idly stroking her. "In a difficult negotiation," he said, "always try to figure out what the other guy is feeling deep inside. Then name it. Say it out loud. It can help you win him over and change his mind about you. Get him to do what you want. He may even thank you for it."

She stared at the boardroom door, conjuring up the things Jack must be feeling.

She had caused so many people to be fired. She knew what happened to them. Their trauma. Their feelings of being devalued. Their shame. Their mourning for who they used to be, their sudden disorientation at being rootless, tribeless, without an identity. They were literally, for months afterward, lost souls. She had disciplined herself not to think about their pain. At least, not too much. She knew it must be even worse for Jack because he had been banished from his business forever because of her. She would have to handle him with extra care.

She told herself, Name what he's feeling. He's probably too injured to notice that I'm using his own technique on him.

She knocked.

Jack said, "Come in."

She opened the door and stepped into the boardroom.

Jack did not turn around. He was watching a video on the big screen, the logo sequence of the MacArthur Foundation playing over and over.

Angela spoke to his back. "A wise man once told me you can always make points with the boss by asking the video editor to add ten more frames to the final dissolve."

Jack turned around slowly. Very, very slowly. "What the fuck?" he sputtered.

Angela saw in his face his shock, rage, and confusion.

"W-w-what the f-f-fuck are *you* doing here?" he said again.

"Jack, Charlie Townsend is my friend." She spoke urgently, hoping that would stop him from throwing her out. "That's how I got here. I can explain everything. I can, I promise."

She sat down in the chair beside him. Raised one hand as if to touch him comfortingly on the back, but held it back a few inches. "But first, Jack, I want to hear about you."

286

"What? You? *You?* Here? What the fuck?"

"Jack, please hear me out. I can only imagine how angry you must be."

"Really now? Can you?" He was fidgeting with rage, maybe holding himself back from hitting her. Just barely. "Can you now, really?"

Very softly she said, "I can try. Please, let me explain. Please?"

She let her hand down slowly, letting it rest tentatively on his shoulder. He seemed to accept it. At least, he didn't push her away.

For a nanosecond, she thought of all the ways her hands had once touched him. Then let that thought evaporate. She focused on the palm of her hand and willed it to communicate compassion. Make him feel compassion. Compassion, goddammit. Compassion.

"Jack, I think I know what you must be feeling. You must be exploding with anger at what happened, the brutal way the agency treated you, the horrible injustice of it all. After all you did for them. It was so unfair. So incredibly unfair. You have to believe me, I had nothing to do with it. They said it was policy. I felt so bad for you, really. I asked them to cut you a break, but they said no. You *have* to believe me."

He was biting his lower lip. She could tell he was listening. It's working, she thought.

She remembered him teaching her how to lie with a straight face. How to lie while looking the other person in the eye and not blinking. A vital skill in the corporate world, he told her. He used to practice with her. They would stand naked together in front of the mirror. Staring each other down until one of them finally blinked. Then collapsing with laughter onto the bed and making love again as they joked, telling bigger and bigger lies to each other.

"I really can imagine how you are feeling, Jack." She took his chin in her hand and turned his face to her. "Betrayed. Lost. Stripped of

287

your dignity. People refusing to take your calls, people who used to call themselves your friends. Feeling like you've been robbed of your future. Feeling like the whole world is out to shatter your confidence. Worst of all, alone. Oh, Jack, it must be terrible for you."

He stared at her. No longer with rage, she hoped. He just looked tired.

He raised his index finger. A timid gesture, asking a question.

"That night at Vlad's," he said hesitantly. "I had a thought later on. I couldn't help but wonder, uh . . . if you . . . ?" He looked away.

Of course, she thought, he needs to know what he did because he knows he was too drunk to remember for certain. This is the moment for my big lie. I need to make sure he believes me.

She gave his shoulder a little squeeze of compassion. She paused, holding her breath for a long beat. Yes, this was the moment. This is the decisive play that would end in her victory or her defeat. The championship, the gold medal, the prize she was betting her entire life on hung in the balance, awaiting her next move.

She took his face in both her hands, willing them to communicate caring and truth. Not truth itself, just the feeling of truth. She peered into his eyes. This would be the test of how well she had mastered the lessons Jack had taught her when he was strong and confident, propped up by his big paycheck, the trappings of his position, and the bits of power he wielded inside his little world.

She held his gaze and did not blink. She saw his sadness, his shame, his guilt. His eyes seemed to be telling her that his heart was an open sore.

Perfect, she thought.

"No, Jack, no," she said in her softest, kindest tone. So very sad to break this news to him. "You really did grope me." Be convincing, she told herself. He absolutely *must* believe me. "I'm

288

afraid you were drunk. Very drunk. I'm sorry, but you were awful. It wasn't like you. You attacked me. Tore my clothes. Grabbed me. Hurt me."

He turned his head, breaking away from her hands.

She was sure she had him right where she wanted him. As she sniffed back tears, she touched his cheek tenderly. "I want you to know something," she said. "Something important."

He stared at the wall.

"Look at me, Jack. Please? I want you to understand something." He obeyed, turning his head to her.

She took his chin and stared into his eyes. He stared back.

"I forgive you," she said, willing herself to hold her gaze steady. *Don't blink*, she commanded herself. *Not even for an instant.*

"I forgave you later that night. And I forgive you now. I realize now that I should not have forced you to take that first drink. That was wrong. I'm sorry. Really, I'm sorry about that. But I'm afraid you did the rest."

He looked down again. Yes, he must be feeling all the guilt and shame she wanted him to feel. She picked up his chin again.

He looked at her. Took a deep breath. Then spoke haltingly. To Angela it sounded like he was begging for approval, for affirmation.

"I've, uh, I've, sworn off alcohol, you know," he said. "For real this time. There's, there's, there's this bar in my stateroom. Got every expensive booze in the world. I haven't even gone near it."

"That's great," she smiled. He desperately needs a hug, she thought, and a pat on the back. But they shouldn't come from me. I can't try to heal his wounds; I need to *use* them.

She let go of his chin and sat back in her chair, not moving away from him so much as giving him back his own space.

He shook his head as if to clear it. "Now, what are you doing here?"

This was just the cue she had hoped for. She had crafted and rehearsed this storyline carefully. The perfect blend of truth and lies.

"Jack, I'm afraid it's a bit complicated. You see, Charlie Townsend and I got to be friends in London. You know, after I took the job at Globalcom." She paused.

He nodded.

She continued, "You see, for several months Charlie had been asking me to help her find a marketing creative, a freelancer, to help her persuade her father to set up a charitable foundation. In my travels, I would ask around casually, but nobody appropriate seemed to turn up. When I got to New York, it was still on my list, but I would never have thought of you for it. I mean, you're so successful; you'd never take an assignment like this. "But once the, uh, incident, happened, well, I had this inspiration. Suddenly Jack Price was available. *The* Jack Price. The most creative guy in the whole business.

"I remembered that your favorite headhunter was Dale Waldman, so I called Charlie, who then called Cliff's company to call Dale and add him to the list of recruiters working on the assignment. I knew that Dale would be sure to call you, especially after what happened. They were putting on a real executive search, very professional, quite a number of candidates, all thoroughly screened. Are you with me?"

She stopped and waited for him to respond. She put her hand on his shoulder. Compassionately again. He nodded a reluctant yes. He seemed to be buying it all. She had designed it to mislead him just enough while at the same time helping him regain a few shards of the dignity he had lost.

"Jack, I really did want to help you. I mean, after all we'd been through. But all I did was put your name in for consideration. You have to understand that. You got the job yourself. You got it on your own merits. Of all the candidates, Cliff and Charlie liked you the best. Really, you got the job on your own. All I did was get you the chance to get the interview. I really hope this gig gives you a new start in the business, away from those stupid agencies."

Jack seemed neutral, but okay. Yes, she thought, he is too injured to recognize his own techniques being used against him. She took his hand and smiled. He did not recoil. He gave her a tentative smile in return.

She let go of him.

"How are you doing with the pitch?" She looked around the boardroom. "Say, where's Charlie?" Now that she thought of it, where the hell *was* she? "Isn't she reviewing your presentation before the meeting? She was so excited to have someone with your credentials working to help her get the foundation."

Jack shrugged. "Charlie left for St. Barth's a few days ago, without a word. I haven't seen or heard from her since then. I've put together a dynamite presentation without her. At this point I don't know what I'd do if she walked in and wanted to change any of it."

Angela shrugged. "She must be coming later today. I can't believe she'd miss tomorrow. It's *her* meeting."

"Well, I think she's a strange one. If you say she's your friend, okay. But what do you make of it?"

Angela wrinkled her forehead, once again genuinely puzzled by her flighty gal pal.

"I'm guessing here, but if she takes no ownership of your presentation, and it bombs with her father, she can throw you under the bus. She can disavow the whole thing. You are expendable if you have to be. If you're a hit, she wins anyway, so she didn't need to get involved. You know how rich people can be. They have to win no matter what. Everything has to be done their way."

Jack snickered. "Yeah, tell me about it." He waved his arm around to indicate the boardroom, the yacht, the whole thing. "This world of the Townsends is pretty unbelievable."

"Oh, Jack," she said, suddenly gushing, "can I tell you my news?" She took both his hands in hers. "Can I?"

She felt the sudden need to unload with *someone*. Why not Jack? She had no one else. After all, she had defused him as a possible threat, and it seemed he had bought her lies. It was safe to share with him. They were old intimates again—sort of. And even in his diminished state, he might still be able to offer good advice.

"Uh, sure." He took back his hands and gave her a puzzled look.

"Cliff has asked me to marry him," she blurted out.

"Huh?" he asked in amazement. "He's, like, old enough to be—to be your grandfather!"

"I know!"

She was talking to him with the gossipy enthusiasm best girl-friends use with each other. It felt good. And why not? She'd had no one to talk to. She dared not let Eric in until the deal was sealed; he could be too chatty. But now she had Jack back on her side. Sort of. Well, enough for her purposes.

"Hey, as you well know, I've always had a thing for, uh, older men." She gave him a little wink.

He shrugged. "Uh, thanks."

"Jack, you must know what I've always wanted. What I've always been looking for."

He leaned back in his chair as if to inspect her from a distance.

"Actually, Angela, I have absolutely no idea what you've always wanted. Not a clue."

She leaned in close and whispered softly, "I want to feel safe. That's all I've ever wanted. Cliff makes me feel safe."

"But how on earth?"

"Charlie and I were hanging out in London, doing girl stuff together. But Cliff, whose flat in Mayfair isn't that far from Charlie's place, in Chelsea, started insisting on having company. He can't stand being alone. Well, one thing led to another. He's asked me several times and I've told him I'm thinking about it. I really think I'm prepared to say yes, I really do. Charlie's in favor of it, too. She told me all about the prenup he makes all of his wives sign. It's got, like, the severance plan all built in. But no matter. My life with Cliff will be so much better than working in that awful agency."

Jack raised an eyebrow in skepticism. "You seemed pretty comfortable in your role as chief culture officer."

She poked her index finger in her mouth in the vomit gesture.

"Ugh! It's been awful. And yes, that's my role. But you're right, it's definitely a role. I was acting. My job was to be the phony front man for their desperate cost cutting. Globalcom is a failing business—there's no help for it. The top executives, Reade and Woodleigh, along with their pals, are plundering the ship before it sinks. My job was to help them gouge millions for themselves out of the employees."

"You looked to be doing pretty well by it, too."

"Sure. That's the deal. Corporate life. But my share is nothing compared to what those guys are raking in."

She took his hands in hers again. He did not resist.

"Jack, I'm so grateful to you for everything. You taught me how it all works. How completely amoral the whole thing is. I'll never forget what you told me: 'Angela, you've got so many strikes against you—you need to do whatever it takes to get ahead. Forget right and wrong, there's only effective and not effective. Just look at the people who run the corporate world,' you said. 'It's a joke, who gets ahead. The so-called leaders produced by big corporations. Who are they? Maybe one in a million is the real deal. Mostly, they are the suck-ups, backstabbers, toadies, sandbaggers, and bullies. They're the hangers-on, survivors who kept their heads down. A lot of them are just nitwits who were dumb lucky. Think it's a meritocracy? Think again.' "

Jack seemed a bit bewildered. "Did I teach you all that?"

"You sure did."

"Well, you were my most successful student, that's for sure."

She squeezed his hands tighter. "Tell me, Jack. Are you healing? Is this job helping? I think it can help you get a new career, using your talents in nonprofits."

Of course, she was thinking about helping herself, but she really did want to help Jack. She really did want to make up for at least some of the pain she had caused him. And she felt she could help him recover. If this was not a weird kind of love she felt for Jack Price at this moment, they certainly shared some kind of bond—a feeling they were connected to each other, like it or not, and probably always would be.

"We'll find out tomorrow in the big meeting." He sighed wearily.

She could see how anxious he was. It was his last chance professionally.

"And how's your son? Luke, right?"

She really wanted to know. She liked the sudden feeling of being close to Jack's life again. "He must be almost grown-up by now. Is he even more handsome than his dad?"

Jack pulled his hands from hers and turned away. He spoke in fragments.

"He's in the hospital with a brain injury. Coma. We were hiking in the mountains. He was using the VeRity headset when he was out of my sight. He fell and, uh . . . It was all my fault. All my fault."

She felt heartsick for Jack. It was real emotion this time. She knew how much he adored his son. She was no longer calculating or scheming. All she wanted in that instant was to try to give this man whom she had once adored a little comfort.

She got up from her chair and wrapped her arms around him.

"Oh Jack, I'm so sorry." He let her hug him. She held on tight. This was a hug he really needed and deserved. He buried his face in her shoulder and just breathed. She patted his back gently, hoping he could feel the solace she really wanted to give him.

The door of the boardroom flew open.

Eric charged in and came to a sudden stop. "Well, excuse me. I had no idea."

Angela looked up, visibly annoyed. "What is it?"

"Charlie Townsend just arrived from St. Barth's. She's asking for you, Angela."

CHAPTER 51

Jack begged off the group dinner on the alfresco deck, pleading rehearsal prep. He had Sally bring him a bowl of spaghetti and a salad in the boardroom. Then he went to bed early.

The next morning, he also avoided the breakfast buffet and went straight to the boardroom, where Sally had fruit salad and coffee waiting for him.

Two morning texts to Sandra. Still no news.

At precisely ten, Angela and Charlie came into the boardroom.

"Where would you like us to sit, Jack?" Charlie asked. She was cold. Completely formal.

He pointed to the two chairs, one on either side of the chair where he planned for Cliff to sit, and said, "Ladies." He watched Charlie for any sign of familiarity or intimacy. She was as indifferent as a stranger on a bus. Angela gave him a little thumbs-up.

The women sat down, and Charlie made small talk with Angela as if he were not there.

He thought about breaking in on their conversation with something, anything—maybe a few words in a familiar tone, or maybe even slightly intimate. Then decided not to. He realized he was the help, here to serve his masters.

The women continued chatting, making no effort to include Jack.

Fifteen minutes went by. Jack was getting nervous. The women were getting bored.

Finally, Cliff appeared and took his seat at the head of the giant table. He motioned impatiently for Jack to get started.

Jack noted that Angela's British boy-toy was not in the meeting. He hit the panel that lowered the blinds and dimmed the lights. The big screen lit up with his first slide. In carefully designed presentation type, it read—*Why philanthropy?*

Slide by slide, Jack built his argument for the philanthropic Townsend Foundation. He showed a review of the branding elements of established foundations, along with the video signatures they used in television shows and Internet presentations. He reviewed their assets, their grants, their missions, their pet social issues, statements of their differing views of philanthropic responsibilities. Jack had all the most famous names in foundation giving—Rockefeller, Ford, MacArthur, Bloomberg, Carnegie, and Mellon—along with others not quite so famous but making an impact and gaining in public recognition. It was a formal business presentation worthy of any boardroom.

Jack watched Cliff. He was unreactive, except for occasionally stroking Angela as if she were his pet cat. He watched Charlie. Charlie was riveted on Cliff. Jack thought she looked incredibly tense.

"So that's our overview of the business of foundation giving among the majors," he said. "And a snapshot of what their brands stand for."

Then Jack clicked to a slide in a bright new color with text in a font that looked like handwritten magic marker. It read—*Enough of the bullshit!*

Cliff chuckled. Angela mimicked his laugh. Charlie gave a little gasp.

Jack turned to Cliff and asked, "The big question is, How should a potential philanthropist evaluate what charitable causes *really* have to offer him?"

Cliff seemed to be with him. "I dunno, Mr. Madison Avenue," he said with an amused smirk. "Why don't you tell us? Now that we're done with the bullshit."

Jack smiled back. "I thought you'd never ask. I would like to propose the first rating system that tells the truth, the whole truth, and nothing but. This innovative philanthropic rating system has only two categories." The first image that appeared on the screen was a cartoon graphic of a teary face with a Kleenex over the nose.

"I call the first category 'hankies,' " Jack announced. "Hankies rate how many tears the cause inspires. How deep is the suffering we're talking about? How piteous is it? Are there starving children? That's a three-hankie cause. Are there starving *crippled* children? That's a four-hankie. Are there starving, crippled children in a country with no water, no natural resources, and absolutely no hope?" The screen filled with a row of five hankies, lined up like stars in a restaurant review. "Now, that's what we call a five-hankie cause!"

He added another line to the chart and announced the results.

"Is there a horrible disease? Two hankies. But if it's a horrible disease that affects children in a way that looks really great on a

299

poster, it could raise it to a four-hankie or even a five-, depending on how cute and pathetic the afflicted kids are. Is there terrible injustice brought about by bad laws and backward-looking policies? If it's in a foreign country where all the laws are bad, it's two hankies. But if it's here at home, where we should know better, and the people who've been wronged look good on camera, it could go to five hankies. What kind of tragedy are we talking about? Just how bottomless are the bottomless agonies our foundation intends to fix? Now, for the first time, we have a system to rate and compare them."

Jack turned to Cliff.

"Mr. Townsend, you're a businessman. You've made your considerable fortune by being able to measure opportunities. Our intention here is to give you the tools to do the same thing as a philanthropist."

Cliff smirked. He was clearly amused. "Keep going," he said.

Charlie's eyes darted back and forth between Cliff and Jack.

"Now to the other side of our evaluation criteria," Jack said. "What's in it for the philanthropist? I'm talking about the philanthropist's enjoyment, ego gratification, and level of personal excitement. On the philanthropic cause side, we rate the opportunity with hankies. On the philanthropist's enjoyment side, we rate the opportunity with . . ."

Jack paused and clicked on the next slide. The hankie symbol was on the left side with a blank space on the right. Suddenly, the blank space on the right was filled with two cartoon testicles supporting a very erect cartoon penis.

". . . hard-ons! The other metric every philanthropist needs."

Cliff gave a hearty laugh.

Jack continued, deadpan. "How big a boner will the giver get from the charity? How hard, how tall will his dick get when they

300

stroke his ego and dedicate lengthy tributes to his selfless generosity? How many hard-ons from the naming opportunities, the buildings, museum galleries, mercy ships, hospital wings, and other places where his name will be carved in stone? How much glory? Just how exciting is this giving opportunity? How thrilling will it be to exchange money for a shot at immortality?

"Now, at long last, the philanthropist has a useful, no-bullshit scorecard for evaluating where and how to give his money. What the worthy cause will get. And just as important, if not more important, what the worthy philanthropist will get in return."

Charlie was wide-eyed and openmouthed, watching Cliff.

Cliff was shaking with laughter. "Price, I like the way you think," he said. "I had you figured for one of those Madison Avenue candyasses. But you're okay."

Jack turned to Charlie. "Charlie, as we discussed when you and Cliff interviewed me, with a Townsend Foundation done right, we can do good, feel good, *and* look good. You can have it all. And so much more. I can envision a day when the Townsend Foundation can be a peer among names like Rockefeller, Carnegie, and, yes, even Gates. Earlier I showed you how these distinguished foundations distinguish their brands in video. Let me show you how I think the Townsend Foundation could do the same."

Jack hit the switch. The room went pitch black. The big screen lit up with a flashing, rapid-fire montage of sad, pitiful, needy people around the world. A very elegant British male voice intoned in a pure BBC accent, "Towns*end* Foundation," stressing the "end" syllable. Suddenly, the faces of the people from around the world looked happy, well-fed, and glowing with fulfillment. The BBC voice concluded, "Towns*end*, where a better future for humanity begins." There was a stirring musical ending as the Townsend logo slowly faded off the screen into blackness.

Jack brought the lights back up to full brightness. Everyone was blinking and squinting.

"That's beautiful, Jack," Charlie said, visibly choked with emotion, "just beautiful. Don't you agree, Angela?"

Angela nodded yes emphatically. Then she and Charlie turned to Cliff.

Cliff was silent. Folded his arms across his chest. "Nice job, Price. Nice job."

Charlie sat up in her chair. It was all she could do to keep from leaping out of it.

"So, Cliff—don't you see what we can accomplish? What we can do for the world? And for our family name?"

Cliff bit his lower lip. Said nothing. One by one, he gave all three people a good, long silent stare, first Angela, then Charlie, then Jack, creating a long moment of suspenseful silence. And milked the hell out of it.

Then he made a big, unpleasant snorting sound in his nose.

"I'm thinking," he said to his lap. "Thinking." He looked at his watch as if he were waiting for something. The only sound in the room was Cliff tapping his foot under the table. He sat in silence, studying his watch.

There was a knock on the conference room door.

Cliff jumped to his feet.

CHAPTER 52

Douglas, the yacht's steward, leaned partially into the boardroom, holding the door half-closed.

"Mr. Townsend," he said, "Mr. Beresford from the Chartered Bank of Antigua is here."

Cliff looked delighted. "Well, what are you waiting for? Send him in!"

Douglas opened the door fully and stepped aside. A studious-looking Black man in tortoiseshell spectacles entered. He wore crisp Bermuda shorts and a linen shirt.

Cliff bounded over to him and gave him a hug.

Charlie was horrified. That's him, she thought. The man who's laundering *my* money and making it disappear to God-knows-where. She sputtered, "But what about our meeting? I've been planning this for months. Months!"

"Enough work for today," Cliff said with a grin. He put an arm around his friend. "*Miss*-ter Beresford, I'm so glad to see you."

Beresford, a good five inches shorter than Townsend, looked up and said with the same playful intonation, "*Miss*-ter Townsend, always a pleasure."

"No, no, *Miss*-ter Beresford, the pleasure is all mine."

Charlie hated when they played this silly game. They sounded like stupid vaudeville comedians to her. It was clear they thought they were hysterical.

"My dear Clifford," Beresford said with a theatrical bow, "may I interest you in a bit of fishing?"

"My dear Thomas," Cliff said with an even deeper bow, "you most certainly may." He turned back to the boardroom. "We can pick this up again over dinner."

With one arm over his friend's shoulder, Cliff and his banker walked out to the deck. The steward closed the door behind them.

Charlie, Angela, and Jack looked at each other in stunned silence. Then Charlie barked, "That's the banker I was talking about! Cliff's money goes into that man's offshore bank and it disappears."

"Do we think he liked the presentation?" Jack asked, sounding tentative. "You guys know him. He seemed positive, didn't he?"

Charlie continued sputtering her frustration. "We know fuck-all. He's a master poker player who plays his cards very close to the vest. He's a bluffer, a faker, and a world-class liar. There's no way to know what he's really thinking until he comes out and tells you. If ever."

"But he seemed to like the presentation?" Jack ventured. "Am I wrong about that?"

Charlie was fuming. "Oh, shut up, Jack. Just shut up!"

The boardroom door opened partially. Douglas stuck his head inside. "Mr. Townsend wants to know if Mr. Price would be interested in joining him and Mr. Beresford on their fishing trip."

Charlie saw Jack looking at her. "Yes, goddammit!" she barked. "He certainly would."

She glared at Jack, waved a finger at him, pointing him toward the door. "He'll be right there. We'll let him go in just a minute." Then she glared at the steward. "You! Go tell my father not to leave without him. Go!" He turned and closed the boardroom door.

Charlie stormed over to Jack and started yelling in his face like a drill sergeant.

"Now listen, Jack. Your job on this little male bonding excursion is to find out everything you can. Everything! And report back to me. You are a spy. *My* spy. You got that, James Bond?"

Jack took a half-step back from her. "Yeah, got it."

Charlie moved forward to put herself back in Jack's face.

"Now, just in case Cliff tries to charm you and make you think he's your buddy, remember this. You work for *me*, understand? *I'm* paying your salary. *I'm* going to decide if you get a bonus. *I'm* going to decide whether or not you get a good reference. Or whether you get fired with nothing in your hand but that sorry dick of yours. Got it?" she sneered. "Buddy?"

She turned to Angela. "Now let's escort James Bond down to his fishing boat." She grabbed Jack's arm and led him out into the sunshine. She put her arm through his, tugging him roughly as they made their way down the three levels to the deck at the waterline, Angela tagging silently behind.

Quietly, through gritted teeth, Charlie muttered to Jack, "Just remember what I told you. I've got you by the short hairs."

As Josef helped Jack into Beresford's small fishing boat, Cliff announced loud enough for all to hear, "No talking business while we're fishing. That's the rule, you understand! Fishing is sacred."

Charlie watched the boat putter away. She was filled with anger and racked with indecision. Was it finally time to use the nuclear option with the old man?

CHAPTER 53

The walkaround cabin fishing boat, about twenty-five feet long, had an open cabin and fishing rods poised and ready on the stern, port, and starboard sides. The pilot and owner, Beresford said, was his brother-in-law Ezekiel. Cliff, Beresford, and Jack were the only guests.

As the boat pulled away from *King of Pawns* and headed out toward the open waters, beyond Silver Point, Cliff stayed in the cabin, joking with Ezekiel.

Beresford gave Jack a little tour of the various types of fishing gear.

"Every time Cliff Townsend comes down here," he explained, "we fish. Going on twenty years now. Of course, Cliff didn't always have a big yacht. Back then, he rented a little Catamaran on his vacations. And Ezekiel had just a twelve-foot open whaler. So many good times we've had together."

Jack hoped he could learn more about Townsend from his long-time friend and banker. "Has Mr. Townsend changed a lot over the years?" he asked.

"Well," Beresford said, taking off his fishing hat and pointing to the gray hair around his temples, "we've all gotten older. But he still seems the same to me. A regular guy. No bullshit. He's just like he was back then. Only more so."

"Really? What part of him is more so?"

Beresford pulled his hat back on. "Oh, that's easy. His generosity. Cliff Townsend is one of the most generous men I've ever known. He was generous when I first knew him, and he didn't have much money. And now, well, now his generosity is even more so. Mr. Townsend has friends all around these islands."

"Like over there?" Jack asked, pointing to the little village clinging to the hill on the leeward side of Silver Point.

Beresford nodded. "That village got destroyed in the hurricane three years ago. Completely leveled. Now look at it."

Jack saw a prosperous-looking community of modest, brightly painted homes with neat yards and gardens, satellite dishes, late-model cars and trucks parked on well-paved roads, a school festooned with colorful outdoor murals and several playgrounds.

"Destroyed?" Jack asked.

"Yes, completely. And you know how little insurance pays after hurricanes."

"Not personally," Jack said, "but I'm sure it doesn't cover much."

Beresford nodded. He looked at Cliff joking around with Ezekiel. "When Cliff Townsend decides to care about people, he really cares. More than most people could ever imagine."

Jack was surprised. All the articles he'd read about Cliff described him as ruthless, tightfisted, and heartless in his pursuit of every nickel he could squeeze out of every deal.

Cliff wandered back to the stern where Jack and Beresford were. Jack thought they all looked a bit silly in their floppy, wide-brimmed fishing hats. On Cliff, Jack thought, the hat defanged his normally fearsome aging-raptor looks.

Cliff leaned into Jack's face. "You ready for some world-class fishing?"

"You bet," Jack said. "Can't wait to get out there and try my luck." He nodded at the open sea beyond Silver Point. He was trying to sound like a seasoned old salt, which he was not.

"Take a good look at these waters," Cliff said to him. "Tonight we're going to take the *King of Pawns* on a little moonlight dinner cruise through this channel and back again to the mooring. A favorite route of mine. I like to sit down on the swim deck at the water's edge and have a cognac or two after dinner. Nothing like it, I'm telling you, nothing. You want to join me?"

"Well, of course," Jack said, "that'd be great."

"You up for a little excitement?" Cliff put his hands over Jack's shoulders and shook him gently. He felt Jack's arms from his biceps to his wrists, then picked up his hands in his. "Make a fist," he said curtly. Jack made two fists. "Now resist me with all your might." Cliff held Jack's arms tightly by the wrists. Jack thought he was doing some kind of inspection of his strength. He tried to show the power he held in his arms.

"Good," Cliff said. He let go of him. "Now, did Charlie tell you that you work for *her?*"

Jack hesitated, unsure of the answer and fearful of potential complications behind it.

"Well, did she?"

"Uh, yes."

Cliff made a sound like a game-show buzzer. "Wrong! You work for me. Everyone on that yacht works for me."

"Uh, sure." Jack tried to get on board with him. "Of course—naturally. We all do."

"Then here's what I want you to do tonight—without letting on to Charlie or Angie or that assistant of hers, or anyone on the crew. Don't tell anyone. Anyone, got that?"

"Yes. Got it. Hundred percent. Got it. What do you want me to do?"

Cliff grinned. "I want you to pick a fight with me. Do you think you can do that?"

"W-w-why would I do that? You're my boss. You're everyone's boss."

"Because I'm your boss and that's what I'm telling you to do. I want to have a little experiment. I want to stage a little—what do they call it?—a little psychodrama. You and I are going to have a knock-down, drag-out fight. I'm going to start it by insulting you. And I want you to insult me back. If we do our psychodrama right, you're going to end up taking a swing at me. And I'll take a swing at you."

Jack was even more confused. "But you're my boss. You just said so. How do you expect me to take a swing at my boss and still keep my job?"

"Because I will fire your ass if you don't. Come on, doesn't every employee secretly want to take a swing at their boss? Back when I had to work for somebody else, I could've—well, never mind."

Jack shrugged okay.

"I'll give you a signal. Let's say when I call you Mr. Madison Avenue, I will start insulting you. Think of a good insult I can hurl at a guy like you. What's the worst thing I could call someone in your business?

310

Jack said, "A hack."

"Okay, I will call you Mr. Madison Avenue and say you're a hack. That's when our free-for-all will begin. Now, what are you going to call me?"

Jack shrugged again. This conversation was getting weird, and dangerous.

"Don't be afraid," Cliff said. "Why don't you start with what everyone already calls me: the King of Sleaze. You could say I fuck over poor people, that I suck their blood, all that stuff. I've heard it all. I can take it. You can talk shit to me. And I'm going to give it right back to you just as good. By the time I go down to the swim deck, we're going to end up duking it out. Like a movie fight."

"But how could a fight like this break out between a billionaire and a lowly freelancer? I mean, we don't even know each other."

"How? Alcohol, that's how! We're both going to be drunk!"

Jack winced. Not alcohol. Please.

Cliff put a fatherly hand on Jack's shoulder. "I heard from Angie that you're on the wagon."

"Yes. I have stopped drinking. Sworn off it. It's really important to me."

"Okay, no problem." Cliff patted him as if to calm him down. "I will make sure that the cocktail you drink has no alcohol in it, I promise. You and I will drink the *King of Pawns* signature cocktail. It's called the Pawn Broker. It's got passionfruit and guava and a bunch of other stuff in it. I'll tell the bartender to make yours nonalcoholic. Don't worry. But you've got to act like you're getting drunk. Think you can you do that?"

"Yes," Jack said. "I can do that. No problem."

"Just don't let the women in on it. If you blow our cover, I really will fire your ass. Right on the spot. You got it?"

"I got it."

Cliff turned to Beresford, who had stood by silently.

"Now, what do you say we go out there and catch some fish?" The old friends high-fived.

Jack pretended he could communicate telepathically with Luke's backpack.

What the fuck? his mind screamed in silence. *What . . . the . . . fuck?*

CHAPTER 54

Charlie watched the fishing boat approach the yacht. She stayed on the second deck as the men disembarked. She watched the crew members taking their catch to be brought to the galley. She watched Cliff and his goddamn banker high-five for the umpteenth time. Then watched the damn boat putter away toward that village on Silver Point.

She was convinced that the village had been rebuilt with drug trafficking money. How else could it have been done so fast? She shuddered to think how Beresford was laundering *her* millions along with drug lord money. She vowed to remove Beresford and his offshore bank from everything that could possibly be connected to the Townsend Foundation. The very day it was established.

She watched Cliff go up to his master suite. She knew it would be naptime for him after a long afternoon out on the water. She watched Jack make his way up to the moonroof suite. She followed him, keeping out of sight, waiting for him to close the door.

Then she burst inside.

"Oh, Jack," she cried, "I am so sorry. So, so, so sorry."

Jack turned around, surprised.

She took his hands in hers. She spoke to him rapid-fire. "I was an ass. An evil woman. A shrew. I'm so sorry I said all those awful things to you. I was crazy, simply crazy, with Cliff blowing us off like that. After all the work we put into that presentation. I mean, that you put into that presentation. And it was great. Really great. You are brilliant—so brilliant!"

She took his face in both of her hands. "I told you that, right? I told you what a genius you are. If I didn't, well, shame on me. I was thinking that the whole time, I swear to you. All I could think of was, What a genius Jack Price is. You will forgive me, won't you? I didn't mean any of it, not one word. That was my anger talking. My madness, my years of frustration and shame. It wasn't me talking. Do you understand? Do you? You beautiful hunk of manhood. I want you to forgive me. I need you to forgive me. Please, Jack, please."

She fumbled with his belt, undid it, along with his button and fly, and yanked his shorts down. She dropped to her knees and started sucking him. "Jack. Darling," she muttered with her mouth full of him. She remembered all the techniques Angela had told her about. She tried them one by one, thinking, if I had two mouths to work on him, I could do them all at once.

He was getting hard. Excellent! She yanked off her linen blouse and bra and stepped out of her shorts and panties. Then got him naked. And pushed him across the room to the giant bed.

When they fell onto the bed, she started kissing his mouth and using her hand on his penis. She climbed over him and rubbed herself against him in long strokes.

314

"Do you want to eat me before we fuck?" she asked in his ear. "You don't have to. I'm just asking what you want. Whatever *you* want. Just tell me what you want and how you want it."

She had gotten him hard. He wasn't resisting her. He hadn't thrown her out of his bed. He was even getting a little hot in his kisses and the way he touched her. She had gotten him all-systems-go as far as she was concerned.

"Do you like cowgirl?" she asked, panting. "We don't have to do cowgirl just because we did it last time. You like doggie better? Or missionary? Just tell me. I'm up for anything. What gives *you* the most pleasure?"

"Cowgirl's nice," he said softly. "I like to watch you come."

"I will, Jack, I will," she said. "You make me come. It's you, it's all you."

She moved into place, straddling and sliding him inside her. She started grinding against him. Then stuck her right index finger in his mouth to get it wet. Then began using it to manually stimulate herself. Back and forth between his mouth and her pussy. Again and again. She knew he liked the taste. She also knew she was not going to come. She was trying too hard. Fortunately she was still lubricating. But no orgasm, no way. He was still hard inside her. She did her Kegel squeezes. He seemed to respond with more excitement.

Fake it, she decided. Just fake it.

She began her simulated orgasm. Her breathing. Her head rocking. Her hip grinding. Her panting. She thought that if she rocked him inside her in just the right way she could make him come and convince him that they were coming together. The ultimate. She could really make hay with a simultaneous orgasm to flatter him and his manhood—and get what she wanted out of him.

315

After a few minutes of more grinding and bouncing, they were both finished. Jack with his actual ejaculation inside her. She with her fake climax on top of him.

She fell down beside him and took him in her arms.

Breaking up her sentences with deep tongue kisses, she wrapped both legs around him and began to question him.

"What did you learn?" she asked, with the coquettish up-speak accent of a teenage girl. "On your fishing excursion?"

Jack sighed. "Nada. Absolutely nada. You heard what he said about no business talk while fishing."

"But what did you boys talk about?"

"Fishing." He gave her kisses that felt like consolation kisses. "Just fishing. End of story. Honest."

She tried and tried. All the way through another blow job and a quick missionary penetration. All to no avail.

"You mean you really can't tell your best girl anything more?" she asked, in her final plea.

"I've already told you everything. Honest." Kisses and strokes. Strokes and kisses. "Honest."

She climbed on top of him one last time, sitting down to press her wet lady parts against his belly. She knew he really liked those sensations.

"Honest," he said as he slid out from underneath her. "Cliff told all of us he'd give us his answer at dinner tonight. I heard what you heard. That's all I know."

She got off the bed, lifted her clothes off the floor, put them on sloppily, and walked out.

She could murder Jack Price with her bare hands. That lying fuck. Maybe someday she would.

CHAPTER 55

Angela was on the very small deck atop the pilothouse, the highest vantage point on the yacht. She watched Charlie below as she stomped out of Jack's stateroom. Her hair was a mess, her clothes even worse. Charlie had been in there almost forty minutes. Enough time to—well, Angela didn't want to think about what Charlie and Jack might have been doing. She needed to keep a clear head about her interest in Jack Price.

She walked down to Jack's deck. Stood outside his stateroom. Put her ear to the door. She heard the sound of the shower. She walked inside and went straight to the bathroom.

The combination shower/steam room was billowing clouds everywhere. Jack was a smudgy shadow moving behind the thick glass doors and the dense mist.

Angela took the towel he had placed near the shower door and walked to the far side of the bathroom. She hoisted herself up and sat on the marble countertop, just waiting.

Finally, the water and steam stopped. Jack's hand emerged from behind the glass door, feeling around for the towel he had left. The towel was not there. Jack's hand reached out farther. Confused. Then Jack stepped out into the bathroom. Dripping wet. Naked. His body looked the same as she remembered.

Jack looked at her. Then down at his nakedness. "Je-sus, Angela," he said.

She held the towel up in the air. She did not move from the countertop. A part of her was hoping he might get hard for her the way he once did. He did not.

"Oh, please," she said dismissively, doing her best to show she was not noticing anything. "If you want your towel, tell me about your male bonding experience. I need the scoop. The whole scoop."

He grabbed the towel and wrapped it around his waist.

"You heard what Cliff said," Jack snapped at her. He took out another towel and began drying his hair, then his chest. "He said no business talk. We didn't talk any business. Just fishing." He was poking the second towel in his ear. "And you know how passionate I am about fishing." He opened his medicine cabinet and began applying his stick deodorant. She noticed it was the same brand he used to take with him on their hotel trysts five years before.

"Yeah, right," she said sarcastically, "your lifelong passion for fishing."

She followed him as he walked out of the bathroom. She made sure to steer clear of the messy unmade bed. She stood, leaning against a far wall. He kept his back to her as he slipped on under-shorts and a T-shirt. He walked to the closet, extracted a pair of

318

Bermuda shorts and a fresh linen shirt, and began to dress, not looking at her, as if she were not there.

"Cliff must have told you guys *something*," she said to his back.

Again, part of her was disappointed that he could be naked in front of her and show not even a hint of desire. After all, it wasn't long ago that they could hardly keep their hands off each other when they were near a bed.

She soldiered on with her business agenda, telling herself to ignore her injured vanity.

"Come on, Jack. Cliff seemed to like your pitch. What did he say?"

He turned around and faced her. "Nothing. Absolutely nothing." She watched him gazing around the room, looking for something. He walked over to the heap of clothes on the floor. He picked up the shorts, extracted the belt, dropped them back onto the floor, and began to thread his belt through the loops.

"Charlie said you were supposed to be her spy—her James Bond. You agreed, right?" She watched him closely for a reaction, any reaction. He showed none. Just the motions of getting dressed. "Come on, Jack, we're all in this together. Out with it."

He put his hands on his hips. He seemed about to explode.

"What do *you* care? The foundation is Charlie's problem. Even more important, it's *my* problem. If he doesn't buy my pitch, I'm totally fucked. If I can't get the old man to set up this stupid foundation, I've got nothing to show for my efforts. And I'm right back where I was that night outside Vlad's. Nobody but nobody is going to hire me for anything. That's what I'm worried about, thank you very much."

He walked back to the pile of clothes on the floor, picked them up, and brought them to the hamper in the closet.

"Please, Jack—I'm way over my head here."

Jack had taught her that, when all else fails, paint yourself as desperate and throw yourself on the mercy of the other guy. She was appealing to the power he once had as her mentor, but this time she wasn't acting; she really was desperate for his advice.

"Jack, I really need your help. They didn't teach us about prenups and trust funds in the projects. Cliff's got a fucking army of lawyers I'm supposed to deal with. And Charlie, she's crazy jealous about Cliff's estate and that banker you went fishing with. One minute she's my BFF, the next minute she's like that girl in *The Exorcist* whose head spins around—without the pea soup vomit. I'm a stranger in this world here, just like you. There must be *something* you can tell me about what Cliff is planning. Something? Anything? I helped you, Jack. Come on, can't you help me just a little?"

He stormed across the room.

"Forgive me if I'm a little short on sympathy for you." He was angry, very angry. "Let me be the first to congratulate you, Angela Hanson. You've finally made it. What you've got are rich people problems. Like whether you'll be crazy-ass rich or only a little bit rich. I mean, you *are* going to accept the old man's proposal and marry him, right?"

She nodded. "And once I'm his wife, I'll be able to help you. Be your ally." She hoped he could see that she meant this. That she really was telling the truth. Her pleading was real. "Jack, I need to know what you know, right now. Please, Jack, please!"

He grabbed her by the shoulders. "I told you, goddammit! I don't know what he's got up his sleeve." He stared into her eyes. Unblinking. The way he'd once taught her. She couldn't tell if he was lying or not. "Look at me, Angela! Look deep inside of me. I know nothing. Absolutely nothing. Honest."

He shook her for a second. Roughly. Then let her go. Stepped back from her, visibly scared, she thought, by what he'd almost done. "Uh, sorry," he said, looking down.

"All right, all right, I believe you," she said, thinking maybe she did. "See you at dinner."

He seemed stronger than he was the day before.

Maybe he was telling the truth. Or maybe not. Maybe he had recovered some of his strength—along with the lying skills he'd taught her.

CHAPTER 56

After texting Sandra and getting the usual reply, Jack put his phone in his pocket and walked to the alfresco deck and took his place at the table. The night sky glittered with a million stars. He sat across from Cliff, Charlie, and Angela. The women sat on either side of Cliff. Jack looked at the empty chair beside him. "Where's Eric?" he asked.

"Yeah, Angie," Cliff said, "where's your little English buddy?"

"He's gone over to St. John's," Angela said. "Looking for some nightlife."

"Well, I hope he gets lucky," Cliff said cheerfully. He appeared to be in a jaunty mood.

He turned to Charlie. "And what are my ladies drinking tonight?"

Charlie waved her crystal goblet high in the air. "Badoit and lime for me," she announced for Sally's benefit. "Maybe later, a little champagne. Depending."

"Same for me," Angela said, looking over her shoulder to where Sally was already scurrying over with the green bottle of French mineral water.

"Well, Badoit is fine," Cliff said, "but my new fishing buddy and I are going to drink Pawn Brokers." He waved at the bartender. Then whispered to Angela, "That's our signature drink on board here. Created especially for us by, uh, some mixologist guy who used to work here. It's delicious." The bartender put Cliff's frosty red cocktail in front of him and walked around the table to give Jack his.

Cliff raised his glass to Jack. "Here's to fishing."

Jack raised his Pawn Broker. "To fishing."

The two men took their first sips simultaneously.

Jack liked the taste. It was very dense with fruit pulp. More viscous than liquid. With overpowering tropical fruit flavors. The cloying sweetness of guava, the tart bite of passionfruit. Cliff had promised him there would be no alcohol in his cocktail. He couldn't detect that familiar alcohol sting, but with all the intense fruitiness, who could tell?

He raised his glass to Cliff again.

Cliff raised his glass and gave him a little wink.

Did he trust the old guy's promise? Hah, what a question. Maybe. Sort of. Or maybe not. Oh shit, who knew? Jack took another sip. Alcohol or no, this much was true—the drink was absolutely delicious. Jack was thirsty. And hungry. And full of anxiety. He downed his first Pawn Broker. Cliff nodded to him and downed his.

Cliff ordered another round for the men. And soon after, another.

For a good twenty minutes, the dinner-table conversation skirted around the topic on everyone's mind.

Jack was starting to relax. Maybe there was just a touch of alcohol in the drink. Or maybe he was just feeling a bit of confidence. After all, he and Cliff had a secret plan. The women had no clue; he finally had something to lord over both of them. And he would get to pretend to deck the old man. This dinner was about to become more enjoyable.

Finally, Cliff spoke up.

"Why the hell is everyone afraid to talk about what they really want to talk about? You all want to know my decision." He looked around the table. Silence—100 percent attention. It was clear to Jack that Cliff was enjoying keeping everyone on tenterhooks.

"Well, I'll get to it in a bit," he said with a smile.

He motioned for another round of Pawn Brokers for himself and Jack.

Cliff leaned back in his chair. "You know, right now," he said, slurring a bit, drawing out every word extra slowly, "my whole estate is up in the air. If I were to drop dead right here at this table, do you realize that I would die intestate?"

He chuckled. A hiccup slipped out.

"You know what *intestate* means? When I first heard the word, I thought it was some kind of medical condition—you know, in a man's balls. But no. It actually means not having a will." Playfully, he put a finger over his lips. "Shhh. Don't let my lawyers know that I told you. I was supposed to keep that a secret. If I die intestate, you guys would have to duke it out with the lawyers and the courts. Funny thought, no? You guys fighting over how to split up my billions."

Charlie was visibly upset. "I didn't know that."

Angela looked down at her plate.

"Don't worry, my dear dependents," Cliff said reassuringly. "I'll be signing my new will in a couple of days. Flying the lawyers down here special to do it. I'll have all my money organized and businesslike. But here's what's more important: I've got a lot more living to do."

Jack watched with amusement as Charlie and Angela jumped all over Cliff, making goo-goo talk about him never dying, living forever. How they couldn't go on without him. He seemed to enjoy their bull-shit. He winked at Jack a couple of times as they slobbered over him.

The steaks arrived. Cliff went silent, except for the abundant noises he made chewing and slurping up the juices.

For a while, no one else took a bite. They just watched Cliff. And listened.

Finally, he noticed. He looked up from his plate.

"Come on, you guys, let's eat up. This is great steak. If you're not hungry, just pass yours over to me." He dove back in with gusto.

Jack started cutting his steak. Angela followed suit. Charlie just picked up an asparagus spear and nibbled on it.

With a big sigh of satisfaction, Cliff finished his last bite and, with a big clang, dropped his fork and knife onto his plate.

"Okay," he announced. "I'll tell you what I've decided."

All the other forks and knives dropped. The table went silent.

Jack nervously downed the last bit of his Pawn Broker.

Cliff nodded approvingly and downed his. Then motioned for two refills.

A part of Jack hoped there was alcohol in his next glass, if there hadn't been before.

Cliff leaned back in his chair. He seemed like he was getting ready to philosophize, not reveal a simple yes-or-no decision.

"You know, there are days when I look at how rich I've gotten, and I have to pinch myself. I can hardly believe it. Me? When I look in the mirror, I have no illusions. I've got the face of a mule skinner and the manners to match. Only good part is this: All my life people have underestimated me. And I've always said, 'Go ahead, underestimate me. Just you go ahead.' Made it work for me. Time after time. Nobody expected a lug like me to have the moves I ended up having. But I did. And here I am, sitting on four billion dollars."

Charlie tapped him on the arm. "I'm pretty sure it's five, Dad."

Jack thought this was the first time he'd heard her call him "Dad."

"Actually, my dear daughter, it's 5.3 billion and change, as of today's market close. But who's counting?"

Cliff raised his drink to Jack. Winked at him again. Jack raised his drink in return.

"Here's to more money than anybody can spend," Cliff said. "More money than anybody deserves." He downed his Pawn Broker. Jack followed his lead.

Cliff kept rambling on.

By now, Jack knew damn well that the old man had lied. There had been alcohol in every one of his Pawn Brokers. Lots. Just masked in tropical nectars. He knew the sensation oh so well. The way it crept up imperceptibly, then hit you all at once. It felt so fucking good. This was his one and only slip off the wagon, and he'd been tricked, so he wasn't responsible. No points against him—this time. Besides, he was feeling . . . just fine. No, better than fine.

He looked across the table at the two women who had fucked him and fucked with him. He looked at Cliff, the Big Liar, who kept droning on. He felt the urge to jump over the railing behind him and swim the fuck away from all this. But he knew better.

Besides, he was waiting for his cue to take a swing at Old Man Townsend. His official, top-secret job. Yes, the evening was about to get more interesting.

Cliff cleared his throat.

"I'll tell you what I learned running a pawn shop. Everybody with something they need to hock walks in thinking of the deal they want, the deal they deserve. But guess what? It's not the deal they get. They walk out with the deal I give them. End of story. They learn to learn to live with it.

"If you guys think I'm going to reallocate all my assets so I can give them away to strangers and pretend to change the world, you're wrong. I'll play nice. I'll tell you guys you did a great job trying. But I'm not buying it."

Cliff stood up.

"Here are my decisions. No foundation for Charlie. It's the wrong thing to do for her, and for the world of philanthropy. You might as well know the score: I give my money away in secret. And lots of it. Have done for years. And I plan to continue doing so long after I'm gone. No credit, no naming opportunities. Ask my banker, Mr. Beresford. He's my agent. That's my version of a Townsend Foundation.

"I'm not against charity, mind you. But in the pawn shop I learned that if you help someone with a handout, you don't tell the world about it. It's not good for the person in need. It's embarrassing. And it makes other people think you're a soft touch. Far as I'm concerned, what are all those names carved on buildings? A lot of ego bullshit. Just another form of greed. I may be a bootstrap boor, but in my book, plastering your name all over is, well . . ."—he paused and put on a pretentious accent with a very broad "a"—"in exceptionally baaad taste."

He turned to Angela.

"Next up, no wedding for me and Angela. It's the wrong thing for Angela. Sure, I'd like to have her in my bed every night. Sure, I'd like her to stay with me to push my wheelchair around and wipe the dribble off my chin and even give me an occasional tickle down there, if my heart can stand it. But she deserves better. She's strong and independent, already making it on her own just fine.

She's exactly what a young modern woman should be. She shouldn't waste her youth and beauty on a saggy-ass old fart like me."

He looked across the table.

"And Jack? Mr. Madison Avenue? That's right—I'm talking to you, Mr. Madison Avenue!"

Jack got his cue. Twice, no less. Now it begins, he thought. With the buzz he was feeling, he was up for it. Oh, was he ever!

"Well, Jack, here, he gets fired. Fired, you hear? My lawyers are going to figure out a breach of contract. All he gets is a kill fee of one dollar for all his services."

Cliff reached into his pocket, pulled out a dollar bill, and flung it at Jack.

"Oh, and before I forget, a coach ticket home tomorrow. Middle seat!"

He stepped away from the table and headed for the stairway.

"Now I'm going down to have my cognac and look at the stars from my favorite spot in the whole world. Down on the swim deck. Who wants to join me?"

Jack was stunned.

And confused.

And drunk.

This was *not* the deal.

CHAPTER 57

Jack heard Charlie's shrill voice piercing through his alcohol haze. She was hollering about what was hers. What she wanted, what she deserved, what she was entitled to. Hollering at Angela, calling her a gold-digging sex worker. Hollering at Jack, calling him a useless piece of shit.

He tuned her out. It was just noise. She was just noise. Static.

He saw Angela just sitting there in silence, looking down at her lap.

He thought, Now I'm supposed to go down to the swim deck and duke it out with the old man. But before I go, let me give these women a piece of my mind.

He stood up. Or tried to. He found himself back in his chair. He felt the boat rocking and swaying. That *was* the boat, wasn't it? Maybe it was a combination of him rocking and the boat rocking.

He tried to get up again. This time very slowly, holding on to the arms of the chair like a very old man.

Jack heard himself start yelling. "That fucker! He lied to me. He spiked my drinks. He wasn't supposed to fire me like that. Fucking liar. I oughta kill the lying fuck. Kill him!"

His words sounded distant, as if it were somebody else talking. He wondered, why was that? Then it hit him. Because it *was* somebody else. It was that *other* guy. That drunk guy. Yeah, him. He could hear the drunk guy yelling, slurring his words, see him listing from side to side. Boy, was that guy wasted.

He saw the guy turn to Angela. How could she have tricked him into this snake pit? Why? What the fuck was she doing? What did she fucking want from him? He screamed that she had ruined his life. Not just once, but twice. Fucking *twice!*

Then he went after Charlie. How could Charlie have used him so badly? Literally fucked him over! Now he's left with nothing. Nothing!

And who the fuck does Cliff think he is, anyway? That lying son of a bitch. He was going to give Cliff Townsend exactly what he had coming to him.

Stumbling together, Jack and the drunk guy somehow found their way down to the swim deck. It took the two of them to do it. In a moment like this, two selves were better than one. Fuck me and the drunk guy, Jack thought. That guy, yeah, he's my superpower.

At the swim deck, Jack found Cliff in his chair by the water's edge, a plastic cognac snifter in hand. Jack and the drunk guy were totally confused. What about the charade? The psychodrama? Cliff's promise not to put booze in his drinks? Was their deal still on? If it was still on, Jack and the drunk guy had better go back to the script.

Drunk guy screamed at Cliff that he was the King of Sleaze. A swindler who had made his money gouging poor people. A parasite, a scumbag predator, a cannibal! And a fucking liar!

Cliff stood up. Drunk guy and Jack weren't the only wobbly ones on the swim deck. Cliff seemed to wobble, too. Everybody was lit.

"Oh, yeah?" Cliff shouted. "You're a has-been flimflam man who's too goddamn old to get work anymore. You were done years ago and didn't even know it. You couldn't sell ice water in the Sahara. Why? Because you are a hack. A *hack!*"

Jack, the drunk guy, and Cliff started exchanging punches. It was all a blur.

Jack felt himself land a punch to Cliff's face.

Jack felt one punch hit his gut, then two to his head.

Jack and the drunk guy tasted blood. Their fists hurt like hell.

Suddenly Jack and the drunk guy got smashed in the face. By the swim deck.

Big pain, much blood.

That was the last thing they remembered.

CHAPTER 58

Angela was trying to think as fast as she could, frantically remembering what Jack Price had taught her. There were times when you should watch carefully and take time to consider. There were other times when you had to act, and act instantly. In this crazy moment, she knew she had to figure out a way to do both.

She considered her next steps. She had not yet quit her job. She could go back to London, back to work, and look for her next opportunity, whatever that turned out to be. After all, she was no worse off than she'd been when she first met Charlie and decided to get her hooks into her. And she had learned so much from these awful people.

She knew this was a moment to be careful. Everything was happening too fast. She did not want to get into this family fight until she could calculate her next—and best—move.

She could not get Charlie to stop screaming and focus.

Then, shit! She saw Eric out of the corner of her eye. He was walking down the deck toward them. He waved hello cheerfully. Not now! Oh, Jesus, not now!

She turned away from Charlie and waved one hand behind her back. Frantically waving Eric away. Not now, please, not now! She glanced backward. He was walking away, vanishing down the long deck. He had seen her signal. Close call. She turned back to Charlie.

Charlie started shouting that she was going to the swim deck to tell Cliff something she'd been waiting to tell him for a long time.

Angela played dumb. She knew this must be the letter from Julia Townsend.

"What's that, Charlie?" she asked. "What do you want to tell Cliff?" She tried to hug Charlie protectively, the way a good little sister would.

Charlie yanked herself free. "Come and see," she huffed, and headed for the stairway.

When they got down to the swim deck, Jack was passed out in a pool of blood. Cliff stood above him, bloodied and a little shaky. Someone had turned the stereo up very loud.

"You bastard!" Charlie screamed in his face, and started throwing wild punches at him.

Angela stood back. Just watch, she told herself. Just watch and evaluate the situation.

Cliff, taller and stronger, grabbed hold of Charlie's wrists and kept her punches at bay.

"Charlie, Charlie," he said, "I have given you too much. Spoiled you rotten. I can't give you a foundation. I have given you enough. More than enough. You need to grow up and get a life. I should have done this years ago."

Charlie screamed that she was finally going to do it. Finally!

"Do what? Cliff asked, holding her arms far apart.

"Expose your crime," she said. She started crying. "The murder you committed. The murder you confessed to when Mommy was on her deathbed."

Cliff gave her a concerned look. "What on earth are you talking about, Charlie?" He suddenly sounded kind, concerned for Charlie's well-being.

"You know goddamn well," she sneered. "The letter, the law firm, the Dictaphone recording Mommy made in her hospital bed. She hid it under the covers, the little thingy, the, the, Dictamite. She told me never to use this unless I was desperate, really and truly desperate. Well, now I am. And I'm going to contact the law firm that's been holding it for safekeeping all these years."

She stopped trying to punch him. Let her arms fall. Cliff held onto her wrists just the same. She sniffed, "The lawyers will release the recording of you admitting to Mom that you murdered Michael de Furia—my real father! You murdered him that night. You forced him off the road and into the tree. You paid off the Westchester police to get them to say it was an accident. But you murdered him—you did, you did! There's no statute of limitations on murder in New York. Mommy and I will expose your crime. Your own confession! Your own words! Think you can say no to me? Huh? Not now. Not ever again."

Cliff stood still. He shook his head sadly. He let go of one wrist. Reached out and touched Charlie's cheek in a gesture of tenderness.

She yanked her arm away from him, trembling, Angela thought, from the awful revelation she had finally made after thirty years of holding back its awful power.

"Charlie, Charlie, Charlie," he said softly, "the things you don't know."

"Oh yeah? I know everything. *Everything!*"

Cliff sighed. "Charlie, as your mother lay dying, she dictated a lot of letters like the one you're talking about. The cancer had metastasized. It was attacking her everywhere. Including her brain. It's what happens in the final stages. She was deluded, demented—imagining all sorts of crazy things."

He went to touch her cheek again. Again, she recoiled.

"Charlie, it's true that I'm not your biological father. I've been sterile my whole life. Your mom and I didn't know that until after we got married. But we both wanted a baby. You. And yes, Michael de Furia was a man she loved before she met me. But he was not your father. We got your mom pregnant from an anonymous donor at a sperm bank. We only had the most basic amount of information about the donor—a strong, healthy Caucasian with no known diseases or bad conditions. That's how sperm banks worked in those days. There was no dramatic encounter at the house. No car chases. No fatal crash. Michael de Furia was long gone at the time you were conceived. He'd moved out west somewhere, no one knows where, or what happened to him."

"Oh yeah?" Charlie howled.

"I'm afraid so," Cliff said with flat calm. "There was no Dictaphone, no Dictamite. There never was."

Yet Angela knew that Julia Townsend *had* owned a Dictamite. She'd seen the user's manual next to her draft of the blackmail letter.

"The lawyers," Charlie said. "Mom's lawyers. Just you wait!"

Cliff shook his head sadly. "Charlie, do you have any idea how many law firms I keep on retainer? Do you really think your poor dying mother would have been able to hire a law firm without my knowing about it? Without my help?"

Charlie was starting to quiet down.

"It was all a delusion of her last dying days. So sad. I've given you everything because your mother made me promise to. And I've kept my word to her. She's the only woman I've ever really loved, the only true wife I've ever had."

Behind his glasses, Cliff's eyes filled with tears. He reached for Charlie's hand. This time, she let him take it. "Believe me, Charlie. Everything I'm telling you is the truth. The God's honest truth."

Charlie stood still, letting Cliff hold her hand.

Angela watched carefully. She saw what was happening! Cliff was lying to Charlie about everything. Absolutely everything. He must have bought the venal lawyers. Was Angela surprised that the sacred trust of the lawyers was for sale? No way. He must have paid them off and destroyed all the evidence. He had *bought* his innocence. His money had the power to change the facts and cover up the worst crime a human being can commit. And he was lying with complete conviction to Charlie. What a performance, she thought. Tears and all.

Angela stood frozen, peeling through the layers of deception between father and daughter. Angela knew how to lie, but this was a whole new level of skill. She thought of what Cliff had said a few minutes before at the table. She, like so many others, had underestimated him.

She could learn from this man.

OMG, could she learn from him! Even if he refused to marry her, she could still learn from him.

The game was not over yet—at least, she hoped not.

"Charlie, believe me," Cliff went on. Angela studied him, admiring his technique. "I indulged you out of love. Not fear. Love for your mother, for the promises she asked of me before her brain went batty and the cancer killed her. Accept my decision. It's made

339

out of love. I've spoiled you. Your mother and I spoiled you. There it is. You'll see the wisdom of it in time."

Suddenly, Charlie began hitting him, more violently than before. He held her wrists, but she got one hand free. She grabbed his eyeglasses, threw them onto the deck, and smashed them under her heel. Cliff was momentarily disoriented. He let go of her other wrist and tried to focus.

Then, in one furious motion, Charlie shoved him into the water. The yacht was moving. Moving away from him. He was thrashing about in the water.

He had to be more than a little drunk after all those Pawn Brokers, Angela thought. The yacht was moving away from him. The stereo was covering his cries for help.

Charlie stood for an instant, watching him. Then she stormed away, right past Angela. As if she were not even there.

Angela struggled with the frenzy of calculations flooding her brain. One way or the other, I can learn from this man. Even if he won't marry me. Maybe he's testing us. All of us. Everybody wants unconditional love, everybody. I can give him unconditional love. Or something that looks like it. Who knows when I'll get this close to a billionaire again?

She jumped into the water and started to swim toward him.

She thought she heard him whimpering and splashing in the darkness.

She struggled in the blackness. She was not a strong swimmer. The water was cold, colder than she thought it would be. She started kicking furiously. Water got into her mouth. Her legs started to cramp. She was swallowing more water. Gagging. She was starting to sink.

Suddenly an arm reached under her and wrapped across her chest. Pulled her up to the surface. As she retched and gasped for air, a man pulled her through the chill water back toward the yacht.

It was Eric.

CHAPTER 59

Jack felt a foot nudging him in the ribs. Where was he? Why was he lying flat on his face? How did he get here? His face felt broken. His right hand stung. He could hardly see through the slits he had for eyes. He was flat against wooden deck planking. He heard water sloshing nearby.

The foot nudged him again. Harder this time. Turned him over onto his back. The sky above was black and starry. Floodlights hurt his eyes. He suddenly realized he was on the swim deck. How did he get here? The last thing he remembered was people yelling at the dinner table. If that really was what he remembered. He wasn't sure.

He could see people standing over him. Charlie. Angela. Eric. Josef, and some fellow deckhands.

Charlie held smashed eyeglasses in her hand. She was shouting. "These are Cliff's! Cliff's glasses!" She squatted down and yelled in Jack's face. Her stale breath made him nauseous. "What did you do to him? He never goes anywhere without his glasses. Where is he? What did you do to my father?"

She stood. "Hold him right there, Josef!"

Josef and his buddy grabbed Jack and yanked him to his feet. Held his arms behind his back.

"You were the last person to see Cliff alive. You must have punched him out and knocked him overboard. You must have. Do you remember what you did? You threatened to kill him. Everyone heard you. You threatened him. I heard you were an angry drunk. We all know about your history of violence when you're drunk."

She turned to Angela. Angela looked down. "Isn't that right, Angela? Right? He gets violent when he's drunk." She grabbed Angela by the chin. "Isn't that right? Come on, you're going to have to tell the police. He gets violent when he's drunk, right?"

Jack was alert, if a bit shaky. His head ached with his hangover and his confusion about what was happening. He watched Angela carefully.

Charlie gave Angela's head a yank. "Out with it, girl!" she screamed, "out with it!"

"Yes," Angela whimpered, "he can be violent when he drinks. He can, er, uh, sometimes."

Charlie let go of Angela's jaw and again waved the eyeglasses in front of Jack. "He never goes anywhere without these. Ever! The old man's seventy-five, for God's sake!"

Josef and his goon friend grabbed Jack's arms even tighter.

"I'm calling the police," she announced, taking her phone from her shoulder-strap handbag. She turned her back to the group but blasted her side of the call like a public announcement.

She bellowed that Clifford Townsend was missing from his yacht. Yes, *the* Clifford Townsend. She played her imperial highness, the billionaire's daughter, to its fullest. The grieving, panicky billion-aire's daughter. This was an international crisis happening right here. She was demanding a search of all the waters. Everywhere! Yes—choking up—assumed dead. His smashed glasses left behind. No, he never goes anywhere without his glasses. Bloodstains on the deck. Blood on the broken hands of the last person who saw Cliff alive. Jack Price.

Jack Price, a drunk with a history of violence. Just a half-hour ago he was threatening to kill Cliff. Everyone heard him. He was the last person anyone saw with Cliff. Someone must have beaten him up and thrown him overboard. Tears, hysterics. Who else could it be? My father, my poor father!

She listened, sobbing and nodding from time to time. Then hung up.

She turned to Josef. "The police are on their way. Hold him right here, Josef. They will take him into custody and bring him over to St. John's."

Jack, now awake enough to know he could not remember what had happened.

Just a haze of anger and confusion.

He wondered, Could I have done it? I don't think I did. I can't imagine that I would. But—and that "but" ran over him like a freight train—I was so damn drunk.

I have no way of knowing.

CHAPTER 60

Angela, Charlie, and Eric were having coffee on the alfresco deck, huddled under the shade of the big umbrella. The late-morning sun was a blinding furnace. There were empty chairs where Cliff and Jack had sat the night before.

Everyone stared deep inside their coffee cups. No one spoke.

Angela had had no sleep. She assumed no one else had, either.

How could *anyone* have slept?

In the space of those few minutes of madness last night, everything had exploded.

Cliff had surely died. Angela herself had nearly died. And afterward, she had lied with her silence while Charlie had Jack sent to prison, and likely the gallows, for the crime that Angela witnessed *Charlie* commit. To boot, she had lost her shot at joining the Billionaire Wives Club. It was back to London and her life as a salary slave, a bitter disappointment.

She had paced around Cliff's master suite all alone for hours, creeped out by the old man's empty space on the giant bed. She could not sit down for more than a few seconds at a time. She was haunted by the ghosts of drowned Cliff and soon-to-be-hanged Jack. Their blood was on her hands, their deaths on her conscience forever. She got her first waking taste of the nightmares she knew would torment her for the rest of her life.

At the same time, she wasn't dead. She owed her life to Eric. Her Eric. Her kid brother, her devoted amanuensis, her sidekick, and so much more. How could she ever pay him back?

She tormented herself with *Why*. Why had she lied to the police with her silence? Why had she not screamed the truth in the face of Charlie's blatant lie? Why had she done nothing to save Jack? Nothing? Why? *Why?*

The best she could tell herself was that, like Jack, she, too, was a prisoner. A prisoner on Charlie's yacht where Charlie's money made the rules. How could she have challenged Charlotte Townsend when the local cops showed the billionaire's daughter so much deference? The crew members backed up the boss's daughter by verifying that they had heard Jack's threats of murder.

No one had seen the actual crime. The only two eyewitnesses were Angela and Charlie. Charlie was so fanatical about her accusation, she had not dared to speak. Who would they believe? Surely not the nobody who had mooched her way on board *King of Pawns*? She was the ruthless gold-digger who had just been publicly dumped by Cliff. Talk about a murder motive. No, Angela kept silent and backed up Charlie. She was afraid—afraid because she really *was* innocent, and afraid that, in a panic, Charlie might accuse her as well.

As soon as the police had left with Jack in handcuffs, Angela saw Charlie transform. She dropped the grieving-daughter histrionics and became the empress. Haughty, cold, imperious, and clearly preparing herself to preside over Cliff's immense fortune, she had ordered everyone back to their rooms.

For the rest of the night, Angela kept telling herself, Somehow, I'll find a way to rescue Jack. Yes, I *will* find a way, she repeated over and over until the sun finally rose.

She really did hope she would find a way once things began to sort themselves out. Although how that would ever happen, she had no clue.

The uneasy silence at the breakfast table was shattered by the ringtone of Charlie's phone, the cool driving instrumental intro to a Drake song. Its hip urban sound was especially jarring in this uncomfortable moment.

She reached down into the Louis Vuitton carryall at her feet.

"This is Charlotte Townsend," she said, with icy formality. She listened to the caller and, at first, did not show any reaction. Then her face seemed to get more and more serious as she heard more.

Charlie rang off and dropped the phone back into her bag. She paused and took a deep breath. "Well, it seems they have found a body," she announced.

Angela stared at her, looking for some kind of direction, a reaction to guide her own.

Charlie looked away.

Angela felt another wave of panic rising inside her. She was Charlie's star witness who had turned Charlie's lie into the truth. She was worried that things might get out of control. But she could not let herself do anything in haste. That would absolutely lead to serious mistakes.

She summoned up one of Jack Price's life lessons: Sometimes, when you know you can't control things, the best thing to do is sit back and do nothing. Just see what the universe has in store for you.

Angela took slow, deep breaths, hoping her face revealed nothing. Charlie talked at the horizon with a flat, robotic affect.

"They are bringing the body here for us to identify before they take it to the morgue in St. John's." Charlie's manner did not invite comments or questions.

Angela gave Eric a covert little no-no nod of the head to make sure he kept his mouth shut. He lowered his eyelids to let her know he got the message.

The table fell into silence again. Nobody looked at anybody else.

A few minutes later, they heard a motorboat approaching.

"Should we go down to meet it?" Eric asked, trying to sound helpful.

Angela kicked him under the table. He looked at her. She glared. He looked down.

"No," Charlie said. "The officer told me he would come up here to meet us first."

Soon there were noisy footsteps on the stairway. Several people climbing together. Then, a familiar voice boomed, "Can you identify *this* body?"

Cliff Townsend stepped onto the deck. He looked fine. Fresh clothes. Well-groomed. Big eyeglasses in perfect condition. Except for a small bruise on his right cheek, just like nothing had happened.

Angela held her breath. She was dumbstruck. There was literally nothing she could do except sit there and gape at what the universe had brought her.

All she could do was ask herself, Do I dare believe my luck?

"Hello, Charlie, my dear loving girl," Cliff said with angry, ironic affection.

Charlie sat frozen and silent. Mouth open, no sound able to come out.

Angela sat watching, perfectly still, closemouthed and wide-eyed.

Cliff smiled at the men who had come up the stairs with him. Two cops, Beresford and the man who had piloted the fishing boat the day before. "Thank you for your help, gentlemen. And Charlie, in case you're wondering, I had a change of clothes waiting for me with my friends in the village on Silver Point."

He turned to Beresford. "Please thank Mrs. Jenkins again for her hospitality. My good night's rest was just what the doctor ordered." He turned back to Charlie. "As for you, I needed to see just how far you would go to get at my money."

"D-d-d-a—" Charlie tried to speak.

"Not a word, Charlie," he barked at her. "Not one word out of you. I've got better lawyers and more of them and deeper pockets and more patience and more friends in high places than you can imagine. So just keep your mouth shut and listen to me for the last time. Believe me, this is the last time."

Charlie looked away. She bit her lower lip shut.

"I was born poor," Cliff said, "and I felt poor for a long time. Even long after I got rich. But now, I've been rich long enough to be, well, accustomed to it. I've learned some of those things that people who were born rich get with their mother's milk. It's something the wealthy are often forced to do. They have to test the people around them. To see who's using them for their money—and who actually cares about them."

Charlie turned back and opened her mouth to speak. Cliff raised a hand to silence her.

Cliff walked over to Angela.

She had no idea what to do. She did not move, barely able to breathe.

He bent down and kissed her gently on the top of her head. He placed his hands on her shoulders and gave them a possessive little squeeze.

"In this short life," he said, "a beautiful woman is one of the few things you can never get too much of. Angie, you risked your life to save me."

Angela let herself exhale. She smiled meekly at no one in particular, asking herself, How do you say thank you to the universe?

Cliff let go of her and gave Eric a mock punch on the shoulder.

"If it hadn't been for your English buddy here, we might have lost you. We saw you struggling from Ezekiel's boat, but it would have been an impossible maneuver. The tide was rushing out against us. The currents there are very strong. Good work, huh, Eric? It's Eric, right?"

"Yes, sir," Eric said, beaming up at Cliff. "It's Eric."

"Well done. You rescued the woman I want to marry. That is, if she'll still have me."

Angela gasped.

Charlie groaned like an animal in mortal pain.

"Charlie," Cliff said, his voice cold and hard, "I've advised the authorities that I won't press charges against you. But I am separating the trust funds you have from the rest of my estate. You are officially disinherited. Dead to me. And by the way, I wasn't about to die intestate. My estate is in apple-pie order, believe me. I just said that to raise the ante on last night's game.

"Charlie, you're on your own now. It's nowhere near the billion-dollar deal you were hoping for. But it's more than most people ever dare to dream about. If you're not stupid with your money, you'll be rich enough your whole life. That's the deal you get. And that's final. When the boat drops you at the dock in St. John's, you'll be on your own nickel. Fly commercial, take the bus, swim back to London or New York, I don't care. Now get out of my sight. And out of my life. Go pack your bags."

Charlie glared at Angela with murderous hatred. She grabbed her designer tote bag and stormed off toward her stateroom.

Cliff reached down and stroked the side of Angela's face. She leaned her head back to rest it against him.

"My girl," he sighed contentedly.

Angela leapt to her feet and threw her arms around Cliff, hugging him literally for dear life. Her dear life that, until a few seconds ago, she thought was ruined. She buried her face in his neck and kissed him, oblivious to the cops, crew members, Eric, and Cliff's Antiguan buddies. She really did feel happy to see him. And even happier that her plans were 100 percent back on track. She was about to get everything she had been hoping for, working for. Working harder, she felt, than anyone had ever worked at any job.

Suddenly Cliff broke away from Angela's kiss. He looked around the deck, puzzled.

"Hey," he bellowed, "where's Mr. Madison Avenue?"

Angela blurted out, "Oh! Let me go get him! Let me bring him back to us!"

Even though she was giddy with relief, she was also calculating at top speed. It was essential that she see Jack before anyone else on *King of Pawns* did. She had to try to anticipate as many angles and outcomes as she could. Exactly what truths did Jack need to hear? Exactly what lies did he need to hear and be convinced of in order to keep him from making trouble?

She scared herself for an instant when she almost spoke the words she was thinking, "I know exactly what to tell him."

CHAPTER 61

Jack shuddered when he saw Angela's face smiling down at him as he lay on the prison-cell floor. She helped put him in this hellhole. She told the police everything Charlie demanded of her. His murder threat, his history of drunken violence, how he was the last person anyone saw with Cliff, the works. Angela had given Charlie all the ammunition she needed.

The guards had pointed out the gallows in the courtyard as they threw him into the communal holding pen. They joked about them. The way convicted murderers bounced in the air and shit themselves as the rope snapped tight. That's what the number-one suspect in the murder of one of the island's best-liked billionaires could expect. They laughed.

Now Angela was smiling down at him. How could this be?

"It's okay, Jack," she said soothingly. "Everything is okay. I'm here to take you home, home to the yacht. Everything is okay. You're free. You're innocent. Cliff is fine. Everything is okay."

He felt Angela taking his arm. Gently helping him up off the floor. As soon as he was standing, he felt her giving him a hug. He was too much of a wreck to resist, or care.

"We can talk in the car. Let's just get you out of here now."

She steadied him as they walked out into the courtyard, then out past the guards to the desk, where they signed him out and gave him back his plastic bag of personal items. Then out to a waiting black SUV. Air-conditioned, Jack found, to his immense relief.

Angela sat beside him in the backseat.

He fumbled for his phone in the plastic bag. His hands were shaking as he jammed the power button repeatedly. He wanted to text Sandra. Desperately. But his phone was dead. No juice at all. He thought he might burst into tears. But not in front of Angela, he told himself, not in front of her. No fucking way.

He felt her stroking his arm soothingly, maternally.

"We're going straight back to the yacht," she said softly. "This was all a terrible mistake. Charlie was so evil to accuse you. You wouldn't harm a flea. She's gone now. Gone. Cliff is back. He was never really missing. And we want to make up for all the trouble you've had. Cliff and I, we have a wonderful plan to make it all up to you."

Jack was confused, unable to process the meaning behind the things she'd just said.

"What the—? Cliff's not dead? Charlie's gone?"

The way she'd said "we" was so damn cozy. And the "Cliff and I." What was *that* about? He had so many questions. But he could barely withstand the overpowering urge to sleep.

"You look like you're ready to crash," she said. "You can't even keep your eyes open. Just rest, okay. Just rest."

"Uh-huh," he said, as he closed his eyes.

He woke up briefly when the SUV arrived at the dock. Then promptly fell back asleep once they were in the back of the boat. He woke up about halfway across the channel as *King of Pawns* came into view.

"What's this about Cliff?" he asked, groggy and bewildered.

Angela gave him another maternal pat.

"He was safe with his friends in Silver Point all along. He told us about your fake fight. He was testing Charlie—and she failed his test."

Jack exhaled noisily, slowly feeling himself rejoining the human race. "I guess she did."

Angela kept stroking him. Soothing, calming, concerned.

"Cliff says he owes you big-time. *We* owe you. He's going to make it up to you. *We're* going to make it up to you. We've got a great new job for you. It could make you a lot of money. A lot. Really. More than you ever would have made at that stupid agency. I could tell you all about it, but Cliff wants to tell you himself. We're going to make it all up to you. Okay?"

Jack noted the emphatic *we* again. This must mean she had gotten Cliff right where she wanted him. She had her hooks into his multibillion-dollar fortune. And Charlie was gone. Angela had it all to herself now. No wonder she was so sweet and cuddly.

Jack wanted to grab her by the throat and scream in her face that she was the most despicable person he had ever known. A few hours ago she'd been happy to incriminate him for murder. She would have let him swing on the gallows, dancing in the air and shitting himself.

He wanted to tell her he was done forever with her lying and her heartless ways of using people. He wanted to pick her up and throw her overboard and let the outboard's propeller tear her body

355

to shreds, turning the water red with her blood. He desperately wanted to rid himself and the rest of humanity of the scourge that was Angela Hanson.

But she said she had a job for him.

For him, a man who was unemployable. A job that would make him lots of money.

So, instead of resetting the scales of justice where they were supposed to be, instead of destroying her to save the world from more of her evil, he just mumbled, "Okay."

Because, well, he really needed a job.

CHAPTER 62

Cliff was waiting on the swim deck, waving enthusiastically as the boat approached.

When Jack stepped onto the deck, Cliff gave him a big bear hug.

Jack stared at him in wonder. And confusion.

"You are a hero," Cliff said, "you and my Angie here. Do you realize that she jumped into the water to rescue me? Can you imagine! This girl can hardly swim. She risked her life to save this old geezer! My bride-to-be. The next—and last—Mrs. Clifford Townsend."

He hugged her to him.

"And none of that prenup bullshit. When I finally go, she's going to inherit everything, the way a real wife should. But in the meantime, this old codger is going to milk the bejesus out of every single day."

Jack stared at the two of them in a combination of astonishment and horror.

Cliff put his arm around Jack for a confidential aside. "I'm sorry you had to get hurt. My doctor's here; he'll fix you up like new. Here's the thing: I couldn't risk letting you know any more about the plan. And I had to spike your drinks. Sorry about that too. I had no choice but to lie.

"I'm the one who got the virgin Pawn Brokers. After all, I had to be absolutely clearheaded and rational. But I had to be sure you were good and toasted. I must say, even in your cups, you landed some damn good punches before you hit the mat. Good thing that planking is wood. Softer landing. Believe me, I know. I've passed out there more than a few times myself."

He grinned and raised an imaginary glass.

He put his arm through Jack's, escorting him up the stairs. Angela followed behind.

"It was Charlie who threw me overboard. As I figured it would be. But I had Ezekiel and Beresford waiting just out of sight to fish me out. That's why I arranged the midnight cruise so they could follow behind us and not attract attention. I needed to see how far she would go to get her hands on my money. She was ready to kill me and let you hang for her crime. She's gone now. Gone."

They stopped on the first-level sundeck. Cliff turned and faced Jack.

"Now, you and I need to talk about getting square. I owe you big-time. First, I want to add an extra bonus on top of the money in your contract. Got that?"

"Sure," Jack said, his head reeling, working to process all the revelations.

Cliff motioned for Angela to come to him. "Angie here, with her head for business, she gave me a brilliant idea." He hugged her. Angela beamed.

Jack watched them, speechless. There she was, launching herself into yet another new life. Shedding her old skin and transforming

358

herself into a whole new kind of snake. Bigger, more powerful, and, no doubt, more poisonous. Again! She was already looking comfortable in her new role as the old billionaire's young wife.

"I'm selling off my companies," Cliff explained. "I need a really good bullshit artist to tell the stories to potential buyers. You'll get a fee for your time. Reasonable, plus a percentage if you can get me my price. Sliding scale. The better I do, the better you'll do. If you do a good job, it could make you rich. Little rich, not big rich, mind you. Interested?"

"Yes," Jack said, "definitely interested." He felt confident he could do a great job. Even in his exhausted state, he knew he was still a great salesman-for-hire.

Angela stared into his eyes for a long moment. Then smiled.

He thought her smile seemed to be saying two things.

The first was, See? I took care of you. And maybe, in her crazy, destructive, fucked-up way, she had.

The second was, In return for getting your life back, you *will* keep your mouth shut about me and everything I've done. Understand?

He gave her a nod of obedience. Yes, Angela, I get it. The whole fucked-up arrangement.

"Jack, they're good companies," Cliff said, oblivious to the silent communication going on between his fiancée and his employee. "These companies are filled with hardworking people. Great value for the right buyers. Can you paint that picture for me?"

"Sure," Jack said, turning away from Angela to focus on Cliff, "I can paint any picture you want."

"But, here's the thing, Mr. Madison Avenue," Cliff said, "this is different. These stories are all true. Think you can handle that?"

"Yes," Jack said, "I'm pretty sure I can."

CHAPTER 63

After a week of pampering on the *King of Pawns*, Jack was physically recovered. But he was still beside himself with worry. There had been no change in Luke's condition. Jack was filled with dread for his son. Dread at the prospect of seeing him again in person, lost in that coma. At the same time, as his own cuts and bruises healed, he developed this crazy hope that when he returned to Luke's bedside, his presence might help spark a recovery. A miracle of paternal love. He knew it was delusional, but it made him feel more optimistic.

A deckhand took his packed bags and was loading them onto the boat to take him to St. John's and his flight to New York on the Townsend jet.

Angela was on the swim deck in a bathing suit, wrapped in a towel. She was dripping wet, her hair matted down. She waved for Jack to come say good-bye.

When he got down to her, he thought she looked different somehow. Younger and more vulnerable than the hard-driving executive who had barged into his office and dynamited his life. Her bubbly mood and eagerness reminded him of the girl he had met so long ago. The girl with earnest energy and sincerity, wide-eyed at the prospect of the great world ahead of her. Sweet and innocent in her longing to succeed, if only she could figure out how. The Angela he once knew. The Angela he had mentored and, yes, once loved.

She thanked him for everything and apologized again for all his troubles.

"I'll never forget," she said, looking up at him with the eager eyes of her younger self, "that *you're* the one who taught me how the world really works. I owe you so much—so much. I've tried to pay you back in some small ways. I hope you know that."

She stood on tiptoe and gave him a sisterly kiss on the cheek and a damp hug of what seemed to be genuine warmth.

Jack wanted to be skeptical, cynical. Suspicious of what she might be up to next. But it felt like she was sincere.

And her promise of the new job was true. He really was set up with a great deal where he could use his skills and rake in a lot more than he ever would have gotten at the agency. For once, she wasn't lying or manipulating him. At least, as far as he could see. She seemed like the sweet Angela he thought he once knew so long ago.

Jack looked deep into her blue eyes. He was pretty sure what he saw was happiness. He gestured at the fabulous surroundings and the enormous engagement ring glittering on her finger.

"So, Angela, do you finally have everything you want?" he asked.

She gave him a mischievous little grin. Looked all around—the yacht and all its trappings. "Almost," she said.

He wondered for a nanosecond what it would be like to strangle her and throw her lifeless body overboard. He knew he could do it. He had the physical capacity. And more than enough pent-up rage.

But then, he'd lose his new job. To say nothing of going back to the gallows in Her Majesty's Prison.

He told himself to file that impulse away. Suck it up—just like every other employee who ever had the secret wish to kill their boss.

So he smiled and waved at her as he got into the motorboat to go home.

He knew that his phone would have a sketchy signal on the ride to St. John's. He powered it off and did not bother to power it back on until he was on the jet, flying back to New York, where he knew he would have reliable Wi-Fi.

When the phone powered up, he saw a flood of urgent texts from Sandra:

> Luke is conscious!
> He's back!! He's talking!!
> Where R U???
> !!!!?????!!!!!!?????!!!!!!

He called her immediately.

Sandra was breathless. "Luke has recovered consciousness! The doctors say he will be all right. They're confident he will fully recover and get on with his life. A month or two of physical therapy and then back to normal. The VR helmet cushioned his fall, saved his brain and his life. How lucky is that?"

"Very lucky," Jack said quietly. Guilt still weighed heavily on his heart.

363

"No, I mean it," she said. "Really lucky. It really did save his life. You should feel good about that. Honest."

Jack was silent.

"Jack," she said, reading his silence and his mind, "you don't have to feel guilty anymore. You understand?"

"Yes, Sandra, I understand. I'll work on it. Can I talk to Luke?"

"Not right now. He slips in and out of sleep. The doctors say it's normal."

"I'll land in New York in a few hours."

"Then get your ass to the hospital and talk to your son. You were the first thing he asked about when he woke up. I told him you were in the Caribbean on an adventure—you know, the private jet, the yacht. He can't wait to hear all about it."

"I'll tell him. All the gory details." Jack was smiling inside and out.

"He'll love it, I'm sure," she said.

He decided this was not the time to tell her about his complications and mishaps. He thought about telling her that he had a great new job lined up. That he would work like crazy, stay off the sauce, make money, and be able to pay for Luke's education.

He wanted to tell her he was going to become a great dad to Luke. The greatest dad ever.

He wanted to tell her that he had undergone a transformation on the floor of Her Majesty's Prison. He'd been terrified, humiliated, reduced to a creature that was barely human. When he was released and exonerated, he felt like he had died and come back as a new man. He saw himself and his life and all his mistakes in a whole new light. Surviving those desperate hours showed him how his selfishness, his narcissism, his vanity—all the weaknesses that had driven him into the affair with Angela—had almost ruined his life and his family.

He would not blow this second chance. No way. He wanted her to know he really was on the wagon, and this time he would make it stick. No more escaping into the false comfort of the bottle. This time it was for real, all of it.

A new Jack Price, humbled, chastened, frightened beyond all imagining. And stronger for it. Changed for the rest of the time he was lucky enough to have.

But no. He could not tell her all that now. Not over the phone.

He knew what he wanted to say to her at this moment. Had to say.

"Sandra?" he asked haltingly.

"Yes?"

"I'm glad you've found someone who's really good for you."

Pause.

"Thanks, Jack," she said, with genuine warmth in her voice. "I hope you find someone, too."

"Sandra," he said softly, "I'll always love you."

But she had already hung up.

CHAPTER 64

Six months later ~

Angela and Cliff were in bathing suits, sunning themselves on a double-width chaise on the third deck of *King of Pawns*. The yacht was moored just off the tropical paradise of the Seychelles, in the southern Indian Ocean.

Cliff was asleep, snoring loudly, one arm resting across Angela's bare midriff.

Very carefully, she moved Cliff's arm aside and got up from the chaise.

She had grown so used to Cliff's clumsy touch that it hardly bothered her anymore. Marriage did change everything, she decided. The unrelenting intimacy with the same person would create that comforting boredom, no matter who your mate was. Yes, she thought, all cats really are gray in the dark. It had been so long since she'd made love to a man close to her own age, she was almost 100 percent convinced that her cats-mantra was true. Almost.

Anyone could see from the sight of Cliff happily snoring that he planned to relax into his new life with his hot young bride. What no one could see was that his hot young bride was secretly making other plans of her own.

Angela, bored and lonely this afternoon, would have liked to play with Eric. But he was playing ashore on Mahé Island and might not return for a day or two. She was delighted with Cliff's grateful generosity to the dear man who had saved her life. What Cliff called "the little private bank account for your English buddy" was a gift of more money than Eric had ever dared to imagine. She enjoyed seeing him flourish. He was relaxed and confident. Now, when he slipped out of his posh accent and into his Derbyshire twang, or vice versa, he did it intentionally and with amused irony.

She waved to Josef two decks below. Mouthed "kayak" with exaggerated clarity and pointed toward the water. She headed down to the giant hold that contained the yacht's many flotation toys and watercraft.

By the time she arrived, Josef had the sea kayak in the water for her. He offered his hand to steady her as she moved to step down into the long, narrow, tippy boat. As she put one foot inside the kayak, it bucked and sent her off balance.

Josef caught her in his arms and kept her from falling.

Angela smiled at him.

Holding her in the air, he said, "Careful. On boat is many ways to die."

Angela lingered in Josef's strong arms for a moment. She thought of how stupid Charlotte had been, to use Josef for sex. She knew that winning the loyalty of a man like Josef could pay dividends infinitely more valuable than a roll in the sheets.

She glanced up at Cliff, snoring on the deck above, and frowned. Then gave Josef a long look.

As he steadied her down into the kayak, she said, "Thank you for reminding me, Josef. I do try to be careful. Always."

CHAPTER 65

One year later ~

Angela stood on the far side of her old corner in New York City. Before her was the building that had once housed the crazy-rich prep school. Behind her were the projects where she grew up.

She looked up at the shiny bronze letters over the archway of the main entrance.

Sonia Hanson Memorial
Girls Community Center

"It's perfect," she said to the man at her side. He was middle-aged and preppy-looking, with tortoiseshell glasses and longish, unkempt sandy hair. He wore an ill-fitting tan suit and a stained blue necktie emblazoned with Y's from his alma mater, Yale. His brown shoes were cracked and worn down at the heels.

"How do you think your mother would feel," he asked, "seeing her name like this in big letters?"

Angela was wearing about $100,000 in designer goods—Carolina Herrera houndstooth pantsuit, black patent-leather Jimmy Choo pumps, Clash de Cartier necklace, rings, bracelets, and earrings. She was carrying a vintage ostrich Birkin.

She took off her big, round Jackie O sunglasses to look him in the eye.

"My mother would be confused and a little embarrassed. But so happy to know she was helping girls in the neighborhood get a better start."

The man touched her arm gently. "Are you sure you don't want a small credit for the Townsend Foundation up there, along with the tribute to your mother?"

She shook her head emphatically no. "My late husband was insistent on this. We take no public recognition for our giving. He considered it to be in poor taste."

"But in the short time since you organized the foundation, you've already done so much good. And really, nobody knows about it."

"I plan to keep it that way."

"About Mr. Townsend . . ." he paused awkwardly. "May I ask, did they ever find any traces of the—?"

Angela sniffed back a little sob. "No, nothing. Just vanished at sea. I was always afraid out there. I used to beg Cliff not to go down to the swim deck to look at the stars, especially after he'd had a few drinks. But he was so headstrong."

She tried but failed to hold back tears.

"I . . . I'll always regret," she stammered, catching her breath, "I'll always wish I had gone with him on that Atlantic crossing. Maybe I might have kept him from . . . maybe he'd still be here."

She choked on her tears. Paused to catch her breath. Waved a hand to sweep away her profound emotions.

"I'm selling that damn yacht," she muttered. "Boats on the ocean—so many ways to die."

She shuddered. Then took a deep breath. There now.

With regal grace, she extended her right hand.

The man took it in both of his and held onto it.

"Thank you, Mrs. Townsend—thank you *so* much."

"Please," she said with a smile, "call me Angela."

She withdrew her hand before the man was done squeezing it, making clear she did not get too familiar with the help.

"Well, then, Angela it is," he said, smiling.

She smiled back. "I'm just one of the girls from the neighborhood." She put her sunglasses back on.

"Angela," he said, "your philanthropy will make a big difference in so many lives. The world would be such a better place if there were more people like you."

"More people like me?" she asked without a trace of irony. Then smiled graciously. "You really are too kind."

The man started to say something more.

She raised a finger to her lips.

He stopped.

She turned and walked toward her waiting Range Rover.

She remembered the pep talk she had given her nervous, doubting self in the elevator of the Four Seasons Hotel the night of her first dinner with Cliff—"You are an actress. Not just any actress. A great actress. A great actress about to audition for the role of a lifetime." I got the role, she thought, and my performance has been brilliant.

She heard a text ping inside her handbag. She stopped on the sidewalk, took out her phone, and looked. It was from Susanna Stratsman:

> Angela,
> On behalf of all of the members, I want to welcome you to the benefit committee.
> In all my years of chairing it, I have never seen anyone elected with a 100 percent vote.
> It's clear you were born to be one of us.
> XOXO
> Susanna

Smiling to herself, she turned Susanna's words over in her head. *You were born to be one of us.* Susanna Stratsman, the aristocrat's aristocrat, had just told her that she had joined their exclusive tribe. That she was *born* to be one of them.

Poor dimwitted Charlie, Angela thought. Try as she might, she was never meant to be one of them.

And as for Charlie's legal challenges? Cliff's army of lawyers—now, Angela's army of lawyers—assured her that Charlotte's claims would never amount to anything. She would be a mere fly that would occasionally buzz into view. No worries. Angela's loyal attorneys were there to swat her away.

She put the phone back into her Birkin.

She stopped and did what she had not dared to do when she had arrived for the little dedication ceremony. She looked across the broad avenue at the grimy brick towers of the projects. She let herself stare at them for a long moment. A flood of memories washed over her. From playing with dolls as a little girl to Eva's skull exploding in blood to countless hours of her mother telling her she could do anything she put her mind to. *Anything!*

She imagined a little ghost across that avenue, standing on that very curbstone. Her tween-age self, staring at the rich kids, pleading with the universe in her naive fury, "Why not me? Why not *me?*"

Angela, the wealthy woman, finally had the universe's answer for that anguished young girl. There *was* no reason why not. Since no one was born deserving anything, why *not* you, little girl? Why *NOT*?

Now, when Angela met people who had grown up with advantages she'd never had, she could fight back that feeling of intimidation. Her stomach didn't twist into knots, her armpits didn't break out in sweat. The scared, undeserving little girl inside her seemed to have been silenced once and for all.

She had followed Jack Price's counsel and done whatever it took.

Did she feel guilty about the things she'd done? Sometimes. But hadn't she learned that everyone cuts corners once in a while? Didn't everyone lose some sleep every now and then?

Angela had her share of nightmares. But she did her best not to let them ruin her days.

With each new line she had crossed, she had worried about getting caught. Paying the price. The black specter hunting her down. But it never happened. And by now, she was pretty sure it never would. The universe seemed to have decided in her favor. No lightning bolts had struck her down. No divine retribution had been visited upon her. Not a single criminal suspicion had even been hinted at. Only good things had come her way.

At first, she thought her cold cunning was something she had learned from the entitled people she had tried to copy in her ascent. But now she realized it had been there all along. The block of ice inside her where other people—weaker people—had a heart. It had been her strength, her rock, her foundation.

Just as Susanna Stratsman said, she was *born* to be one of them. If there was such a thing as destiny, she had found hers, and fulfilled it. She had become the powerful, confident, unassailable woman of the world she was meant to be.

Maybe it was time to think about the daughter she would have someday. Of course, she would have to find the right man. No, not a husband. Not now. Not after what she'd had to endure living with Cliff.

Maybe Jack Price? Now that selling off Cliff's empire had made him a little bit rich.

She smiled at the thought. She wondered what a girl with her genes and Jack Price's might look like.

She walked the rest of the way to her waiting Range Rover. Her brawny driver was holding the rear door open for her.

"Thank you, Josef," she said as he ushered her inside.

Eric slid across the backseat to give her the place with the extra leg room. She settled in, pulled down the center armrest, and placed her bag on it. Everyone snapped their seat belts, and Josef steered them out into the traffic.

She stared out the window, lost in thought about her someday daughter. Would she call her Sonia, after her mother? No, there was too much sadness in that name. Besides, she was leaving Sonia here at the projects to help the girls who really needed her.

Eric touched her arm. "May I ask Her Royal Highness a little question?"

She was thinking about a letter she would write to her daughter. Yes, a letter about her hopes and dreams for her. She would tell her why she had made sure her girl would grow up able to afford everything she never could. Most of all, she wanted to make sure that her daughter possessed the one priceless luxury Angela knew *she* could never afford—the luxury of giving in to the power of love.

"*Angela*," Eric barked, "I'm talking to you."

She turned to him, annoyed at having her reverie interrupted. "Yes?"

"Don't you feel a wee bit of a letdown? Now that you've finally gotten everything you ever wanted. I mean, what's left for you?"

She yanked off her sunglasses. "What are you talking about? I'm just getting started."

Quickly catching her misstep, she gave Eric a big smile and Josef a fond little tap on the shoulder. "What I mean is—*we're* just getting started. We're a team, the three of us."

Of course, she knew that one day she might have to get rid of these men. Even dear darling Eric, as much as she loved him.

They knew too much. And she had no illusions about their loyalty to her. It was another thing she had bought.

Now that she had extracted everything that dear departed Cliff had to offer—his gigantic mountain of money and all his dirty secrets—she was sure she had internalized the credo of the very rich: Never let anyone, no matter who they are or what you think they mean to you, come between you and your money. She was confident she had the clearheaded, cold-blooded ability to get away with just about anything – if she had to.

Even the occasional murder.

Angela Townsend left behind the girl she had once been and rode away from the projects, looking at the world through her Jackie O sunglasses.

Just as her mother had told her to do, she never looked back.

ACKNOWLEDGMENTS

These days, the journey to publication is so daunting that the word "acknowledgements" does not do justice to the debts one owes.

First, my indomitable agent Linda Langton and her right arm, Lindsay Watson.

At Woodhall Press, David LeGere, the visionary who has literally done the impossible and built this vibrant independent imprint. His teammates, Matt Winkler, Christopher Madden, Colin Hosten, Jayne Bryer, irreplaceable intern Jillian Gallagher, and Jessica Dionne Wright, cover designer *extraordinaire*.

For insight-driven marketing and PR executed with aplomb and elegance, Claire McKinney of Claire McKinney Public Relations and her digital wizard Sonya Dalton.

For invaluable help along the way: John Paine (for the second time), editor of my primordial ooze. Rebecca Uberti, whose graphic artistry inspired me and elevated my words from the very beginning of this footslog to its culmination. Judy Katz, publishing force of nature, who led me to Linda. Marina Aris – writer, publisher, Authors Guild powerhouse connector and generous advisor. Alison Holtzschue, a regular reader of my drafts and always an honest and helpful critic. Mark Morril, counselor, reader, cheerleader. Arthur Klebanoff, font of publishing wisdom. Michael Kubin for generosity with his network. Barry Mills for the old college try

Finally, my wife Evelyn, for more than words could ever describe.

ABOUT THE AUTHOR

Glenn Kaplan is the NY Times bestselling author of *Evil Inc* and two other novels, *Poison Pill* and *All For Money,* as well as *The Big Time,* a non-fiction business book. He worked in the international art world and as creative director in global advertising agencies and a Fortune 500 company. A graduate of Bowdoin College, he is married and lives in New York City.